PRAISE FOR *SONS AND ____*

"*Hays makes sure that the historical aspects of the story are as compelling as the murder mystery at its heart. . . . A smart Swiss procedural that keeps its mystery ticking.*"

—*Kirkus*

"*The second outing of Linder and Donatelli is as crisp and skilled as the first, with our police duo digging beneath the beauty of Bern to the shadows beneath. Old scandals and new conflicts are investigated by realistic, complicated people, whom the reader fears might not always make the right choices. Brisk plot, depth of character, great setting—what's not to love?*"

—Laurie R. King, Edgar Award-winning author of thirty novels, including the Mary Russell-Sherlock Holmes series

"*Kim Hays balances winter-keen psychological insight with the warmth and beauty of the most charming canton of Switzerland, methodically revealing the small tragedies of class and family, uneasy marriages and toxic workplaces. Giuliana Linder and Renzo Donatelli are compassionate, conflicted, and utterly compelling.* Sons and Brothers *is a must-read.*"

—Julia Spencer-Fleming, *New York Times* and *USA Today* bestselling author

"Sons and Brothers *features an intriguing murder case well worth sinking your teeth into . . . Recommended for fans of both detective mysteries and police procedurals.*"

—*Crime Fiction Critic*

PRAISE FOR *PESTICIDE*

"Swiss detectives dig into the cutthroat world of organic farming in Hays's twisty murder mystery . . . The result is an engrossing page-turner . . . [and] an entertaining whodunit."

—*Kirkus* (starred review)

". . . A tense, character-driven crime debut perfect for fans of thoughtful police procedurals."

—*BookLife (Publishers Weekly)*

Sons
and
Brothers

Sons and Brothers

A POLIZEI BERN NOVEL

KIM HAYS

SEVENTH
STREET
BOOKS®

Inquiries should be addressed to
Start Science Fiction
221 River Street, 9th Floor
Hoboken, New Jersey 07030
PHONE: 212-431-5454
WWW.SEVENTHSTREETBOOKS.COM

10 9 8 7 6 5 4 3 2 1

978-1-64506-058-1 (paperback)
978-1-64506-074-1 (ebook)

Printed in the United States of America

Dedicated to my dear mother

Joy Kramer Hays
1929–2011

who taught me to enjoy
art museums, English history, looking things up,
and, above all, reading mysteries!

Foreword

Bern and Its German

K eeping all the characters in a novel straight can be a challenge. Several readers of *Pesticide*, the first Polizei Bern book, have pointed out that their task was made harder by almost everyone being called by a first name, a last name, *and* a nickname at various points in the story. So I decided to see if I could offer a bit of assistance when it came to *Sons and Brothers*.

Nicknames are often far from reasonable. Calling a William Will makes sense, but Peggy for Margaret? Jack for John? Pancho for Francisco? In Bern, men's nicknames tend to end in "u," women's in "i," "e," or "a," and there is often a change in the sound of the main vowel.

Below, I've listed in alphabetical order by last name all the characters in *Sons and Brothers* who are referred to by their first name and a nickname, and also the characters who are simply called by some version of their name throughout the book.

Assume these names are pronounced so that a = ah, e = eh, i = Tina, o = roll, and u = moon.

Name	*Nickname or First Name*
Amsler, *Jakob*	Köbi (ö = like the "i" in "bird" with no "r" sound)
Arm, *Arnold*	Noldi
Balmer, *Hansruedi*	Hansruedi may be short for Hans-Rudolf or be a name in itself
Beck, *Peter*	Pesche
Brand, *Isabelle*	Isa
Brand, *Lukas*	Lüku (ü = a French "u," with very pursed lips)
Brand, *Ueli*	Ueli is his full first name, but it can be short for Ulrich
Donatelli, *Fränzi*	Fränzi's real name is Franziska (ä = the "a" in "France")
Donatelli, *Renzo*	Renzo is a nickname for Lorenzo
Emmi	Emmi is a nickname for Emma
Franz	Fränzu
Gurtner, *Charlotte*	Lotti
Gurtner, *Johann Karl*	Hannes or Karli (many other nicknames are possible)
Gurtner, *Markus*	Märku
Gurtner, *Patrick*	Pädu
Gurtner, *Philipp*	Fippu
Katharina	Käthi
Linder, *Giuliana*	Giule
Linder, *Paolo*	Giuliana sometimes calls her brother Lolo

Michael	Michu (the "ch" is said deep in the throat)
Rieder, *Brigitte*	Bri
Rieder, *Heinz*	Hene
Rossel, *Toni*	Toni's full name is Antoine
Sämu	short for Samuel
Stettler, *Ändu*	short for Andreas (so is Res)
Stettler, *Heidi*	Here, short for Adelheid, although Heidi can be a first name
Thomas	Tömu

Men of any age sometimes call each other *Alter*, which means "old man."

1
Before

Bern's Mattenhof neighborhood in October, over a year before Johann Karl Gurtner's death

Markus Gurtner had taken photographs in many homes since he'd started the portraiture assignment: seventeen pictures were finished, with only six to go. This living room was one of the most attractive he'd been in, free of the dark wood paneling, squatting sofas, and massive sideboards that so many of his elderly subjects favored. Here, instead, were pale-green paint, olive-and-white striped curtains framing glass doors that opened onto a balcony, and scattered armchairs that weren't too heavy to be moved.

He'd just turned his own chair to face the subject of his next portrait, Jakob Amsler, a giant of a man who sat upright and silent, an unlikely moment of autumn sun lighting his lined face and bringing out his dark-blue eyes. To Markus, the man seemed neither nervous about the photography session nor eager for it. He was simply ready for whatever came next.

"I know the sponsors have already had you talking for hours," Markus began, "but I've only read the summaries. So, before we get started, do you mind a couple of questions? At sixty-nine, you're one of the youngest people I'm working with. Where did you grow up? Before you were taken away, I mean."

Amsler nodded and leaned forward, clasping his huge hands and resting them on one thigh. "I was born here in the city and grew up on Altenbergstrasse."

Markus knew the neighborhood along the river. "Lots of brothers and sisters?" he asked.

"I was the second of six children when the social worker took me, but my mother might have had more kids afterward. I wouldn't be surprised."

Markus had been listening to these stories for weeks now: one child after another wrenched away from parents judged neglectful or immoral. Sometimes it had been the parents themselves who hadn't been able to cope and sent their kids away to work. Each new recital of facts gave Markus access to the secrets that had shaped his subjects' wrinkled faces and hunched bodies. "Who were your parents?" he asked.

Amsler's face was set, his voice hard. "My younger sister Anna and I had the same father, our mother's husband. The other children had other fathers. After mine left, when I was four, my mother started to drink. She wasn't exactly a whore"—Markus's breath caught, momentarily, at the word—"because she wasn't organized enough. She just drank and slept with men, and some of them must have given her money, because we didn't starve." He laughed, a dark sound. "I'm probably the only Swiss contract child alive who agrees with the officials—my mother *was* unfit to raise us. Unfortunately, their solution was worse than the problem."

Markus considered the many emotions—sadness, acceptance, self-pity, rage—that he'd heard from other *Verdingkinder*. Detachment like this was new to him.

He continued to probe. "They sent you to work on a farm in the Emmental when you were nine, yet by sixteen you were apprenticed at Bern's biggest telecom firm. You became an engineer. It's—impressive. Most *Verdingkinder* never managed to get any proper training at all." He spoke in admiration; too late, he heard another possible interpretation of his words: What have *you* got to complain about?

Amsler rose abruptly and walked to the balcony doors, which

he opened wide. For a moment he stood with his back to the room. Beyond him, Markus saw the turbulent autumn sky and the neighborhood's cluster of low-rise apartment buildings. Cold air rushed in, and Amsler seemed to lean into the wind before closing the doors.

He turned to face Markus, his enormous frame almost obscuring the view. "Yes, I've been lucky beyond anything I deserved."

The smile that should have accompanied these words was absent, and Markus longed to capture the bleakness of the old man's expression as he spoke of luck. God, how would he ever get Amsler to look that way again, once he had his lighting set up? Maybe he ought to forgo this chat and get straight to photographing.

As Markus started to suggest this, Amsler's face transformed. The grim lines around his mouth vanished, and he smiled. "I hear my wife. She's home early from school—she's a teacher." He started toward the front door, as if welcoming his wife home from work was a daily highlight. Perhaps it was. "Now you'll see how truly lucky I am."

Markus heard their voices in the hall, and Amsler returned with a white-haired woman at his side, as straight-backed and strong looking as he was. She was tall, too, though still small next to her husband.

Markus stood, and she moved forward, hand outstretched, as Amsler said, "This is Renata Lanz, my wife."

So she uses her own last name, Markus thought. Not so common at her age. "I'm glad to meet you, Frau Lanz," he said.

She shook hands with vigor, but her eyes held more curiosity than warmth. "Thank you, Herr Gurtner. Don't worry, I won't get in your way. It's painful for me to hear about Jakob's childhood in Heidmatt, even after all these years."

"Heidmatt? On the Emme?" Markus turned to Amsler. "You were a *Verdingbueb* in Heidmatt? The village on my list is—" He pulled a sheet of paper out of his back pocket, unfolded it, and read, "Schönenbach."

"Oh, Schönenbach's no village, just a clump of farmhouses," Amsler told him with a shrug. "It's part of Heidmatt."

"But my father was born in Heidmatt. He grew up there." Markus heard himself grow louder in his excitement.

Amsler nodded. "I know," he said. "Karli Gurtner, the boy in the castle."

So Amsler had done his own research—Markus felt the strange, almost dizzying sensation of the lens turned back on himself, for once. "Yes, I suppose that's right. Aunt Lotti's castle," Markus echoed. "Did you . . . did you ever meet my father?"

"We were in the same class for several years," Amsler answered.

Apart from his grandparents and aunts, Markus had never met anyone who'd known his old man as a child. He tried to imagine him as a schoolboy, playing with other children. "A friend of my father's," he breathed.

Renata Lanz, still standing at her husband's side, gave a small snort. Then she touched Markus's arm, as if to make up for her derision. "I'm off to put the groceries away," she said. "Let me know if you need anything."

What he needed was to speak—to let the questions about his father pour out of him. Instead, he had a portrait to produce.

Swallowing his curiosity, he began to discuss the practical aspects of setting up the shots. Perhaps later they would have more time to talk.

2

At the Dählhölzli park, Bern, Monday,
November 23, 5:12 p.m.

She'd been answering 117 for almost two years now. She'd managed giggling teenagers trying to send cops to nonexistent addresses, drunk men whispering obscenities, crazies babbling about neighbors trying to poison them, lonely folks just calling to chat. She'd learned to handle all of that, not to mention all the people who misused the emergency number to complain about a speeding ticket. But mostly, she dealt with panic.

This call was one of those. The person on the other end of the line was so out of breath that at first he—it sounded like a man—couldn't say a word. He gasped for air in shaky moans and panted it out again; it was hard to tell if he were hyperventilating or simply exhausted.

"This is the Emergency Service," she repeated. "Breathe as deeply as you can. Long breaths, now. In through the nose, out through the mouth. That's right. Can you manage to tell me your name?"

As she waited, she checked where the call was coming from: a landline at the Dählhölzli restaurant by the river. It was only five-fifteen, early for dinner guests, but . . .

The man spoke at last, and his words flowed together. "Listen. I need you to send rescuers to Dählhölzli, near the restaurant. Now, right now. A man's drowning in the Aare. I tried to get him out, but I couldn't see . . . God, I'm sorry. I'm afraid the guy is . . . You've got to hurry."

"I will, but first I need your na—" She'd already shifted into action as she registered a sound she hadn't heard for a long time: the old-fashioned click of a receiver being replaced in a holder. Then she thought about nothing beyond making sure that six of the nearest uniformed police were on their way, along with an ambulance. If they needed more rescue personnel and divers, someone would let her know.

A picture formed in her head as she worked: a man struggling weakly against the racing black waters of the river, on a rainy night in temperatures just above freezing. Then the phone rang again.

"Emergency Service," she recited. The drowning man dropped from her mind.

3

Dählhölzli, Monday,
November 23, 8:30 p.m.

The footbridge over the Aare River was slick in the heavy rain, but Renzo Donatelli sprinted it anyway. It might only shave seconds off the time his colleagues had to wait around getting soaked, but Renzo hadn't been a *Fahnder* so long that he'd forgotten what it was like to be a uniformed cop, standing guard at a crime scene in a downpour. If it *was* a crime scene. That's what he was here to decide.

The tent over the body was lit from inside, and as he got closer Renzo could make out the heavyset form of Michael Graber. It was Michael's partner Fritz who had called Renzo; Fritz must be taking a break somewhere dry. On a night like this, it didn't make much sense to have *two* men standing guard against the occasional conscientious dog walker or poncho-draped bike rider.

"Ciao, Michu," yelled Renzo over the roar of rain and river. "Is there room for us in the tent?" Michael scattered drops from his hood as he shook his head, so Renzo opened his umbrella over both of them. "Okay. You found the body on the bank here, couldn't resuscitate, and called the doc. She reckons he was thrown in—is that right?"

Under the shelter of the umbrella, Michael tucked his flashlight under one arm and pulled a pack of tissues out of his jacket pocket. He extracted one with wet hands, giving the limp bit of paper a disgusted look before blowing his nose. "I asked the doctor to wait for you, but . . ." He rolled his eyes.

Renzo also wished she could've hung around to brief him herself, but in this weather . . . "It's okay. What am I looking for?"

"It's pretty clear," Michael said. "Swollen knuckles and a bruised eye, for a start."

"So, there was a bit of a punch-up." Renzo shifted, glad his boots were keeping his feet dry. So far.

"Yeah, plus scraped shins and fingermarks on one shoulder. Welts on the wrists, too."

"From rope?" Renzo asked. That would be a macabre development.

"No, no; just someone holding his wrists tightly. That stuff's nothing compared to the head wound, though—it was obviously a hell of a bang." Michael put one hand up to his own hooded head as he said this and rubbed his crown, wincing in sympathy. "Guess he could've hit a rock when he went into the river."

Renzo knew how stony the steep banks of the Aare were. "Any idea yet where that happened?"

"Nope," said the other man, gesturing with his flashlight as if to remind Renzo what the weather was like. "When we got here around five-thirty it was already dark and pissing down."

They both turned and looked at the Aare, which was a roiling mass of black barely broken by the flashlight's pathetic beam. "I've only seen the river this high a couple of times before," said Michael, "not counting those floods when people were boating down Gerberngasse."

"It's amazing you managed to find the corpse at all in this rain," said Renzo, reaching for the tent flap. Then he lowered it again. He wanted to form his own opinions about the dead man, but not yet. First, he asked, "Do we know who he is?"

"Johann Karl Gurtner, a seventy-two-year-old doctor at the Insel Hospital. His ID was in his wallet, along with plenty of money, so this wasn't a mugging. He isn't wearing a watch, though, which for a guy his age is—"

Renzo interrupted. "An elderly doctor got into a fight walking along the Aare?"

Michael laughed. "Hard to imagine, huh? So, shall I call now, while you're having a look, and tell them we're ready for a pick-up?"

"Go ahead," said Renzo. "You and Fritz and the doc took photos before you messed with him, right?" Michael nodded, and Renzo passed him the umbrella, ducking through the tent opening.

As he crawled into the shelter, he was already planning for the long night ahead. He'd have to make sure the paths on both sides of the river were blocked off and that a team was ready at first light to search the banks for the spot where the man—or the body, if he was already dead by then—had gone into the Aare. They'd need forensics, plus a team on door-to-door inquiries, and . . . . One thing at a time, he told himself, and focused on the corpse.

The body lay face up in only underpants on a sheet of bright yellow plastic, its sodden clothes beside it in a large sealed bag. The shoes appeared to be missing. Renzo's lips tightened at the sight of the narrow, vulnerable-looking feet, before his eyes moved to take in the whole man. Experience told him that the doctor must have been at least six feet tall and quite broad chested for a seventy-two-year-old, but his half-naked corpse looked small and fragile.

Renzo fished a pair of latex gloves from his jacket pocket and wrestled his damp hands into them. Then he crouched by the body and gently lifted and turned the legs, arms, hands, and torso to study their bruises and scratches. Bent over the face, he noted the puffy flesh around one eye, then took the head in both hands, feeling the place where the skull bone gave way and pierced the brain. Finally, he laid the head down.

Who had this doctor been? Given his age and job, he was a man who'd spent the last four decades of his life working to keep other people's hearts beating. Given his wedding ring, he probably had a wife and children and grandchildren. And, given his wounds, he was almost certainly the victim of a hateful crime. A man, Renzo concluded, whose death he'd be only too glad to devote as many hours as necessary to investigating.

He crawled out of the tent and stood, stretching his back.

"Pick-up is on the way," Michael said, passing the umbrella back to Renzo as he fumbled with his flashlight. "Straight to the institute for a full post-mortem, right?"

"Yep," Renzo confirmed. "I'm going to phone this in to homicide from here. Go find Fritz wherever he's taking shelter and dry out a bit with him. Just come back when you hear the siren."

"Thanks, Renzo." Michael threw the words over his shoulder as he jogged away down the path to the bridge. Renzo reached for his phone to call Erwin.

4

Giuliana had claimed the entire sofa and lay with her back propped against the armrest and her laptop on her stomach, rereading interview transcripts for an upcoming trial. She glanced away from her screen at Ueli, who was sprawled in an armchair across from her, feet on the coffee table, also staring at his laptop. He was doing background research for a new article; something about an architect who designed low-energy buildings. She hoped his reading material was more interesting than hers: of course she wanted the man she'd arrested for killing his ex-wife to be put away for a long time, but after so many months of trial prep, she'd grown bored with the details.

She'd just decided that she'd earned a mug of tea when her mobile rang, and she leaned precariously forward to grab it off the coffee table. When she saw who was calling, she said, "Hey, Renzo. Don't tell me you've been out in this rain. What's up?"

"I'm wrecking your quiet evening. I've just given Erwin a body, and he asked me to fill you in."

"Hang on." She headed to the kitchen, which still smelled like the chicken-and-mushroom casserole they'd had for supper. She took paper and pen from the cookbook shelf and sat at the round kitchen table. "Okay," she said.

Taking notes, she noticed again how skilled Renzo was at summarizing what she needed to know. That wasn't the only reason she loved working with him, of course, but . . .

"Sorry, I missed that. Something about scratches?"

"Yeah, on his left hand, like a metal strap was torn off in a hurry, so we need to check if he wore a watch. Mobile's also missing. But not his wallet, and he had over three hundred francs in it."

"What about the call to Emergency?"

"A male voice. Believe it or not, there's still a pay phone on the wall outside the zoo restaurant, and that's what he used. But no one was there when the cops arrived. A rescue pole from one of those stands along the Aare was lying on the bank. But that was it."

"Odd," Giuliana said. She tucked the phone under her chin as she filled the kettle and reached for the jar of ginger tea. "What about the family?"

"The wife called just after eight to report her husband missing, four hours after he went out to walk the dog. By then the body was already on its way to the examiner. She and the son were informed an hour ago, but Erwin hasn't had a chance to interview them. He'd like you to meet him at the institute, but before that . . ."

She turned off the kettle, realizing there was no point making tea. "He wants me to talk to the widow and son."

"Exactly. They live about ten minutes from your place. Nicole Gurtner at Frikartweg thirty-two. That's in the Elfenau. Son's Philipp, eighteen. There are two older sons, too, by an ex-wife, plus a daughter-in-law and some grandkids."

She bent over the table to scribble the names and address. "You said this heart surgeon, Johann Karl Gurtner"—she read the full name out to be sure she had it right—"was walking his dog. Anyone find it?"

"No dog so far. Dead or alive."

"Anything else?"

"Yeah, something important. The boy and his mother still think

Gurtner's death was an accident. So, Erwin would like you to break the news."

"Good," said Giuliana.

She was already planning her approach when Renzo said, "Good luck. And—great to be working with you on this."

"Yeah. Same for me," she said and paused too long before hurrying to add, "Hope your Aare search goes well. Bye." She hung up and stood for a moment staring at the phone, her other hand pressed to her cheek.

Then she went into high gear, changing her jeans and oversized sweater for tailored black trousers, a light-gray blazer, and a white blouse, brushing her hair and putting the heavy mass of curls into a loose knot at the back of her neck. She stared out of the bedroom window at the sheets of rain falling in the arc of light from the streetlamp. Shit. They'd had a week of this icy rain now. When was it going to snow?

Back in the living room, she perched on the arm of Ueli's chair and put a hand on his shoulder.

"Oh, no," he groaned as he took in her change of clothes. "Don't tell me you have to go back out into this weather."

She shrugged. "There's a drowned man; looks like he was beaten up. Erwin's in charge, but I'm on the roster as second detective. Sounds interesting. I'll probably be out for the rest of the night. Depending on how things go, I might not make it home until tomorrow evening. You going to be okay?"

They both knew what that meant: can you get the kids up and out the door, make sure they eat all their meals, and check on any after-school appointments? At least Isabelle was sixteen now. She was pretty good at looking after herself, and not bad at helping to supervise her brother, Lukas.

Ueli frowned. "I've got a ton of writing to do." She waited, even though she needed to call the widow, until he looked up at her and smiled. "It'll be fine. I have two interviews scheduled for tomorrow, but they're while Lukas is at school. We'll work it out."

"Thanks, love. Sorry to mess you around again." She kissed him and he stroked her cheek; then she moved to the sofa to pull on her boots.

Ueli glanced over at her and asked, "Who's dead?"

"A heart surgeon." Her laptop was right next to her; transferring it to her knees, she looked up her victim. He was a big deal, according to the first article she found—a professor at the University of Bern medical school who'd been recognized with some kind of Swiss-wide award for his work as a surgeon. Also an active member of one of the city's trade guilds. She assumed he'd bought himself into the guild system, until she noticed toward the end of the article that his mother had been a von Eichwil. That meant he belonged to the closest thing Switzerland had to an aristocracy. And he was over seventy. How the hell had someone like that managed to get himself socked in the eye?

"I'm guessing inheritance," she said. "Sounds like he might have had a stack of money."

The rain was easing off as she left the apartment. The light from the streetlamps was muted by mist, with the temperature hovering around freezing. Shivering despite her thick wool coat and scarf, Giuliana got into her car and typed Nicole Gurtner's address into her GPS. Then, before she backed out, she called the woman's landline. It rang for a long time, and she hoped the bereaved mother and son hadn't fallen asleep.

"Gurtner." The voice was as deep as a man's, but . . .

"Is this Philipp?" she asked. Correct procedure required her to call eighteen-year-olds "Herr" or "Frau," but she didn't think the boy needed formality right now.

He gave a "Yes" that sounded half-strangled.

"Philipp, this is Giuliana Linder with the police. I'm sorry to bother you so late, but I have some questions that I'd like to ask you and your mother in person. Is she awake?"

She heard nothing for a minute or so, and she began to wonder if he'd just abandoned the call. Then he was back. "She says you should come over."

"I'll be there in a few minutes," said Giuliana and started the car.

Despite her eagerness to learn more about the dead man, she drove slowly on the icy roads, wondering about the scratches on the victim's arm suggesting that his watch had been torn off. Could it have fallen off in the river? What about the emergency caller? Suppose the surgeon had turned on the slick path to get away from someone trying to rob him, then slipped and fallen into the river. A mugger with a conscience might have called for help and then run.

Her mind drifted to Renzo. She'd had breakfast with him just that morning: Monday at six-thirty, their current weekly gym date, when they'd chat about cases over coffee and croissants. A once-a-week workout for her; an almost-daily routine for him. That morning he'd tried something new. She could see him, a heavy dumbbell gripped in both hands, slowly raising and lowering his upper body on the unfamiliar machine, his light-brown hair darkened by sweat, his skin gleaming. She hadn't been able to stop watching him.

She let go of the image as the GPS identified Gurtner's house, its ground floor lit up. It was a three-story villa in one of Bern's poshest neighborhoods, which made sense for a medical school professor who was also a von Eichwil. She walked through a gate set into the tall boxwood hedge, along a path edged by two rows of carefully shaped box plants, and up three steps to the front door. In the faint light of the streetlamps, Giuliana noted the elegance of the small front garden. The Gurtner family's wealth seemed tastefully displayed, but the signs were there. And money was always a strong motive for murder.

Giuliana rang the bell. The door was opened almost immediately by a tall blonde woman of about fifty who would have been attractive if her face hadn't been puffy and blotched. She stood back to let Giuliana in: a slim figure dark against the cream-colored walls in the hall. Her silky T-shirt and black trousers were stylish but muted.

"Frau Linder," the widow said, her voice tight with control. "Please come in." Giuliana hadn't expected the woman to remember her name. That told her a lot. Here was someone who scribbled down details and made a point of recalling them; her system worked even when she was stunned by grief. Giuliana filed this away for future consideration.

Giuliana walked through into what turned out to be a sleek living/dining/kitchen area that took up most of the ground floor. A figure was slumped at the granite-topped kitchen table.

"Philipp," came Nicole's voice from behind her, and the teenager straightened slightly. "Frau Linder is here to ask us some questions."

Was there something cautionary in her tone? Giuliana wasn't sure, but she remained alert to every nuance she could take in.

The teenager stood, then stared down at her through shaggy dark-blond hair, mouth tight, and said nothing.

"I'm so sorry for your loss," Giuliana told him, and he took the hand she offered without meeting her eyes. Adding, "My condolences to you, too, Frau Gurtner," she turned to Nicole and saw that the woman's self-command had drained away; she stood by the table swaying. Moving quickly, Giuliana took her by the arm, maneuvered her to one of the chrome-and-black chairs at the table and more or less pushed her into it.

Nicole clutched her arms around herself, shivering.

Giuliana turned to her son. "Philipp, could you get your mother a sweater?" The boy nodded and went upstairs, and Giuliana said to Nicole, "Let me make you a warm drink. Do you need something to eat as well?"

Nicole looked at her with round eyes, as if only just realizing that she had a guest. "No, please, I should . . ." she began.

Giuliana cut in. "Did you eat dinner?" Nicole nodded. "Then what about some tea with milk?" A pause was followed by another nod, so Giuliana filled the lemon-yellow kettle and took it to the huge gas stove. She set it on a burner and opened the cabinet over the sink where, sure enough, she found cups. She lined up three yellow-and-white patterned mugs by the stove, located a flowered cannister half full of tea bags, and was getting spoons out of a drawer when Nicole said, "I'm trying to focus on Hannes, and all I can think about is the funeral. What kind of wife is already working on the guest list for her husband's funeral two hours after she hears of his death?"

"Someone who uses work to distract herself from grief," Giuliana answered, while registering that Nicole had called her husband by the nickname Hannes. She leaned back on the countertop, waiting for the kettle's whistle. Not a sign of that evening's dinner remained in the neat kitchen. "You're obviously organized, and planning helps you stay calm." She smiled at Nicole. "Don't feel bad about something so normal."

Philipp returned and put an oversized black hoodie around his mother's shoulders; it stank of stale cigarette smoke, but she didn't seem to notice. She smiled up at the boy and squeezed his hand.

Giuliana put the three mugs of tea on the table along with a carton of milk and a sugar bowl, then got her notepad and pen out of her bag, and sat down at last. "Frau Gurtner, how long was your husband missing before you called the police?"

"I got home from work at six, and he'd taken the dog for a walk. He usually does . . . did that on Mondays around four and was back by five-thirty at the latest. I just thought he'd run into a friend and was having a drink. At seven I called to see if he'd be home for dinner, and there was one of those messages saying he wasn't available." Nicole was turning the sugar bowl lid round and round in her hands, her forehead wrinkled in concentration, as though even remembering what she had done a few hours earlier was an effort. "So, I started making calls to the older kids, then his hospital colleagues, some of his friends. And finally the police. I knew they'd think I was overreacting, but I wanted them to check the hospitals. An hour or so later, we heard he'd fallen in the Aare."

"And you, Philipp? Where were you all day, and when did you get home?"

The boy met her eyes at last, and she realized she hadn't heard him speak since she'd arrived. His voice, when he answered her, was a mutter. "I was in class until about four, when I biked over to a friend's house. We hung out for a while. I got home a little after Mam, maybe six-fifteen."

"Okay." She gave him an encouraging smile. "Your school?"

"Kirchenfeld," he answered. It was the same *Gymnasium* her daughter Isabelle attended.

Before Giuliana could ask another question, Nicole said, "I'd like to see my husband's body tonight. Can you drive me to . . . wherever he is? Please."

"Have you found Polo?" Philipp snapped. Then his cheeks reddened, and he lowered his voice. "He's a long-haired dachshund, black and tan, and he's old." He gave her a look from under his hair that was almost pleading. He was just a kid, she reminded herself, his dad was dead, and he needed his dog.

"I'm afraid not. But the patrols have been told to keep an eye out, and I'll pass on his description."

"What about seeing my husband?" Nicole asked, and Giuliana knew the time had come to tell them the truth.

"That should be possible," she told the widow, then glanced over to be sure Philipp was listening. "But before I set it up, I need to explain: the police don't think your husband's death was an accident. It looks like he was in a fight before he went into the river."

She was about to mention the head wound when Philipp interrupted. "What? That can't . . ." He broke off, rested his forehead on the table, and covered his head with his arms. His mother moved her chair closer to his and embraced him, murmuring, her head bent over his.

Giuliana was torn between sympathy for Nicole and Philipp's grief, and frustration at not being able to see their faces or hear what Nicole was saying. Before Philipp had put his head down, she'd seen shock in both their expressions. But was it shock at the violence—or shock that the evidence of it had already been discovered?

Either way, Erwin was waiting; she had to hurry things along. "I need to ask both of you if you can think of anyone who might have been angry enough with Herr Doktor Gurtner to want to hurt him."

Philipp didn't raise his head from the table. His mother turned her face to Giuliana, eyes distant. After a moment, she shook her head. "There's no one. Maybe at the hospital, but . . . My husband is . . . was . . . an outstanding surgeon. He could be demanding at times, I know, but they all respected him. That's why he stayed on part-time, even after retirement. I can't believe anyone would . . ."

Without warning, Philipp scraped his chair back and left the kitchen. Nicole stared after him, then got up. "Sorry," she murmured, as she went after him.

Damn. Giuliana was running out of time, and she'd barely begun to question the most obvious suspect: a wife who was over twenty years younger than her husband and very attractive. She still needed to find out where Nicole worked, so they could check what time she'd left that afternoon. She burned to know if Gurtner had really had as much money as she suspected. If he'd gambled, if he'd been a drug user, if he was in debt. And she itched to get her hands on Nicole's phone, to check for signs of another man in her life.

As if to mock her thoughts, a phone rang, and Giuliana realized she was hearing the landline on the kitchen counter. After a moment of hesitation, she got up to answer it.

"Linder at the Gurtners'."

"*Bitte*? Who are you?" The voice was high-pitched with tension.

"Giuliana Linder. And your name, please?" She spoke slowly, trying to project calm.

"I'm Jagoda Gurtner. Where's Nicole? Why are you there? Is there more news about my father-in-law's accident?"

The wife of one of the two older sons. Giuliana hated to tell her by phone that the surgeon's death was no accident, but if she didn't do it now, Jagoda would hear the news from Nicole. She explained.

"He was pushed into the Aare? How could . . .? Do you . . . do you know who did it?"

Giuliana went over the basic facts, and asked a few questions. She learned that Jagoda was married to the oldest son, Patrick, aged thirty-seven. They had two small daughters. Gurtner's other son, Patrick's thirty-five-year-old brother Markus, was single, and Jagoda *thought* he lived alone. The emphasis in her sentence suggested that Jagoda was either unsure about, or unhappy about, Markus's relationship situation. Giuliana wondered which it was.

"I need to tell my husband," Jagoda said, "so he can call his mother." She drew a deep breath, and added shakily, "It must have been a robbery. Oh, God." Her voice broke on a sob. "I wish . . ."

When someone died, people always said, "I wish." They wished they had seen the person more recently, called more often, shared a secret, asked important questions, expressed love and gratitude more openly. Guilt, recriminations, regrets: they were as much a part of death as grief.

"I'll tell Nicole you called" was all Giuliana said.

Jagoda mumbled something and hung up; only after Giuliana had run the sounds over in her head a few times did she decipher the words, "Give Fippu my love."

Fippu: it was a common nickname for Philipp. Giuliana added what she'd learned about Gurtner's older children to her spiral pad, noting that Patrick and Jagoda were clearly close to Gurtner's second family. Then she checked her watch: eleven-forty and Erwin was still waiting for her to check in.

She was debating whether to go looking for Nicole and Philipp when the widow returned to the kitchen and stood, hunched, by the counter. Her face was drawn and blotchy, but she seemed less shaky. Philipp's black hoodie was gone; Nicole had put a long camel-colored cardigan over her black silk shirt, and she was hugging it closed around her waist. "Who was on the phone?" she asked.

"Your daughter-in-law," Giuliana answered and summarized the call.

Nicole nodded. "I already asked her and Patrick to help with the funeral. Thank God we'll be able to do it together." She took a deep breath and smoothed down her cardigan. "When can we go?"

"I just have a couple more things to ask you. Let's sit." They went back to the table, and Giuliana took a gulp of cooling tea before asking, "Do you know if your husband had on a watch when he went out with the dog? If so, what did it look like?"

"Well, I can't be completely sure, since I was at work, but he always wore the same watch, an Audemars Piguet that his mother gave him when he graduated from medical school. It's platinum, with a metal band, and the face is black. Why?"

"It looks like it may have been stolen," Giuliana answered.

Nicole lifted a hand to her mouth. A sob worked its way through her fingers, but she made a fist and pressed it against her lips. "What else?"

"I need a recent photo of your husband."

Nicole went into the adjacent living-room area and brought back a terracotta-colored handbag. She found her mobile and scrolled for a while, then passed Giuliana the phone, with fresh tears in her eyes. "Will this one do?"

Giuliana studied the picture, which showed the upper body of a white-haired man in a polo shirt, smiling expansively into the camera. His eyes were blue, his chin strong, and his neck and arm muscles well defined. A suspicion of jowls blurred his throat, and Giuliana thought she saw something in his smile—an overdose of self-satisfaction, perhaps? Still, all in all, he was a handsome man who looked at least ten years younger than his age.

"That's perfect." Giuliana got a card from her jacket pocket and wrote her cell number on it. "If you could send it there . . . and then tell me about your job."

Nicole forwarded the photo before saying, "I work three days a week as an assistant in a doctors' office; I'll give you the website."

Giuliana passed her notepad over and watched Nicole write. Of course, an alibi provided by a busy doctor might not be airtight. Everything Nicole and Philipp had said about that afternoon and evening would have to be checked. The house would be searched, too— although at this point it was hard to know what they should look for.

"That's enough for now," she said when Nicole passed the notepad back. "Why don't you get ready while I call ahead?"

Despite having said she wanted to get going, Nicole rose slowly, and Giuliana watched how she crept up the stairs, clinging to the banister.

As soon as Nicole was out of sight, Giuliana moved into the small utility room off the kitchen and called Erwin.

"What the hell's going on?" he barked. "I thought you were meeting me here."

"You asked me to interview the wife and son first, remember? I'll be there in another twenty minutes, and I'm bringing the wife to see the body."

"Shit! Can't that wait?"

"Let her get it over with," Giuliana said. It's her right, she felt like adding, and, besides, it was a kindness.

"If you say so. I'll tell the folks here to make sure his brains aren't hanging out."

That was Erwin. Giuliana rolled her eyes despite her fondness for him. "I'll be there as fast as I can."

She walked back into the kitchen to find Philipp leaning against the table, fingers in his pockets and thumbs hooked through his belt loops. "I'm coming with you to . . . where my father is," he said. His voice sounded tough, but his eyes were fearful.

"I think your mother would appreciate that," Giuliana said. "We're going to the Institute of Forensic Medicine. It's across the street from the *Inselspital*."

"Have they . . . cut him up?" His voice was barely more than a whisper.

"A specialist will need to examine the body so we can get more information about how he died, but that hasn't happened yet." She spoke gently. "It's not the signs of violence you need to prepare yourself for. It's that—well, he might not look like himself. A corpse seems . . . empty. The face you know by heart looks strange. You may not even recognize him at first. Don't feel bad if that happens. It's common."

Philipp nodded and looked quickly away.

He went into the entrance hall, as Nicole came downstairs. Whatever she'd done to her face and hair, she looked less ravaged.

"I'm ready," she said.

Five minutes later, Giuliana was driving the three of them through a fresh outbreak of sleet toward the Monbijou Bridge. Beside her, in the front, Nicole was lost in her own thoughts; in the backseat Philipp was shifting his long legs around, trying to get comfortable.

The dark silence of the car ought to give Giuliana a chance to ask Nicole more questions. Having checked her brakes and felt no skidding, she pushed driving to the back of her mind and said, "Tell me about your husband."

At first Nicole said nothing, and Giuliana thought she wouldn't answer. Then she began to talk. Her voice had a storytelling lilt to it, as if she were submerged in her own words and her own world.

"Everyone looks up to Hannes. Dinner parties, conferences, presentations—they're effortless for him. When I met him, he was surrounded by smiling people, like a magnet that had drawn them together. I was drawn to him, too."

Unfortunately he was married and had two children, thought Giuliana, and then chided herself: she didn't know that for sure; maybe he'd already separated from his first wife.

They were driving around a traffic circle that was usually a battleground for trams, buses, and cars; at this hour, it was silent and empty. "How old were you when you met him?"

"I was thirty-one and he was forty-nine, still with his first wife, Kathrin. When she found out three years later that Hannes and I were having an affair, she divorced him. Otherwise, I'm not sure he'd ever have left her. I mean, he seemed perfectly content to juggle a wife and a girlfriend indefinitely." A trace of bitter humor crept into her voice.

Giuliana glanced in her rearview mirror at Philipp's wide eyes. She bet he'd never heard his mother talk like this. Still, if Nicole had temporarily forgotten her son's presence, so much the better. "So, you got married," Giuliana said.

"Yes. Afterward, things changed—but that's normal. Even before we married, I knew that his work was sacred. My father was a doctor. I saw how hard it was for my mother, and still I chose exactly the same life. And Hannes—he grew up in the Emmental with a traditional village GP as a father, who was a god in white. Even at home my father-in-law was a benevolent dictator." She paused. "Actually, I'm not sure how benevolent he was. I never knew him."

"How did your husband find time to keep in touch with his family . . . the older children, for instance?" Giuliana asked, trying not to interrupt the flow of Nicole's thoughts.

"I encouraged those relationships. Once Kathrin and Hannes divorced, I got pregnant with Philipp right away, which Hannes . . ." She broke off and glanced back at Philipp.

Gurtner had just escaped the responsibilities of a home with kids, and Giuliana doubted whether he would have been overjoyed when his beautiful young wife announced she was pregnant. Yes, she really had been beautiful, Giuliana decided, picturing her twenty years younger, relaxed and sparkling instead of gray with grief.

Nicole must have decided to plow on, even in front of Philipp, because she resumed her story. "I wanted Philipp to know his brothers, so I told Hannes I was glad to have his kids around. In fact, I often invited them over myself. It was hard at the beginning, with them being rude and repeating inappropriate comments their mother had made. But then Kathrin met a man herself, and things settled down."

Giuliana made an encouraging noise; in fact, she was struck by the effort Nicole had made with her stepsons—assuming she wasn't just trying to make herself sound good.

Nicole was still talking about Gurtner's family. "Patrick and Markus were teenagers when I married Hannes, so they were at an age when children start seeing less of their father in any case. Patrick stayed in touch, though, and his little girls brought us all closer again. As for Markus, I . . . well, he was a problem before I came along, and he's turned out fine. At least, I . . . I think so." Her voice trailed away.

It was after midnight. Giuliana had been driving deliberately slowly, but they'd be at the institute soon. Then Nicole would see her husband's body, and the full reality of his death would descend upon her.

"What about your husband's medical colleagues?" she asked, deciding that this was not the right moment to ask more about the son named Markus who only *might* be fine.

Nicole sighed. Whatever impulse had made her pour out her feelings seemed to be over, and she looked drained. Then she straightened in her seat and spoke again. Now she sounded dutiful, not eager, and she used the past tense.

"Hannes was senior heart surgeon at the university hospital, so he had a lot of people under him. And even the ones who didn't report to him directly—anesthesiologists and lung specialists and all the rest—were mostly younger than he was."

Giuliana took her eyes off the road long enough to meet Nicole's eyes and nod. "So, he was the boss."

"Exactly." Nicole looked relieved as she shifted back to staring through the windshield. "He was in charge of all the major heart operations, and he expected staff to do things the way he wanted them done. Which I think most of them did. He'd talk about his workday sometimes, and we attended hospital social events, but I can't say I really knew any of his colleagues. You'll have to ask them what they thought of him."

They were pulling into the parking garage next door to the institute. Talking about her husband had taken Nicole's mind off what was coming, but now she was afraid—Giuliana could hear it in her shallow breathing as she spoke.

Giuliana ushered the two of them into the institute's bleak waiting area, a small glass box off the entrance hall. It had two sofas covered in a rusty tweed that was probably supposed to blend with the maize-colored armchairs but didn't. The dog-eared magazines on the end tables featured TV personalities and obscure European royals.

"I know you want to go in to your husband as soon as possible," she told Nicole, "but I need to leave you here for a moment. I'll check in with Erwin Sägesser, the detective who's running the investigation, and be right back." In fact, she mainly wanted to make sure the body was ready for viewing.

Nicole looked less lost now, more determined. She had on a red wool coat, and the bright color seemed to lend her fortitude. She nodded briskly, then took a pad and pen out of her purse. "Fippu, I need your help with the death notice," she said. "We should get something into the newspapers right away. Why don't we try to come up with a draft to show your brothers before we send it off?"

Giuliana admired her, the way she engaged her son's mind to keep it off his fears. She seemed like a loving mother. It sounded like she'd gracefully accepted her other roles over the years, too: active stepmother to two boys who could sometimes hurt her; homemaker and wife to a busy surgeon who was often absent—and all on top of her own job. Nothing about her suggested that she had been looking for a fast way out of her marriage. However, as Giuliana set off to look for Erwin, she reminded herself that Nicole—like the spouse of any homicide victim—was at the top of their list of suspects.

5

Giuliana followed the sound of Erwin's voice to one of the institute's tiny offices. Seeing her in the doorway, he interrupted his phone call to growl, "Finally. Where's the wife? Let's get this over with." Before she could respond, he was booming into the phone again. "I don't give a fuck if their routine is wrecked by the police barriers. Tell him if any of them mess up our crime site, you'll arrest them."

Giuliana suppressed a sigh and waited until he'd ended his conversation, then held out a hand. "Ciao, Erwin."

"Giule." His hand engulfed hers. "It's been eight hours since we found that body, and I feel like everyone but me is standing around with his thumb up his ass. So, did the wife kill him?"

"Too soon to say. She and the son are in the waiting room." That might cause him to lower his voice. Or not.

"I've talked to the pathologist," he went on, scratching at the gray stubble on his cheek. Over twenty years earlier, when she'd joined the cops, Erwin had been all muscles and bad jokes, with brains well hidden. Now the brains were more obvious and the jokes less sexist; some of the muscle had turned to fat, but there was still plenty left.

She broke out of her moment of nostalgia: Erwin was still talking about the pathologist. "She'll do the complete autopsy tomorrow," he said, "but we've got enough to get started. Right now the dead doc is laid out looking pretty, so push the family in there to see him. Then we can get rid of them and work. I want my first orders for the team in place before I go to bed."

It took only ten minutes for mother and son to finish the viewing. Philipp wanted to stay longer and sit with the body, but to Giuliana's relief, Nicole reminded him they'd have time to do that later. For now, it would be best for them to go home and try to get some sleep.

"Will you be able to?" Giuliana asked quietly as she walked Nicole out of the main doors and over to the police car that Erwin had managed to rustle up. Philipp trailed behind. "Do you want me to have the policewoman drive you by the emergency room; shall I get a doctor to prescribe you some sleeping pills?"

Nicole stumbled a little, and Giuliana reached out to steady her.

"Thanks, but I keep stuff at home for bad nights. We'll be all right. A lot of arrangements need to be made." Her face wavered, and she drew a jagged breath. "We'll be all right," she repeated.

Philipp caught up with them at the waiting police car. His eyes were red and swollen from crying, but he looked better, somehow. "I'm going to make flyers about Polo tomorrow and put them around the neighborhood. You'll keep looking for him, right?"

"We will. And try not to worry. He may already be at an animal shelter. Or even waiting at home for you."

Giuliana had never owned a dog; her knowledge of them stemmed from children's books. In those stories, dogs always found their way home, even when they had to cover vast distances. Did they do that in real life? She hoped she wasn't treating Philipp like her own eleven-year-old son.

She extracted a slightly worn-looking card from her handbag and gave it to the boy, before remembering Nicole already had one. Well, Philipp was a legal adult too. "Until I hear from you, we'll keep searching."

* * *

Giuliana and Erwin settled down in the now empty waiting room. Erwin dumped himself into the armchair, while Giuliana took off her boots and curled up on a sofa. Then she summarized what she'd learned from Nicole, which wasn't much to base a homicide investigation on. Finishing her report, she added, "Surely a surgeon has all kinds of opportunities to upset people—fellow doctors, medical students, patients."

"Yeah," said Erwin. He slid deeper into his armchair, hooked one foot under an end table and dragged it forward until he could rest his legs on it, then crossed his arms on his chest. "I'll follow up with the Insel Hospital's legal department, ask about complaints. I've known some doctors I wouldn't mind braining with a rock, the puffed-up bastards. Hmm. How else does a man like Gurtner make enemies? I checked online, and he's a big deal in the *Burgergemeinde*—active for a while in the central organization and now in his own guild, the Cloth Handlers. Maybe the killer was a fellow burgher."

Giuliana nodded. "Yeah, I saw Gurtner was a von Eichwil." The names of the great founding families of the city were familiar to most Bernese: the von Graffenrieds, von Erlachs, and von Eichwils, among others. She smiled at her colleague. "Now, that would be a vision: one elderly patrician pitching another into the Aare. Because of a seven-hundred-year-old family feud, maybe?"

"More likely because of a one-year-old embezzlement scheme. Those fuckers must have all sorts of shady deals going on."

"Then there's his immediate family," Giuliana said. "Why don't you let Renzo and me divide them up between us? We'll need interviews with the older sons, and I'd like to talk to the first wife as well."

"Good. Renzo's interviewing talents are wasted with him running the search along the Aare. I'll get one of the other *Fahnder* to take that over, so you and he can focus on the Gurtner family. Too bad there's no daughter for him to wow."

Giuliana said nothing but winced inwardly, knowing how Renzo resented jokes about his looks. She and Erwin agreed that Renzo should report to her directly on the case. As Erwin went over his plans for the following day, Giuliana reminded him about Polo.

"I forgot the mutt," Erwin admitted. "We'll tell our investigators to ask about a dachshund on the loose—that's something people would notice. I'll make a note to check pawn shops and jewelry stores for the missing watch—and we need to be sure no other valuables were taken from the body. You can ask the family."

"What about the one-one-seven call? We should listen to that, see if we get any leads. It's strange, the caller disappearing. Most people would stick around to be the center of attention. Or at least lend a hand."

"Maybe so. The guy must have known the doc was dead, though. I'm not saying it was the caller's fault. No one in his right mind would have jumped into the Aare in last night's weather, even to rescue a drowning man."

I'll bet *you* would have, Giuliana thought.

"Still," he went on, "the caller probably felt like he'd fucked up, so he snuck off."

Giuliana shook her head. "That call still bothers me." She stared at a spray of silk flowers in a vase perched next to the sofa; they were so dusty and faded she couldn't tell what color they'd originally been. "Suppose a biker crashed into the old guy. Or a jogger. Gurtner may have been seventy-two, but he wasn't frail. I'll bet he didn't suffer fools gladly. Say they started to trade insults, got into a fight, and Gurtner fell in the Aare. The other man tried to save him, made the call, and ran away."

"It's possible," Erwin said. "But the stolen watch doesn't fit with a jogger. And a thief doesn't fit with an attempted rescue."

They sat in silence. Giuliana suddenly found that she couldn't think anymore. She tried vainly to hide a yawn behind her hand.

"It's two-thirty," Erwin said. "We're both beat. I'll figure out who should take Renzo's place on the site and get some other stuff rolling, then I'm off to bed. You go home now and we'll meet tomorrow."

She was at the door of the waiting room when Erwin called out to her back, "By the way." He paused. "Toni Rossel is our prosecutor."

She turned to look at him, eyebrows raised.

"Yeah," he said. He gave her a grimace and a shrug that conveyed how helpless he was to keep the rotation system from occasionally assigning Toni to their cases. Then he disappeared down the hall.

Giuliana walked to her car, teeth gritted, shaking her head. Christ! Now she'd have to deal with that operator Toni. It had been two years since she'd been required to work with him on an investigation, and she supposed she should count herself lucky for that. Well, she'd cope. Maybe MeToo had taught him something.

The icy streets were empty of cars and people, and even driving carefully she was home from the institute in ten minutes. There was no parking near her apartment, but she found a space two blocks away on a street that traversed a steep, tree-covered hillside. A half-hidden staircase between two houses brought her to the top of the hill where a circle of hundred-year-old buildings around a small playground marked her neighborhood. On one side of the hill was Bern's medieval city, invisible beyond the thick trees below her. Looming above her on the other side, where she could still see a few distant lights through the fog, was Bern's own mountain, the Gurten. And twisting through all of it was the Aare. No matter where you stood in Bern, you were never far from its river.

She let herself into the apartment; shed coat, gloves, boots, and scarf; and felt her way into the kitchen, where she turned on the light and drank a glass of water. Then she peeked at her eleven-year-old, Lukas. In the glow of a nightlight, his dark curls were visible on the pillow, but the rest of him was hidden under a duvet covered with spaceships. Next door, his sister Isabelle slept in darkness; Giuliana, sticking her head into the room, could just make out the sleeping teenager's form. She stood there a moment, listening to her daughter's quiet breathing and trying to figure out why her room smelled of limes. Probably a new shampoo.

Closing Isabelle's door, she continued down the hall into her and Ueli's bedroom. As usual, silent as she was, she couldn't get ready for bed and creep under the covers without waking her husband. "You fine?" he mumbled.

"Yeah. It's after three. I'm setting my alarm for eight-fifteen."

"S'okay. I got the kids." He scrunched over to her side of the bed, threw a heavy arm over her and, within seconds, was snoring lightly into her ear.

I'll never get to sleep like this, she thought—and then she was gone.

6

After four hours of sleep, Renzo was back on the Aare path before dawn to supervise the search. Drizzle was falling into the slush on the ground and paths, and the going was slippery for everyone, but at least it wasn't pouring anymore. He'd just finished talking to a jogger whose usual route along the river was blocked when his phone rang.

"Things going smoothly?" asked Erwin.

"Yes. I've got . . ."

Erwin interrupted him. "That's good, because I'm taking you off the crime scene. Be here for a nine-thirty staff meeting."

"*Testa di cazzo*," Renzo said to himself as Erwin hung up. What the fuck? They'd worked well together on the last case they'd shared, so why was the old bastard jerking him around? His first instinct was to call Giuliana to find out if he'd done something wrong, but he stopped himself. She'd been up as late as he had. Besides, if he called her every time he thought of her . . .

He put his phone back in his pocket, found a colleague from the search team to take charge of things, and left the riverbank. Twenty minutes later he stormed onto the homicide floor to find Erwin making coffee.

Before Renzo could say anything, Erwin clapped him on the shoulder and handed him the full cup he was holding. "Black okay?" Erwin poured another for himself. "You set up that detail on the Aare so well I can send Hansruedi down to run it. You're going to do interviews. Giule and I figured that was a better use of your time, huh?"

Renzo puffed out a long breath and tried to flush the anger-induced adrenalin out of his bloodstream. "Jesus, Erwin, I thought you were dragging me back here to chew me out."

"Why would I do that? Come on; let's sit down. I'm starting at nine-thirty sharp, whether Rossel is here or not."

Renzo had been assigned to cases prosecuted by Toni Rossel before, but he'd never worked directly with the man. Rossel won a large majority of his cases, which made him popular, and he was always friendly, slapping backs, shaking hands, and telling jokes. Women liked him, too—he had quite a reputation. Still, Renzo had heard that a lot of the seduction stories came from Toni's own mouth; how many were true, he didn't know. Erwin wasn't a Toni fan, apparently, but then Erwin didn't respond well to charm.

Sitting at the conference table drinking his coffee, Renzo watched Erwin hook his laptop up for a presentation. He respected Erwin enormously, but why couldn't the old man explain himself once in a while, instead of just issuing orders?

As if he'd read Renzo's mind, Erwin looked up at him and said, "You'll be reporting to Giuliana. Got a problem with that?"

Renzo swallowed his grin, but not before Erwin saw it and grinned too. "Okay, then." He started to flick through his presentation notes, while Renzo got up and walked over to the room's one window. His back to Erwin, he let himself feel happy, thinking about all the things he wanted to discuss with Giuliana.

Renzo was still smiling when he heard Rolf Straub, the top homicide detective, greet Erwin; he turned from the window to shake Rolf's hand and sit down. At 9:25, Giuliana and Walter Mosimann, another *Fahnder* like Renzo, arrived; Renzo kept his hellos casual.

At nine-thirty, without Rossel, Erwin began, quickly summarizing the known facts: the emergency call, the finding of the body, the pattern of the wounds and bruises indicating a fight, and, finally, the damage to the head.

"The riverbank upstream from the restaurant is rocky. Easy to pick up a stone, hit Gurtner and toss it in the water. But if Gurtner stumbled headfirst into the river—or was shoved—there are rocks just under the surface that would give him a similar head wound. From the state of the body, it's clear he washed up on the bank soon after he went in, which means the time of death may be right around when the emergency phone call was logged at 5:12 in the evening. We'll know more about all of this soon—the autopsy is going on right now. Giuliana? What about the wife and son?"

Renzo watched Giuliana's eyes turn away from Erwin and pass over the faces at the table, gathering her listeners in. No special eye contact for him, but, well, he was used to that when they worked together. "At the time of that one-one-seven call, Gurtner's wife was at work and his youngest son with a school friend," she said. "That sounds reasonable but hasn't been verified, so those are the first alibis we'll check."

Erwin nodded. "Okay, assignments. I've already sent Hansruedi Balmer to take over at the crime site. Walter, you're going to be in charge of canvassing Gurtner's neighborhood. We need to find people who saw him with the dog. If he left home about four—which his wife says he usually did—and took the path through the meadow here"—from his laptop Erwin projected a map of the area that highlighted the paths leading down to the river—"he'd have been on the Aare by four thirty. Sometime between then and the emergency call, he ended up in the Aare without his dog or his watch. The dog's a long-haired dachshund, and here—" Erwin clicked to a photo of a slim silver-and-black wristwatch. "It's an Audemars Piguet worth about forty thousand Swiss francs."

There was a moment of silence during which Renzo glanced at his own watch, a Tissot he'd bought for almost a thousand francs. Even as he'd chosen it, to celebrate moving out of uniform into plainclothes, he'd known that a Swatch for a tenth of that price would have served him just as well. How could anyone rationalize having a forty-thousand-franc watch?

Into the bubble of quiet around the table burst Toni Rossel. Instead of slipping into a seat, he stood in the doorway, running his hand through his dark-blond curls and beaming unapologetically. It was, thought Renzo, almost as if he expected everyone to applaud or leap up to greet him. Leaning on the doorframe, Rossel took in the projection on the wall of the conference room and drawled, "Just because I'm late doesn't mean I need a new watch, Erwin. My Rolex works fine."

Renzo grinned; he couldn't help it. They all waited for Rossel to take a seat at the table so Erwin could continue, but instead, the prosecutor went around the small room shaking hands and squeezing shoulders. His blue eyes were full of warmth as they met Renzo's, and he said, "It's good to be working with you."

Giuliana was the last to be greeted, and Toni bypassed her outstretched hand and put an arm around her shoulders, kissing her cheeks three times. "You look terrific, Julie," he said. Sitting down, at last, in the empty seat next to her, he leaned toward her as if about to whisper in her ear.

Trying to process the compliment and the way Toni'd called her "Julie," in French, Renzo heard Giuliana murmur to Toni, "*Hör uf.*" Cut it out. Then she turned back to face Walter Mosimann, whom Erwin had put in charge of Gurtner's street, and picked up the briefing as if it had never been interrupted. "While you and your people are knocking on doors, Walter, try to pry out some gossip about the family."

Erwin nodded. "You know the stuff: father yelling at the kid, mother yelling at the father, evidence of battering. Plus even a whisper of either parent having someone on the side."

Renzo stole a glance at Walter, who was nodding as he wiped his glasses on a neatly ironed handkerchief. It was hard to imagine a stick like Walter gossiping about sexual escapades with anyone, let alone perfect strangers, but he was very conscientious, so it would get done.

Still puzzling over Toni's relationship with Giuliana, Renzo heard Erwin say his name. "Renzo, thanks for setting things up on the Aare. Next on your agenda are Gurtner's adult kids: try to see at least one of them this morning. In the afternoon hit the Insel Hospital to talk to Gurtner's colleagues. Not just other docs but anyone who worked with him. By noon I should have a list of names for you to try, and you can add to it. Giuliana is going to interview the first wife as soon as she can, and after that she and I will discuss next steps. Does everyone know enough to get started? Any questions? Rolf?"

"What do we know about the emergency caller?" The homicide boss spoke in his usual deliberate way, hands folded on the table, body held almost at attention.

"Zip," answered Erwin. "Tomorrow the papers will ask anyone who saw Gurtner during his walk to call in, and we're specifically requesting the man who dialed one-one-seven to come forward. I'm going to email all of you a recording of the call. Listen to it and tell me your ideas about the caller. Any other questions? Okay then. Let's get going."

Everyone except Toni stood; as for Giuliana, she was up and gone while the others were still gathering their belongings. So much for the quick chat Renzo had been hoping for.

As he headed for the door, Renzo glanced at Toni, whose lips were pressed together. Rising from his chair he said to Erwin, who was stacking papers, "Ah, too bad. I thought Giuliana would fill me in on what I missed, but I suppose she's too overwhelmed with work, poor girl. Maybe you can . . ."

"You'll get the minutes," Erwin said.

Toni smiled and shrugged.

Then Erwin turned and saw Renzo. "Come with me, and I'll give you the info on Gurtner's kids," he said. Renzo followed him out, leaving the prosecutor still smiling.

* * *

Patrick, the oldest of Gurtner's four children, was an economist who worked for the Federal Chancellery. Renzo had heard it said that, although the Federal Council ran the country, the chancellery ran the Federal Council. So, he was pleasantly surprised when Patrick offered to see him that morning at ten. It was an easy walk from the police station to the chancellery offices, but Renzo knew he'd need his car after the appointment, so he drove, blessing the regulations that allowed him to park illegally on police business.

The Federal Palace where Patrick worked sat on a ridge that towered over the Aare. From its back terrace, the view of the river, the hills beyond, and sometimes—when the weather was clear—the skyline filled with snow-covered Alps was a tourist's dream.

Renzo arrived early and used the time to do something he should have done much sooner: google Johann Gurtner. There were a number of short pieces about his accomplishments as a surgeon and his charitable activities in both the city and canton of Bern. Deciding to read them later, Renzo concentrated first on the pictures that accompanied the articles. They showed a tall, handsome man—first with blond hair, then blond-brown, then white—who projected an air of command. It wasn't just the influence of a white coat, either. One photo from the sixties showed a young, strong-chinned Gurtner in tank top and shorts receiving a trophy. Since there was a Swiss-style punt moored on a riverbank next to him, Renzo deduced it was for boating.

"Hello, sorry I'm late."

Renzo looked up from his phone and saw an older version of the youngster with the trophy. But while the man in the photo looked like he'd stride toward you, hand thrust out, his oldest son was smiling shyly as he ushered Renzo into his office. Though it had a large window, the room was still little more than a cramped space off a narrow corridor. Renzo watched Patrick arrange chairs so the two of them could sit side by side at the window instead of facing each other across an official desk.

"You asked if I could see you today," Patrick said, before Renzo could begin, "and I want to help with your investigation, but I only have half an hour now. Then I've got a meeting with my boss and *his* boss. I can talk to you as long as you'd like another time, but today..."

"I understand," said Renzo. "I'll stick to the most important questions." He couldn't help contrasting the man's pleasant composure to his own devastation the day after his father had died of cancer. And he'd had months to prepare for that. Why hadn't Patrick taken compassionate leave? Renzo hesitated, then said, "Let me offer you my condolences."

Patrick lifted a shoulder in a slight shrug, then leaned forward. "Thank you. But ... well ... my father left my mother when I was seventeen. I ... spent time with him, of course, but ... Anyway, my wife, Jagoda, her parents are Croatian. She believes in family. So, since our girls were born, we've had my father and Nicole to dinner, spent Christmas and Easter with them and Philipp. But the truth is, we weren't close. We haven't been for a long time." He leaned back, his face expressing no apology.

Well, the man was honest, at least. But Renzo's next words came out sharper than he'd intended. "The police think someone killed your father. Does that surprise you?"

"Of course it does," answered Patrick quickly. He paused and looked around his office as if there was something to see in the small, sparse room, and his gaze settled on a poster-sized black-and-white photograph of two girls against a background of leaves and flowers, one about four like Renzo's own Antonietta and the other a couple of years older. The younger girl gazed up at the older, who'd wrapped an arm around the younger's shoulders, looking down. The picture was saved from being saccharine by the mischievous expressions on the girls' faces.

"Your daughters?" Renzo asked.

Patrick nodded, smiling, and seemed to regain his calm. "Jagoda told me last night that the drowning wasn't an accident, and I'm still processing that. I can't imagine how Paps could get into a fight walking Polo. But if I knew of any 'enemies' I'd tell you." His voice made the quotation marks around the word "enemies" perfectly clear.

"Has your father been in a fistfight before?" Renzo asked.

"I know his own father pushed him into boxing classes when he was very young; I suppose those were the days when fighting was considered manly. But as an adult? He was much too concerned with his reputation, I'd say. And his hands. After all, he *was* a surgeon."

Renzo couldn't imagine a man as composed as Patrick punching anyone either, but he still wanted his alibi. First, though, he said, "Your brother Markus hasn't returned my calls. Is he out of town?"

"I'm sure he'll get back to you as soon as he can. He's a professional photographer; his schedule can be tight. He also grew apart from our father after the divorce. Like me."

Something about Patrick's calm, smiling demeanor was so deliberate that Renzo was sure he was holding back. "And Philipp?" he asked, probing in the hope that Patrick's composure would crack. "What do you know about his relationship with your father?"

Patrick shook his head. "He *is* almost twenty years younger than I am, you know. We all get along, when we see each other, but . . ." He shrugged. "I'm sorry not to be more helpful."

Renzo knew his own siblings so well he could have talked about them for hours. But maybe not to the police, he conceded.

Perhaps Patrick realized that his reticence was coming across strangely, since he added, "Markus might be able to tell you more about Philipp; I think they get together for a beer sometimes."

Renzo decided to ask one more question before turning to Patrick's alibi. "I'm going to the Insel to interview people about your father. I want to know what he was like."

Patrick stared out of the window for a moment. When he looked at Renzo, his face was sad. "He was a complicated man. Not very open. I gave up trying to understand him years ago." He smiled wryly. "I never considered psychology as a career—economics and politics were much safer choices." As he spoke, Patrick stood and pushed his chair back behind his desk.

Renzo stood too, and Patrick held an arm out, ushering him smoothly toward the door. But Renzo wouldn't be seen off so easily. "I need to know where you were yesterday between three-thirty and five-thirty in the afternoon," he said, his body in the doorway.

Patrick nodded. "I was here until about four. Then I went out to run some errands. I was back sometime after five-thirty because I had a late meeting at six."

There were paved paths running down from the palace to the riverbank, and from there it was only a short walk to the footbridge at Dählhölzli where Gurtner's corpse had been found. Patrick could easily have walked to any spot along the Aare where his father had been out with the dog, punched him in the eye, pushed him into the river, and been back in his office well before six. But the older man's swollen hand showed he'd thrown a punch as well, and Patrick's face was unmarked. Ribs, maybe? Renzo decided not to ask the man to take off his shirt inside an office made of glass at his place of work. That was something to check out later.

He handed Patrick a card with his email address. "I need you to make a list of every place you went yesterday afternoon, and send it to me by four o'clock. Please."

"I'll do that." Patrick slipped the card into the breast pocket of his shirt, walked Renzo to the staircase, shook his hand, and turned back to his office.

Afterward, walking to his car, Renzo considered what he'd learned—and what he might have missed—talking to Patrick. He'd totally failed to establish a rapport with the man, but that was his own fault; he hadn't been able to disguise his disquiet over Patrick's lack of grief. *So swallow your feelings better next time, dickhead,* he told himself, as he drove toward the Insel hospital. Well, he didn't think he'd missed anything major. He hoped not, anyway.

Patrick had told only part of the truth: he *was* meeting his boss, but not for another half hour. Once the cop had gone, he closed his office door, walked to the window and studied the same view—overcast right now—that a group of tourists below him were photographing. As he stared out, he dialed Markus. No answer—but that was no surprise. His brother rarely answered his phone when he was working, which was most of the time, except when he was out partying, and then he didn't answer it either.

Patrick stayed at the window, face turned away from anyone in the corridor walking by his office. He went over in his mind what he'd said about Markus. All very neutral. He'd probably made himself sound like a heartless shit, but better that than showing Donatelli how much he worried about his brother. Then the cop might have pressed him. As it was, Patrick was amazed he hadn't asked about Markus's eighteen months in juvie prison. That just proved what the family had been promised: that juvenile records were sealed. Not to the police, though. They'd find out soon enough.

He smacked his palm on the window frame. If only there was some way he could keep the cops away from his brother.

He smiled then, imagining Markus telling him, "So pray to Saint Jude for me, *Alter*." The patron saint of lost causes had been a running joke between the two brothers for years, although Patrick couldn't remember which of them had first pointed out that Jude had his work cut out looking after Markus. Not that either of them had ever believed in saints or the power of prayer. But the joke about St. Jude had become part of what connected them.

Christ, what would Nicole say if Donatelli asked *her* about Markus? Suppose she told him about Paps's sixtieth birthday? A family dinner, with his aunts Lotti and Bri and Bri's husband Hene. Patrick had brought Jagoda, although they hadn't known each other long, and she'd sat next to Philipp, then six, who'd been overexcited but trying to behave. And there was Markus.

Nine people sitting around the oval cherrywood table with empty dessert plates in front of them. It was late for Philipp, and now he was cuddling sleepily in Nicole's lap.

What had Paps said? It had been the tone as much as the words—something about getting out of Nicole's lap and not being such a mama's boy. Some kind of threat or punishment had been involved, too, Patrick thought: if Fippu kept acting like such a baby, he wouldn't be allowed to attend grown-up parties again.

Patrick was trying to ignore Paps as he talked to his uncle, and he hadn't noticed Markus leap from his seat. Yet suddenly his younger brother was standing over their father, lowering his face until the two of them were nose-to-nose, and snarling, "Leave Fippu alone, or I swear I'll make you sorry." Paps's chair crashed over as he got to his feet and took a swing at Markus, and Fippu began crying.

Patrick had been first to move. Grabbing Markus from behind and locking his arms around him, he'd dragged his brother away and half-carried him out of the room and down the hall. It hadn't been difficult; under his clothes, Markus had felt like skin and bones. He was sobbing, muttering "Bastard" under his breath.

"Can I let you go?" Patrick remembered asking. Markus had nodded, and with an arm around his brother's shoulders, Patrick had guided him out of the back door into the late March chill of the garden. They'd stood on the damp grass holding each other, while Markus cried on his shoulder. He remembered the smell of wet earth and the feel of his arms encircling his brother's fragile body.

What had he thought about as he'd hugged Markus? He was sure he would've been overwhelmed with the usual jumble of emotions that his brother generated in him: love and sadness, guilt and exasperation, anger and regret. He knew he'd asked, "Are you coked up?"

"I couldn't think of any other way to get myself here," Markus had answered.

"So, don't come next time," Patrick had said. "Don't do it. These family get-togethers—just stop trying to be the son he wants. You can visit Bri and Hene and me alone. Then we won't have to watch you suffer."

He'd stepped back and looked at Markus then, looked right through the slick image the kid projected and into the person who was his brother. He was gaunt. There had been enough light left in the spring sky to see that his pupils were huge, the whites of his eyes bloodshot. Under Patrick's hands, Markus's whole body seemed to jitter—he was probably speeding, too, but what difference did that make, now?

"Hey, man, you've made it through so much shit and you're safe now. So, just . . . hold it together." Patrick's voice had cracked, and he'd taken another step back, letting go of Markus to get a grip on himself, trying to lighten the mood. "What about Saint Jude, huh? All the work he's put into keeping you in one piece—you going to waste that?"

Over twelve years ago now.

Patrick had fetched Markus's coat and he'd left, without coming back into the house. To Patrick's enormous relief, he'd never come to another family gathering. After that, the brothers met a couple of times a year for a beer, and he and Jagoda had invited Markus and his woman-of-the-week to dinner a few times, but he didn't think they'd hugged since that March evening. Markus told the family he took photographs for a living, and recently he'd talked about having some success, but Patrick didn't know whether that was true. He was almost sure his brother had been drug-free for a while now, but he was afraid to ask.

And now their father had been killed, and the police would pay Markus a visit. At least if Markus called him back, Patrick could give him a heads-up. Or maybe he didn't need Patrick's help anymore. Actually, Patrick reminded himself, Markus had a lot more experience dealing with cops than he did.

Still, he picked up his phone again and, leaning back against the window, wrote a text: *Cop (Donatelli) here asking Qs about Paps, family. You're next. Anything I can do?* He sent it along with one of the sappy images of Saint Jude he'd add to a file every now and then, just to make Markus smile. Then he looked at his watch. Less than fifteen minutes until his meeting, and he still had papers to review.

With a sigh, he sat down in his desk chair and attempted to stop worrying about his brother—something he felt like he'd been trying and failing to do for his entire life.

7

After Erwin's early-morning meeting broke up, Giuliana phoned Gurtner's first wife Kathrin and made an appointment to see her at three-thirty. With that to look forward to, she buckled down to her deskwork. She assigned further research on Johann Gurtner and his family to several investigators, read interview notes as they started to come in and summarized them for Erwin, researched answers to questions that arrived from fieldworkers, updated the list of everything that needed doing, and made sure she and Erwin weren't duplicating their labor. In the process, she kept track of an ever-expanding timeline surrounding Gurtner's death.

Meanwhile, she tried to ignore the voice in her head that kept asking why she hadn't played along with Toni that morning. She'd broken the unspoken rule that said, No matter what happens, just laugh it off.

After an hour of driving herself crazy with self-recrimination, she got up to get another cup of coffee and found herself stomping to the espresso machine in the break room. *Calm down*, she told herself, but it wasn't easy. What was she supposed to do, let a man she hadn't been friends with for years paw at her during a meeting in order to keep the peace? Stay around and schmooze with him just to stroke his ego?

The draining board next to the sink was full of clean cups; she took one and turned on the coffee machine. She shouldn't be this upset. She enjoyed working with men and got along in their world; otherwise, she couldn't have joined the police and would never have been promoted. But Toni was a special case. He'd played her well that morning. His display of affection—which had no doubt made everyone in the room wonder just how close their relationship was—had left her unable to put him down without looking like a bitch. Well, she was damned if she was going to take part in his drama. Let them think she was a bitch, if that was what it took to keep him away from her.

By the time her coffee was ready, she was over the worst. Walking back to her desk, she realized it was Renzo, not Toni, who really worried her. She'd tried to avoid his eye during the meeting, but at one point she'd caught him giving her a look, both puzzled and wounded, that had gone to her heart. Surely he couldn't imagine that she'd hold him at arm's length, only to have a fling with Toni? But that was just the sort of thing Toni *wanted* her colleagues to believe. She felt her anger rising again and took a few slow breaths.

At least Erwin would never fall for anything Toni said or implied about her; he appeared to trust the man as little as she did.

Her mobile rang. It was the youngster who'd been checking through official records for any mention of the Gurtners.

"Listen to this," he said. Giuliana could hear the excitement in his voice. "Did you know that Markus Gurtner, the second of the victim's three sons, has a record? He tried to kill someone and went to juvenile prison."

"What?" Giuliana sat up in her chair. Surely Erwin didn't know this either, or he'd have brought it up at the staff meeting. "Tell me what happened."

Erwin wasn't answering his phone, so she sent him a text about the discovery, with a copy to Renzo, and settled back to her paperwork. It was not yet eleven when her phone rang again, and the receptionist asked if she could put through Charlotte Gurtner.

Giuliana had drawn herself an annotated family tree; glancing at the small whiteboard next to her desk, she saw that Charlotte was Gurtner's older sister: seventy-seven, unmarried, living in the Emmentaler village of Heidmatt.

"Good morning, Frau Gurtner. This is Giuliana Linder. I'm very glad you called. Let me—"

The older woman interrupted with a little huff of irritation. "I'm in Bern, and I want to know what's going on with the investigation. How soon can I talk with ...?" She paused, and Giuliana could picture her squinting at a slip of paper as she said, "Herr Sägesser?"

The woman's voice was soft and cultured but braced with rods of steel. Here was a person who wasn't used to hearing the word "no." Luckily, Giuliana didn't want to say no; she was ready for a break from her deskwork and glad to be spared a trip out to Heidmatt to interview Gurtner's older sister.

"Herr Sägesser is going to be out most of the day," she said, knowing Erwin was at the crime site that morning and meeting with Gurtner's lawyer after that. "I'm the second homicide detective assigned to Herr Doktor Gurtner's case, and I can see you right away, if you like."

"Thank you," Charlotte Gurtner said crisply. "Frau Linder, you said? Tell me where to come."

Forty minutes later, Giuliana was shaking hands with a tall woman in a pale-gray wool suit and a lilac-colored silk scarf. Charlotte Gurtner might be seventy-seven but she looked sixty, with a slim, straight figure and carefully maintained ash-blond hair in a chignon. The word "patrician" could have been coined for her, Giuliana thought, as they sat down at a table in the small meeting room on the top floor that Giuliana had hastily reserved. Charlotte had been accompanied by a plump, pleasant-faced woman of about fifty, whom she'd introduced as her secretary, Alice Schwander. Alice was currently in the tearoom across the street, waiting to be summoned.

Charlotte folded her hands on the table, but not before Giuliana noticed their trembling. She was about to reach out and touch the clasped hands, but changed her mind at the last moment. "Before we go any further," she said, "I hope you'll accept my condolences. I'm so sorry for the death of your brother."

"Thank you," said Charlotte, her frown relaxing a fraction.

Giuliana said, "When was the last time you saw him?"

The woman's face tightened again, and Giuliana cursed herself for going in too fast. "It was the second of November. He and my sister-in-law invited me to dinner, along with our younger sister Brigitte and her husband. I haven't seen Karl since then," she paused to draw in a shaky breath, "but we spoke on the phone about a week ago."

"Can you think of anything that might explain why someone would kill him?"

Charlotte bit her lip and fingered the amethyst brooch on the lapel of her wool jacket. Then she gave a slight, exasperated jerk of her head. "Surely this was a robbery. One reads so much about foreign gangs entering the country for a week or two and committing thefts all over Switzerland before driving away. 'Criminal tourism,' isn't that what the papers call it?"

"It exists, especially in the border cantons," Giuliana answered. "But we believe this crime was committed purposefully against your brother, since his wallet wasn't stolen."

Charlotte looked dazed for a moment, then she rallied, her expression even fiercer than before. "That's ridiculous. Why would anyone attack Karl?" She paused, lips pressed together and eyes fixed on Giuliana, as though daring her to argue. When Giuliana said nothing, she went on, "I've telephoned my brother at least once a week since he went away to boarding school at thirteen. He would have told me if he'd had an enemy, and he never said a word about . . . any such thing. It's quite impossible."

Giuliana had heard this response many times over the years "I know my son. He'd never hurt someone." "You've made a mistake; I'd be the first to know if my husband was stealing from his firm." "No, no. My daughter tells me everything." Denial was always easier than recognizing how little we truly understand the lives and hearts of the people we love. So now she just nodded at Charlotte, accepting her statement without question. "You and your brother were close."

"I'm five years older, so I've always felt . . . responsible for him, I suppose. He's truly exceptional. I mean . . ." She paused, covering her mouth with her fingertips. Again Giuliana fought the impulse to reach out a comforting hand; she might have done it with someone else, but she sensed it would be a mistake with Charlotte.

Finally, Charlotte clasped her hands on the table again. "I have always been very fond of him, and proud of him, too. Karl was a fine doctor and a fine man. A very fine man."

"Yes," Giuliana said. "Can you explain something? Both of Herr Doktor Gurtner's wives call him Hannes, but you call him Karl. Why is that?"

Charlotte actually smiled. "Our father was also named Johann, so my brother was called by his middle name as a boy. When he went away to school in Thun, he switched back to using his first name, so his nickname became Hannes. But for my sister and me, he'll always be Karl. Or even Karli, sometimes."

Giuliana tried to imagine how this stern, formal woman might have behaved with her little brother: chuckling at his amusing anecdotes, perhaps, or murmuring sympathetically as he told her his troubles. "What did you and your brother talk about on the phone recently? Was there anything worrying him?"

Charlotte's hands relaxed as she reminisced. "We talked about the three boys and how they were getting on; sometimes he was quite concerned about them. The youngest, Philipp, for example, finishes school next June and wants to do one of these gap years that are so much the fashion. Hannes was against it, unless the boy proposed some truly educational project instead of months of travel and odd jobs." She grimaced at Giuliana, who nodded, although she saw nothing wrong with travel for its own sake. "He also told me about some of the operations he performed. There were doctors and hospital administrators who made his life difficult: people who didn't have his work ethic or envied his position. But nothing specific came up recently. Oh, and we talked about his charity work for the *Burgergemeinde*. Our family has belonged to the Cloth Handler's Guild for generations, and Karl dispensed money to the guild's social cases."

Hmm. Not many doctors found time to do charity work; Gurtner truly had been an impressive man. But making decisions about who got how much money was just the kind of thing that could lead to conflict. Giuliana and Erwin had already decided to assign Renzo to this angle, so, after a pause to let Charlotte reveal anything else that was on her mind, Giuliana said, "Could you tell me more about your childhood. You lived in Heidmatt, right?"

Charlotte frowned. "I can't see how any of that is relevant. Aren't there more important things to think about?"

All Giuliana could do was answer truthfully. "At this stage it's hard to know what's relevant. Anything might be helpful."

Charlotte pursed her lips, then nodded. "Very well then." She paused, as if to gather her thoughts, and said, "Our father was the doctor for the village of Heidmatt and the smaller communities around it, including all the isolated farms. He insisted that the three of us children should attend the village school for our first six years. The other pupils went there until fifteen, when they were either apprenticed to a trade or left to work on the family farm. Since I'm so much older than Karl, we were only in school together during his first year, when he was seven; after that I was a day pupil in Langnau, our nearest town."

The older woman leaned back a little in her chair. Even if she didn't approve of Giuliana's questions about her family, she was clearly enjoying her memories. Giuliana took the opportunity to ask, "What was your brother like as a schoolboy?"

Charlotte chuckled. "The truth is, he was very naughty. You see, he was so intelligent that he got bored, so he got into trouble. The schoolmaster simply couldn't control the class. Karl could be very cheeky to him—and about him, too. Oh, he made my mother and me laugh with his impressions of that foolish man! You must remember that schoolmasters still beat boys back then, and Karl's teacher used to work himself into a frenzy, flailing at pupils right and left. Of course he never dared to beat Karl, but he bellowed at him often enough."

Giuliana found this story surprising. In a small Swiss village in the early sixties, a schoolmaster should have been an authority figure, earning the support and respect of parents. Gurtner's father, the local doctor, would have had considerable clout. Had he too been amused by his son's impudent mimicry of his teacher?

"It sounds like the three of you had good times together," she began.

Charlotte drew herself upright, and the shutters seemed to bang shut again. "Indeed. We were close." She stopped and closed her eyes, biting her lower lip, and when she looked at Giuliana again she was completely composed. "So," she said, "What are you doing to find out how he died?"

Giuliana leaned in. "Right now, at least twenty-five people are searching along the Aare, talking to Herr Gurtner's neighbors in the Elfenau, and going through footage from street cameras near where he walked. This afternoon we'll spread our investigation to the Insel hospital and begin checking the alibis of everyone who worked closely with your brother. One of my colleagues is speaking to Patrick Gurtner this morning; I'd be interested to hear your opinion of your nephews. And your brother's wives."

The older woman pursed her lips again. "Karl's divorce was . . . most unfortunate. I talked to him and Kathrin about staying in their marriage, but . . . things took their course." Giuliana nodded, and Charlotte went on, "That was almost twenty years ago, and today I have a . . . cordial relationship with Nicole. Actually, I've just come from visiting her."

"Are you aware of any problems in her marriage with your brother?"

Charlotte shook her head, frowning, but whether over the marriage or the indelicate question, Giuliana didn't know. She decided to push. "When we investigate a homicide, we always search for different kinds of betrayal. Do you have any reason to suspect that one of them could have been unfaithful?"

Giuliana expected an automatic denial, but instead Charlotte leaned forward and put her chin in her hands. Outside, Giuliana could hear the hum of midday traffic on Nordring; she hoped her hungry stomach wouldn't growl into the silence as well.

When Charlotte sat back, her air of certainty had abandoned her. "I don't know," she admitted. "Nicole would never have told me if she was having an affair, and Karl wouldn't have talked to me if he'd suspected it. Nor would he have confided in me about any . . . liaisons of his own, if there were any. Too many words were said between us when he and Kathrin split up. Maybe if I'd been more understanding then, I'd know more now." She gave a shaky sigh. A moment later, however, she added impatiently, "So, what did you want to ask me about the boys?"

I want to know if one of them might have lost his temper and killed his father, Giuliana thought, but what she said was, "Did they clash with their father over anything?"

"No." Charlotte's self-command was back in full force now. "There is nothing to discuss when it comes to Karl and the children." Giuliana opened her mouth to bring up Markus Gurtner's violent past, but Charlotte anticipated her. "I know you're skulking around Markus's criminal record, so let me set you straight. What's past is past. He's thirty-five now, and he's fine. So," she added with a single clap of her hands, "what can I tell you that will actually help you?"

The handclap made Giuliana feel like she was in the presence of a strict kindergarten teacher. Still, she took her time before answering Charlotte's question. So Markus was fine, was he? She remembered the night before on the way to the forensic institute, when Nicole had also said Markus was "fine." Thanks to her colleague's research, she now knew a lot more about Gurtner's second son, and she'd already decided to take him off Renzo's interview list and talk to him herself the next morning. Until she'd had a chance to form her own opinion, she'd hold back further questions about Markus.

So what *could* Charlotte Gurtner do to help the police? Giuliana took a deep breath and said, "As I told you, we don't think your brother's death was random. He was killed for a reason. You knew him all his life and you were close to him. Go home, reflect, and ask yourself who might have wanted him dead. If you get any ideas, no matter how vague, call me. Please."

Charlotte glanced down at the card Giuliana handed her. When she looked up, her expression was troubled. For the first time since she'd come in, she looked confused, tired, and old.

"No one could have wanted Karl dead," she said. "No one."

Charlotte sat next to Alice on the drive home from Bern to Heidmatt, her eyes closed and her head resting against the window. Alice thought she was asleep, which was what she wanted her to think. And truly, she did feel exhausted. She'd planned to accomplish more on this trip to the city than just a brief visit with Nicole and an interview at the police station. After the detective's questions, though, all she'd wanted to do was go home. She hated to admit it, even to herself, but the interview had upset her. She'd known before she arrived that it wouldn't do to reveal anything about Markus. What an embarrassment that boy was! Still, his bad behavior was nothing to go on about in public—and certainly not to the police.

No, it wasn't skirting around the topic of Markus that had distressed her—she'd been prepared for that. It was what the interview had shown her about her relationship with Karl. For decades she'd seen her brother once every six weeks and spoken with him on the phone every Sunday, but the policewoman's questions had made her feel that she hadn't been close to him. How could you love someone as much as she loved Karl and be so ignorant about his day-to-day life? Did that mean she hadn't really known him? She'd understood him so well when he was a child. But recently? She'd told the woman what an impressive person he'd been. Why hadn't she talked about how clever he was, how funny and charming and full of ideas and plans? "It sounds like the three of you had good times together," the policewoman had said, and she'd answered, "We were close." But she hadn't explained what joy that closeness had brought her—and what sacrifices.

Eyes still closed, she sat in the car remembering herself not as Charlotte, but as Lotti, a skinny thirteen-year-old who had finally managed to establish herself at her new school in Langnau. She remembered her delight at the start of the summer holiday that year. She could ride her pony for hours if she wanted to and play with Karl. Even Bri had become less of a brat since she'd turned three.

On that first school-free day, her father had come home early enough to join the family dinner. Such a thing was rare, and no one was expecting him. The table had been set in the courtyard, where the honeysuckle vines bloomed yellow and white against one wall, releasing a wonderful scent, and purple petunias and pink geraniums mingled in the low beds against the other walls. Dinner had been served at six-thirty as it always was, and Karl, as usual, was late. They'd all—except Karl—just sat down, and she and Bri jumped up and ran to their father when they saw him step through the glass doors. She got there first and he kissed her cheek as she hung on his arm, but it was Bri he swung up in the air, shaking off Lotti's hand in order to do it. She felt a pinch of pain. Then she reminded herself that she was a teenager now and strolled sedately back to her seat. Mother was standing at her place, and Father came over to kiss her cheek, too. The maid, Ida, scurried in with cutlery and glasses for him, and he thanked her and took his seat across from Mother. How pleased Karl will be to see Father, Lotti thought. After supper, Father usually went to his study to write up notes on his patients in a big leather book, and Karl might miss him if he didn't come soon.

She told her father about Foxie, her pony, and he nodded and smiled as he listened. Even as she talked, though, she could tell something was wrong. Her mother was eating more slowly than usual, casting anxious glances at the glass doors between bites, while her father gazed up at her mother from his plate now and then with angry eyes. Finally, he put down his knife and fork in a careful way and said, "Thérèse, is this typical? Do you let the boy come to the table whenever he feels like it? Are you incapable of exerting even the slightest discipline over . . . ?" He broke off as the maid brought out another dish of boiled potatoes.

Now it was her mother's turn to raise hot eyes in her father's direction, and her voice was sharp when she said, "Please, Johann. He's just a boy, and it's the start of school holidays. He'll come in when he's hungry. Now," Mother tried a gay voice, "tell us where you went today—all over the region as usual? Any interesting patients?"

Normally, Lotti was on Mother's side when Father got cross with her. This evening she was surprised to find a spark of anger in herself that echoed her father's. *She* always had to be at the table at six-thirty for dinner. It wasn't just her father's rule, but her mother's as well. Why didn't Mother make Karl come in, too?

Then Bri, who'd only just graduated to the grown-up mealtime, crowed, "All done." Her plate was clean of meat and vegetables, and she raised her arms in Father's direction. "I want to sit on your lap, Vati." She beamed at him, oblivious to the tension at the table.

Father's face cleared as he looked at Bri, stretching her pudgy arms to him across the table. "Brigitte, let your father eat in peace," said her mother, but Father laughed, got up from his unfinished meal, took the little girl in his arms and settled her onto his lap. Awkwardly, he continued to cut up meat and potatoes and eat them. Bri's hand stole out, grabbed a round of cooked carrot from his plate and popped it into her mouth.

"And you talk to me about discipline," she heard her mother say in a soft voice she wasn't sure her father could hear.

Just then Karl rushed into the courtyard, his hands clean but the rest of him dirty from playing out of doors. "Vati," he called as he came toward the table, "Ida told me you were here. Now I can show you the dam I've been building; it's . . ."

"You're twenty minutes late for dinner, Karl," his father said, pointing to the place on his right where Karl was supposed to be. Father's voice was calm. Good—he wasn't angry after all; he was just being stern. Now all Karl had to do was apologize.

"I didn't know *you* were here, Vati," her brother said casually, still not taking his seat, "or I'd have been here sooner."

Her father's mouth tightened. "Your food was put on the table at six-thirty, as it always is. Sit down now and eat it."

Karl looked at the cold vegetables and the sliced veal with its congealing gravy; he turned to the maid waiting by the doors. "I need some new food, Ida," he called out. Ida started to come toward him, but Father held out a hand to stop her.

"You will eat the food on your plate," said Father.

Karl glanced up at his father, and Lotti could see that he'd finally woken up to the fact that he was in trouble. Truly, thought Lotti, it wasn't fair. If her mother never expected Karl to be home on time, then Father should be angry with Mother, not Karl. She waited for her mother to explain that Karl wasn't to blame, but Mother simply took another bite of veal. Slowly her brother sat down, picked up his fork, speared a round of carrot, put it in his mouth, and chewed it. As he ate, he stared, not at their father, but at Bri, who still sat next to him cuddled in their father's lap, no longer looking so cheerful.

Noticing Karl watching her, she said to him, "I ate everything. I like carrots." Her eyebrows drew together in concentration, as if she were trying to understand what was making her big brother unhappy. "I can eat your carrots, if you want," she added. Father, who'd been staring off into the distance, smiled and kissed the top of her head. One of his big hands held her firmly on his lap, while the other picked up his wine glass.

Karl's face turned dark, and he dropped his fork onto the stone floor of the terrace and bent to pick it up. Bri screamed suddenly and burst into tears; Karl was already sitting upright in his seat, fork in hand, calmly eating cold potatoes.

"Bri, what in the world . . .?" said her father, as the little girl's wails rose in pitch. All Lotti could understand through her sobbing was, "Hurt!"

"Ida," their mother called to the maid. "I'll see to the fruit and coffee with Marta . You take the baby upstairs and put her to bed."

Ida carried Bri, whose wails were subsiding, into the house. Lotti had never taken her eyes off her brother since the moment she'd seen him push his fork off the table on purpose. She knew he'd hurt Bri—probably pinched her leg under cover of the tablecloth. Their father, drinking his wine, hadn't even noticed Karl bend over to retrieve his fork. But her mother . . . She turned, frowning, and caught her mother looking at her. *Not a word,* said her mother's expression, as clearly as if she had spoken. When Lotti looked back at Karl, he was smiling at her so lovingly that she couldn't help but smile back.

That night in bed she lay awake, thinking about choosing sides. It wasn't fair that she should have to decide, but, even so, she knew she'd already chosen. She was on Karl's side, always, which meant she had to pick Mother over Father, because Mother loved Karl the most. Mother loved Karl more than she loved Father or Bri or Charlotte. So Charlotte chose to be on Mother's side.

Now, over sixty years later, tears ran down Charlotte Gurtner's face. She stopped pretending to be asleep and sat up. Alice took one hand off the steering wheel to place it briefly on her knee but said nothing. Thank God for Alice. Charlotte pulled a handkerchief out of her jacket pocket, wiped her eyes, blew her nose, and glanced out the window to see they were almost in Heidmatt and it was still raining.

"You've made good time," she said to her secretary. "What are you planning for lunch?"

8

Despite having eaten an excellent lunch of penne with eggplant and ricotta at a restaurant near Bern's teaching hospital complex, Renzo was in a bad mood. Every step of the short distance he walked toward the hospital entrance was reluctant. It was hard to admit even to himself how much he hated the place—its harsh light and antiseptic smell, the rattle of carts on corridor floors and, above all, the voyeuristic glimpses into countless rooms whose beds held people battling pain and death.

Three years earlier, he'd spent what had felt like every spare minute of an eternal six weeks there, watching his sixty-six-year-old father die of lung cancer. Just walking through the automatic double doors into the foyer made his stomach clench, and he couldn't conjure a single smile for the woman who gave him directions to cardiovascular surgery: follow a thick blue floor stripe through the main hall, down two corridors, and up to a bank of elevators. And that was only the first step. It was as if the buildings' architects had been instructed to make the place as confusing as possible, in order to keep visitors intimidated. Renzo gritted his teeth and found the blue line, reminding himself that he was not here this time as a supplicant stumbling through weeks of bewildered grief. He was an authority, with the right to demand information.

The heart surgeon Renzo had an appointment with, Herr Doktor Adrian Brun, was in his late forties; he'd come to the Insel from the University of Zürich's hospital to work under Gurtner ten years earlier. His headshot on the department website showed a receding hairline, thick brows, thin lips, and a serious expression marred by a hint of petulance. Renzo was ushered into Brun's office as soon as he arrived; full points to the man for not keeping him waiting, he thought, as he tried to settle himself comfortably in the dark wood chair across from Brun. The heart surgeon had risen to shake hands and now sat behind his desk, elbows resting on his blotter, fingertips pressed together. Behind him was a large painting, a forest landscape, blandly attractive. "I've got all the department secretaries and several people in the personnel office compiling the lists your Herr Sägesser requested," said Brun. "And now you're here, Herr Donatelli." His mouth formed a smile. "What *else* can we do for you?"

Renzo tried to control his temper. Before he could open his mouth, Brun was working to put him on the defensive. Well, he was damned if he was going to apologize for any trouble that investigating the death of this man's colleague was causing. He was sure Brun himself wasn't going through the past year's surgery schedules to confirm whom Gurtner had dealt with most often.

"Murder is disruptive." Renzo knew that some of his exasperation had crept into his voice, but he didn't care. "I'll..."

Brun interrupted. "I find it hard to believe Herr Gurtner was murdered." He said this with a frown and a small shake of the head, as if he suspected the police of identifying homicides simply to meet their quotas—or relieve boredom.

There was no way to sit comfortably in this hellish chair, Renzo decided, so he perched on its edge, a position that allowed him to rest his hands on Brun's desk. He saw the doctor's face register indignation at this invasion of his territory. Renzo smiled. "All the evidence of a homicide is there, Herr Doktor Brun. Provided by your fellow physician in forensic medicine. Now, since I don't have all the schedules yet, why don't you tell me where you were yesterday between three-thirty and five-thirty in the evening?"

The surgeon raised his eyes to the ceiling before saying, "I was operating until almost four-thirty, as the schedules will show; then I cleaned up and by five I was sitting right here, planning the department's work for the next month until almost seven. Hannes may have insisted on being called head of this department, but he only worked sixty percent."

"It can't have been fun, playing second fiddle to an old man who refused to retire," Renzo countered. "Didn't you come from Zürich expecting to take charge much sooner?"

Brun's eyes opened wide; then he drew his brows together and pursed his lips. Renzo imagined his dignity warring with his longing to complain about how unfairly he'd been treated. "I *was* told when I was hired that Gurtner would be gone by sixty-five at the latest. But it didn't work out that way."

Renzo hitched his chair forward and rested his lower forearms on the surgeon's desk. "Who can confirm that you were here in your office yesterday at five? Your secretary?"

"No. On Mondays she works until three-thirty." As soon as Renzo'd moved forward, Brun had leaned back in his padded leather chair; his hands were now folded over his stomach. It was hard to tell if his raised eyebrows referred to Renzo's question or the contamination of his desk. No point in really pissing him off, though—Brun *was* in charge of providing the scheduling information they needed for the doctors, medical students, nurses, and administrators Gurtner had worked with most often. Renzo dialed down his needling.

"We're grateful for all the work the Insel staff is doing. Once we know where everyone was scheduled to be and with whom, we can check if they were actually in place. The sooner we get the schedules, the sooner we can eliminate suspects. So," Renzo took his arms off the desk and put his hands on his thighs, "tell me why anyone might want to punch your colleague in the eye and push him into the Aare." He paused and looked Brun straight in the face. "Was Hannes Gurtner a man someone would want to kill?"

"Of course not," said Brun quickly. "He was enormously respected, a great . . ."

"Yes, we've heard over and over that he was an excellent surgeon. But that doesn't mean he didn't drive some of the people he worked with crazy."

Renzo watched Brun as he said this and something about the way the doctor's face changed, a flick of an eyebrow, a twist of the mouth, and a kindling in the eyes, suggested that he'd struck home. Not that he was surprised. A top-notch surgeon like Gurtner had to be a prima donna. Especially a surgeon whose mother's family had been helping to run the city of Bern—and the canton, too—since the thirteenth century.

Then, to Renzo's disappointment, Brun got hold of his face and himself. He wasn't about to let some cop know what he and his fellow doctors truly thought about a dead colleague. He sat up straight, hands folded in front of him, and spoke almost as if he were reading a press release. "I wouldn't want you to leave this room imagining even for a minute that anyone at this hospital would wish to confront or hurt our chief cardiac surgeon. You'd be making a huge mistake to push your investigation in that direction."

Renzo stared at Brun, eyebrows raised, hoping to jog him into indiscretion. He wished he had the man sitting across from him at a bistro table with an almost-empty bottle of wine between them. *Then* he'd get some stories. That wasn't going to happen, so he might as well move on. "Thank you for that analysis," he said, then stood up and held his hand out to Brun in farewell.

Renzo hadn't appreciated the surgeon's evasiveness, but he'd enjoyed watching him try to mold his face to fit his script. Brun certainly had a motive to get rid of the man clutching at the job he, Brun, had been hired to do, but if he'd really been in surgery until four-thirty, he couldn't have killed Gurtner in Dählhölzli before five-fifteen. It was people's alibis, not their feelings about the dead surgeon, he had to focus on. At least for the present.

9

G iuliana had a late lunch with Erwin in the police station's crowded basement cafeteria, pleased to find a beet and goat cheese salad next to the steam tables full of meat, vegetables, and potatoes. Erwin had gotten her message about Markus's criminal past, and she'd just finished giving him more detail. "Most of the file is old enough to be on paper," she told him, buttering the whole wheat and sesame seed roll that had come with her salad. "It's on my desk at the moment, but I'll have everything scanned and sent to you. You should have it by three this afternoon at the latest, I think."

"Thanks," grunted Erwin, who was wolfing down meatloaf, cabbage, and mashed potatoes with gravy. "When's Renzo talking to him?"

Giuliana finished her mouthful of roll, crossed her mental fingers, and said, "I'm planning to talk to him myself first thing tomorrow. Unless you'd like to interview him."

"I have a feeling we won't be doing just one round with this guy," Erwin said, picking up his shandy. Giuliana watched him take a sip of what she considered a desecration of good beer before he added, "You get started and see what you can tease out of him, and I'll take him the next time. Okay?"

"Yeah—but first I have to reach him," she said. "If he hasn't responded to all the messages I've left on his cell by the end of the day, I'll go to his place unannounced." She took another bite of the sweet, orange-flavored beets and salty goat cheese and added, "I was thinking about giving Nicole and Philipp another go afterward, but ..."

"Too soon," Erwin interrupted, as he pushed his empty plate away.

"Just what I thought—I'll wait to see what gossip Walter comes up with in the neighborhood first. But with both alibis having checked out ..."

"I'm not sure I trust Philipp's—I bet his pal would lie for him and consider it a great joke." Erwin drained his shandy. "But let's wait a day anyway before we requestion them."

He reached for the cafeteria's dessert of the day, a mound of chestnut puree blanketed in whipped cream. "There's a rumor the commandant has told the cooks to make all the dessert portions smaller, to keep us fit. Look at this! I bet it's true." He dug in his spoon and took a bite before adding, "Let me know if you think Markus Gurtner is actually missing."

"I will," she said and stood, picking up her tray. "Sorry to desert you." He waved his spoon at her benignly, a royal dismissal, and she went back to her deskwork until it was time to leave for her meeting with the first wife.

This interview with Kathrin Gurtner was a get-out-of-jail-free card. She loved working in the field. Deskwork—sorting and digesting the data gathered by other people—was only a necessary evil by comparison. As she left the building, her spirits light, she realized it wasn't raining; that alone was enough to put her in a good mood. At a stoplight, she got out her phone and played the short recording of the emergency call for the second time. The caller, clearly a man, was breathless and agitated. He didn't sound young, but whether he was twenty-five or sixty was unclear. At first he just panted. Then he spoke quite clearly but very fast. "Listen. I need you to send rescuers to Dählhölzli, near the restaurant. Now, right now. A man's drowning in the Aare. I tried to get him out, but I couldn't see anything. God, I'm sorry. I'm afraid

the guy is . . . You've got to hurry." Then he hung up, before the operator could ask any questions.

Playing the call again as she drove past the Rose Garden, she listened this time for anything else besides the actual words that might
give her a clue to the caller's identity. He spoke Bernese dialect like
someone who'd been speaking it since childhood; that was clear. That
didn't tell her much, not even that he was Swiss, just that he'd grown
up not far from Bern. Still, at least she knew he was from the area. She
listened for background noises, breaks in the sentences—anything to
tip her off to who he might be. She sensed the roar of the river, but since
she already knew where the payphone was, that was useless. Sighing,
she played the damned thing a third time. Still no insights.

Then the call went out of her head as she drove over the crest of the
hill, and the Paul Klee Museum came into sight. All girders, glass, and
undulating waves, it was her favorite modern building in Bern. She
admired it anew and then, slowing to a crawl, turned her head to the
right, as she always did on that rise, because it was one of the best places
in the city for viewing the full range of the Bernese Alps—if they were
visible. Today, only a wide swathe of gray-white cloud met her eyes. No
mountains. She sped up and turned toward Kathrin Gurtner's apartment in the Schönberg-Ost complex.

The woman who opened the door was not what Giuliana had
expected. Having seen the tall, thin, effortlessly elegant Nicole, she'd
assumed Gurtner's first wife would be an older version of the same
type. But the woman who greeted her was short and round, with boy-
ishly short gray hair. She wore a red cowl-neck sweater, comfortable-
looking jeans, and oversized slippers with large black-and-white cats'
heads bobbing over her toes as she walked. Kathrin caught Giuliana
eyeing the slippers as they shook hands.

"My son Patrick's little girls gave me these last Christmas. I have a
black-and-white cat, so the girls thought they would be perfect for me.
Pure kitsch, but I can't resist wearing them. Not what people usually
put on for a police interview, though, I guess."

Giuliana grinned. "Nice to have a change," she said. A woman who wore silly slippers because they were a gift from her granddaughters had already won her over.

"How about some lemongrass tea?" the older woman asked and gestured Giuliana to a flowered loveseat in the middle of the living room that faced not only a coffee table and a pair of armchairs but also a wall of glass. Giuliana realized the view was exactly the one she so loved—the spread of snow-covered mountains across the horizon beyond the Klee Museum. The bank of clouds had shifted a little since she'd driven along the crest of the hill, and here and there, a peak showed through the gray.

Kathrin followed her gaze. "Go right ahead: sit on the sofa and stare. I do it all the time. I took this apartment for the view."

By the time Kathrin had bustled back from the kitchen, Giuliana's notepad was out. Kathrin settled the tea things on the table, filled two mugs from a teapot, and deposited herself onto the loveseat next to Giuliana. Giuliana reached for her tea and, before she could ask a question, Kathrin spoke.

"I'm truly sorry Johann is dead. You may suppose I hate him because he cheated on me, but that was years ago." She took a sip of tea, set the mug back down, and impulsively touched Giuliana's leg. "Hanging onto hate is exhausting, so I made myself let it go. Besides, about a year after Hannes left, I realized I was happier without him." She was smiling, but Giuliana still thought she looked sad. "Now that he's dead, though, I've been thinking about the fun we had when we were young. We met in *Gymnasium*, so I've known him since I was thirteen and he was seventeen."

Giuliana took up her pen. "Why don't you tell me about him?"

Kathrin pushed herself up off the deep loveseat, fetched a bulging manila envelope, and plopped back down. "I got out these snapshots when I heard Johann had died. I want to go through them with my sons." Without too much trouble, she fished out a photograph and held it up. "As a teenager, Johann—Hannes, we called him—was beautiful. Here he is with the hiking club. See for yourself."

The young man in the black-and-white picture wore nothing but a pair of shorts. He had the close-clipped back-and-sides haircut of the era, but a shock of longer hair fell dramatically over his forehead. He was standing apart from a small group of boys, looking seriously at the camera and gesturing with one arm at something off to one side. With his intense gaze and well-muscled chest and shoulders, the pose gave him a heroic quality, like a young warrior urging his companions forward into glorious danger.

"You're right." Giuliana held the photo close, her eyes fixed on the young Gurtner's face. "He was magnificent. Everyone must have been in love with him."

"They were! And not just the girls. I don't mean Hannes was bisexual. But everyone—the boys and girls, their parents, the teachers—was under his spell." Kathrin took the snapshot back from Giuliana and studied it again before putting it on the coffee table.

"So, definitely an alpha dog at *Gymnasium*."

"Exactly. He started building a reputation when he arrived in the seventh grade, and it grew. The hiking club, for example," she waved a hand toward the photo, "he revived that and made it cool. The same with punting on the Aare. He won prizes in that."

"How'd you get to know him?" Four years apart in high school. That was a big maturity gap. Her daughter Isabelle's boyfriend Quentin was three years older than she was, and even this age disparity troubled Giuliana and Ueli.

"I'd heard of him even before I started school, because my father taught chemistry at the *Gymnasium*. He told stories about Hannes at the dinner table. He was the boy who played pranks on people—students and teachers. Once he locked the assistant principal in a bicycle shed. The man had to hammer on the door until someone let him out, and it was a very cold day. I remember being surprised that even my father, who was so strict, laughed when he told us that story. Later I learned the assistant principal was unpopular with the teachers as well as the students. Still, the way I remember it, most of Hannes's jokes all through *Gymnasium* were laughed off with 'boys-will-be-boys.' Almost all the teachers were men, don't forget."

Giuliana could imagine the sort of indulgent attitude they'd show, as long as Hannes didn't go too far. "That kind of adolescent usually has a crowd. Did Hannes?"

"Oh yes. He was never on his own at *Gymnasium*, and it was the same when he was a med student. Once he became a doctor . . . well, senior doctors all stride around hospitals trailing a flock of students; that's how the system works. Hannes reveled in it. The higher up the ladder he went, the bigger his audience got. Lots of surgeons are performers at heart, and he was so good at making people laugh." Kathrin was smiling as she spoke.

Giuliana waited, sipping her tea, as Kathrin stared out at the distant mountains half-shrouded in cloud. Then she turned to Giuliana, her cup clasped in both hands. Her eyes were serious now. "There was so much good in him. If only . . ." She paused. When the silence persisted, Giuliana pressed gently. "If only?"

Kathrin only shook her head, her face full of regret, and Giuliana thought she must be contemplating her broken marriage. Which made Giuliana wonder how they'd gotten together in the first place—this cozy-looking granny and the god-like Hannes.

"How did you become a couple?" she asked.

Smiling slyly, as if she could read Giuliana's mind, Kathrin fished another photo out of the manila envelope on the coffee table. This one, in color, showed the young Hannes with his arm around a voluptuous girl. She was dressed demurely and her hair was in a conventional late-sixties flip, but the schoolgirl clothes couldn't hide the breasts that strained at her shirt-buttons, the tiny waist, the full hips filling the short, tight skirt. The boy was fair, with blue eyes and blond hair. The girl's hair and eyes were dark, her lips full. The young Kathrin was not as conventionally beautiful as Hannes, but, even in an old snapshot, her sexiness was palpable. They made a striking pair.

"I developed early," Kathrin commented dryly.

Giuliana laughed. "Well, I can certainly see what brought you together. When was this taken?"

Kathrin flipped over the photo. "It says June 1970, so I was fifteen and Hannes nineteen. We were together during his last two years at *Gymnasium*, but things ended when he went off to Bern for university. Five years later we met at a bus stop in Bern, and we started seeing each other again. We got married when I was twenty-eight."

And twenty years later you found out about Nicole. It was time to ask some more pointed questions. "I'd be grateful if you'd tell me about your and your children's current financial situations," Giuliana said.

Kathrin's eyebrows rose. "Aha, now we're getting to the real police stuff," she said and set the photo down, no longer smiling. "You want to know if I had a motive to kill Hannes for his money. Well, I didn't. I mean, I can't imagine why he'd leave me anything, and I don't need it anyway. When we divorced, we agreed he'd give me a large sum right away, instead of doling out alimony, and he paid child support until the boys finished their education. I assume he's left everything to Nicole and the three kids, but I wouldn't know." Her gaze as she looked at Giuliana was fierce, as if daring her to challenge this account. Since it could all be verified or contradicted by Gurtner's lawyer, Giuliana had no need to do so. But the question hadn't been fully answered.

"One of my colleagues talked to your son Patrick," said Giuliana, "but Markus hasn't gotten back to us yet. I know about his time in juvenile detention, but not about his life right now. How is he doing?"

"Markus is a professional photographer," Kathrin said, looking out at the mountains again. Her voice was clipped. "I'm not supporting him and I'm sure Hannes wasn't, so I assume he's getting along, financially at least."

"It sounds like you and he aren't close."

There was almost a minute's silence, while Kathrin stared out the window. When she spoke, her face was still turned away, and her voice shook. She set her mug down on the table very carefully.

"That's not my choice, believe me. I would . . ." She stopped and turned, at last, to Giuliana, hands covering her nose and mouth. After a moment she was able to speak again.

"Markus had a difficult childhood and a worse adolescence. After juvenile prison, he had to fight drug dependence, so . . . well, it wasn't until his late twenties that he pulled himself together."

She gave Giuliana a look that pleaded for understanding and then looked away again before going on. "One of the ways he was able to . . . make progress was by breaking with . . . with his family. With his father especially, but also with me. Which was very painful. It still is. But I understand he had to do whatever would help him heal. That's why I don't know much about his life now. It's not because I . . . ever gave up on him."

Kathrin picked up the teapot and disappeared into the kitchen. Giuliana gave her space. She looked around, surprised that a room with so much glass could still feel snug. It was the rugs, she decided. Instead of keeping the parquet flooring exposed, Kathrin had used large, colorful rugs and clusters of furniture to divide the open living space into rooms. She moved over to another window, this one facing away from the mountains. She didn't notice the new view. She was too busy imagining Lukas or Isabelle in ten years' time, addicted to drugs and rejecting her help. How would she live with something like that? The unimaginable pain? The helplessness? How could Kathrin bear it?

Kathrin came back looking calmer and set down the fresh pot of tea. "Have a seat and let's go on. What else can I tell you about myself and the kids?"

She was attempting a cheerful matter-of-factness now. Giuliana kept sympathy at bay and continued her questioning. "Why was Markus's childhood so bad?"

Kathrin sighed but kept her expression under control. "Basically, because he was a disappointment to his father. Before Markus had time to do more than be a baby, Hannes decided he was . . . I don't think it's too strong to say that Hannes considered him flawed before he walked. Which he did late. Later than Patrick, anyway. Which for Hannes meant he had failed. He was always pointing out to the family how much better Patrick was at everything than Markus."

What assholes parents could be, Giuliana thought. Markus must have grown up not only angry with his father but resenting his brother, too. "Second children often have it hard, don't they?" was all she said.

Kathrin leaned forward, stirred the tea in the pot and refilled their mugs. A comforting citrus smell enveloped Giuliana as she picked hers up and drank. When Kathrin began to speak, she'd become more fluent, as if she'd grown determined to make things clear. "That was part of it, the birth order. But it was more than that. Patrick was a quiet baby and a sturdy, self-contained little boy, pleased when his father played with him and resigned when he didn't. Whereas Markus was colicky. Does that mean something to you?"

"It does," Giuliana said. A friend's baby had developed colic; she could still hear the infant's thin, never-ending wails and feel the mother's desperation. It had given Giuliana a whole new understanding of why some parents shook their babies to death.

"Well, then, you know what colicky babies are like," Kathrin continued. "When Markus was three weeks old, he started to cry day and night. I had no idea what to do except carry him around and pray he'd fall asleep. Three months later, the crying stopped, just like that, but it was too late. By then Hannes despised Markus, and he just kept on rejecting him. He'd decided Markus was—broken. Second-rate. A bad deal." Kathrin laughed bitterly. "Talk about a self-fulfilling prophecy!"

Giuliana, hands folded in her lap, sat quietly, waiting to see what would come next.

"Markus grew up wanting his father's attention more than anything, so he tried to please him. He got good grades and brought Hannes little gifts from woodworking class. When that didn't work, he tried sports: football and running and skiing. By thirteen he could ski like a bat out of hell; he won racing cups. Hannes just didn't care. So Markus began to make trouble. That certainly brought him attention from his father. Of a kind." Kathrin barked another humorless laugh. "Until he ended up in juvie, as you know."

"Yes, I do." Giuliana thought how well Markus's mother was building a case for why Markus might be guilty of killing his father.

"Well, enough of that," said Kathrin, miming lightness. "I've gotten completely off track. What happened to Markus and how much Hannes was responsible for it still eats at my soul, but it's not exactly relevant. Let's see. You asked about the children's finances, didn't you? As I said, Markus appears to be self-supporting, and Patrick works full time and makes a good salary. What else can I tell you?"

She crossed her arms across her chest and leaned away from Giuliana, who kept surprise off her face with an effort. How could Markus's bad relationship with his father be irrelevant to their homicide investigation? Apparently, his mother was in denial, and Giuliana decided to leave it that way until she'd talked to Markus herself. She smiled at the older woman, noticing deep lines on either side of her mouth that hadn't been as prominent before. Kathrin was tiring; it was time to move on. "Why don't you describe your work," said Giuliana.

Kathrin uncrossed her arms and reached again for her tea. "I'm an accountant. I keep books and do financial advising for the hairdressing profession. Not that I know how to cut hair, but I do know what makes for a successful salon, so when I see a promising one that needs capital, I invest in it. I make a good living, and I also help women who run small businesses." Relaxed again, Kathrin leaned toward Giuliana to add, "Believe me, I have no need for Hannes's money."

"Where were you yesterday afternoon between three-thirty and five-thirty?"

Kathrin seemed to find the question amusing instead of threatening. "I was here alone, working. I made several calls from my landline, which I think should give me an alibi."

Someone was already collecting the family members' phone records; Giuliana would check them soon. "What about some background on your former sisters-in-law?" she asked. "I've only spoken with Charlotte so far. She's formidable."

"Yes," Kathrin said with a smile, "Charlotte can be quite scary. Hannes called her Lotti and teased her, so I saw her at her most relaxed, but still I felt she kept me at a distance. The younger sister Brigitte and I are close, though. There's ten years between her and Charlotte, with Johann in the middle. Bri was a teenager during the seventies;

Charlotte allied herself with her parents' generation. Bri has a laptop and uses it all the time; Charlotte avoids computers. Bri's married, Charlotte isn't. Neither had children, which I think they both regret." Kathrin's expression had grown sad, and she sighed heavily. "Charlotte adored Hannes, too. His death must be terrible for her. I need to call her; I need to call both of them."

Giuliana felt her time was up. She gathered notepad and pen, took a last peek at the Alps on the horizon, thanked Kathrin, and left. Driving back to the station, her thoughts drifted from what Kathrin had said about Johann and Markus Gurtner to relationships between fathers and sons generally. Ueli spent more time with Lukas and Isabelle than she did, and as far as she could tell, he was an excellent parent to their son. And what about her own father and brother? Was it healthy that Paolo had worked for their father since law school and then taken charge of the defense practice when the old man cut back? Had their father pressured Paolo into these choices? She didn't know. But Paolo seemed content.

She drove once again past Bern's rose garden; it stood high on a hill overlooking the Aare and the Old City. Now, in November's gray rain, the park was bare of color, but by late March, there would be snowdrops and crocuses, followed by blankets of daffodils and later a tumult of purple wisteria. Only four more months of gloom to get through. Didn't Bri, Gurtner's younger sister, live near the *Rosengarten*? Thoughts of Brigitte Rieder reminded Giuliana that not only fathers and sons had their troubles. What about her own aborted career as a lawyer, first defending and then prosecuting? What had *she* been trying to prove to her father? Even her final choice of the police had been a message for him—although what, exactly, she'd never figured out, unless it was meant to show him that there were other ways of fighting for a fair society than defending people accused of crimes.

Giuliana imagined that her mother probably had a lot of insight into her daughter's decisions, but Aurelia Linder did not share her wisdom with her children unless they wanted it. Maybe, when this case was over, she'd ask.

* * *

Kathrin Gurtner had several calls to make, but instead of sitting down at her desk to study her client list, she walked to her wall of glass. More peaks had emerged from the cloud cover, but Kathrin didn't see them. In her mind she was in the house where the boys had grown up. It was Sunday night, and she waited in a doorway between a dark hall and a dimly lit room: Markus's room, where she was trying to talk to him about the weekend he'd just spent with his father and Nicole at a ski resort in the Bernese Alps. She'd already heard Patrick's laconic description—snow excellent, food good, Nicole bearable, Paps as usual—but seventeen-year-old Markus had said nothing. Now, sprawled on his bed and refusing to look at her, he declared in a voice that was almost, but not quite, a yell, "I won't talk about it, so stop asking me. Besides, what's the point? You'll get a report from Paps soon enough about how badly I behaved." Kathrin sighed quietly. Markus was right. It would have been helpful to hear his side, though.

"You know Nicole's having a baby, right?" Without waiting for her to answer, he added, "She told us it's another boy. Poor little fucker. Or maybe Paps'll be a *good* father to this one. Wouldn't that be a laugh?"

She wanted to sit down on the bed, gather Markus into her arms and rock him, but he'd never stand for it. He just stared at the ceiling, while she hovered in the doorway saying nothing. After endless seconds, she was about to turn away when she heard him say, "Mam?" The sarcasm seemed to have leaked away; he sounded tentative.

"What is it, dear heart?" she answered softly, trying not to spook him.

"I know this isn't a question a guy should ask his mother, but are you sure I'm..." He stopped, and she heard him breathing hard. "Does Paps think I'm not his son?"

She steadied herself on the doorframe and then took the few steps that brought her to the edge of the bed, where she sat, daring to put a hand on Markus's shoulder. He continued to stare at the ceiling, but he didn't shake her hand off.

"I've thought about it a lot," he said slowly, "and it would make sense of everything, you know? If you'd been having an affair and he didn't want a scandal and decided to raise me as his own kid, it would explain . . . And I don't look at all like him, you know that, and Patrick does. So . . ." He paused and finally turned his head to look at her. When he spoke, his eyes were hard and his voice harsh. "Tell me, for fuck's sake—I *have* to know."

She wouldn't cry; he deserved a calm answer. "I swear to you that if there were any chance you weren't Paps's son, I would tell you. But in all the years Hannes and I were married, I never had an affair; I've never even had a male friend. There's been no one in our lives for him to suspect, and it wouldn't occur to him that I would . . . look for someone else. That's not the way he thinks."

Hand still on Markus's shoulder, she spoke gently to him and tried to catch his eyes, but they were back on the ceiling. His hands were in fists at his sides, his body rigid, his lower lip caught between his teeth.

"I wanted so much for it to be true," he whispered at last. "I even imagined going to court and demanding a paternity test. Although that wouldn't be very nice for you, would it? Besides," he added, before she could say anything, "I'd have to be eighteen to make the request."

"I'll support you," she said, "if you want to do it. But the truth is that he has to be your father. I wish I could give you another answer, but it would be a lie."

Another heavy silence before Markus said, his eyes closed, "He barely yells at me anymore, you know? Just ignores me. I tested it by skiing across his path. It was a close thing, but I didn't touch him. He fell from the shock. I walked back to him, but he wouldn't let me help him up. He knew I'd done it on purpose, but he never said a word. Maybe I scared him. God, that would make me happy, to think he was too afraid of me to tell me what a little shit I am, like he usually does."

Markus rose from bed in what seemed like a single swift movement. That was what his skiing was like: lithe and effortless. She stood as well, trying to ignore the fear that his last words had generated. He'd been challenging his father's authority since he was a toddler. Was he going to start challenging him physically now, too? Causing Hannes to fall on the *piste* was very dangerous. Maybe Markus hadn't succeeded in scaring his father, but he was certainly scaring *her*. Not that she'd let him know that.

"Markus," she said and stopped. He came closer, put his arms around her, and hugged her, and she felt tears start in her eyes. "It's okay, Mam. Don't worry. I won't . . ." He dropped his arms to his sides and turned away, toward his desk. "I can handle things," he said.

But that hadn't been true. Kathrin, still standing in front of her window, registered at last that the entire horizon was now a display of snow-covered mountains under a band of blue-gray cloud. Markus hadn't been able to handle things. Shortly after that conversation he was in juvenile prison, a violent offender. And now, eighteen years after their conversation that Sunday night? How was he handling things at the age of thirty-five?

10

Dählhölzli,
Tuesday evening, November 24

B y six that evening Renzo had given up on the hospital's coffee and
sat drinking mineral water in one of its cafés. He was pleased with
what he'd accomplished. A combination of charm and badgering had
finally resulted in detailed work schedules for scores of people, and
now a team of cops back at the station were on the phones doing alibi
checks. With the help of the personnel director, he'd also ferreted out
twelve men and women who'd worked with Gurtner especially often.
All had expressed praise and regret but nothing that sounded like genuine grief at the man's death.

The most refreshing interview had been with an anesthesiologist,
a short, plump, forty-something-year-old woman with a face full of
laugh lines who'd said, "I couldn't stand the man. He was everything
I expect an old-school male surgeon to be: stuck-up, bossy, blatantly
sexist, inconsiderate of anyone's feelings. I could go on. The point is
there are hundreds like him out there in the world of medicine; thank
God they keep on retiring. I will say one thing for him, though—he
kept up professionally. No matter how obsolete his way of treating
women was, he was *not* old-fashioned in his methods. Kill him? Well,
I've seen him drive med students and junior docs to tears with his

criticisms, but would one of them retaliate by pushing him into the Aare? I doubt it."

Renzo doubted it, too, but only because of the practicalities, not because he didn't believe most people capable of it. A chance encounter, one nasty comment escalating into blows, followed by that tiny slip over the edge of reason that was responsible for so many crimes of violence: in this case, a quick shove into a fast, cold river.

"Do you think he was particularly cruel, compared to others like him?" Renzo asked.

The anesthesiologist was in scrubs and hadn't taken the time to sit when he'd tracked her down. The two of them were slouched against a wall in a long corridor, leaning toward each other. At Renzo's question, she shook her head emphatically and poked her glasses back up her nose. "Oh, believe me, they come worse."

"And, when you say he was sexist, do you mean he was abusive?"

"No, no," she countered immediately, pushing herself off the wall and facing Renzo, her good-humored face serious. "I didn't mean to give you the wrong idea. He could never bring himself to take women seriously, but I haven't heard a murmur of gossip about inappropriate behavior—sexual innuendos, too much touching, or anything like that."

Now Renzo sat in a molded plastic chair by a cafeteria window, his head turned so he could stare out into the dark. He'd slept only a few hours the night before, and he was beat. He couldn't even remember what he'd planned to do next. On impulse, he pulled his phone out of his pocket and dialed Giuliana.

"Hey, Renzo," she said. "Tell me you aren't still at the hospital."

"Only if you tell me you aren't still in the office," he countered. "And then we'd both be lying. I already told Fränzi two hours ago that I didn't know when I'd be home."

Since the birth of his kids, Renzo had sometimes walked out of meetings to get home in time to bathe Antonietta and Angelo, now four and five, and put them to bed, even when it meant turning right around and driving back to the station afterward. He'd come to terms with the fact that he was a lousy husband, at least in his wife's eyes, but he'd be damned if he was also going to let his job turn him into a bad father. But today, the first day on a new case, he'd already decided to miss bedtime.

"Ueli's not expecting me, either. Shall we meet?"

Renzo felt his whole body relax. "That's why I called, to see if you felt like reviewing the case."

"Sure. I have a suggestion of where to get a drink, too: the zoo restaurant, so I can walk the path where Gurtner went into the Aare and see where his body was found. Although I know you must have spent hours there last night . . ."

"I don't mind taking another look," Renzo said quickly. "Let's meet there in fifteen minutes and walk before it starts raining again. Bring your flashlight."

Twenty minutes later they stood on the riverbank path, their powerful lights trained on the river that twisted its way around Bern on its way to the Rhine. The opposite bank was invisible in the November dark. As he and Giuliana picked their way around puddles, Renzo fastened the top button of his sheepskin coat, then shivered as a drop of water fell on his cheek from one of the trees arching overhead. He shifted his flashlight to the other hand, playing it around the area, and lit up a giant boar, snuffling in the mud behind the wall of his pen. Only a faint smell of wild animal reached Renzo; the rain seemed to be washing the zoo odors away.

Giuliana walked slightly behind him, stepping carefully; she'd had the sense to put on rubber boots. He had a pair in the car, too, but had been too vain to wear them. Stupid decision. It was half a mile to where they believed Johann Gurtner had come downhill to the river path. About halfway there, they reached a tiny footbridge; it spanned a stream that crossed the path and flowed into the Aare. Renzo stopped and raised his voice so Giuliana could hear him.

"You know I was here at first light this morning, before Erwin called me in for the staff meeting?"

Giuliana's hood hid her face, but he saw her nod.

"I walked along here then and decided Gurtner couldn't have entered the river beyond this point. For his body to have ended up where it did, he'd have to have gone in along the stretch we've just walked, where the drop from the path to the river is steep, and the current is fast right up to the bank. From here on, until well past Gurtner's house, there are mainly quiet pools right below the path. You'll have to take my word for it, in the dark."

"Given the weather, I'm glad to take your word for it," said Giuliana. "Let's turn around."

Slowly, they retraced their steps back toward the restaurant, shining their lights all along the bank, with Renzo pointing out the most likely locations for the fight. On one side of the narrow path was forest, and, where the walkway widened, there were enclosures for small groups of indigenous animals: mountain goats, chamois, deer, and boars. On the other side of the path, the steep riverbank was overgrown with shrubs and small trees. They passed the restaurant in order to reach a wide footbridge that led to the opposite bank. Less than thirty feet downriver from the other end of the bridge, Renzo's flashlight revealed the crime-scene tape that marked the spot where the police had found Gurtner's body.

"We're so lucky he didn't float all the way to Schwellenmätteli and over the weir," Renzo said and then wished he hadn't. Giuliana had likely been searching for bodies in the Aare when he was still a kid. But she didn't seem annoyed at him for stating the obvious; instead, she added, "And lucky he ended up so close to a restaurant. Let's get our drink."

They walked back to the old-fashioned two-story wooden building. It was set well back from the path to leave room for its enormous terrace. Four months earlier, the tables, now stacked and shrouded in tarpaulins, had been filled with families eating sausages and fries as they watched people stroll the riverside paths. But that had been July. On this cold November night, there was not a person to be seen.

Five minutes later they were settled at an upstairs table in the almost empty restaurant, nursing glasses of red wine. Giuliana sighed, combed her dark hair back from her forehead with all ten fingers, further displacing her already lopsided bun, and smiled at Renzo. It was a smile that had attracted him to her the first time they'd worked together, when he was twenty-eight and not yet married, and it still turned his heart over six years later.

"Tell me what you thought of Patrick Gurtner," she said.

He summarized the content of the interview and then went to the heart of her question. "Patrick's alibi will be hard to confirm—shopping downtown in various stores—but we're working on it. He wasn't sad about his father's death and had the sense not to fake it. When I brought up Markus, he defended him. I'd say Patrick's smart enough to kill someone and get away with it, and his office looks down on the Aare. But what would his motive be? Something to do with money?"

A bald waiter who looked well beyond retirement age shuffled over to their table and asked if they wanted to have more wine and order dinner; they declined both. Renzo's glass was long empty; Giuliana still had an inch in hers. She took a sip before saying, "I checked with Nicole Gurtner's boss, too, who says she was at her desk at 4:50 p.m., when he passed her on his way to the waiting room to fetch his last patient. Then he wrote up notes and returned phone calls, and by the time he left his office again at five-thirty, she was gone. It's just possible for her to have driven from there to the Aare in twenty minutes, but she'd need to have had fantastic luck with the traffic."

"Yeah," Renzo broke in. "She could have parked at her own house and run down the hill to the river; she'd need to have set up a meeting place with Gurtner to find him so quickly. Unless we dig up a motive, like the boyfriend Erwin is hoping for, it just doesn't seem likely. What about the youngest son?"

"The school friend confirms Philipp's times of arrival and departure," she said, "but that's all we have to go on so far."

The creak of a door, a burble of voices, and a blast of outside air startled them into silence. Giuliana, who was facing the door at the top of the stairway, smiled, and Renzo turned around to see tourists in matching hats crowding into the restaurant. Each seemed determined to stop just inside the entrance to peer around the long, narrow dining room, only to be elbowed aside by the next person trying to get into the room. In the meantime, a young man, apparently their guide, was imploring them to move further into the space and get out of each other's way. At least, that was what they assumed he was saying, from his gestures. His voice grew louder and louder in his frustration, and his charges' answers grew shriller. In the meantime, from a back office, a portly man, surely the restaurant manager, surged forward, two waitresses flanking him like tugs escorting a barge.

Renzo turned back to Giuliana and opened his mouth to speak, but the noise in the room had reached a level that made it difficult for them to hear each other. At least now all the guests—there must have been fifty of them—were inside and being maneuvered skillfully past rows of tables and into what must have been a private dining room. In twos and threes, still talking, they vanished, and, in a surprisingly short time, the room was quiet again, although no longer completely silent; the faint sound of animated speech could be heard from behind the room's double doors.

Their eyes met, they started to giggle, and then Giuliana leant her head back and burst into laughter. As she laughed, she reached out, grabbed Renzo's hand, and squeezed it. "Did you see the second tour guide? The tall, thin one who came indoors at the very end looking so cross and bedraggled? He was desperate to get them into that room. I thought he was going to nip at their calves like a sheepdog."

Renzo continued to grin, but he was no longer picturing the tourist invasion. He was feeling Giuliana hold his hand and seeing the line of her throat disappear down the V of her blouse as she leaned her head back and laughed. Something in his face must have given his thoughts away, because she dropped his hand and folded her arms on the table.

"Well, back to business," she said. "Markus Gurtner finally phoned me back, and we've set up a time to talk. Luckily, his files have arrived from juvenile court. Has Erwin had a chance to tell you about the crime?" Despite her return to seriousness, the last bit of laughter was still visible in her face. Renzo was glad.

"No," he answered, not hiding his own smile at all.

"A class of Bernese *Gymnasium* students were on a two-day trip to Geneva. Six boys high on cocaine and alcohol went out to a park at night and, for no reason at all, dragged a fifty-two-year-old passerby off his bicycle and began beating him. They hit him repeatedly and, once he was down, kicked him in the gut and head. Someone saw the attack and called the police, who arrived in time to save the man's life."

Renzo's smile was gone. He knew too many stories like this one to be surprised, but he could still be shocked. Just the week before in Bern a middle-aged man had asked three teenage boys sitting on the train station steps to move, since they were blocking his way, and they'd cursed him and grabbed at his legs, and he'd fallen down the stairs. Miraculously, he'd been bruised and shocked but not seriously hurt, and people in the station had come to his aid. But no one had dared do more than yell at the boys, who were gone by the time the police arrived. He'd thought these kind of random attacks were recent, but Markus's story was eighteen years old. He and Markus were almost the same age. Had any of *his* friends been that casually violent as teenagers?

"Brain damage?" Renzo asked.

"Even after several operations and over a year of treatment and rehab right after the attack, the man is handicapped. Only mildly, or the boys' punishments would have been worse. There was a ringleader, of course: there always is in situations like that. It wasn't Gurtner—he was sentenced to eighteen months. After he was released, he became an alcoholic and got heavily into drugs. Stopped right on the edge of heroin addiction, though. According to the last entry in his records, he's clean now, but who knows?"

"And we're going to go talk to him right after tomorrow's briefing, right?"

Giuliana's mouth tightened, and he recognized the determined expression she got when she was about to insist on something.

"I'd like to do the first interview by myself."

Renzo had a sense of déjà vu. This wasn't the first time Giuliana had conducted a potentially dangerous interview alone, and she hated the implication that she couldn't protect herself. He knew better than to question her judgment. Still... in as mild a voice as he could manage, he asked, "Why take the risk?"

"I *know* protocol says interviews should be done with two of us present, and there are good reasons for that, but people reveal much more when they're approached alone."

"Fine," he said, since there was nothing else he could say. "Do you have time for me to brief you about the hospital?"

She looked at her watch. "Let's take fifteen more minutes."

Renzo nodded. If he was home by eight-thirty, there might still be a chance of eating with Fränzi, and he thought she'd appreciate that. He was never sure these days what he could do to please his wife, except work eight to five, instead of day and night, and he didn't see how he could make that happen. Even if he'd wanted to.

"We now have a pretty good idea of which medical people Gurtner had the most contact with during the past two years, and I've got a team on the phones and, if needed, going around the city finding out what those people were doing yesterday between four and five-thirty. Any enemies he made earlier than two years ago who stalked him to the river or happened to pass him on his walk will be harder to identify."

Giuliana nodded. "That's an excellent start. Did anyone seem to be lying?"

Renzo snorted. "Are you kidding? All of them were lying. Such regret over the death of a man they didn't much care about." He shook his head. "I know what you mean, though. If I talked to his killer today, I couldn't tell; at least, none of my inner alarms went off."

Giuliana nodded and bent to retrieve her handbag from the floor. "See anyone with a fat lip?" she asked.

"No, I didn't, but that reminds me—I need to ask the autopsy doc if the bruise on Gurtner's hand could have been made by an arm or a shoulder blade. Or ribs. If so, we're going to have to start asking everyone who knew Gurtner to strip to the waist." He was thinking of Patrick. "And don't forget that our riverbank killer hit Gurtner in the eye, which probably left *him* with bruised knuckles, too. Or her. Didn't see any of those today, and I was looking, but they're not that hard to cover with extra-long sleeves or even make-up."

Giuliana nodded and made a note. "I'll check on the stuff about bruising for you tomorrow. My turn to pay this time," she added, walking off to find someone to take her money. While she was gone, he thought about his next steps. Erwin wanted him to visit Gurtner's guild, the Cloth Handlers, to find out what the doctor's responsibilities had been. He'd need to do some research on that before he talked to anyone there.

"So, you'll interview Markus tomorrow morning," he said when Giuliana returned from paying and started to put on her jacket.

She nodded. "And Gurtner's younger sister on Thursday. I don't think she saw him as often as the older sister, but she may still give us something useful." Renzo nodded and got up slowly, reluctant to leave.

"Oh, yeah," Giuliana said, "the emergency call. Any ideas about that?"

"Haven't listened to it yet."

"Let me know if you pick something up. This afternoon I sent it to a language specialist at the university. She's going to let us know more about the caller's dialect."

Renzo, standing next to her as he put on his own jacket, sang softly, in English, "The rain in Spain stays mainly in the plain," which elicited a puzzled look. "We're getting help from a Swiss Henry Higgins," he explained.

"I never thought of it like that. How come you know a song from *My Fair Lady*?"

"Because I have a mother and two sisters. I can remember Bianca, who's six years older than me, waltzing me around the living room to 'I Could Have Danced All Night.' The three of them watched videos of all kinds of girly musicals, and no one ever told me boys weren't supposed to watch *The Sound of Music* or *Grease*. I loved *Grease* when I was small."

"It made *me* desperate to go to a drive-in movie theater,"

commented Giuliana, as they walked toward the door together, "but by the time I got to the US in my twenties, I couldn't find one."

Opening the door, they were greeted by the sound of rain, so they paused under the portico. "Shit," said Renzo. "It's pouring again. See you tomorrow." He resisted the urge to pull her body into his arms, but he still couldn't stop himself from grasping her shoulders and kissing her on the lips. Then he smiled into her eyes and ran to his car, umbrella unopened in his hand. Only when he was settled in the driver's seat did he glance back to the doorway. She was already gone.

11

Giuliana stood in the hall outside her apartment, in no hurry to unlock the door. She always considered these few minutes to be her rebooting time, a pause to allow the mother/wife program to download. This evening the process was taking longer than usual; she was berating herself for the way she'd acted with Renzo. Just because she had mixed feelings didn't mean she had to indulge in sending mixed messages. She'd once begged Renzo to pretend that he didn't know how she felt, which was that she'd jump into bed with him if it weren't for her husband and kids. She'd promised to let him know if she ever changed her mind about her marriage. But she hadn't changed her mind—so why put the careful balance they'd achieved at risk?

By the time she'd gotten the door open, she was ready. As she stepped into the foyer, calling out a hello, Lukas ran to her from the living room, where his Legos were scattered across the floor, grabbed her around the waist in a hug, and asked, "Did you know Leonardo da Vinci invented cannons? And parachutes? And helicopters? Did you know that?" Isabelle yelled, "Hey, Mam," over the music blaring out of her room, and from the kitchen Ueli called, "We're having soup. Lukas, you can set the table now."

She was home.

The soup was filled with peas, sliced carrots, and cubes of celery root as well as chunks of chicken. It probably also contained all the leftovers that had been lurking in the refrigerator for days. By the time the family sat down to eat it with slabs of seven-grain bread and a garlicky salad, Giuliana was well into mother mode, listening to Lukas talk about a new fifth-grade project on da Vinci, and Isabelle describe plans for a demonstration on Human Rights Day in December. It wasn't until Isabelle went back to her room to study for a geography test and Lukas wandered off to find his English homework that she and Ueli had a moment alone.

She smiled across the table at him and once again wondered why red hair was called ginger. Ueli's hair, rising wildly around his head, was the color of marigolds, terracotta pots, basketballs, traffic cones, papayas, sunsets. Since the first time she'd seen him, with his closely trimmed orange beard, yellow-brown eyes, and freckled skin, she'd come up with so many comparisons—but never ginger. Nothing made her smile like Ueli's hair. Grinning back, he poured them each a little more red wine.

"Thanks for getting the kids out this morning. I really needed the sleep," she said. In the small window of time that morning between dragging herself out of bed and racing off to work, she'd barely spoken to him. "What'd you work on today?"

Ueli's expression grew instantly focused, as it always did when he talked about his writing. "I'm doing a piece about a young couple in the Emmental who won a national prize for their cheese. It gives me a chance to talk about how family farms survive by finding niches where they can market themselves successfully. Quality not quantity. That sort of thing. Then I'm broadening it to describe a few other small farming-related businesses that meet a special need." Now he wasn't at the table with her anymore, but somewhere in his head, with his unfinished article. She was used to it and kicked him gently in the shin with her toe to get his attention.

"Make sure they give you a big Emmentaler," she said.

Ueli came back to earth, smiled, and stretched extravagantly in his chair. He wasn't a tall man, but he was bulky, mostly with muscle and now, approaching fifty, with some extra padding, too. "Of course—their biggest and best wheel of cheese."

She'd been joking, and now he was, too. Ueli wouldn't take a gift from anyone he wrote about; he had strong convictions about honesty and fairness. Not that his code of morality always ran exactly parallel to the law. Her values had been very similar to his twenty-five years earlier. Then she'd ended up in the police.

"What about you? How's your case coming along?" he asked her.

He always asked, and he was truly interested—as her husband and as a journalist—but she was invariably selective about what she told him. Now, for example, she'd have liked to pour out her worries about Toni Rossel's attempt to undermine her authority. But she couldn't. Ueli didn't know anything about Toni.

"We don't have much to go on yet. The drowned man's named Johann Karl Gurtner. Ring any bells?"

Ueli shook his head.

"Adult kids Patrick and Markus Gurtner." It was worth asking; Ueli's work meant that he knew all sorts of odd facts about people all over Switzerland.

"Nothing comes to mind." Ueli drained his wine glass, pushed himself to his feet with a small groan and came around the table to give her a quick kiss on the lips. "I'm going back to the computer for . . . oh, wait a minute. I got an email from Lukas's teacher. There's an emergency meeting on Thursday night for parents and kids. Apparently, a girl is being bullied." He shook his head. "I thought this kind of thing happened between girls in, like, the seventh or eighth grade, not the fifth."

"Does Frau Tanner give any details in her mail?" Giuliana asked, frowning. Ueli shook his head. "Or Lukas?"

"He said, 'That's girls' stuff,' in a disgusted voice and refused to say more."

They raised their eyebrows at each other. "I was planning to ask him to help me load the dishwasher," Giuliana said. "I'll see if I can get anything out of him."

"Great," Ueli murmured; he was already walking away, and she could tell from the vagueness in his voice that his mind was back on prize-winning cheese and small Swiss farming businesses.

Giuliana finished her wine, cleared the table, ladled leftover soup into a plastic container, and went to the door of Lukas's small bedroom. It had stars-and-planets wallpaper and blue-and-white painted IKEA bunk beds, a wardrobe, and a desk. Moving to a room of his own three years earlier and choosing his own décor had been a big event, and he loved the colorful space he'd created. He lay draped over a red beanbag chair, stomach down, head hanging, writing in his English workbook.

"I'd like you to help me in the kitchen," said Giuliana, leaning her head into the room.

"Do I haaaaave to?" She stood there, waiting, saying nothing. "I'll just finish this, then," he added, resigned. As he wrote, he read aloud, "'I walk to school. Do you walk to school? No, I don't. Yes, I do.'" He closed the workbook and scrambled to his feet. "Mam, this 'do' word is dumb. Why can't I ask someone, 'Walk you to school?' like in German?"

Giuliana pondered the question. She knew how to say most things in English but not why. "I don't know, love. English used to sound more like German, before it got mixed up with French and changed a lot. Maybe that's when the 'do' came in." But probably not, she told herself, since French reversed words to form a question just like German. Luckily, Lukas didn't pursue the subject. He followed her into the kitchen and started rinsing and loading the plates she'd stacked for him.

"What's the name of the girl in your class that the other girls are picking on?"

"Salomé," he said. "We . . . um . . . the girls call her Salami. Someone put a salami in her desk last week. A really smelly one." He giggled.

Giuliana noticed the giggle and the word "we" before the "um." She started wiping down the kitchen counter, watching Lukas's profile as he stood at the sink. "Why do they pick on her, do you think?"

"Because she's fat. And weird-looking," he said casually, as if it had nothing to do with him. His face remained untroubled.

A tight band squeezed Giuliana's chest. Could this be her sweet son talking?

"Is Salomé a good student?"

"I guess so. She doesn't talk much in class, but when she does, she answers right. Especially word problems in math. Like two trains are passing and what time do they meet, the kind I hate most."

"Has she ever done anything bad to you or hurt your feelings?" Giuliana asked.

Lukas was squirting too much green detergent into a pot and swishing the sponge around without scrubbing. "Sit down a minute," she added. "I'll do the pots later." He sprawled into one of the kitchen chairs, and she sat down across from him. "Did you hear my question?"

"Of course she hasn't been mean to me. She never even talks to me."

"So, why do you call her 'Salami' when you know it must make her feel bad? Why do you tell me she's weird?"

"But she *is* weird, Ma—and everyone calls her Salami."

"I'd act weird, too, if my whole class was picking on me. So would you, Lukas." She heard her voice rising and lowered it carefully, groping for a reasonable tone. "You know perfectly well that she's being bullied and that you're part of it. Can't you imagine how sad it must make her feel?" *What is wrong with you*, she felt like yelling at him. She kept those words inside, where they twisted in her stomach.

Lukas stood up and folded his arms across his chest. His dark eyes, so much like her own, were fiery, and his chin jutted toward her. "I don't care if she's sad," he said, his voice getting louder as he went on. "And I don't care what you say. I'm not going to be friends with some . . . some *fucking* girl just to make you and Vati think what a 'good boy' I am." He ran out of the kitchen and into his room, slamming the door so hard that the air in the house shivered. Giuliana sat, shocked into stillness, replaying the way Lukas had said "good boy" in a high-pitched, namby-pamby voice, as if it was the suckiest thing he could imagine. And saying "fucking" right to her face. Of course she knew he used the word, but up until now that had been with friends, never with her.

Isabelle appeared in the kitchen doorway, laughing. "Jeez, Mam, that was wild. You're talking to Lüku about fucking girls?"

Frowning, she shook her head. "I'm trying to get him to tell me why he's helping to bully a girl in his class."

Isabelle shrugged and made a face that Giuliana hoped was meant to show support, just as Ueli came up behind his daughter and leaned on the other side of the doorframe. Ueli's expression was torn between sympathy with her and irritation with Lukas. Unless it was the other way around—she hoped not.

"You want me to deal with him?" Ueli asked. "He shouldn't curse when he talks to you. I don't want him to get away with that."

She looked at her two redheads, side by side in the doorway, their faces very similar as they studied her, despite Ueli's beard. She sighed and stood up. "No, I'll give him some time to calm down while I finish the pots; then I'll talk to him."

While she worked in the kitchen, Lukas slipped in and out of his room in his pajamas, going to the bathroom to get ready for bed and ignoring every member of his family. At eight-thirty, just before he was supposed to turn out the lights, she went into his room. He was in the lower bunk now, under the covers; she sat down on the edge of the bed. Before she could talk, he blurted, "I know I'm not supposed to say fuck to you. It came out. Sorry."

She smiled at him and put her hand on his chest. "Thank you. And I didn't mean to upset you so much, although I think what we were talking about is important."

"What *you* were talking about," he countered.

She kissed his cheek. "Just think about it," she said and left before he could say something else to annoy her. She was very relieved Lukas's teacher had called this meeting; maybe she'd get some tips on how to talk to him about bullying. She just hoped she'd be able to be there.

She settled into an armchair across the room from Ueli, opened her laptop, and started to prepare for her interview with Markus

Gurtner the next morning. Now *there* was someone who was very likely to say fuck to her, she thought, and not because it just "came out." She hoped Markus wouldn't turn violent. She was confident she could handle him if he did, but afterward her boss Rolf, not to mention Renzo, would give her an even harder time about interviewing people one-on-one in their homes.

She'd just have to make damn sure that Markus didn't jump her.

12

Markus Gurtner lived in Bethlehem. The neighborhood was about as far away from the Gurtners' elegant Elfenau address as a person could be and still live in Bern, in terms of both distance and atmosphere. Despite using her GPS, Giuliana must have made a wrong turn, because she found herself unable to drive across the tram tracks to Markus's building. She parked where she was and, following a footpath that took her over the tracks, passed a once-attractive fountain; the basin had "Fuck the police" scrawled on it in giant black letters. Something to be expected in this part of town. Soon, though, she began to see that even in this defiantly working-class area, gentrification was underway. Scattered among the seedy five-story walk-ups were freshly renovated buildings and even a few brand-new ones.

Markus's place turned out to be a renovation, recently painted and still free from graffiti, with larger windows than many neighboring buildings. His name, displayed next to the street-level bell push, was printed on off-white cardstock in a crisp font. That didn't jibe with the pathetic, semi-employed, perhaps still alcoholic or drug-addicted figure that she and Renzo had envisioned. Giuliana rang the bell and was buzzed in. "Take the elevator to the fifth floor," a voice called down. She'd expected to have to climb stairs.

When she stepped out onto the fifth-floor landing, he was waiting in the doorway. "Markus Gurtner," he said, holding out his hand. As she shook it, she took him in.

She knew from the autopsy that Johann Gurtner had been tall and from Renzo that Patrick was, too. Markus was medium height, slim but well built. His straight brown hair was cut close on the sides and in back but left long in the front and on the crown and pulled into a high ponytail. It could have looked silly, but it didn't. His one earring, a thin silvery bar hanging halfway to his shoulder, didn't look silly either. Nor did the blue tattoo around one wrist—not the usual dragons or Celtic symbols, but something that reminded her of the patterns on Arabic tiles. He wore dark gray jeans and a pale gray V-necked sweater with the sleeves pushed up. Sloppy black socks on his feet somehow kept the whole ensemble from looking too dapper.

She stepped into the apartment and glanced down the short hall into the living room. Both rooms, painted stark white, were bright with sunlight. Like Markus's clothes, everything she could see from where she was standing—furniture, upholstery, rugs, curtains—was either white, gray, or black. As she was unbuttoning her blue coat to hand it to Markus, she was aware of how bright it seemed in that monochromatic room, where the only other spot of color was a pair of gloves, also blue, lying on the chest of drawers next to the coatrack. Then she noticed the photograph on the far wall. It was filled with color. It showed an almost life-sized naked woman, and, although she was standing on a small round rug, not a shell, her stance was exactly that of Botticelli's Venus. The echo was unmistakable—the way the body inclined toward the left, with only the toes of the right foot touching the ground, the right hand at her breast, the left hand at her crotch. Even the extravagant coppery-blond hair that tossed around her face was reminiscent of the Botticelli painting. The expression on this Venus's face was not serene; instead, she was blatantly aroused, lips parted, eyes heavy, cheeks flushed. The fingers at her nipple and between her legs were clearly not there out of modesty. It was an exceptionally erotic photograph and not a comfortable image with which to confront guests in the foyer.

"What an amazing picture," she said to Markus, as he hung her coat on the rack. "The goddess of love—that's very clever."

"Thank you." Markus said, his back to her. They moved into the living room, and she sat on the charcoal-colored sofa while Markus got them coffee. More large bright photographs hung on the walls. These were all of food and reminiscent of Dutch still lifes, both the austere ones with lemons, nuts, and wine goblets, and the opulent ones with pies, dead rabbits, and bowls of gleaming fruit. There was no direct attempt to imitate a particular artist's work, as far as she could tell, but these were unmistakably an homage to the seventeenth-century paintings. The details gave it away: the curl of lemon peel, the squares of sunlight reflected in a wine glass, the fall of a white tablecloth. They were beautiful.

"Herr Gurtner, are these your photographs?"

"Yes," he answered, from the kitchen. "What do you take in your coffee?"

"Milk, no sugar, please." He carried in two cups of coffee, one black and one with her splash of milk, and set them down on the glass table in front of the sofa. Then he dropped into an armchair across from her—plain black wood with gray cushions, she noticed—and waited for her to begin.

She couldn't get over the contrast between what she had anticipated and what she was confronting.

"Your mother said you were a freelance photographer. I wasn't expecting . . . this."

His smile was bitter. "It has taken me a long time to build up my business. Switzerland is full of professional photographers, and most don't have a past as . . . colorful as mine. But things are good now. I've been getting assignments from Nestlé to do food pictures. And I have a gallery that shows my work."

"In Bern?"

"In London."

She kept her astonishment to herself. "Why doesn't your family know how successful you are?"

"My brothers do. Well, more or less. And one of my aunts. My father found out recently but . . . well, I don't think he . . ." Markus's voice trailed off.

She took a deep breath. Time to get to the point.

"Tell me when you last saw your father."

Markus looked up, and, although his face was composed, his eyes were beyond his control. There was something defenseless in them, but what she mainly saw was rage. He leaned forward and took her wrist, gripping it. She tensed, getting ready to spring out of the chair and pin him to the floor—but not yet. Instead, she waited to see what would happen.

"Frau Linder," he said, his oddly light-colored eyes locked onto hers. "I did not kill my father."

"Let go of me *now*."

He released her and sat back instantly, both hands in his lap. "I'm sorry," he said, but he wasn't sorry, although he certainly seemed to be in the grip of various other emotions. All the while, he kept staring into her eyes, and Giuliana didn't break the stare. "When you were seventeen years old," she said, "you and your friends beat and kicked a random passerby almost to death, simply for fun. I look at you now, eighteen years later, and see a man who is still in the grip of anger. I know from your mother that you had a difficult relationship with your father. It is easy for me to imagine you killing him."

"Terrific. My mother tells a cop she suspects me of murder."

Poor Kathrin. Filled with love for this lost boy of hers, and he was so quick to accuse her of betrayal. Giuliana fought to control her temper.

"It hasn't occurred to your mother that you could have anything to do with your father's death. That's why she talked so openly to me about your relationship with him."

Markus looked down, and when he looked up again, everything

about him was calm. His self-command was astonishing. Abruptly, he got up and walked across the room. His back to her, he gazed out the window, and she spoke softly to him. "Herr Gurtner, you say you didn't kill your father. Why should I believe you? Family members kill each other all the time, as you know from the news. Your father's homicide resembles an unpremeditated killing caused by rage, which you appear to be full of. And you told our investigator on the phone that you have no verifiable alibi for the time of his death." She chose her next words carefully. "I'm here to listen to you, so it's time for you to talk. Before you do, I need to warn you that what you say can be used against you in court. In addition, you have the right to have a lawyer present."

"Fuck lawyers," he murmured, still looking out the window. Giuliana waited in silence, her notebook in her lap, pen in hand. Slowly, Markus came back from the window and sat down again in the armchair. Deliberately, he took a sip of coffee, set his cup down gently, and leaned back in his chair before opening his mouth.

"You want me to talk. I know how to talk. Imagine how many therapists I've been to. Psychologists, psychiatrists, social workers, parole officers, career advisers, drug- and alcohol-abuse counselors. Before prison, during prison, after prison. Before and after I dropped out of university. I can't say a word about my relationship to my father that has a ring of truth to it. It all sounds like bullshit, especially to me."

Smart move, Giuliana thought; he's creating a context for whatever he tells me that allows him to reinterpret it later. But she wasn't going to be manipulated. She leaned forward and met his eyes.

"I'm a cop. That means I've heard as much bullshit as any psychiatrist, probably more. So, let's get back to my question—when was the last time you saw your father?"

"It was four or five weeks ago, at the Bellevue Hotel bar."

"I need time and date." After he'd used his phone to figure it out, she said, "Tell me about it."

He paused a moment before beginning and took a deep breath. "I'd just gotten the invitation cards for my second London show, and

I wanted to celebrate, so I took Ada—that's the woman in the Venus photo—to the Bellevue bar and bought us a bottle of champagne. We drank and talked, and then Ada got a work call and went to the hotel lobby to handle it, so when my father walked by on his way out, I was alone. I hadn't seen him for at least a year and hadn't noticed him at the other end of the room. He was with a couple of men his age. I got up, shook everyone's hand, and asked them to join the celebration. I even gave out cards for the opening. Portrait of the artist as a delightful son—that was me."

Markus drank some more coffee. His face was expressionless.

"My father's colleagues left. They'd insisted he stay and have a drink with me, and he must have thought it would look . . . bizarre if he didn't. So he sat down, and I filled his glass. It clearly made him uncomfortable to be there, and the more upset he got, the more I wanted him to stay."

Markus stopped abruptly, his lips a thin line. "Surely you don't want to hear this crap."

"On the contrary, I'm very interested. Please go on. What happened after your father joined you?"

Markus's voice, when he finally answered, was not quite steady. "He spent about ten minutes at my table, and everything he said was an insult. He made a crack about me being alone; when I told him Ada was in the lobby, he suggested that the women I hung out with were trashy, followed by a hint that my photos were . . . effete. Odd contradiction there, don't you think? I guess he's always assumed that I survive by getting the rare job photographing clothes and food. He couldn't believe it when I explained about my one-man show at the gallery. Not that he was pleased for me. He called the photo on the invitation card disgusting."

To Giuliana's surprise, Markus chuckled, before adding, "In his defense, I have to say that it *is* disgusting—it's based on those *memento mori* still lifes the Dutch did. It shows a woman's hands holding a bouquet, and both the hands and the flowers are covered in maggots. He didn't ask any questions about the show or the work. Still, I told him about my plans for that show. Also my work as a commercial photographer and how successful my sales are these days. I even mentioned the great reviews my first London show got. I'm embarrassed by how much I bragged to him, and he just sat there, gripping his glass. As soon as Ada came back, he used that as an excuse to leave. And that was it."

He paused. The silence stretched. "I haven't seen him since," he finally added. "I haven't talked to him, either." With that, to Giuliana's annoyance, he got up and went over to look out the window again.

Giuliana thought of Kathrin's description of the little boy who could never gain his father's love. Markus's story filled her with sympathy for him, but she kept her voice cool as she asked, "Why do you think your father wasn't pleased by your professional success?"

Markus turned from his view of the street and leaned back against the glass, watching her.

"What you're asking is part of what I've spent years trying to understand, alone and in therapy. It's not something I'm going to talk to the police about. But I'll tell you this much: it has to do with control. You've been investigating my father for twenty-four hours, right? By now, it shouldn't surprise you to hear that he needed to be in charge of things—and of people. Over the last ten years I've been trying to learn not to let myself be one of those people."

Markus had his eyes fixed on Giuliana as he spoke, and she stared right back. At the door he'd come across as self-possessed, and the anger he carried around gave him a quality of menace. Now the sunlight exposed the hollows of his face, the taut tendons in his neck, his rigid shoulders. He'd learned to keep his hands still, but his whole body still spoke of anxiety and vulnerability. A year older than Renzo, she reminded herself, but Renzo hadn't retained such adolescent neediness. Now Markus seemed to expect her to speak, but she stayed silent, so he continued.

"When I don't . . . When I didn't respond to my father the way he expected me to, I denied him control over me. That's one reason why, in the Bellevue bar, I kept telling him about my photos when he was critical, instead of getting defensive. It broke his . . . his grip. I wish that were the only reason, but I guess . . . some part of me never stopped hoping he'd throw his arms around me and say, 'Märku, what great news! I'm so happy for you, so proud of your success. Tell me all about it.'" Markus's laugh was a bark. "Well, I'm rid of those fantasies at last, thank God—with him gone."

There was a long silence, and then Giuliana heard a stifled sob. Markus walked out of the living room and into what she assumed was his bedroom, closing the door behind him.

She was alone for about ten minutes. She read through her notes on the interview so far and added clarification. She carried the cups with their half-drunk, cold coffee into the kitchen and left them by the sink, filling two glasses with water instead. As she turned to carry them into the living room, she noticed a large photo on one wall. It showed a very old woman with crooked arthritic fingers peeling potatoes onto a newspaper spread on a kitchen table. The woman's head was bent over her work, but she'd raised it just enough for the photographer to catch her eyes.

Giuliana knew this photo. She remembered seeing those eyes. The longer she'd looked into them, the more the woman's age and frailty had fallen away, until all that was left was determination—the will to carry on—and the conviction that it was enough. Examining the picture now and feeling again the pull of those eyes, Giuliana recalled that she'd seen it in September at a city-sponsored exhibition on *Verdingkinder*. She'd known about Switzerland's indentured or "contract" children for years but considered them a nineteenth-century abomination, like child factory workers or chimney sweeps. It had shocked her to learn that Swiss boys and girls had been removed by local officials from parents deemed unfit and forced to labor for their keep, chiefly on farms, as late as the 1970s, although by then it was rare. The children's "caretakers," although paid a fee by the state to feed and house them, had often treated them worse than livestock, forcing them to work long hours in dangerous conditions and barely giving them enough to eat. And then there was the physical and sexual abuse they endured.

Giuliana had found the exhibition fascinating. She'd listened to recordings of former contract children describing their lives on farms and studied old photographs of the attics or lofts they'd slept in, examples of the tools they'd used, and collections of the meagre belongings they'd cherished. Most powerful of all had been the photographs of twenty or more old people who'd survived the experience. Because not all of them had. Giuliana grasped now that the photographer who'd created those portraits must have been Markus Gurtner.

Markus strolled out of his bedroom and met her in the kitchen. Except for a trace of redness around his eyes, he looked as cool as when he'd opened the apartment door. She handed him one of the glasses of water and went back to where she'd been sitting.

"I apologize," said Markus, taking his own seat. "Let's go on."

"Could you hold out your hands, palms down, Herr Gurtner?" Looking puzzled, he complied without hesitation. *Well-acted if he's the killer*, she thought. There was no bruising at all on the knuckles—but marks from gloves had been found on the rescue pole and the telephone. With his prison sentence for assault, she might be able to get permission to search for those gloves.

"According to the officers who spoke with you on the telephone yesterday, you were at home Monday afternoon and early evening. Is that correct?"

"Yes. I had a set of photographs due, fashion shots for a magazine, so I was at the computer all day. I didn't see anyone until I went out to get groceries just before the stores closed at seven. I sat here tinkering with the pictures until six-thirty."

She frowned. "Did you go out of the apartment to get the newspaper or pick up your mail? Did you play music or make any noise? Could anyone have seen or heard you while you were working here? Think about it."

Markus sat perfectly still, and again she was struck by his ability not to fidget. He shook his head. "I got my mail and played music, but no one noticed, as far as I know."

"We'll check. In the meantime, try to think of someone who could alibi you."

She stood up, and so did he. She caught no gleam of relief in his eyes that the interview was almost over, no shift in his expression at all. She wondered if she could change that. "Who do *you* think killed your father?" she asked and saw at last some strong emotion lash across his face, gone before she could say exactly what it had been.

"You really think it was someone who knew him? Not a random nutcase?"

"It looks that way."

Once more, Markus remained motionless as he thought.

"I've barely been in my father's house over the past ten years—by choice, I should tell you—and I know nothing about the people he associated with, except that I imagine they had something to do with the hospital or with the *Burgergemeinde* and our family's guild. I'm sorry. I can't answer your question."

They were still standing in the living room. Giuliana went on. "What do you know about your father's childhood?"

Markus's eyes widened and his eyebrows went up. "His childhood? He never talked about his childhood. Sometimes he told stories about the time after he went away to boarding school in Thun, but he was already a teenager then. If you want to know about when he was really young, you'll have to ask his big sister Charlotte. Watch out for her, though; she'll tell you whatever makes us sound good. By 'us' I mean our family—*Tante* Lotti thinks all von Eichwils rank just below archangels and far above every other patrician in Bern, not to mention normal mortals. Brigitte, Paps's younger sister, is my godmother; she's completely different—I like her. But she was little when Paps went away to school, so I don't know what she'd remember about him as a child."

Markus was trying to move Giuliana toward the foyer as he spoke, but she held her ground. "I've already talked to Charlotte Gurtner, and, as you say, she's loyal to her relatives. She even defended *you*." She gave him a twitch of a smile as she said this, and, to her surprise, he grinned back as one eyebrow shot up. It was all she could do not to grab his shoulders and shake him as she continued. "Whatever your aunt claims, you're still a suspect in this homicide. If you didn't do it, then help us give you an alibi. Also, if you have more thoughts about who might have killed your father, let me know. Call me any time at work or on my mobile."

She handed him a card from her purse. Then she said, "I saw the picture of the old woman in your kitchen. That was in the *Verding-kinder* exhibition this past September, wasn't it? Did you do all the portraits?" When he nodded, she went on. "They're brilliant. I don't know how you managed to make each person look strong and broken at the same time. The photo of the tall man in front of the open window—that was another of my favorites."

"Thanks." He gave no second smile, but she got the impression he was pleased. Then, before she could change her mind, she added, "Show your mother your work. Tell her how successful you are. She deserves to know." She regretted how emphatic her voice sounded in her own ears—and probably even more so in his—but she wasn't sorry for the words. She kept his gaze and refused to look away, expecting to see the anger reappear in his pale eyes, but they stayed blank. "I'll think about it," he murmured.

Together, silently, they walked to his front door. He got her coat off the rack, helped her into it and held out his hand. "I've known a lot of cops," he said, as they shook hands. "You're not what I expected. Which has been . . . interesting." He'd closed the door even before she turned toward the elevator, leaving her wondering if she'd received a compliment. Thinking, too, that she might have glimpsed him smiling just as the door closed.

Markus locked the door and went back to the kitchen, where he stared at the photograph of Edith Neuhaus peeling potatoes. It surprised him that the woman cop had recognized it from the show. That was because he didn't think of cops as people, he realized, with a life separate from dealing with criminals, a life in which they could go to exhibitions and be struck by pictures. Or empathize with his mother. Or, perhaps, get someone reminiscing about his father's childhood and naming his contemporaries. Like Norbert Wittwer. What a pity Norbert was an uncommon name: it stuck in people's minds.

It had stuck in *his* mind when he'd heard it at the Kornfeld art gallery about a year and a half earlier. He'd shown up at the gala opening that evening in order to charm the various gallery owners who might display his photographs and the rich people who might buy them—but also to admire the extraordinary collection Kornfeld was exhibiting before his annual auction. Strolling into a roomful of prints and small paintings by Emil Nolde, he'd seen his father and Nicole. They were talking to a middle-aged couple and didn't notice him, and he began to turn away, determined to avoid a confrontation. Then some force he couldn't explain made him approach the four sleekly dressed people holding champagne flutes and greet them warmly. As usual, Nicole couldn't hide the flash of fear that crossed her face before she smiled and bent forward to exchange cheek kisses with him. That made him sad; at some point during the past twenty years he'd become fond of her, mainly because Philipp loved her, but also because she'd raised his half-brother to be such a good kid.

The conversation had been courteous and short. Almost an hour later, he was drinking his own well-earned glass of champagne in the darkness of the gallery terrace when, from an even darker corner, he'd heard his father's voice. Approaching quietly, he saw his old man half-hidden by a row of large bushes, phone to his ear.

"I can't talk, Norbert. I'm surrounded by people." Pause. "No, I won't speak with you now, not even about that. I'll call when I can." Pause. "I told you, when I can. I don't know when that'll be." Pause. "I see. Still, don't call me like this again. You know the way you're supposed to get in touch with me. We have a deal, and you need to stick to it." As his father's hand moved away from his ear, he growled a curse and slipped the phone into a trouser pocket. Then he walked back across the terrace and into the gallery, leaving Markus to stand in the dark and wonder. Who would his father speak to so rudely? No one from his professional world, surely. And what about "You know the way you're supposed to get in touch with me"? That was plain weird.

The old man's voice had been odd, too—not just angry, but different, somehow. Was it his pronunciation? Markus only knew that the whole conversation had been strange. So, who was Norbert?

When he thought about the call the next day, he considered asking his aunts about the name or mentioning what he'd heard to Patrick the next time they had a beer together. But he decided to keep it all to himself. His father's words and tone of voice had made the relationship with this Norbert seem like a secret, and the idea that his self-righteous father might have a hidden vice or a shady past intrigued him. He'd reminded himself that it was all a fantasy of his own concoction, based on one strange phone call. Still, he hadn't been able to let go of the idea that there was something to know about this Norbert, something that could be useful to him.

13
Before

J akob Amsler, the man who'd gone to school with his father, phoned Markus ten days after having his picture taken for the exhibition. He suggested they have a beer. Markus was intrigued. Some people, especially lonely ones, confused professional sociability with friendship. With a wife, two daughters, and a grandson in Bern, Amsler wasn't lonely, and he was too smart to misread Markus's attentiveness during the shoot. Markus hoped he was calling so that they could talk more about his father's childhood in Heidmatt. Besides, he'd liked the man.

He accepted the invitation.

They met at a small restaurant near Loryplatz, more or less midway between their homes. The place had two rooms, one on either side of the front door: one for meals and the other for snacks and alcohol. It was popular with locals in the summer because of a large back garden. Now, on a cold, clear October night, all that mattered was its location. Arriving a little before their nine-thirty appointment, Markus was surprised to find the place simple and uncluttered, with several good lagers and ales on tap, and a few fresh flowers on each table, even in the bar area. He sat down at a corner table and amused himself by covertly examining the other seven people in the room. All of them stared at

Amsler when he arrived. With his great size, he had to be used to the attention, and yet he looked about him shyly, Markus noticed, his face only relaxing when he recognized Markus in his corner.

"I really like the feel of this place," Markus told the older man as he sat down. "It's a great find." Amsler nodded. "It's got a nice atmosphere, hasn't it?" he agreed. "After fifty years in Bern, you get to know all the good meeting places." They each ordered a pint of beer and smiled at each other as they touched glasses. "Call me Jakob," Amsler said; "I'm already thinking of you as Markus." Markus clinked his glass against Jakob's a second time, in acknowledgement of their new first-name status.

During the hours they'd spent together at the photography session, Markus had heard a lot about the two-and-a-half years Jakob had spent working under terrible conditions on the farm of a couple called Haldemann, before he was transferred at eleven to another farm, where life had been better. After that first mention of Markus's father, Jakob hadn't talked about him again, and Markus was determined to get more out of him this time. First, though, they chatted about the exhibition on *Verdingkinder* where the photographs would be displayed; both were disappointed that the show had been postponed until September.

"But I guess it's worth waiting until we can get the Käfigturm as a place to hold it," Jakob said. "It should bring in a lot more people, being so central."

"I think the show will attract attention no matter what. It's a topic that really grips people: so many children suffering and no one doing anything about it. The fact that the authorities were to blame makes it . . . all the juicier."

Jakob laughed. "Yes, it's a story with a lot of villains. Still, in some ways it sounds worse than it really was. I mean, everyone treated children badly back then. Even Haldemann and his wife, my *Meischter* and *Meischterin*, weren't exactly monsters. Yes, I worked extremely hard; yes, Haldemann hit me; yes, I slept in the hayloft and was cold in the winter and always hungry. But that wasn't just because I was a *Verdingbueb*; it was because Haldemann was a mean son-of-a-bitch. He beat his wife while I was there, and I bet he bashed up his own kids plenty, which would explain why they almost never came home to visit from wherever they'd gone off to as soon as they were old enough to get away. It was a bad placement with a bad master. There were good ones, though."

Markus found that hard to believe. From what he'd learned from Jakob on the day he'd photographed him, these Haldemanns, the man and woman who'd cursed him, begrudged him every mouthful he ate, and tried to keep him from attending school, had not even called him by his name. To them, he was always just *Bueb*: Boy. Yet here he was, not just a survivor but a retired professional with a successful engineering career behind him. And still working, too—although he understood that Jakob's small business as an electrician was "just to keep his hand in," as he'd said. The man probably couldn't imagine a life that didn't include hard physical labor.

Thinking all this, Markus smiled at Jakob and lifted his glass to him in silent salute before taking a drink. In the warm room, the cold beer filled Markus's mouth with a sharp, vital taste. "Did you actually know kids who worked for decent families?" he asked.

"One girl, Heidi, lived with the couple that owned and ran the inn. She worked hard—their own kids did, too—but the whole family was kind to her, and she married one of the innkeepers' sons." He paused, taking a long pull at his own beer. "There was another boy, Pesche, a couple of years older than me, whose family came to love him like one of their own eight kids. But that's the kind of story that doesn't get told."

"So tell me," said Markus.

Jakob sat next to Pesche, beaming at everyone around the table. When he wasn't smiling, he was eating, and when he wasn't eating, he was being served more food. Pesche's master, Herr Fankhauser, kept cutting him slices of bread, and Frau Fankhauser filled his bowl over and over with thick pea soup. The soup had rings of onion and bits of bacon, and the bread was fresh and chewy. When he finished the soup, he knew there would be blackberries and custard. Tonight, he was allowed to eat as much as he could hold—and he would, too.

Such luck! With Haldemann away until late that night, Herr Fankhauser had come to help with the evening's milking. Inside the barn, where they'd murmured to the cows as they milked, the man paid no attention to Jakob. Afterward, though, in the smoky kitchen, he'd put a hand on Jakob's shoulder and said to the *Meischterin*, "Now why should you fix food for this youngster when your old man's not here? I'll take Köbi home with me and send him back to you later on, and you'll get a quiet evening to yourself. I know how much my wife likes it when there are no menfolk underfoot."

"With eight children, I doubt your wife ever gets a quiet evening," sniffed Frau Haldemann. Then she'd turned to Jakob. "Well, boy, you know what will happen to you if you leave chores undone. If you want to risk it, go ahead. It's no skin off my nose."

Considering that the *Meischter* had given her a banged-up nose a couple of weeks earlier, Jakob found this a strange choice of words. But he said nothing. He was suddenly so happy he couldn't keep still, so he dashed over to where Fankhauser had left his bicycle leaning up against the side of the barn.

"Think you can balance on the back of my bike?" Pesche's master asked.

The path to the Fankhausers' farm was uphill; Jakob doubted the man could pedal home with an eleven-year-old boy perched behind him. It didn't matter. He could run all the way to Pesche's in less than ten minutes—he'd done it before.

"That's okay, *Meischter*. I'll walk along beside you." *And try not to run ahead of you.* He didn't know which made him want to go faster, joy or hunger.

Now the hunger was satisfied. After the berries, the girls cleared the table, and one started to sweep the floor, while an older boy rounded up the little ones to get them washed and into bed. Herr Fankhauser's father moved to an armchair to smoke his pipe and read the

newspaper, but everyone else bustled around. Jakob hoped he wouldn't
be sent away yet.

Frau Fankhauser seemed to understand exactly how he felt. "Pesche,
why don't you take Köbi out to the barn and show him Lulu's puppies?
Just be back by eight. You, too, Köbi. Come in here to the kitchen before
you leave. I bet you'll be hungry again by then; maybe I'll have a little
something for you!" She smiled at him, and he felt tears in his eyes. For
one horrible second, he yearned to throw his arms around her waist,
hide his face against her chest, and cry like a baby. Luckily, she already
had a baby over one shoulder and no arms free to hold him.

He and Pesche went outside, and the stupid feeling passed. Now
that it was September, the sky was still blue after supper, but the breeze
blew cold, stirring the tops of potato plants still waiting to be har-
vested. Inside the barn, the dairy cows, light brown with white faces,
stood twitching and shifting side by side, the air around them warm
and scented. Pesche skirted the cows to make for a corner of the room
barely lit by the open door, where he stood to wait for Jakob.

"Go quietly, now," said Pesche as they started to move forward,
their eyes adjusting to the gloom. "Lulu's calmer than she was when
the pups were first born, but she doesn't know you like she knows me."

Jakob could see Lulu lying in the straw panting, and he could hear
the small warning growls she made as she watched them approach.
Baled hay had been piled to enclose the corner—Lulu could scramble
out easily enough, but her puppies couldn't, which kept them safe from
the cows' horns and hoofs.

"There were six," Pesche told him, "but one was born dead and
one died after a day. These four are doing fine. They're just over three
weeks old."

The boys sat on the hay bales and watched the puppies clamber
over their mother. Lulu was doing her best to ignore being scaled like
a mountain. Then one of the pups gnawed on her ear, and she shook
her head furiously, throwing him off her neck and into the straw that
covered the barn floor. He lay on his side for a while before staggering
to his feet and weaving toward Pesche and Jakob.

Lulu was champion at bringing in the cows, but she wasn't much to look at, and it was impossible to know what kind of dog had fathered her litter. The pup lurching toward them was a dirty shade of brown with some lighter yellowish-brown patches. His legs looked too short for his body, his tail and ears too long. Still, his eyes were bright and he seemed to be grinning at them—Jakob felt sure he was a male. He put out a hand so the pup could sniff his fingers. Raising her head, Lulu growled louder, and Pesche crooned to her. Standing up to defend the puppy was apparently too much trouble, so she watched warily but kept her peace. Jakob stroked the small head with his finger and giggled as the pup tried to chew on him. He knew better than to jerk his hand back and startle Lulu, so he deftly kept his fingers out of reach of the puppy's new teeth and patted him again gently.

"Do you know what your *Meischter* is going to do with them?"

"I know he's keeping one to help Lulu with the cows. I guess he'll either find homes for the rest or drown them. That's what happened to the last litter."

"I wish he'd give Haldemann one."

"He's not going to give that bastard anything."

"Don't call him that," Jakob said, keeping his voice down as he stroked the drowsy puppy.

Pesche turned amazed eyes to him. "A bastard? Why not? You expecting a stack of Christmas presents from him this year?" He snorted and glanced at Jakob's clothes—a filthy oversized shirt missing most of its buttons and torn, too-short trousers—before looking away.

"Ever since you told me what 'bastard' really means, I've stopped using that word for him. In my head, I mean. Because there's nothing wrong with bastards if you're one."

"Okay. What shall we call him then?"

By the time they had run through Pig-Pizzle, Turd-Fresser, Stumpy-Dick, Dung-Fucker, Wobbly-Ass, and a few more, they were lying in the hay weak with laughter. The puppy hadn't been scared off by all the noise; he was draped over one of Jakob's wooden clogs, fast asleep.

The boys sat up, side by side, and began to try shoving each other off the hay bale with their bottoms. After more giggling, they were quiet at last. Jakob listened to Pesche's breathing, the cows' low moos, and the puppies' whines, punctuated by his stomach making funny churning noises. He felt better than he had in a long, long time.

Pesche turned toward him. "Remember last week in class when I begged Müller to read us more of that great story he'd started the week before?"

"Yeah, I thought you were an idiot—it was such a boring book. Then Müller kept looking for it until it was time to go home. God, we were lucky!"

"He couldn't find it because I'd hidden it."

"No wonder you asked him to read it," Jakob crowed.

Pesche's eyes went from laughing to serious. "Remember how Müller said he was going to make Fränzu read out loud at the end of the day, even though he mixes up letters and gets the words wrong. That's why I hid the book. I like Fränzu. If that bast . . . shithead Müller's going to force Fränzu to read to the class just to make him look stupid in front of everyone, then I'm going to do the same to him."

The puppy on Jakob's wooden clog woke up and nibbled at his ankle. Jakob wished he could cuddle him but was afraid Lulu would have a fit.

"Yeah, you *do* make Müller look stupid, and he hates you for it," he told Pesche. "Maybe if you sucked up to him instead, he'd be nicer to you."

"No, he wouldn't. Don't you get it? The only kids in that class that Müller is even halfway decent to are the ones whose fathers are important. Like Karli. He'd never dare to hit Karli, because of who his parents are."

Before Jakob could respond, he heard Frau Fankhauser calling: it must be eight o'clock already. He moved the puppy gently off his foot and jumped up, thinking about what else Pesche's *Meischterin* might produce for him to eat before he went home. Half an hour later, having added a handful of roasted chestnuts to all the food in his belly, Jakob trotted home, carrying a small smoked sausage and a bag of dried apple slices. He was going to hide them in the loft. He wondered how long he could make them last. Maybe if he ate one tiny bite of sausage and one apple slice every night before he went to sleep . . . it would be hard not to gobble them up, though. Some nights he was so hungry his stomach hurt.

Markus's beer mug sat empty in front of him as he listened; not once during Jakob's story did he catch himself longing for more than the pint he'd decided to allow himself. Jakob was eleven in the tale he'd just told; when Markus was eleven, his mother had had trouble getting him to fold his duvet each morning and put his toys and books back on the shelf. As far as he could remember, that was all the work he tackled as a child. At that same age, Jakob had spent most of each day digging, planting, weeding, milking, shoveling shit, chopping wood, fixing fences, and God knew what else. It was another world. It seemed impossibly long ago and far away to him, and yet his father had grown up in it.

"So you and Pesche saw each other at school, too? Not just on the Fankhauser farm."

"Yes, Pesche was two years older, but we were both in the same class, along with your father. None of us called him Johann, you know—we called him Karli. Everyone did."

"I'd forgotten that: both his sisters still call him by his middle name, Karl. I wonder when he switched to using his first name." He was just formulating another question about his father when Jakob said, "It's good to see you. I'm going to take off now, but I hope you'll get in touch if you want to have another drink. I'm sure you want to hear more about your father, but I'm doing some wiring on a construction site these days, so I have to get up early tomorrow."

Markus stood, too, thinking maybe he'd call Ada and ask if she wanted to meet him in town; he certainly wasn't ready to go home yet. Jakob had already paid, so the men put on their jackets and went out into the cold night. Towering over him, Jakob extended his hand. As he took it, Markus noticed an awkwardness about the old man that hadn't been there before, as if he needed reassuring. "I enjoyed this evening," Markus told him. "I'll call you so we can do it again." It surprised him to realize that he meant his words with all his heart; he was disappointed their drink had ended so soon.

"I'd like that," Jakob said softly. His smile was wide, but his eyes were still uncertain. He turned away to walk home, and Markus watched him for a while before reaching for his phone. He wondered if Ada would like the idea of his spending the night.

14

All the way back to the police station, Giuliana thought about her interview with Markus. Gurtner's middle son was the perfect suspect. The man's police record showed he was capable of brutality, his history of drug and alcohol dependence indicated his instability, his grip on her wrist confirmed that he still acted on angry impulse, and his own words proved how fraught his relationship with his father had been. Johann Gurtner had excelled in provoking his middle son, something she imagined Markus's brother Patrick would confirm, if put under pressure. Although Markus lived nowhere near the section of the Aare where his father's body had been found, there were all kinds of reasons he might have been by the river at Dählhölzli. Perhaps he'd been planning a fashion shoot at the zoo or in the adjacent forest. Or, despite their animosity, father and son might have made an appointment. Based on what she'd learned about their relationship, Markus hitting and then killing his father made sense, and that son might be one of the few people the surgeon would have taken a swing at.

She'd have liked to discuss the interview with Renzo while it was fresh in her mind, but she'd have to write it up instead. Her morning alone with Markus had released Renzo to do other things, so she'd sent him out with several photographs of Gurtner's missing Audemars Piguet watch. Lots of jewelry stores in the city bought old watches, and even the stores that didn't might have appraised Gurtner's watch since it had disappeared. And then there were pawnshops to visit and Bern's best-known fences to talk to. Some of the questioning was being done on the phone by other investigators, but Renzo was handling the more difficult approaches in person.

What should be her next steps for dealing with Markus? She'd think about it over lunch, before discussing it with Erwin. She parked in the lot behind the police station and went around the building and across Nordring to the bakery café. There she ordered a mushroom omelet with a green salad and waited for it to arrive at one of the round tables in the back room. From there she could look out onto a tiny courtyard; the baker had made an effort to fight November's gloom by planting some straggly pink heather along a back wall. On that chilly day, the view was still bleak. At least it didn't include rain, she reminded herself and smiled at the waitress who brought her omelet.

She knew why she was overthinking her interview with Markus— it was because of Toni. Had she been working with another of the prosecutors she knew, her next steps would have been clear: write up a report on the suspicious interview, discuss the evidence and her gut feelings with her homicide partner and perhaps with their boss Rolf, and immediately afterward consult the prosecutor. There might not be perfect consensus on the steps that would follow, but at least everyone would be on board. But Toni Rossel prided himself on being—she sneered as she considered some of the clichés favored by the newspaper articles she'd seen—ahead of the pack, a risk-taker, a lone wolf. In other words, a loose cannon. She stared at the last leaves of arugula on her plate, sighed deeply, and ate them, deciding to forget about coffee and talk to Erwin as soon as possible. Maybe he'd say her distrust of Toni's reactions was unnecessary. She hoped he would.

A glance around the noisy homicide room showed her that Erwin wasn't back from his morning with Gurtner's lawyer and banker. So she put her laptop under her arm and walked toward the end of the corridor to the case office: the room that brand-new homicide cases were shifted into if the crime wasn't solved within the first forty-eight hours. The space was small and completely utilitarian: two desks, two padded desk chairs, and one filing cabinet took up most of the room. On one wall, there was a whiteboard, on another, an expanse of cork for pinning up photos and notes. Impersonal as it looked, Giuliana loved working there—it helped her to focus. Erwin had scattered paper on one desk, so she sat down at the other, her back to the door. She texted Erwin an urgent request to talk, plugged in her laptop, and began to write up the interview with Markus.

She heard the door open and looked around to be confronted with Toni. Damn. How had he tracked her down—and what did he want from her? As her case's prosecutor, he had a perfect right to talk to her any time, although most colleagues would have had the courtesy to call before interrupting her—or at least knock on the closed door. "Julie," he sang out, making his private nickname for her sound as throatily French as possible. "I'm so glad you're here alone, so we can have a private chat." He grabbed Erwin's desk chair and turned it around, pushing it across the space between the two desks and settling himself in it, so that, when she turned her chair to face him, their knees were less than a foot apart.

With his eyes on hers, he leaned forward, and she found herself looking at him closely, which she'd made a point of not doing in the meeting the day before. He had a couple of years on her—was he already fifty?—but she could imagine women still finding him sexy, with that combination of curly blond hair—which she'd bet a month's salary was now dyed—and sleepy blue eyes, along with a still more-or-less trim body. The boyish charm that had attracted her to him when they'd first met was still there, too, and it seemed as fake to her now as a bad toupée. God, how could she have let him touch her? But she had. Over twenty years ago, on an office sofa, with one alcohol-fueled and totally consensual late-night fuck—she wouldn't dignify the encounter with a nicer word—she'd given this man power over her. She couldn't even be angry with her younger self. At that age she'd been much too naïve to grasp the danger of what she was doing. At least she'd had the sense to turn him down firmly from then on. Still, he'd never let her forget the incident, despite all the affairs he was rumored to have had since.

"So," said Toni, "how are things going? Do you think Erwin's running the case well? Letting that bear loose among the *Burger*—they must be laughing up their sleeves at him." He waited a moment, perhaps for an obliging giggle from her, but she made her face stone, so he went on. "You were supposed to talk to the middle son this morning, the one who already tried to murder someone eighteen years ago. What's the story?" He was still leaning forward. Despite her instinct to lean back and get him out of her face, she stayed put, thinking furiously. He persisted. "You going to bring him in later this afternoon?"

It was now or never—either she'd be a good girl to preserve the peace, or she'd make her position clear. There was no middle ground.

She put both hands on the arms of Toni's chair and pushed it back until they were at least a yard apart. That gave her the room to stand up, which she did, pushing her own chair out of the way and then leaning back against her desk. She made herself smile at him and said, "That's more like it," then went on before he could say something snide. "Now, about Markus. I'll send you and Erwin my report the moment it's done, but I can sum up by telling you that we haven't got a speck of evidence yet that would justify picking him up."

Toni returned to his charming smile; it was his default mode. "But you agree he's our prime suspect, right?"

"Yes," she said. "But . . ."

He made a sad face. "Everything's always 'don't' and 'but' with you now that you're a homicide detective. You used to be . . ."

"Look, Toni." She forced another smile. "We work together now, that's all. Let's lay our history to rest. Okay?"

His eyes were hard now, but his own smile remained. "Well, you're still special to me. What do you expect, when all I have to do is close my eyes to see you lying there . . .?"

She couldn't stand it, especially since she could remember it, too, and didn't want to. Talking over him, she said, "I don't want to talk about the past. Stop dragging it up, for Christ's sake, and let's get back to work. Please don't call me Julie, either—I didn't like it then, and I don't like it now."

"Or what, Julie?" His smile now was genuine. How he loved feeling that he had her in his grip. "You can't stop me reminiscing. Maybe I'll share the details with a few of your colleagues here. I bet they'd love to hear our little story. Why not? You may think times have changed, but not by much."

She tried to keep her face blank, but he must have seen something there, because he said, "No? You don't like that idea? Well, in that case, the least you can do is cooperate. If I decide it's time to arrest Markus Gurtner or anyone else, then it's time. That prick Erwin's goal in life is to make me look bad, but I can trust you to back me up. Right?"

She stood up straight. "Time for you to leave."

He got up, too, and opened his mouth to say more, but something stopped him. Instead, he moved to the door. Just as she thought she was rid of him, he turned and said, "I know why you've got no time for *me* anymore. You've found yourself a new sofa buddy, haven't you— that bit of beefcake at the meeting yesterday, the *Tschingg*. I saw him watching you. What do you imagine your colleagues think about that, hmm?"

He was out the door and gone at last. Giuliana sank back into the chair and turned it around to face the desk. Hands clasped tightly on its surface, she worked to slow her breathing and ease the tightness in her chest. How dare he call Renzo a *Tschingg*? It was a slur on Italians she'd have thought no educated person would use. She couldn't remember the last time she'd been so angry. God. She'd have to warn Renzo to watch out for Toni.

As she stared at the laptop screen, trying to force her thoughts back to the report on Markus, her phone rang. Erwin said, "Let's talk. I'm in the office. Where are you?"

"I'm in the new case room." Click. Thirty seconds later, he was there. He, too, pulled the free chair over to her side of the room and sat down, leaning back as far as he could to put his feet on her desk. *Interesting*, she thought. He was invading her space, too, but there was no hostility in it, no disrespect. It was comfortable.

Before she could open her mouth to tell him about Toni or the interview with Markus, Erwin began to describe his morning with Gurtner's lawyer and banker, who'd been evasive about his affairs.

"I'm asking about unlikely sums of money being paid into or out of Gurtner's various accounts, unexpected investments, recent changes to his will, bitter personal lawsuits he's involved in—all the stuff any cop would look for. Meanwhile, these two wiseasses nod nonstop like dashboard bobbleheads and explain that research takes time, they are checking the records carefully, and they will get back to me as soon as they can. Pure bullshit. After that, the lawyer has the balls to hint that I should tread carefully because of Gurtner's connections to the *Burgergemeinde*. I almost trod on *him*."

"I can imagine," Giuliana said, smiling as she pictured the scene. Blunt to a fault as he was, Erwin hated pussyfooting. He also hated bankers. To him they were crooks. It amused her that Erwin, who voted right of center, and her husband Ueli, who voted far left, shared this vehement distrust of Switzerland's iconic profession.

"So, I think we'll see results from those two tomorrow." Erwin smiled smugly. "The other development I'm still hoping for is dirt on Nicole Gurtner."

"Has Walter turned up any gossip about Nicole and a lover?"

"Nope," growled Erwin. "Not a fucking word." He brightened momentarily. "Get it? A fucking word. Ha-ha!" Giuliana lifted an eyebrow in his direction, and he subsided. "Still, we're just getting started. I've got investigators poking around asking questions at her office and among her friends. If she was cheating on her husband, someone is bound to know and let it slip. Now," he added, "tell me about the bad seed—whatshisname—Markus."

Looking at her notepad as she talked, she recounted the interview, then said, "Before I give you my take on all that, why don't you tell me yours?"

"No alibi for the time of his father's death. Let's go arrest him," Erwin said. Although his voice was gruff, she knew him well enough to hear the joke behind it and rolled her eyes. He grinned and went on. "I think you and I probably agree about what our next steps should be. This guy's a good possibility, and we should talk to him again, probably search his place, and try to find someone who saw him leave home that afternoon. Also check his father's phone records for calls from him, ask Nicole about him—do everything we can think of to turn up more signs that he's our killer. But we don't have enough evidence to arrest him, so we want to keep looking. Gurtner might have a girlfriend with a jealous husband; he might have been fiddling the Cloth Handler's books; he might have been mugged. Now tell me what *you* think."

Giuliana had smiled all through Erwin's words, and now she got up and gave him a high-five before sitting down again and saying, "Exactly. We don't have enough evidence. There's this, too: he's exceptionally vulnerable to having his life disrupted by police attention—as an ex-con and ex-drug abuser who's trying to build up a business. If he's guilty, too bad. But if he isn't . . ." She frowned at Erwin. "The worst of it is, I just had Toni here and, before I could even tell him about the interview, he asked if we were picking Markus up this afternoon."

Erwin jerked his feet off her desk and brought them down to the floor with a bang. "That viper would love the limelight he could focus on such a juicy suspect. Patricide is dramatic as hell, plus there's the guy's wild past, his burgher background—Toni'd squeeze the story for every drop of hype."

Giuliana moved away from her desk. There wasn't any room among the furniture to pace, so she just walked to the window and back a few times as she said, "He wants me to support *him* if you make a decision he doesn't like." She shook her head. "Can you believe that? He thinks he can get me to undermine you!"

He must have sensed something behind her words, because he sat up even straighter and asked, "Did he threaten you, Giule?"

"Yes." The word came out before she could think it through.

To her surprise, he didn't ask for details, just shook his head and said, "He's a prick."

She smiled grimly. "That's just what he called you. But let's get back to Markus. I have to send Toni my report on the interview, and you have to brief him, but I think we agree that we'll play Markus down as much as we can while we see what evidence we can find. Can you think of anything else we—?"

Erwin interrupted. "Toni's not a fool. He'll know there isn't enough evidence. The fact that Gurtner's a von Eichwil works both ways. All the more media coverage if the arrest is a good one, but a shitload more trouble if it isn't. And if something new comes in that makes Markus look guiltier, well, even you'll want him picked up then."

"Of course I will. But I'd still like to avoid a media carnival."

"Fat chance of that," said Erwin. Still, he followed the words with a nod in her direction and added, "I'll do my best." He scooted his chair back to his desk and hauled himself out of it. "Why all this drama about Markus, anyway? You got the hots for the guy?"

When Giuliana had first started working with Erwin, years before, comments like this had set her on fire with rage. Now they ran off her like water. "He *is* sexy, it's true, but that's not why I'm worried for him." She gave Erwin's question serious thought. Under his banter, he was asking for her instinctive take on the man. "I guess I respect him for turning his life around. He's angry and messed up, which makes him dangerous, but he's interesting, too. And he's a fabulous photographer. His portraits—the ones I've seen—they're beautiful, and they also . . . um . . . they honor their subjects. I like him for that, at least."

Erwin was silent, nodding very slightly, a frown on his face. He was processing her words, she knew, even if he didn't comment. "Good. I'm off. Wait, no, let me check with you about Renzo. I've asked him to spend some time at the Cloth Handler's Guild, finding out what Gurtner did there. That fine with you?"

"Of course," Giuliana said. "But isn't there still stuff to do at the hospital?"

"He can fit the guild research in along with that. Plus I've got a couple of women working the hospital staff now, trying to squeeze gossip about Gurtner's love life out of his favorite nurses. If anyone knows about his playing the field, you'd think they would."

With those words, Erwin was out the door, no goodbye; she knew his mind was already on something else. Her thoughts shifted, too, to Renzo. She'd have to tell him about Toni soon. He might need to protect himself from the man. She needed to do that, too, but she hadn't yet figured out how. At the very least, though, she could go back to her desk in the homicide office instead of isolating herself in the case room.

Five minutes later, in the presence of two colleagues and Rolf, she opened her laptop and continued writing about Markus as accurately and neutrally as she could, imagining Toni reading every word.

At home she asked Lukas no questions about the bullied girl Salomé, and the evening was peaceful. Isabelle had two exams the following day and, except for raiding the refrigerator twice and groaning about her teachers' cruelty, stayed in her room. Once Lukas was in bed, Ueli went back to writing in the living room, and Giuliana sat in the kitchen using part of her mind to go over reports about door-to-door inquiries while another part considered what tomorrow's interview with Gurtner's sister Brigitte might reveal. A third part tried to repress all thoughts of Toni and was unsuccessful. She got up to make herself a pot of mint tea and saw it wasn't yet ten. She grabbed her phone and dialed Renzo, who answered quickly.

"Hi, what's up? Something you want me to do?"

"Are you going to be at the gym in the morning?"

"Sure. At six, like always. Want to join me? With all this Gurtner stuff going on, we may not get in our Monday workout-and-breakfast next week."

"Breakfast is what I called about. Do you mind cutting your

routine short? If I meet you at six-forty-five, we'll have an hour before Erwin's briefing. I've got something . . . to tell you."

"Sure," said Renzo. He sounded surprised but didn't ask questions. "I'll see you at the gym at a quarter to seven. Why don't we . . ."

Almost in her ear she heard Fränzi say, "Who are you talking to?" with the bite of resentment in her voice. Then there was a throaty murmur and a sharp intake of Renzo's breath, before he said, "Got to hang up. See you." He was gone, leaving an echo of his eagerness in her ear. Lucky Renzo. Mouth twisted, she slumped over her reports again. At ten-thirty, she went to stand behind Ueli, hands on his shoulders, and bent to kiss his neck. Seductive murmurs were not her style. "Come to bed," she said.

Ueli leaned his head back so that it rested just below her breasts, and she bent over again and brushed her lips on his ear. She waited to hear him say, "I'll just finish this," but he didn't. He saved his file, closed the lid of the laptop, and stood up. Together, they checked on Lukas. His duvet had slipped, and Giuliana tucked it firmly around him. Standing in the dark hall outside Isabelle's room, they noticed dim light shimmering under her door.

"Good night, Isa," Ueli called. "Stop texting and go to sleep."

"Sleep well, sweetheart," Giuliana threw in, before their daughter could voice any protests, adding softly to Ueli, "She'll probably just keep doing it."

"Of course she will," said Ueli cheerfully, "but I like to remind her every once in a while that her parents aren't *completely* clueless." They went into their bedroom. Ueli closed the door quietly, turned, and put his arms around Giuliana. For a moment, resting her head on his shoulder and feeling the pressure of his arms, she considered telling him all about Toni Rossel. Then he kissed her, and the thought blackened and crumbled to dust.

15

Renzo slipped out at 5:40 a.m., wearing sweats. In the still-quiet garage, he slung his gym bag onto the car's passenger seat and hung his work clothes for the day, black trousers and a white shirt, on a hook in the back. He was at the gym by six, as he was at least three mornings a week. Usually he started with free weights and then switched to the machines, but with Giuliana coming in forty-five minutes, he decided to do only floor work. He was finishing a last set of pushups when he saw her standing in the doorway across the room. He caught her eye and did five jump pushups in rapid succession, clapping his hands between each one, then watched her shake her head and raise her eyes to the ceiling in derision. It was so like her that he laughed aloud. While he showered, shaved, and dressed with efficient speed, Renzo thought, not for the first time, how much Giuliana reminded him of his older sister Bianca, partly because of their dark southern-Italian looks but mainly because both of them could tease him without making him doubt their love. Love. The word came into his mind without hesitation, a given. He knew Giuliana loved him. Just not more than her family.

She was waiting for him in the narrow, shampoo-smelling lobby, still in her coat. "Sometimes I can't resist showing off," he said with a tilt of his head and a grin as he approached her.

"And sometimes I can't resist making fun of you—even though I'm impressed," she countered, hooking her hand under his arm and almost dragging him out the door. "Come on, let's get breakfast."

In the bakery, over hot milk coffee and still-warm croissants, she quietly summarized her interview with Markus. "I've sent you, Erwin, and Toni a copy of the report. Erwin likes him for the killing and so do I, but there just isn't enough evidence."

"What about your gut feeling when you were with him?" Renzo asked, biting off the tip of his second croissant and smiling at the crumbs on Giuliana's lips.

She must have caught the direction of his eyes, because she wiped her mouth vigorously with a napkin. "I don't listen much to my gut, because it makes so many mistakes—you know that," she said. "He is a very angry man, yet some part of me liked him. If we find out he lied about his alibi, though, that will be more important than any impression of mine. What's worrying me is Toni Rossel."

Renzo, coffee cup halfway to his lips, put it back in the saucer. Should he tell her what he'd overheard Toni say to Erwin after their meeting about the case overwhelming her—and about the contemptuous way he'd said it? No, but at least he could warn her. "Do you . . . um . . . do you consider Toni a friend? Because my impression from the meeting yesterday morning and something he said afterward is that he's . . . somewhat hostile to you. And to Erwin."

Giuliana gave a snort of laughter and reached out across the small bistro table to pat his arm. "Thanks for your tact. What you mean to say is that he's out to get me. We despise each other. Erwin and Toni also can't stand each other, although I don't know the history behind that." He saw her face grow serious, fast. "Toni and I had a confrontation yesterday, and he threatened me. Along the way, he accused us—you and me—of having an affair. He may not really believe that, no matter what he says, but he'd use it anyway if he thought it would get him something he wanted. So, that's why I wanted us to have this breakfast—to warn you. Because of me, you're in his crosshairs now. I'm really sorry about that."

Renzo felt her words like a punch in the gut. He didn't give a shit about Toni—although maybe he should, a small voice told him—but he knew how much Giuliana feared sexual gossip. Which she should. There were a couple of policewomen in other departments whose male colleagues sniggered about them, and . . . had he ever doubted that they were the sluts rumor said they were? It shocked him to realize that he'd always assumed the bulk of those kinds of stories were true. No smoke without fire, and all that shit. His worry must have shown in his expression because she leaned toward him, face full of concern, and added, "I don't think he can hurt your career; you're completely out of his chain of command. And I can't imagine he'd send Fränzi an anonymous letter or . . ."

"Wait," he said, his voice ringing in the little room, and Giuliana leaned back, startled. They were sitting in their usual corner, where they could discuss police business in private, but two women at the closest table were staring. They looked hastily away as he frowned at them. Not cops, though. Good. Glancing around, he didn't see anyone he recognized from the station.

Voice much quieter now, he said, "Sorry. What I meant was, let's worry about *you* now, not my career. What do you mean, he threatened you? With what? What can he do?"

She sighed and looked down at her empty coffee cup as she spoke. "I think he's worried that Erwin and I will try to keep him out of the loop in some way—and, even though he's wrong, there's something in what he says, because we both think he's more interested in looking important than conducting a tight investigation. Anyway," she glanced up as Renzo nodded his agreement to her assessment of Toni, "he told me if the case isn't handled the way he wants, he'll make sure the whole shop knows that he and I had sex together . . . hey, don't look at me like that," she added. Renzo had no idea what expression was on his face, but he did his best to force his features into blankness. "It was over twenty years ago. We went back to the office after a work party and ended up on a sofa in the break room. It was all over in minutes, and we both pretended afterward that it never happened. Or, at least, I did. I was already with Ueli—not married, but together—and Toni had a girlfriend, too. It was one of those things that's best forgotten. The problem was that he didn't want to forget about it—not then, because he kept pushing me for a repeat, and not now either, I guess because it's such a good tool to use against me."

Renzo's brain burned with questions, and he was afraid all of them would upset her. Instead, he blurted out, "So that's why he called you *'Julie'* like that, in French. His name's Antoine, so I guess it's his mother tongue. It seemed very... intimate. Do you speak French with him when...?"

Giuliana interrupted, her eyebrows climbing almost to her hairline. "Renzo, for God's sake," she said. "The thing with Toni happened over two decades ago. I was—what?—twenty-five? I'd gone into my father's defense practice straight out of law school, and things... didn't work out. After two years with him, I spent... maybe six months at the courthouse. I was miserable. I figured out pretty quickly that the only reason I was trying to become a prosecutor, was... well, I guess it was mainly to thumb my nose at my father."

Renzo leaned forward, fascinated by these revelations. He knew Giuliana had joined the police after working with her lawyer father for a while, but he'd never heard any details.

Giuliana fussed with the crumbs on her plate, obviously avoiding his eyes. "Toni befriended me when I was feeling bad . . . especially about myself. That oily charm of his seemed real to me then. Turned out he was in charge of prosecuting someone my father was defending and hoping to pump me for info. I was so naïve, I thought he was trying to help me fit in." She frowned at her watch. "We've got to go; staff meeting's in ten minutes."

"No, wait." Renzo almost reached across the table for her arm. A week earlier, he wouldn't have thought twice about doing that, but now he was cautious about touching her. He had to keep her out of trouble, and he was part of that trouble. "We'll talk more about this." She shook her head, but he went on. "Later, I mean. Right now I've got two questions."

"Okay, ask. I'll give short answers." She had a smile on her face, but everything about the rest of her looked weary, as if she hadn't slept and didn't know when she would.

"Why does he think we're having an affair? Did someone say . . .?" She interrupted. "He says it was because of the way you look at me, but don't worry about that. He's just saying whatever comes into his head."

Renzo appreciated her attempt to comfort him, but the guilt didn't go away. Nor the shame. Jesus, he'd probably stared at her all through the staff meeting like a starving lion watching an antelope, and everybody'd seen it. His face burned. Did he give himself away every time they were together at work? And he thought he was discreet. *Cazzo!*

"Don't blame yourself," she said softly. "I . . . look at you, too." He glanced up quickly, but she was already out of her chair, putting on her warm jacket, adjusting the shoulder strap of her purse, glancing around the room. He sat unmoving. What was she telling him? She'd never chewed him out for kissing her on the lips Tuesday night—and now this. Had she reconsidered, after making it so clear in June that she wouldn't sleep with him?

She was already walking away. "We're late," she called over her shoulder. He grabbed his jacket off the back of the chair and followed her. They were crossing the street when she asked, "What's your second question?"

For a moment, he couldn't remember. Oh, yes—Toni. "It sounds like Toni's out to get you personally. Do you know why? I mean, what has he got against you?"

They reached the heavy station door, and Renzo moved closer to her to open it. As she walked by him into the building, she turned to look up into his face.

"I don't know," she said, before they took off for their meeting.

"Honestly, I don't. Unless it's that . . . all I've done since that one time we . . . had sex was turn him down. Along the lines of never, ever again. Maybe . . . maybe he took that personally."

Renzo almost laughed. He and Toni had something in common. Only he'd never even gotten a first time.

16

oni Rossel did not appear at the eight o'clock briefing, and Giuliana only became aware of how much she'd been dreading having to deal with him when she felt her pen wobble in her hand and understood that her trembling fingers were caused by relief. Today there were three *Fahnder*—Hansruedi, Walter, and Renzo—and three homicide detectives—Erwin, Giuliana, and Rolf—sitting around the conference table. Erwin took an evidence bag out of his jacket pocket and laid it gently in the middle of the table. A watch with a pale metal band showed through the clear plastic.

Giuliana expected Erwin to look triumphant; if the watch had turned up at a shop, they might have a description of whoever had sold it or even a CCTV shot. But Erwin seemed, if anything, a bit puzzled. "Yesterday at noon, a woman turned this in at the zoo's ticket office, and it made its way to me. The finder says she noticed it glinting in the bushes along the river as she was cleaning up after her dog. The glass is broken, but it's still running. Never went into the Aare. Have a look—there's a bit of blue thread caught in the band."

He handed the plastic bag to Rolf, and it went around the table. The blue material—Giuliana guessed wool—was lodged between the links. Looking closely at the watch, she saw an inscription on the underside of the face.

"What does the writing say?" she asked.

Erwin picked up a scrap of paper and read, "*For my beloved son—another special watch at last. You know I've always believed in you. Mami. June 1975.*"

There was silence and then Hansruedi Balmer said, "Mami? How old was he when he got this forty-thousand-franc watch? Five?" The other men at the table snorted.

Giuliana found the inscription intriguing rather than funny. Remembering what Nicole Gurtner had told her, she took Hansruedi's question at face value. "It was when he passed his medical finals, so he was at least twenty-five. His father was alive then, and his parents never separated. So, why is the watch just from his mother?"

No one answered; Renzo diverted their thoughts by saying, "I saw Gurtner's clothes right after his body was found, and I don't remember a sweater or anything in that shade of blue. If we're lucky, that thread came from the killer."

Erwin nodded. "I'll call the wife as soon as we finish here and ask if Gurtner owned anything that color. A scarf that washed off in the Aare, maybe? But I hope you're right, Renzo. Hansruedi, find out exactly where along the riverbank this watch was found and see if that tells us anything about where the fight took place. I'll give you the phone number of the finder. Now," he glanced around the table, "how do you think this watch ended up in some bushes? Plausible scenarios, anyone?"

Giuliana couldn't imagine, and the more she considered it, the less she could explain it. The watch hadn't gone into the Aare with Gurtner nor been stolen, nor could she see how it could have come loose during the fight: the band wasn't broken, and there was no catch to come undone.

"The thief dropped it and then couldn't find it in the dark?" suggested Walter Mosimann.

"That's about all I can come up with myself," Erwin agreed. "But eventually I hope we'll be able to do better." He paused and looked down at his notes, then glanced at Giuliana before continuing. "We may have a suspect: Markus Gurtner, the middle son of our victim. So far there's nothing to put him on the banks of the Aare on Monday afternoon. What we've got is a man with a criminal background, a history of conflict with Gurtner, and no verifiable alibi. He says he was at home in Bethlehem when his father was killed. Walter, I'd like you and a couple of your people to talk to his neighbors and see if anyone saw him going out when he says he was in. Check the local cameras, too. Not enough evidence for a search warrant yet, but Toni's going to set up access to his past calls. Questions?"

He looked at Giuliana when he said this, and she shook her head. "Sounds good to me." Which it did. Markus had to be further investigated, and Erwin was going about it intelligently. She couldn't help sympathizing with their prime suspect, but that didn't mean he hadn't done it. *You're a cop on this case, Linder,* she reminded herself, *not defending counsel.* Still, she hoped that something else—someone else, ideally—would turn up to divert attention from Markus. Especially Toni's attention. She considered his threat to expose her and hoped she could get out of the meeting room soon, in case he put in a last-minute appearance.

"Now, what else? There are a couple of investigators still nosing around to make sure we know all we can about the Gurtners' marriage and finances, and we've got people checking alibis for Gurtner's hospital connections. Renzo's looking at the man's burgher connections, and Giuliana's going for the younger sister. Right?"

She nodded. "Appointment's this afternoon."

"By later today," Erwin paused, glowering, and Giuliana remembered the uncooperative banker and lawyer of the day before, "I *hope* to get one of our accountants started on Gurtner's finances. Renzo will see if he was fiddling the books at the Cloth Handlers' Guild. Anything I'm forgetting? Questions, Rolf? Anyone?"

Giuliana watched heads around the table shake before asking, "Has anything usable come in from the public in response to our requests for information about Monday evening? Did anyone see our emergency caller?"

"Nothing."

"And no word on the dog?"

"Nope."

"I'm still waiting for an analysis of the emergency caller's dialect," Giuliana reminded them. "Any of you guys had new thoughts about the call?"

The five men shrugged or shook their heads again.

Erwin turned to Renzo, grinning. "Before you leave, Renzo, I'd like you to run Gurtner's watch down to Monika"—she was the middle-aged head of forensics—"and persuade her to do it *now*. She knows it's coming, but you'll have far more success convincing her how urgent the tests are than I ever could." He winked broadly at the younger man, and faces around the table filled with grins; Hansruedi made some sort of kissy noise. Giuliana sucked in her breath. She remembered—surely not more than a year ago—when Renzo had been convinced that his looks kept him from being taken seriously; back then, Erwin's request would have made him livid. Now he just gave Erwin a thumbs-up as he grabbed the watch, cocked an eyebrow at Hansruedi, and left. She breathed out. He didn't need her to look out for him, she reminded herself; he could take care of himself. Well, most of the time.

"Thanks, everyone," Erwin said, and the meeting broke up.

Giuliana had a lot to do that morning, and she didn't want to waste time on a confrontation with Toni. It infuriated her to have to skulk around her own building, but fighting with the prosecutor would not only be dangerous for her career—it could threaten her ability to pursue the Gurtner case properly. Slinging her laptop in its case over her shoulder, she walked upstairs to the top floor, which was home to the white-collar crime unit and had several rarely used offices and meeting rooms.

She passed a colleague who specialized in tax crime, sitting surrounded by framed photos of his kids—he had five. She poked her head into his office. "Hi, Sepp. I need a quiet place. Do you know if the room across the hall is free for a couple of hours?"

"Giuliana," he answered, a smile on his large, round face. "It's been a while." He shrugged. "Nothing scheduled that I know of. Make yourself at home."

She had reports to read. But her curiosity about the watch's inscription nagged at her. Settled in the unfamiliar room, she searched online for background about Johann Gurtner's doctor father. Apart from simple biographical information, there wasn't much to find. She reached out to someone who'd know more.

Kathrin answered her phone on the second ring, and Giuliana read her the inscription on her ex-husband's watch. "Were you there when his mother gave it to him?" she asked.

"No," Kathrin told her. "Right after he got his degree, she came into Bern for the day and took him out for lunch, and he came home with the watch. She loved giving him presents. I thought it was a nice thing for her to do. Extravagant, of course, but she always loved spending money. I'm glad you found it. Why are you asking about it?"

"Didn't it strike you as odd that the watch was from his mother and not both parents?"

"Aha!" said Kathrin. "I can see why that would puzzle you. I suppose it says a lot about Hannes's family that I didn't find it strange at all. It was painfully obvious that his mother favored him over his sisters, and don't forget I knew them only as adults, so imagine how bad it must have been when they were small."

Giuliana's thoughts flashed to Charlotte before she asked, "But what about the father?"

"He and Hannes weren't close." Kathrin paused, and Giuliana could almost hear her reflecting. "But it was more complicated than just that. My mother-in-law visited us a lot, my father-in-law almost never. Hannes never talked about it, but I always knew he . . . wanted more from his dad. That the coolness between them was . . . well, not his choice at all. Still, they were distant enough that the watch being his mother's gift alone seemed normal to me. But now you're making me speculate that his father not being involved in the gift probably hurt Hannes's feelings. Maybe a lot."

Giuliana worded her next question carefully. "Do you think your father-in-law was jealous of your husband's professional success? Since he'd remained a country GP all his life, I mean?"

"I doubt that. I think the tension between Hannes and his father went back a long time. It was there before Hannes became a heart surgeon. In fact, it was part of . . . I'd call it a strain within the family. Every year Hannes and I and the boys spent Christmas Eve with his parents in Heidmatt. Charlotte was always there, since she lived with them; sometimes Brigitte and her husband were, too. It was never a relaxed event. Actually, that's a major understatement: the stress used to hum around us all like a high-voltage wire."

Giuliana scribbled a note to herself and then chewed on her pen. "You think Christmas was the only time your husband saw his father?"

"I don't know." Kathrin was silent again. "All I can say is that if he met his father alone, he didn't tell me about it, and he never explained why they were estranged. When the old man died, Hannes was . . . bereft. Such terrible grief—and I couldn't help him with it."

Giuliana thanked Kathrin but felt the phone call had left her with even more questions than before. Charlotte and Brigitte Gurtner would probably have their own opinions about the inscription on the watch and their brother's relationship with his father. The question was would they tell her?

That gave her an idea. She was seeing Brigitte, the younger sister, that afternoon, but Charlotte had been much closer to her brother and, if she remembered correctly, had stayed at home caring for her parents until their deaths.

She found the older sister's telephone number in her mobile and dialed.

17
Before

Bern's Old City,
spanning a nine-month period before Gurtner's death

Markus's agent found him work photographing restored medieval textiles during November. It turned out to be a fascinating but complicated job, and five weeks went by before he set up another drink with Jakob Amsler. This time, they decided to meet at Ringgenberg, a beloved Bernese café on the Kornhausplatz. It was a popular place with good food, so Markus made their reservation for nine-thirty, assuming the dinner crowd would have thinned out. With Saint Nicholas Day on December 6th, the city's storefronts were festooned with white lights; more glowing decorations hung across the streets between shops. Trying to absorb a little of the holiday mood, Markus got out of his tram at the train station and walked down Bern's main shopping street to the restaurant. Every shop window was decked out. One displayed full-sized Christmas trees studded with silver balls; in another, mannequins in hooded red robes trimmed with fur created a row of elegant St. Nicholases.

For Markus, the weeks of Advent did not generate happy memories, although recently he'd begun to enjoy giving gifts to his little nieces. As he headed to Ringgenberg to meet Jakob, the only childhood he was thinking about was his father's and what else he could find out about it. As before, Jakob greeted him warmly, and they ordered half a liter of red wine to share. Before Markus could form a question, the older man asked, "Do you have any family?" and he found himself talking about Patrick and Philipp.

"A high-level federal bureaucrat, and," Jakob paused, deliberately, "a freelance photographer. Does that make you the black sheep?"

Markus laughed. "Is it that obvious?"

"How'd you fall into that role?" Jakob asked. "I bet you were destined to become a doctor, after Patrick didn't."

Markus nodded, smiling. "Of course I was. Until I dropped out of university. But my wool was pitch-black long before that."

"Tell me," said the older man. So Markus did. He started out just reciting facts about his boyhood and adolescence, trying to suppress any emotion but irony, but at some point he realized the tone of the story had changed. Perhaps it changed when, after hearing about the attack on the man in Geneva, Jakob asked, "This group of teenagers who were arrested: was one boy in charge?"

"Yeah. A kid called Sämu." He'd pushed Sämu out of his head a long time ago, but now he saw him as he was then: the pale, mobile, androgynous face; the long, dark hair; the eyes full of laughter and scorn. Sämu had been eighteen at the time of the crime, so he'd gone into a man's prison, not a boy's, and served a longer sentence than Markus. Since the trial, they'd never met or spoken again.

"What was it about him that made you do what he said?" Jakob asked.

Markus searched the other man's face for the contempt he expected to see there, the look that went with the questions he'd heard so many times. How could you let yourself be swept into a crime? Why didn't you just walk away? Don't you have any moral courage? But there was no contempt; the old man was asking a different question, one he'd never been asked before, even by his lawyer. Markus thought about Sämu's electric personality and answered, "I wanted to be part of the group of boys that Sämu dominated, because . . . I guess because he was fascinating. He seemed totally in control of himself, and yet it felt like he could go out of control between one second and the next and get away with anything."

Jakob was paying close attention, nodding at his words. "Yes, I know what you mean. I imagine this Sämu was intelligent."

"Yes, that was part of why I admired him: his cleverness, his coolness. I was afraid of him, too. One minute he'd be warm and funny, the next minute detached, and a minute after that, in front of everyone, he could dig his claws into one of his so-called friends—verbally, I mean. It was extraordinary how fast he could become cruel and rejecting. Still, we were all drawn to him. Especially girls. Maybe I thought some of *that* would rub off on me if I hung around with him. There was nothing I wanted more than to attract girls." He laughed and drank some wine, knowing he was laughing because of his discomfort at revealing so much truth to someone he barely knew.

Jakob nodded again. "So, when he expected you to do something, like kick a man in the head, the dangers of not doing it probably seemed . . . huge. Especially when you were too drunk to think beyond the moment. To consider . . . the penalties for getting caught."

"That's it; that's exactly it. But the penalties did arrive—they came fast and kept on coming, even after I got out of juvie. First failing university and then . . . well, I got into drugs. Alcohol, too. I was taking photos by then and starting to make money, but . . . I was a mess."

"Yeah, I know what that's like. It's such a cliché for us *Verding-kinder* to have alcohol problems, but I fit right in—I hit the bottle just before and after our first baby was born—our Anna." Jakob raised his eyebrows. "I'm okay now, as you see." He pointed to the glass of wine he'd been sipping slowly, then to Markus's, which wasn't even half-empty. "Guess you're over it, too."

"I hope so," said Markus. He kept his head down for a moment, so the old man wouldn't see the surprise in his face. Jakob a recovering alcoholic? He seemed so—what was it? Centered? Self-contained? "Didn't you want children?" Markus asked. Flustered, he added, "Sorry. That's none of my . . ."

"It's okay. My problem was the opposite. I wanted kids, desperately, and I planned to be a perfect father. But I couldn't remember my own father, and I'd had a bad . . . a really bad childhood. I don't mean as an indentured kid, but before that. My mother . . . locked me up a lot." Markus started, but Jakob was staring at his wine glass, so he kept quiet.

"I was afraid," said Jakob. "Suppose I neglected Anna or hit her or shook her to death? I told Renata how scared I was of fucking up fatherhood and she . . . she was incredulous. She tried to talk me out of it, but I just drank more. Poor Renata. She'd just had a baby, and her husband was losing his marbles and becoming a boozer. So, she went home to live with her parents until I got a grip on myself. It was the best thing she could have done, because I was frantic to get her and Anna back. So I . . . I pulled myself together." Jakob, his head still bent, took a deep breath, blew it out and then looked up to smile at Markus. "Now tell me how *you* beat the dependency. Not one of the twelve-step programs, or you wouldn't be drinking at all."

Markus kept talking, warmed by the older man's interest, even as a small piece of him looked for the catch. This wasn't a scam; his every instinct told him that. So, why the kindness? After a while Jakob asked, "What kind of photos do you take, besides portraits?" And Markus let go, temporarily, of his suspicions, and talked on, explaining the development of his work and basking in the attention of someone who truly seemed to want to listen.

At some point Markus saw how few guests were still in the restaurant and flushed. "I've been jabbering. Forgive me."

His companion reached out and rested a warm hand on Markus's forearm. "Nothing to forgive. I'm interested in your photos, and you were answering my questions."

Markus glanced out one of the two big windows opening onto the street. Under the streetlights, he watched the no. 9 tram unload a few figures in coats and take on the larger crowd heading home after an evening in the city. Turning back to Jakob, he said, "I'm sorry I talked so much, because I meant to ask you more about my father. You said you went to school with him."

"Yes, for two years," Jakob said. "The school had only three class-rooms for pupils between seven and fifteen. I was with him in the middle grade."

"What was he like then?" Markus asked and was ashamed of his breathlessness.

"Remember how you described Sämu? The boy whose group you were so desperate to join in high school? Well, you could have been describing your father. A younger version, of course; he left our school before fourteen, so I never knew him as a teenager."

Markus leaned across the table, transfixed. "Did he have a group, too?"

Jakob nodded. "They were nicknamed the Three Bears, because their names were Bernhard, Albert, and Norbert."

"Norbert," Markus repeated. The name he'd heard at Kornfeld's gallery months earlier. What else could he find out? "These three bears, my father's friends. Were they contract boys, too?"

Jakob was smiling at a handholding young couple at the next table; he looked back at Markus and said, "No, no. The bears were local kids. Let's see what I can remember. Albert's father was a farmer with a lot of land—he could pay for hired help and didn't need *Verdingkinder* to work for him. Bernhard . . . I don't recall anything about his parents, but he wore warm clothes in the winter and good boots, so they weren't poor. He could draw well, too; I remember that about him."

For a moment, the older man seemed to lose himself in his memories. Get on with it, Markus thought, just as Jakob said, "As for Norbert, I knew he was different the moment I met him, almost as outcast as a *Verdingbueb*. His mother lived in a rundown cottage on the edge of the village and worked as a cleaner, although I didn't know that then. No one had a clue about his father, including him. He was older than the rest of us but smaller and . . . not bright. He could read and write, but I don't know if he learned much else from school."

"And this . . . Norbert was one of my father's best friends?" His father, who entertained dinner guests with tales of his medical col-leagues' mildest mistakes or misunderstandings; who expected perfection from his three sons in any task they undertook—this man had had a childhood friend who was simple?

Jakob shrugged. Something in his smile told Markus he understood the reason for his incredulity. "Norbert had his place in your father's group, and he was certainly the most devoted of the bears. Grateful for your father's attention, completely loyal, ready to do or say whatever was asked of him. Unfortunately, since then he's had a hard life—serious drinking, unemployment, illness. I'd see him now and then when I was back in Heidmatt visiting friends, but we only recently got to talking again."

Markus considered telling Jakob about the one-sided conversation he'd heard at the gallery, which had made it sound as if his father had some sort of arrangement with Norbert. Would Jakob know anything about that? The conversation shifted to another of the man's friends in Heidmatt, and Markus didn't bring it up.

Their young waiter asked if they wanted refills. Smiling inwardly at the green earplugs piercing the boy's lobes, which made him feel old, Markus said no and paid the bill.

"Thanks," said Jakob. "I'll contact *you* for our next drink. That is," he added, his voice suddenly gruff and uncertain, "if you'd like to meet up again."

Markus leaned forward and clapped Jakob's bicep. "Let's make it soon."

Over the next nine months, the two men met twelve times. Markus enjoyed telling Jakob about his changing photography projects, including a big assignment to record historic Swiss buildings that had fallen into obscurity. He listened with pleasure to Jakob's anecdotes about working as an electrician, but the old man talked about the past as well, not only about his years as a *Verdingbueb*, but also about the early years of his marriage. Over one of their beers together Markus finally mentioned his father's phone call with Norbert, but Jakob seemed as puzzled as he did about what the two men had been discussing.

In September the exhibition featuring Markus's portraits of *Verdingkinder* opened to strong media attention: talk of reparations for survivors of the indenturing system was a hot political topic. Jakob came to the opening with his wife Renata and both his grown daughters, and Markus introduced them to Ada, whom he knew he should call his girlfriend but never did. After the speeches and Prosecco, Markus took Jakob, Renata, and Ada out to dinner at Café Fédéral.

"Why wasn't any of your family at the opening?" Jakob asked Markus once they'd ordered their food. "Didn't you tell them about the exhibition?"

Ada glanced at him, and Markus gave her an appreciative smile. He loved the way she dressed; she always managed to look both slutty and elegant. Tonight she had on skin-tight black trousers and a discretely sequined peacock-blue top. She looked over at Jakob, sighed, and rolled her eyes. "I'm so glad someone else is talking to him about this. I've given up."

"Patrick knows," said Markus, trying not to sound defensive.

"Your brother?" confirmed Renata. Markus thought she looked elegant, too, in an old-lady way, with her sleek white hair, rust-colored dress, and strings of amber beads.

"Yes, my older brother. I'll take him around the exhibition next week, when it isn't crowded. He and my aunt Brigitte—my godmother—are the only ones in the family I've told. That's . . . just the way it is." Markus heard how roughly he'd spoken and was sorry, but he wasn't going to get into the subject of his family at this celebratory dinner. Jakob brought up his father over coffee, though, sliding into the topic while the two women were immersed in a comparison of favorite films.

"We've talked a couple of times about Norbert Wittwer, and I was wondering if you wanted to meet him. Not to be melodramatic, but if you don't do it soon, it may be too late. I told you he had liver cancer, didn't I? Well, it's worse. I figured maybe the next time I drove out to Heidmatt, you could come with me. If you want to, that is."

Although he heard no pathos in the man's voice, Markus said,

"I'm sorry to hear he's so ill." The other shrugged. "He's seventy-four—I never imagined he'd make it this far, given the way he's lived." They were seated upstairs at a window and Jakob turned to look out over the square below, where at least twenty people, mostly men, stood around a chess game with giant pieces. When Jakob looked back at Markus, he was smiling crookedly. "I apologize if I sound callous—I guess it's the ex-drinker in me lacking sympathy for someone who couldn't stop boozing. But we all have our terrors. I guess we fight them whatever way we can. And . . . sometimes we lose. Norbert never stood a chance."

Markus was thinking. Going to Heidmatt, this time not to his Aunt Charlotte's castle for a dutiful visit, but to the village itself, and meeting a man who'd cared about his father as a boy. What could it possibly bring him? It had taken him a long time to learn to expect nothing from his father—or at least nothing good. He remembered the combination of fear, hope, and puzzlement that had filled him as a child whenever he'd approached his father with even the simplest question or anecdote. Eventually, he'd begun to drown these feelings in cynicism, wondering before every encounter how the old man would put him down this time. Patrick had helped him cope with it. The anguish in his mother's eyes was too much for Markus to bear, but Patrick made a game of it, lifting one eyebrow as Markus turned to their father and then waiting for the response to whatever Markus said with the fake eagerness of a game show host listening for a competitor's answer. Afterward, when they were alone together for a moment, Patrick would shake his head and say, "The old man's slipping. He sounded almost pleasant that time," or, giving Markus a high-five and a grin, "That was a good one. You really know how to make him lose his shit." God, he'd been grateful to Patrick for that. He was still.

This childish humor had helped Markus to cope, yes, but not to understand. Something about the idea of meeting his father's friend made him hopeful again. Maybe Norbert, despite his limitations, had a memory of the old man that would offer Markus a piece or two of the puzzle that was his father. Or one of Norbert's stories might give him leverage over the old man, the next time he had to deal with him. It was worth a try.

Markus registered that he'd been quiet for at least a minute; Jakob had joined Ada and Renata's conversation about a recent Korean movie that had impressed them. Sensing Markus's focus upon him again, Jakob turned and said, "If you want to meet Norbert, I'll tell you what. You give me a couple of evenings when you're free, and I'll set things up with him and drive us out to Heidmatt. If he isn't already hospitalized, I'll suggest we meet in the local inn, The Lion. It's run by Heidi Stettler's family. I told you about her once—she was also *verdingt* and married the innkeepers' son Ändu. You can meet them, too."

"That would be great," said Markus and reached for his phone to check his calendar. No matter how little he found out about his father's childhood—a time which he was starting to think his father had deliberately kept quiet about all these years—an evening in Heidmatt with his father's former classmates was bound to give him something he could use against his old man. The idea made him smile.

18

Giuliana's drive to Charlotte Gurtner's home in the village of Heidmatt took less than an hour, but she felt as guilty as the class goody-goody cutting school. She knew that part of why she'd decided to reinterview Gurtner's older sister in her home instead of by phone was because it was a great way to avoid both Toni and her paperwork. Besides, she loved the Emme valley. Even on this cloudy day, the sun popped out intermittently to warm the land, and, in its glow, the valley's rounded hills, forest-bordered fields, and lonely farms lost their wintry dullness. Some scenes she passed remained gray and gloomy; others, suddenly touched by the fitful sun, seemed to gleam like miniatures from a medieval Book of Hours. Many hills were topped with a single, enormous tree, bare-branched and spidery against the sky, and groups of brown-and-white cows grazed on sparse patches of grass that hadn't yet succumbed to winter. Here and there the towers of small village churches marked the skyline. Giuliana, who knew the Emmental well, was struck again by the region's beauty. Thoughts of both Gurtner's death and Toni's hostility faded into the background.

For all her family forays into the Emmental, she'd never been to Heidmatt. The farming community had about a thousand people spread over a lot of land and was, she'd just read, known chiefly for two things—its covered bridges and its castle. That castle—or some earlier version of it—had belonged to a branch of the von Eichwils since the 1300s and remained theirs even after the family lost their role as regional overlords. Johann Karl Gurtner had grown up in it, and now his sister Charlotte lived there alone. Giuliana could scarcely believe she was getting a chance to see inside it.

After the interview, she'd planned as a courtesy to introduce herself to the local cop, but a quick online check revealed there wasn't one. The town of Langnau, a fifteen-minute drive away, sent someone to Heidmatt once a week for a couple of hours to staff a police office and meet with anyone who showed up. "The place hasn't had any crime in ages," a Langnau colleague had explained on the phone. "There are some fights, broken up by whoever's around, and there's spousal abuse. I know through the grapevine which men beat their wives—and there's one wife who's a slugger herself—but there's nothing we can do unless we get a complaint." The sigh that followed encompassed years of frustration. "Let's see," he continued. "What else? Shoplifting, vandalism. Kids' stuff." He wished her luck with her case, and that was that.

Since the village of Signau, Giuliana's road had off and on run parallel to the Emme. Approaching Heidmatt and the covered bridge that led into the village, she saw that her route had curved away from the big river again, and it was something smaller that the little wooden bridge crossed. Apparently, the heart of Heidmatt was nestled between these two arms of water, the Emme and the Dornbach. She creaked slowly over the rustic bridge, and from then on kept a curious eye on the place where Gurtner was born. Heidmatt announced itself as a farming community with its first shop, which sold tractors, along with the tillers, harvesters, winnowers, and other attachments that went along with agriculture. Following her GPS to the castle, she passed a gas station, general store, bank, post office, and several small, modern office and apartment buildings, not to mention a metalworking business that offered to shoe horses. Then came an inn, The Lion; beside it, a sign pointed toward the town hall—useful information, that.

Soon after, she began to climb, and five minutes later she'd reached Charlotte Gurtner's home, perched on one of the steep, wooded bluffs above Heidmatt.

It wasn't just an oversized house with a few crumbling medieval bits that she found herself staring at, but an honest-to-God castle. A discreet sign on the side of the road revealed that the building dated back to the mid-fourteen hundreds but had been expanded in the eighteenth century and renovated in the twentieth. It was built of whitewashed stone, with some half-timbering, and a mixture of slit windows in the oldest parts and shuttered casements in the newer sections. There was a large, arched doorway that showed off the building's extremely thick walls, and nearby was a round tower topped with a colorfully tiled octagonal roof. It was a small place, for a castle, and Giuliana liked it all the more for that. It had character.

She parked in a neat gravel lot fifty feet along the road and walked back to the door under the arch. The arch was round, not pointed, and had a lion's head as a keystone. The door had enormous hinges and was carved with vines and leaves. As she touched the button mounted on the wall beside it, the Heidmatt church bells struck eleven. *Hope the old lady likes punctuality*, she thought, and waited for someone to let her in.

The door was answered by the middle-aged woman who'd brought Charlotte Gurtner to the police station; she reintroduced herself as Alice Schwander, Frau Gurtner's secretary. Her voice and manner were subdued but not unfriendly. "Let me take your coat," she said, and Giuliana handed over her thigh-length car coat, which Schwander hung in the hall wardrobe before saying, "Frau Gurtner is waiting for you in her sitting room, if you could come with me." Giuliana followed her down a dark hall lined with windows that had been built for the exit of arrows rather than the entrance of sun. After a longer walk than Giuliana had expected, the secretary opened a door off the passage, and they stood on the threshold of a large room whose far wall contained glass doors leading to an inner courtyard.

Although there wasn't much light coming into the room from the gray sky, only one lamp was lit. It sat on top of an elegant little desk where Charlotte Gurtner was working, her back to the door. Now she got up and came across the room to greet Giuliana. No suit this time—she wore a navy wool skirt, navy pumps with low heels, and a twin sweater set in pale coral. As she shook hands with the older woman, Giuliana decided the set was cashmere; all that was missing was the traditional single strand of pearls. Instead, Charlotte wore a small pearl brooch pinned to her cardigan, a pearl ring, and a matching set of earrings.

"Thank you for seeing me at such short notice, Frau Gurtner. I'm sure you could have answered my questions on the phone, but I'm pleased to have a chance to see where your brother grew up."

"As I've said, I'm eager to help," Charlotte said, "and I certainly prefer talking about something so important in person, so thank you for coming. Coffee?" At Giuliana's "No, thank you," the door closed behind Alice, while Charlotte escorted Giuliana to the large rectangular table on the window side of the room, seated herself at its head and pointed her visitor into a chair at her right. Giuliana removed not only her usual spiral notebook and pen from her purse but also several close-up photographs of Gurtner's watch and took a quick look around the room. The chandelier over the table and the two decorative sideboards against the wall indicated that this had probably once been a dining room. Now the fireplace on one wall had two easy chairs in front of it, and the escritoire where Charlotte had been sitting had a modern lamp. Perhaps she had turned this large space into a combination study-dining-sitting-room and spent most of each day in here. Giuliana felt sad, trying to imagine what it was like to be the single inhabitant of a castle meant to hold a medieval family and all its retainers. At least Charlotte had Alice.

She put one of the 8½ -by-11 photographs in front of Charlotte, who examined it and said, "This looks exactly like Karl's watch." She glanced up, frowning. "Surely if there's any doubt you can have it examined for fingerprints."

Was she pretending not to know about the writing on the back?

"When we talked on Tuesday," Giuliana said, "you told me that you and your mother and Karl were very close."

"Particularly Karl and my mother, I'd say. Brigitte was closest to my father." She didn't seem to notice having left herself out of the equation.

"What about your brother's relationship with your father?" Giuliana knew she was fishing. Honestly, what did this have to do with Gurtner's death? Still, she was determined to get to the bottom of the words on the watch.

Charlotte frowned. Was she about to object to the question? After a moment's thought, she said, "Our father was very busy—he was the only doctor for miles around—but he spent time with us children when he could. He was strict, as fathers were in those days, but he could also be generous and kind. He believed my mother spoiled Karl; it was because he was worried about the mischief Karl got up to with the village children and the schoolmaster that he decided to take him out of the local school after Christmas the year he turned thirteen, instead of waiting until the end of the school year. I went to a day school in Langnau—so did Brigitte—but Father sent Karl to boarding school in Thun. My mother begged him not to, but Father felt Karl needed discipline. And look how well Karl turned out! Who could be more disciplined than a heart surgeon?"

From among the photographs, Giuliana produced a piece of paper with the watch's inscription on it. "I told you on the phone that we found your brother's watch by the side of the path not too far from where he may have gone into the Aare. This was written on the back. I notice the gift is only from your mother."

The slip of paper in her hand, Charlotte got up from the table and walked to her desk, where she pulled down the lid that formed the writing surface, put her hand in a pigeonhole and pulled out a soft case containing a pair of glasses. Giuliana was impressed at such organization. Her own mother, efficient in so many ways, became frantic at least once a week as she searched for her reading glasses in every room of the large apartment where she lived with Giuliana's father. Charlotte put on the glasses, read the words Giuliana had given her, and stood still, her eyes apparently fixed on the painting over the desk. It was an oil portrait of a young woman with shoulder length hair and a small pillbox hat decorated with a feather. The colors were warm pinks, blues and greens, the background monochrome but textured by square, distinct brushstrokes. The more Giuliana stared at it, just as Charlotte was doing, the more it resembled a work by Cuno Amiet. A copy, surely. Or would someone who lived in a castle be able to fill it with Amiets, Hodlers, and Giovanni Giacomettis? Real ones.

Giuliana shifted her attention from the painting to Charlotte, who was returning to the table, smiling. "I've seen this watch on my brother's wrist many times, but I didn't know its history, and I've never read the inscription. It's all so like my mother. That's her portrait over my desk, done when she was in her early twenties, after she and my father were married but before I was born. She was twelve years younger than he was, and she sometimes seemed more like a friend to Karl and me than a mother. She teased us, played games with us. I loved her very much. I can just imagine her spending a lot of money on a present for Karl and not wanting Father to know she'd been so extravagant."

Giuliana thought it sounded plausible, too, especially since Gurtner's von Eichwil mother had surely had her own money, even in those days when Swiss women couldn't open a bank account without their husbands' permission.

"Do you know why your mother writes about giving your brother 'another special watch at last'?"

Charlotte seated herself again at the head of the table, but she didn't relax into her chair. "That's because . . . well, it shows you what an impressive person my brother was, even as a child. One November, a boy fell off a bridge and drowned. One of the Fankhauser children, I think he was. Karl saw him and went into the Emme to try to save him, but the boy was carried away by the current. Karl was wearing a watch my father gave him for his thirteenth birthday—a watch that had belonged to our paternal grandfather and meant a lot to my father—

and it got lost in the river while Karl was trying to grab the boy. Father was very angry and told Karl he wouldn't buy him another to replace it, and he forbade my mother to do so. That's probably another reason she didn't want my father to know about her gift to Karl, even though it was twelve years later."

Giuliana remembered Kathrin, Gurtner's first wife, saying that Gurtner and his father were estranged but that when the older man died the younger was devastated. Why would the elder Gurtner be so unforgiving when he should have been proud? "I'm surprised your father was angry, considering the circumstances in which the watch was lost."

Charlotte shrugged. "I told you my father was strict. Karl was supposed to wear the watch on special occasions only; that day was a regular school day, so he was disobeying. No attempted rescue could make up for that, not in our father's eyes."

Was that the whole story? The father's behavior still seemed unreasonable. Before Giuliana could formulate another question that wouldn't sound rude, Charlotte frowned. "All this talk of the past: it's a waste of time. I want to know what you have been doing to find out who attacked my brother."

Hmm. Giuliana was not going to tell Markus's aunt that her middle nephew was the crime's main suspect. The older woman's frown became a glare. She leaned toward Giuliana and when she spoke her voice was softer, not louder, and all the more formidable. "I need to hear what progress you've made on this case, Frau Linder."

Giuliana had no obligation to report to the old woman but, intimidating as she was, Giuliana could sympathize with her anger. "I know you're frustrated, Frau Gurtner," she said at last, "but all I can tell you is that the investigation is continuing. Teams of police are looking into your brother's finances and legal affairs, his guild work, his recent experiences at the hospital, and his home life. I believe his past is important, too—it offers us insights into his character. Also, sometimes we uncover people from a victim's past who carry a grudge or believe they have some claim on him. We can't neglect that possibility."

From the courtyard came the sound of raindrops beating against the glass doors. The erratic sun that had lit up the farms and fields that morning was gone, and the day had turned dark. The room, too, had darkened to the point of needing more lamplight, but Charlotte did not get up and turn on the lights. She continued to gaze at Giuliana, all of her seventy-seven years showing in her face.

"I'm not aware of anyone from my brother's past who'd want to hurt him. But I can see why you had to ask. Thank you for coming here to speak with me. Please . . ." she paused, and Giuliana thought how exhausted she looked, "please keep me informed."

"I'll do my best," Giuliana said. "Thank you for seeing me."

Despite the way her body had just drooped in the chair, the older woman stood gracefully and walked over to her desk, where the lamp still burned. There was an intercom on the top of the escritoire; she pressed a button and said, "We're finished, Frau Schwander." Moments later, the secretary opened the door. Giuliana moved to where Charlotte stood and shook her hand, allowing herself a swift glance at the portrait before she turned away. Her eye caught the raised brushstrokes on the canvas and the characteristic "CA" in the lower right-hand corner, followed by "42." The pretty young woman in the small feathered hat, Gurtner's mother, had indeed been painted by Cuno Amiet.

"Goodbye, Frau Gurtner," Giuliana said.

The older woman had moved from her place by the desk to the glass doors. "Goodbye, Frau Linder," she said, turning away to stare into the sodden courtyard.

19

As Giuliana drove back down the steep track from the castle to the village center, she tried to persuade herself that she hadn't been wasting time. In driving rain, she passed the scrollwork gates leading to the village graveyard, which she'd missed on her way uphill, the austere parish church, and the elegant-looking parsonage. Then came the inn at the crossroads. "*Gasthof Löwen,*" read the blue sign over the door. The Lion was a large, old-fashioned wooden building, several stories high. It was white with forest-green shutters, topped with a steep, brown-tiled roof. Giuliana found herself turning into its small parking lot. What was the harm in having a quick lunch here? She was hungry and discouraged—and she needed a bathroom. Maybe it wouldn't still be pouring when she was ready to drive back.

Inside, the wide, red-carpeted corridor, lit by hanging brass lamps, was warm and dry, and the wooden furniture glowed in the lamplight. Giuliana passed several closed doors and found the one marked *Damen*. Back in the corridor after her stop in the bathroom, she headed for the door with *Gaststube* on it. As she got closer she could hear voices but was still surprised to find at least twenty people, mostly small groups of men but also several couples and a pair of women, eating lunch in the dining room on this chilly, rainy day. The smell of roasted meat hovered around her, but overriding it was the delicious odor of something sweet baking—cake, perhaps, or fruit pie. A young woman was just coming through a swinging door with a tray full of plates; she looked startled to see Giuliana and called out a greeting. Moving back to press her bottom against the door until it opened a crack, she bellowed "Frau Stettler, another guest," over her shoulder, smiled at Giuliana, and carried her plates toward a round table full of men in blue overalls.

The woman who emerged next through the swinging door was white-haired and solidly built, with large blue eyes and a smile that glowed. She had once been very pretty, that was clear, but the best word to describe her now would be motherly. "*Grüessech*," she greeted Giuliana. "You must be so glad to be out of that cold rain. May we give you some lunch?" As she spoke, she guided her guest to a small table and pulled it back, so Giuliana could sit down on the wooden bench that ran along two of the room's four walls. It was cushioned in a dark red that matched the corridor's carpet.

"Our lunch special today is beef tongue in caper sauce with mashed turnips and potatoes gratin. But if you'd rather have something lighter, we have Gruyère-and-leek pie and a mixed salad. The pie's still warm from the oven, and the salad dressing's a homemade mustard vinaigrette. If neither of those appeals, I'll be glad to bring you the lunch menu."

"No, pie and salad sounds delicious," Giuliana said. "Is this your restaurant?"

The woman beamed. "I act like it is, don't I? It was mine and my husband's for ages, till we turned it over to our daughter and son-in-law a couple of years back. But they let me do the baking anytime I feel like it." She lowered her voice as if she were revealing a secret. "I started working here when I was eight, and I guess I don't know how to get along without the place." She laughed, and the sound made Giuliana smile. This woman's laugh would make anyone smile. "Now, what can I get you to drink? A *Ballon* of red against this chill?"

"No wine, thanks. How about a large glass of sparkling water?"

Waiting for her food, Giuliana looked around the dining room. The lower half of its walls were dark wood paneling, the upper half covered with a fading beige-and-white striped wallpaper. The effect could have been dreary, but she found it snug. In one corner of the room, an old-fashioned green tile stove radiated heat; cowbells hung by leather straps from a nearby beam, and next to the swinging door a mounted deer's head stared at her. Someone had framed reproductions of Albert Anker paintings and hung them on the walls. Giuliana could see several images she knew well, as many Swiss did: a young girl of about twelve in an apron, blond braids pinned up on the back of her head, peeling potatoes; a boy in a blue farmer's smock, even younger, reading aloud to a very old man propped in a pillow-lined chair; a flock of eager chickens surrounding a young woman feeding them grain. Another of his famous paintings was of his own little son laid out for burial—Giuliana didn't see that anywhere in the room. Thank God for antibiotics and vaccines, she was thinking, just as the motherly woman came through the swinging door with a tray. Giuliana considered her age: around seventy was her guess. Could she have known Johann Gurtner? And if she had, did it matter? Could this contemporary of his know something that would help Giuliana figure out who'd killed him? Well, it wouldn't hurt to ask.

Frau Stettler—Giuliana remembered the name the young waitress had called through the door—placed a generous wedge of pie surrounded by green salad in front of her, then set down a tall glass and filled it with bubbling water from a large bottle. "Can I get you anything else?" she asked.

"No, this looks delicious," Giuliana said, "but I was wondering if you have time for a question. Can you take a minute to sit down?"

The other woman's friendly face took on a wary look, but she pulled out the chair across from Giuliana and took a seat. "Just for a moment. I have meringues in the oven."

"Let me introduce myself," Giuliana said. "I'm Giuliana Linder. I'm a detective with the cantonal police. Based in the city."

"Heidi Stettler," the woman replied. "So, you're from the police . . ."

Giuliana went on. "This past Monday Johann Gurtner drowned in Bern, and I'm investigating his death. He lived here as a boy and went to the village school until he was thirteen. You said something about working here at the inn since you were a child . . . so, I wondered if you knew him."

Heidi Stettler frowned as soon as she heard the name Johann Gurtner, and the rest of Giuliana's words were spoken to her bowed head. After a moment, she looked up and said, "Of course I knew about the Gurtner family, and Karli—that's what he was called then—was in my class at school for a year or two, but we were never friends. The castle folk kept their distance from the village, and I wasn't even a regular villager. I was . . . a *Verdingmeitschi*."

"Oh, that explains why you said you started working here when you were so young," Giuliana said, forgetting Gurtner for the moment in her fascination at meeting someone who'd been a contract child. "In September there was an exhibition about *Verdingkinder* at the Käfigturm in Bern. Was your portrait in it?"

"No. I was asked, but I . . . I declined. A friend's picture was there, though, so I went to see it. I tell you, that whole show made me feel blessed. I had one or two . . . unpleasant incidents growing up here, but mostly I was well looked after, especially by the innkeepers I worked for. Who became my in-laws. Yes," she continued, resting her hands on the table in preparation for pushing herself out of the chair, "I was luckier than you can imagine."

"If I wanted to ask anyone in the village about Herr Doktor Gurtner's childhood—besides his two sisters, I mean—who would you recommend that I talk to?" Giuliana spoke quickly, before the other woman could go back into the kitchen.

Heidi Stettler answered just as quickly, "I'm sorry, but I have no idea. It's been such a long time. Now I've got to check on my meringues." Standing, she resumed her professional role. "What about your pie?—you haven't had a bite while we've been talking. Would you like me to warm it up?"

Giuliana stood, too, and put out her hand. "No, no; I'm sure it's fine as it is. Thanks for speaking with me, Frau Stettler." They shook hands, and the older woman's warm smile reappeared at last. "No trouble at all," she answered, before disappearing through the swinging door. Giuliana took a bite of her pie. The crust was crumbly and still warm, and the sharp taste of aged Gruyère mingled with the mild oniony flavor of the leeks in a smooth, firm custard with a touch of nutmeg. She took another bite.

Large homemade meringues piled with fresh whipped cream were an Emmentaler specialty that had been served at the inn not only since Heidi was a child there, but also long before her time. She always did the meringues last in her baking day, because they had to cool in the oven before being put away. Now, seeing that all three baking sheets-full were done, she turned off the heat. While they cooled, she'd ice her cakes. Melting chocolate for the first of the frostings, she thought about what she'd said to the policewoman. *I was luckier than you can imagine.* But still she hadn't wanted to talk with the academics and activists who'd put on the exhibition. How could you explain what you'd suffered when others had suffered so much more? That was why she'd refused to take part. They'd talked about breaking down the walls of silence and even seeking reparations, and she didn't disagree. But answering questions about her life before she'd married Ändu . . . well, it was fine to add to the Stettler family's reminiscences with a few anecdotes of her own about burnt stews and spilt beers, but she kept her feelings about those years to herself. No one, not even Ändu, knew how miserable she'd been after her mother died. No one alive now, anyway.

She'd been six, and the loneliness and grief had begun the moment she understood that she'd never see her mother again. Two months later, her father gave her to a great-aunt to raise. Night after night, she'd lain in bed at her aunt's, wondering why Father had kept both her older brothers but not her. What had she done wrong? A little over a year later, she'd been transferred to an orphanage. She couldn't understand what it was about her that made everyone send her away. Then, after a year and a half of learning to fit in at the orphanage and finding a few grown-ups there who were good to her, she'd been moved again, this time to live and work at the Stettler's inn and go to the village school in Heidmatt with three of the innkeepers' six children.

The first two years at the inn had been bad, not because anyone had mistreated her but because she'd been terrified of making a mistake and getting pushed out yet again. Her terror had made her stiff and silent, but she'd worked as hard as she could, hoping that if she made herself useful enough, she'd be kept. One day, drying and stacking plates, she'd tripped and broken eight of them. The crash had brought both Frau Stettlers, the Mistress and her mother-in-law, running into the kitchen to find ten-year-old Heidi sitting cross-legged among the shards of porcelain, wildly crying. Heidi could still remember the younger woman's loud "What in God's name . . .?" cut off by the older woman's "Shhh." Then the Master's mother was pulling her gently to her feet, placing an arm around her shoulders, and leading her upstairs to her own bedroom, where Heidi's fear of being sent away had finally spilled out in a few choked sentences. "We'll never send you away, my little sparrow," the woman had told her, "never. I'll tell my son and his wife what I've promised you, and they won't disobey me. You are a very good girl, and we're lucky to have you. So, let's wash your face and go downstairs. And remember, if anyone is mean to you, here at the inn or out in the village, you come tell me right away, and I'll deal with it." She'd led Heidi to the small bathroom on the adults' hall, where she'd never been before, muttering, "Poor little rabbit. Passed round like a lost package. No wonder she's been scared stiff."

After that, Heidi grew less shy with the Master and Mistress and began to have fun with the Stettler children, who ranged in age from two to fifteen. When she wasn't going to school, cleaning bedrooms, or working in the kitchen, she was expected to look after the two- and four-year-old little Stettlers, which she considered a treat, not a job. At eleven, she still shared a classroom with the seven-to-nine-year-olds; their teacher, Fräulein Kämpf, a spinster in her fifties, let her help with the youngest pupils. She hadn't been so happy since before her mother died.

Then she was promoted to Herr Müller's class.

Even now, so many decades later, Heidi's fear of Herr Müller rose in her throat. How she'd loathed him—the feeling filled her anew, seemingly fresh after over sixty years. He'd brought the old shame back to haunt her—the feeling that she must be doing something wrong to deserve the way he treated her. Spreading orange-flavored buttercream frosting on the second of her cakes, Heidi felt the spatula shake in her hand, and she had to set it down to let her rage subside. Blaming the victim: that was the phrase they used now. She had been the victim, and she'd blamed herself.

20
Before

"Adelheid, stand up."

Heidi's chest tightened so she couldn't breathe. Emmi, who shared the double desk with her, gave her a look of agonized sympathy.

"I know you play dumb in this class, Adelheid, but have you grown deaf, too? I told you to stand up."

Her desk was in the back of the class, so heads were turning to look at her, and she heard a few nervous titters. She looked for Pesche's eyes; they were the only ones she wanted to see. All those faces: some pitying, some curious, some hungry for what would happen next. Only Pesche gave her a true smile, willing her to be brave. She stood up, hands clasped so tightly at her waist that they hurt.

"There she is. Our little barmaid. Bursting her buttons as usual."

Heidi's face burnt. The older Frau Stettler had been promising to make over some hand-me-downs for her and take her to buy her first bra, but she'd gone to Luzern two weeks earlier to help her daughter with a new baby, so Heidi had to keep fastening her school blouse and cardigan with safety pins. All she could do was cross her arms over her chest and wait for this to be over.

"Now, Adelheid, I'm sure you did your homework last night, so you'll have no trouble coming to the board to solve this equation for us." He paused, and when she didn't move, his voice lashed out: "Don't dawdle, girl." She forced herself to move to the front of the room, arms still hiding her breasts, afraid to look around, even at Pesche. As she walked, she stared at the blackboard, where she saw $x + 9 = 18 - 2x$ written large and white. At the board, she had to uncross her arms to pick up a piece of chalk. Ändu had shown his brother and her a few equations like this the week before and explained how to figure them out. You had to make sure you got the x alone on one side. But how? Her mind was blank. Herr Müller stood right behind her, smelling like the little cigars he smoked. She heard him move and felt his arm go around her shoulders and his fingers touch the top of her breast. Even through her cardigan, blouse, and undershirt, she could feel those fingers moving across her skin, and she started to sweat. Oh God, what could she do? The algebra problem was forgotten as she tried to turn out of his grasp, but his other hand grabbed her other shoulder. "Now, then. Let's see if I can help you do this problem," he said, using his fake nice voice again. They both had their backs to the class, and he was so close now that his thigh was touching her bottom. And not just his thigh, she realized with horror, as she felt something hard prodding at her. Her whole body shook as he pressed . . .

"Are you showing her your . . . *algebra*, Herr Müller?" Karli Gurtner called out. "Looks as if you're teaching her physical education, not math."

Herr Müller stepped back so fast he almost stumbled, and as his hands left her shoulders, she ran back to her seat, not caring how much her breasts wobbled. She put her head down on her desk and felt Emmi's arm around her. How comforting that was, so different from Müller's arm. She took deep breaths—she wouldn't cry in class.

"That's enough from you, Karl," she heard Müller say. If any other boy had spoken to him like that, he would have dragged him to the front of the class and beaten him with his cane. Still, Müller's tone was hateful. "Thomas," he growled, "come up here and solve this problem, now." Tömu was good at math, but still Müller would make him suffer.

Finally, the church bells rang, releasing them for the ninety-minute lunch break. Like almost all the children, she went home to eat and do chores before heading back to the school for two more hours of afternoon lessons. She whispered a quick goodbye to Emmi, whose route home lay in the opposite direction, and was halfway across the schoolyard when she felt a hand on her shoulder. She tore her body out of the grasp and whipped around to find not Herr Müller but Karli. As usual, he was staring at her chest, so she immediately crossed her arms again. Then she remembered what he'd said to the teacher to make him leave her alone and gave him a small smile. When he smiled back, she thought about how handsome he was. He was one of the few boys in the class who was taller than she was, and he had thick blond hair, golden rather than yellow-white like hers, and wavy, too. "Heidi," he said, a little out of breath with chasing her, "That pig shouldn't be able to . . . bother you. It's disgusting. Listen, I'm going to make him stop."

She'd have laughed, but she didn't want to hurt his feelings. He was trying to be nice—she couldn't imagine why. Not Karli—although when she thought about it, he *had* tried to talk to her a few times recently in the yard, but she'd been so sure he was going to make fun of her that she'd hung her head and backed away. Now she looked directly into his eyes, perhaps for the first time in her life.

"Don't say anything to him, Karli. Please! He's already mad about this morning. It'll get both of us into more trouble." Feeling daring, she reached out and touched his hand, to show him that she was grateful. His hand moved with a jerk, grabbing hers, first hard and then with a softer pressure. She thought about pulling it back, but there it stayed, snug and warm in his.

Still holding her hand, he started to pull her back toward the schoolhouse. "Come on. Müller's still at his desk. He's afraid of my parents, just like everyone else. You'll see. I'll tell him to leave you alone, and he'll end up trembling like a rabbit." As he spoke, he pressed her to his side, one arm around her waist, pushing her almost to the schoolroom door. She stopped dead and stood her ground at last, and his face turned sulky—more like the Karli she knew. "I know you want to help," she said, "but I'm not brave like you, and I can't go back in there. I can't stand up to him. I hate it when he gets angry."

His smile was back. "What a little mouse you are! You stand in the cloakroom, then, where he can't see you. Once I've told him to leave you alone, I'll walk you home, okay?"

"What about your lunch? Aren't you supposed to go home to eat?"

Karli waved a dismissive hand. "I told the driver to take Bri home and not come back for me. I can skip lunch for once—or maybe I'll have it at the inn, since I'm going to walk there with you. We can eat together."

Her stomach hurt at the thought: Karli walking her home and eating at the inn. It would impress everyone who saw him, sure, but they'd tease her afterward. And what would they think she was up to? Karli was only thirteen, a year younger than she was, but still she knew what they'd think. As for sitting down at a table and eating lunch with him—that was daft. They needed her in the kitchen, right now! If she was late, she might not get lunch at all.

But she wasn't there, she was here, at the schoolhouse, so she planted herself at one side of the classroom door and peered around it. Karli sauntered toward the teacher's desk. As Herr Müller looked up and noticed him, Heidi drew back and waited.

"Müller," said Karli cheerfully, and she cringed at the way he left off the teacher's title. This could not go well; she knew it. Still, she kept listening. "I didn't like what you were doing with Heidi at the blackboard this morning. You'd better leave her alone, or I'm going to tell my parents what you were up to."

She heard Herr Müller push back his chair and pictured him standing up. When he spoke, his voice was like spitting. "How dare you, you little turd!" There was silence. When the teacher spoke again, his voice was different, smoother and scarier. "So, you're trying to come to the girl's rescue? And you think you can use your parents as a weapon? Well, that's funny, because in this case, your mother and father are on my side, not yours. Do you honestly think they care what happens to a *Verdingmeitschi*? You stupid boy—don't you understand that no one gives a damn about a girl like that?"

Heidi covered her face with her hands. Karli said, "What are you talking about?" More than defiant, he sounded genuinely puzzled.

"I'm talking about you keeping your mouth shut, or I'll go to your mother with some very disturbing news that I'm sure she'll want to hear. *I'm ashamed even to mention such a distasteful business to you, Frau Gurtner, but are you aware that Karl is sniffing around a kitchen maid from The Lion? He's only thirteen, yes, but so advanced for his age; who knows what could be happening? A contract girl like that, working in a bar: such a corrupting influence.*" He broke off this one-sided conversation, which he'd been conducting in a cooing singsong, and laughed.

Heidi wanted to run all the way back to the inn, but she stayed where she was, waiting to hear what Karli had to say. She thought she could hear his feet moving, almost as if he were shuffling.

"You would *never* say that to my mother," he said, but there was no fire in his voice. She'd never heard him sound so unsure of himself.

Herr Müller laughed again, even louder. "You're too young for these games, you little fool, and too naïve. Believe me, your mother would thank me and then take you out of this school so fast you wouldn't have time to draw breath. Or she'd get Heidi sent away!"

There was a sound of protest from Karli, but the teacher talked right over him. "I know why you're playing the hero, boy. I understand exactly what you are after better than you do yourself. However, you'd better back off now. Lord it over the other kids as much as you like but never over me. Do you understand? Say 'Yes, Herr Müller.' Say it, boy!"

Heidi heard nothing. Then Karli murmured.

"Now get out of my sight, and don't you ever try something like that again, you little shit," said the teacher.

Heidi heard Karli running, but she ran, too, and was out the schoolhouse door before he was. She heard his feet coming after her, but she went on until they were a good distance from the school. Then she turned, and he caught up with her. They were both panting, but his face was red and twisted with more than just exertion. She saw the shame in his eyes before he looked down, not at her breasts this time but at his own feet.

"I'm sorry, Karli," she whispered. "I know you tried. You did your best."

For a moment, he said nothing; then he glared at her. "You'd better leave me alone," he spat out, before turning and walking away. She ran all the way to the inn, wondering what excuse she'd offer for being late.

She worked as fast as she could in the time that was left before afternoon school and begged Mistress to let her stay home. She was told not to be ridiculous and to get back to school and not try any tricks. That was what Mistress said to her own children when they tried to play hooky, so it was what Heidi expected. For the next two hours, she sat at her desk as quiet as death. Herr Müller didn't call on her, although she caught him staring. Then, just before it was time to go home, he banged his pointer on the desk. Everyone stared at him.

"When classes end, everyone is free to leave except Adelheid, who will stay after school. She needs some special lessons in algebra."

Heidi reached out and grabbed Emmi's hand. She started to pant, trying to think. She'd run, that's what she'd do. Before she could steel herself to leap up, she heard the class murmur. Then Pesche stood up. He was not a big boy, but his voice was deep and strong. "I'm not leaving unless Heidi leaves with us. You can't keep her here alone."

Herr Müller's face turned white. "Are you telling me what I can and can't do, you piece of filth?" He started toward Pesche with his cane. Immediately, Köbi jumped up. He was followed by Tömu, Noldi, the Fankhauser twins, and even Bernhard, who didn't usually budge without Karli's say-so. Then Emmi, who was usually as quiet as Heidi in class, said in a shrill voice, "You aren't allowed to hit girls or keep us after school alone. My Mam said. She said if you ever hurt one of us girls to tell her right away, and she'd tell my Paps."

"Shut up," roared Herr Müller, just as the church bells rang four, time for everyone to go home. No one moved. Müller stood frozen, his cane raised, and glowered at Pesche. Heidi could see he'd forgotten her in his hatred for this other *Verdingkind*. The look in Herr Müller's eyes scared her. He hit all the boys except Karli, and Pesche got beaten most of all. But she'd never before seen him look at Pesche like he wanted to beat him to death. Three other boys stood up, and so did Emmi and another girl. Everyone stared at Müller, while he glared at Pesche. Then he screamed, "Get out, all of you. Out! Now!" And the spell broke.

Heidi gave Emmi a squeeze to thank her for speaking up, and then she grabbed her book bag and once again raced toward the inn. She was first out the door and thought she was safe, but she heard feet pounding behind her. Again! This time she knew it wasn't Karli. "Heidi. Stop," a voice called. It was Pesche. She paused, breathless. Barely slowing down, he grabbed her hand and pulled her off the road and down a bank into a tangle of bushes and trees between two farmhouses. Only when they were standing close together in a tiny clearing in the undergrowth did he let go of her hand. "Müller's gone crazy," he said. "What are we going to do?"

At that, Heidi started crying and couldn't make herself stop. She put up her hands to her face and wailed, "Why is this happening? What did I do wrong?"

Pesche moved nearer, but he didn't touch her. They were exactly the same height, and she could feel the warmth of his body. She knew they were hidden by bushes on all sides, and she shivered, but not with fear. "Heidi, you didn't do anything wrong," Pesche said, speaking softly into her ear. "Nothing! Müller's going after you because he's a sack of shit and because you work at the inn. And because . . . because you're so pretty—but being pretty's not wrong! It's the way you are— pretty and nice and . . ." He broke off and gently stroked her hair a few times before dropping his hands to his sides.

"But . . . but . . . what should I do?" Heidi kept her face covered but peered through her fingers at Pesche, with his serious brown eyes, thick black eyebrows, and springy dark hair. She saw him raise his hands so he could grasp her upper arms. She breathed the great sigh that had been waiting inside her and put her arms around his waist, resting her head on his shoulder. His arms slid around her back, and then he was hugging her. For a long time, they stood there, holding each other close, the bushes pressing around them to make a little cave of green shot through with sunlight. Finally, they moved apart, but only a little. Heidi knew her face was a mess of snot, spit, and tears—and so was Pesche's shirt. She had no handkerchief, so she bent over and used her petticoat to clean her face; Pesche kept his hand on her waist. When she finished, she looked at him, smiling shyly. He smiled back, then grew serious as he said, "Didn't you used to help Fräulein Kämpf with the baby class?" She nodded. "Was she good to you?"

"Always," Heidi answered. She was too breathless to say more.

Pesche took her hand again. "We're going to her house, and you're going to tell her everything Herr Müller has said and done today—and anything that happened before, too."

"But she'll think I'm a bad girl," Heidi said. "That's why I haven't told Master and Mistress. I think I could tell Old Mistress, but she's away in Luzern."

Pesche had already turned away to lead them out of the bushes, but he turned back and gave her a kiss on the cheek. Then he put his hands on either side of her face and, standing very close to her again, he touched his lips to hers. He was blushing, and she felt her face heat up, too. But they kept looking into each other's eyes and smiling.

"You're not a bad girl, Heidi," he said. "Everyone who knows you knows that. It's that Müller's a bad man. Everyone knows that, too, but no one does anything about it. Maybe now someone will. Come on, let's go see if Fräulein Kämpf's home."

Decades later, in the kitchen of The Lion, all three cakes stood iced, and the bowls and pans Heidi had used for her baking were washed and dried. The meringues had cooled, and she was putting them away in a set of large, old-fashioned tins whose lids were decorated with scenes of famous Swiss mountain peaks. She could remember Old Mistress putting her meringues into the same tins. It wasn't the old lady she was seeing in her mind's eye, though, but Pesche.

How many times had they kissed after that? Not many, but if she concentrated she could probably picture every kiss. Remembering Pesche made her happy and melancholy at the same time; it always turned into a series of what-ifs. She reminded herself that Ändu was part of this story, too. After Fräulein Kämpf had heard, with many promptings, confirmations, and additions from Pesche, everything that Herr Müller had said and done (although not what he'd said to Karli); after the Fräulein had put her arms around Heidi and hugged her in a way she'd never done before and assured her that none of this was her fault; after she'd praised Pesche and sent him back to the farm; after she'd walked Heidi to the inn to confront her Master and Mistress with the story; after Heidi was told she never had to go back to Müller's classroom, because Fräulein Kämpf would give her lessons at her house; after all that, the Master and Ändu barred Müller from The Lion when he showed up the following Saturday night for a drink and gave him a beating. No one ever reproached them for it, not even knowing it had been two against one and that Ändu was Heidmatt's best wrestler and as strong as a bull. By spring, the class had a new teacher, and Müller and his wife and kids moved away.

Sometime after she'd married Ändu and become a Stettler—someone who could truly stay at the inn all her life—he told her what Müller'd said when he and his father confronted him in the dark innyard, the words that had caused Ändu to give him that first punch in the mouth. "She's a *Verdingmeitschi,*" he'd said. "I bet you're both fucking her yourselves."

It was all very long ago, and the federal government had recently apologized for over one hundred years of officials putting children in orphanages, even when they had parents, or placing them with farmers and then not caring what happened to them. That apology meant something to Heidi; of course it did. But no one and nothing could take it away completely: that feeling of shame for something you'd done or something you were. Or maybe it was more like a spot of foulness inside you that would never heal. Heidi took off her apron, hung it on a hook behind the kitchen door and leaned her forehead against the kitchen cabinet, her arms crossed on the counter. For just a moment, before she said goodbye to the inn staff and went home to Ändu and their own kitchen, she thought about the last time she and Pesche had kissed.

21

The Old City,
Thursday morning, November 26

Renzo was almost finished with a summary of the alibis generated by two days of calls to scores of doctors, nurses, and hospital orderlies. He glanced at his watch and cursed—he wasn't going to get it done now. He needed to be at the office of Gurtner's guild at eleven for an appointment with the treasurer. That meant driving to the Old City *and* finding a parking place. Or walking fast. He decided to walk—or rather, given how late he was, to jog.

The Society of Cloth Handlers had first appeared in the city's records in 1358. Its members hadn't just been cloth merchants, as Renzo had assumed, but weavers, tailors, dyers, and, by the 1500s, some landowners and high political officials. Including the Eichwils. Over the centuries, the Cloth Handlers or *Tuchleute* had shrunk to become one of the city's smallest guilds, with only four hundred and seventy-two members. Taken all together, the city's various guilds formed the Community of Burghers of Bern—the *Burgergemeinde*. Only a few of the modern guild members were descended from the master bakers, stonemasons, and tanners who'd run the medieval city. The rest had joined since then, paying a lot of money for the privilege, and now there were over a thousand men, women, and children belonging to the *Burgergemeinde*. Like everyone in Bern, Renzo understood that the burghers had power, but he didn't know how much. What was certain was that as a group they owned enormous chunks of the land in and around Bern and hundreds of the city's buildings.

The *Tuchleute*'s building—each of the guilds had one somewhere downtown—was in the medieval section of the city; parts of it dated back to the fifteenth century. To get there, Renzo crossed the Aare by the Lorraine Bridge, hurried to Waisenhausplatz, and zigzagged through narrow streets until he was jogging under the arcades on Rathausgasse and down a narrow alleyway to Kramgasse and the guild house. The ground floor of the narrow stone building held an expensive-looking dress shop, which seemed appropriate for a place dedicated for hundreds of years to the making and selling of cloth.

Despite being two minutes late, Renzo took another minute to slow his breathing before pressing a buzzer labelled "Reception: *Tuchleute*." He identified himself to the male voice that answered. "Please come up to the fourth floor, Herr Donatelli," the voice said. "I'll meet you there."

Climbing the staircase, Renzo admired the decorative stucco on its ceiling. People told him that Gurtner had loved practicing surgery, but Renzo thought how much more agreeable it would be to work in this quiet, history-soaked place rather than the frantic Insel hospital. As a surgeon, Gurtner might have saved people's lives, but he probably never had time to think about his patients as more than a collection of body parts. Maybe in this setting, he'd actually found time for friends.

A man in thick glasses waited for Renzo on the fourth floor by a pair of double doors. As he got closer, Renzo saw that the dark wood panels above and below the gilt door handles were identically carved with the paraphernalia of the cloth trade. He'd identified a loom, bolts of cloth, and a spinning wheel before courtesy forced him to look at the man in front of the panels. The Cloth Handlers' treasurer was medium-sized and very thin, with a mostly bald head. He wore a white shirt, tweed blazer, well-creased trousers, and highly polished shoes, and looked to be around seventy. Renzo was preparing himself for a stiffly formal interview when the man offered a warm smile and said, "What? Not panting after climbing four flights? I'm impressed. I got here early just so I could get my breath back before you arrived." Without waiting for Renzo's response, he thrust out his hand. "I'm Georg Nägeli, the *Seckelmeister.* Come in."

As Nägeli opened the right-hand paneled door, Renzo considered the treasurer's old-fashioned title: *Seckelmeister.* It had been a long time since any man in Bern had carried money in a *Seckel* or little sack. Johann Gurtner's equally medieval-sounding title had been *Almosner,* because he distributed alms.

The room the men walked into was large, with colored-glass chandeliers, painted ceilings, and spindly-legged chairs and tables. It didn't encourage the visitor to settle down; Renzo decided it must be an entrance chamber. Before he could take in more of the elaborate décor, Nägeli led him out a far door, down a hall, and into a smaller room. This one had no gilt ornamentation, just winged armchairs, polished side tables, and beautiful wood paneling below silk-covered walls. The elegance of the room was slightly marred by a wool overcoat draped over the arm of one chair. Nägeli relieved Renzo of his sheepskin jacket to place it over the chair's other arm, then pointed his guest toward one of the deep armchairs pulled up in front of a—sadly unlit—fireplace. Renzo lowered himself gently into the chair, thinking, *So this is where the burghers have their little business meetings.*

Nägeli took the armchair on Renzo's right, turned it so the two men could see each other well, and said, "I'm so glad you got in touch. I've been upset about Hannes's death. It's a comfort to help with your investigation, even if there isn't much I can do. Please, ask me anything you'd like to know."

"Thank you," said Renzo, who was luxuriating in the soft warmth of the chair. "First, I'd like you to explain to me what Herr Doktor Gurtner did here as your almoner."

Nägeli rubbed his hands together, as if he couldn't wait to get on with his explanation, but first he asked his own question. "Do you know anything about the *Burgergemeinde* and its social service responsibilities already, Herr Donatelli?"

Renzo was grateful for his online research of the night before. "I know that each guild used to spend its own money to look after its members if they fell on hard times. But today, everyone in the *Burgergemeinde* pays taxes and gets the same benefits as any other citizen: unemployment insurance and all the rest. The difference is that when one of the burghers needs advice or financial help, they go to their guild's social-services expert—this person you call an almoner. These days the almoner administers the government's funds, not the guild's, but still in a personalized way."

"That's very well put," said Nägeli, smiling, and Renzo was surprised not to feel patronized by the praise. The man was simply too kind to give offense. "Let me continue from there. The guilds still have money, from investments, rents, and membership fees, which are used for scholarships or special charities. As far as actual social welfare goes, though, the almoner has no say in who gets it. That's decided by government regulation, just like it is for anyone."

Renzo felt his tentative hypothesis grow iffier. He'd hoped that Gurtner, in this role as the Cloth Handlers' dispenser of money for hard cases, would have made enemies. "What do you mean, you need help because you can't find a job in your field?" he'd imagined Gurtner saying. "You studied sociology, didn't you? Well, what did you expect? Get a job as a barman or a taxi driver, or go sign up for an apprenticeship at a bank. Why should the guild take responsibility for your foolish decisions?" There must be lots of older Bern burghers who reasoned like that; sometimes—Renzo shuddered at this sign of his growing stodginess—he caught *himself* thinking those thoughts. Which was exactly why an *Almosner* like Gurtner had to follow the same rules as any bureaucrat in the unemployment office: to avoid prejudicial or arbitrary choices about who got help.

"Can you give me an example or two of the kinds of situations Herr Doktor Gurtner handled?" Renzo asked, not ready to give up yet.

"Let me think," Nägeli said but went on quickly to say, "One of the most common problems he dealt with was elderly parents. Middle-aged guild members came to Hannes at their wits' ends because their mother had died and, two years later, their eighty-eight-year-old father was living in squalor and refusing to eat the meals his home-care helpers prepared. That's the kind of situation where our small guild can truly help. Hannes got advice from social workers at the *Burgerspital*, so he could make recommendations. Sometimes he went to talk to the elderly father or mother himself, if he knew the family. Since he was a doctor, the old people weren't as likely to take offense, and he could sometimes get them to agree to more assistance. Of course, if dementia had set in, then it was more difficult . . ." Nägeli shook his head and leaned toward Renzo. "He was good at handling these situations, very gentle."

Here was a brand-new picture of Hannes Gurtner. It had been Renzo himself who'd summarized the hospital staff's verdict: that Gurtner was impatient and even cutting in his dealings with medical colleagues. What he was hearing now implied patience and kindness.

"It sounds like you respected him," he said to Nägeli.

"I did. He took this job as almoner seriously and did it well, as far as I could tell. Not that he gossiped with me about the people who came to see him for advice. But we've known each other since we were teenagers—through annual guild events with families—and we're about the same age, so he took me into his confidence now and then."

Of course, Renzo thought. The whole Society of Bern Burghers is a family affair. As an outsider, he thought of it as a political and financial institution—it even had its own bank—but for members, its social functions must be important, especially for making sure their children made appropriate friends.

Renzo decided to be blunt. "I'm sure you realize that I'm here in the hope of hearing about someone who might have wanted to kill him. Did he ever tell you about an advice session that ended badly?" It was his turn to lean forward in his chair, eager to be sure that the *Seckelmeister* understood the importance of what he was asking. Suppose he took offence at the idea of one of his fellow Cloth Handlers as a murderer?

Nägeli's grave face told Renzo there was no danger of that. "As soon as you made this appointment with me, I started thinking about our membership, particularly anyone who might have financial problems. It's quite odd to have to consider people you know as potential murderers, but I did my best." He allowed himself a small smile at that point. "Still, my best wasn't good enough—I didn't come up with any names."

Renzo hadn't been expecting a miraculous revelation, but he couldn't help but feel disappointed. "Could you at least talk to me some more about why people came to see him?"

Nägeli pressed his fingertips together and gazed at them for a moment before answering. "In a small guild like ours, where we know each other and have for generations, shame is a big problem. Think about the things someone might have wanted to discuss with Hannes: mental illness; a teenager out of control, maybe starting to take drugs; a husband who gets violent when he drinks; being out of a job for so long that the usual unemployment insurance has run out. These are common problems in our guild, just like they are for everyone, but our members are deeply ashamed of them, and they're terrified of other guild members' gossip."

Now Renzo risked a small smile of his own. "You're destroying my grand illusions about Bern's patrician families."

This comment caused Nägeli to bounce a little in his chair. "That's it! Illusions. See, we burghers believe these same myths about ourselves, and that's what makes everyone so ashamed of having a mother who drinks or a brother who's lost his money on a foolish investment. Everyone is convinced no one else in the guild has these problems—and they *want* to believe that. Because who wants to accept the truth: that the people in the exclusive club they belong to are just like everyone else, except richer? And some of them aren't even rich, because plenty of burgher families haven't had money for generations."

Renzo tried to put himself in Gurtner's place as almoner. "You're saying that lots of the people who came to see Herr Doktor Gurtner were deeply ashamed of being here. He must have shown a lot of sensitivity, dealing with that."

Nägeli grimaced. "Hmm. If Gurtner had a fault, it was that . . . well, sometimes he wasn't as . . . delicate as he could have been with people's feelings of embarrassment. When folks who had trouble asking for help finally came to Hannes, he didn't show sympathy for their ordeal. He just got on with his job of figuring out what needed to be done to alleviate their problems. Generally, that was fine, but a few of the more delicate souls complained about his insensitivity. Never a formal complaint, just gossip that made the rounds." Nägeli paused. "No, that's not true." He was smiling now, as if at a private joke. "I remember there was one formal complaint to the head of the guild, the *Obfrau*, from Frau Schmalz."

"Can you tell me about it?" Renzo had his notebook out and his pen poised. It was past noon now, and he was starting to get hungry.

"I shouldn't, really—but I will." Nägeli's smile was positively mischievous now. "First, you have to know that Frau Schmalz is quite overweight. Her doctor has recommended several diets. That's not good enough for her, though; she wants to go to a clinic for three weeks where she can have massages and nutritional advice and special meals. So, a few months ago she asked her doctor to write her a prescription for a place like that. He apparently said if she wanted to splurge on a fat farm, she was welcome to do it, but he wasn't going to prescribe it, and no health insurance company would pay for it in any case, even with a prescription. So, she came along to Hannes and told him there was no point being a member of the *Burgergemeinde* and the Cloth Handlers' Guild, nor in having an *Almosner* who was not only a famous surgeon but also a von Eichwil, if he couldn't get her into a particularly fancy weight-loss clinic in the Alps near Zürich. Which, by the way, cost twenty-thousand francs per week!"

"Ha!" Renzo's laugh was brief, but he kept grinning. "What happened?"

"Hannes got on his high horse and, believe me, when he did that he could really tower over a person. He said she could pay to attend any clinic she liked, but the Cloth Handlers' Guild dealt with cases of real suffering, and she should be ashamed to come to him with so ridiculous a demand. As a doctor *and* a von Eichwil, he told her, he'd never lift a finger to do anything so . . . shady, and he was insulted that she could expect such a thing of him. I imagine she felt reduced to the size of a mosquito—only figuratively speaking, unfortunately—and buzzed away. Afterward she wrote the guild *Obfrau* a letter about her 'terrible experience,' threatening to lodge a complaint with the board. A soothing answer was sent out, and that was the end of it, as far as I know."

"How did you find out about all this?" asked Renzo.

"I told you Hannes was discreet—and he was. This was one case, however, where as soon as Frau Schmalz left, he came upstairs to where I and a few other guild volunteers were working at our desks and . . . spilled the beans. He was fuming, but the more he told us, the more we laughed, so finally he started laughing, too."

Johann Gurtner laughing with a group of friends—it was a picture of him that neither Renzo's talks with his hospital colleagues nor with his family had conveyed. Perhaps with them he'd been too conscious of his authority to laugh. It was useful to see the man in this new light. As for uncovering a threat, though . . . "Can you imagine Frau Schmalz and Herr Doktor Gurtner punching each other and her pushing him into the Aare after hitting him in the head with a rock?"

Nägeli gave a great guffaw and then looked guiltily at Renzo, shaking his head. "It's a terrible death, not funny at all, I know, but I've known Frau Schmalz for years. She isn't just fat; she's short, and she wheezes. She waddles, too, when she walks. She couldn't even lift a big rock, let alone reach high enough to bang Hannes on the head with it. No, Herr Donatelli, I think you can be quite sure our Frau Schmalz did not kill him."

Dismissing Frau Schmalz with a clap of his hands on his thighs, Nägeli stretched his legs toward the empty fireplace and reached with one hand to pick up a slim leather briefcase propped against his chair. He laid it across his lap and said to Renzo, "So, you've asked me about

Gurtner's work as almoner. But I'm sure you also want to ask me about money."

Delighted that he wasn't going to have to approach his next question on eggshells, Renzo nodded. "Yes, I'm hoping you'll tell me if you noticed signs of Herr Doktor Gurtner misusing funds."

The smile on Nägeli's lined face was knowing, and Renzo was just starting to feel annoyed when the older man said, "Come now. What you want to know is if either of us was an embezzler. In fact, the real question is whether he caught *me* fiddling the books, because then I'd have a good reason to kill him before he exposed me. Right?"

"Absolutely right," admitted Renzo. He felt slightly irritated at having his questions preempted, but the old boy was having so much fun, Renzo couldn't hold it against him. "I see you've given this thought."

"Of course I have," Nägeli said. "I'm a forensic accountant—I only retired from Credit Suisse a few years ago. Figuring out who's fudging the books is my meat and drink. And Hannes wasn't. He didn't know how. Besides, there wasn't much of anything lying around for him to take. He had access to a small discretionary fund to handle any emergencies our members might have. It usually contained about ten thousand francs, and he kept scrupulous track of how that money was spent during his three years as almoner."

Renzo was about to break in, but Nägeli continued. "As for the guild's rather substantial investments . . ." The treasurer laced his fingers together and laid his clasped hands down softly on the briefcase in his lap. His face remained placid. "I can safely say that on my watch our accounts have never been tampered with, not only because of my oversight, but also because there is an annual audit. However, I'd be happy to have a police accountant review the guild's finances."

A preliminary review of the Cloth Handlers' finances would be a good idea, and Renzo would recommend it to Erwin and Giuliana, along with some background research on Georg Nägeli. Still, he didn't believe the man had a dishonest bone in his body. No embezzler would look so calm at the idea of someone going through his books.

Now Nägeli was positively beaming as he held up the leather case that had been on his lap. Fiddling with the combination, he lifted the lid and removed a small stack of printed letter-sized paper before closing the case and setting it at his feet. He's enjoying this piece of theater, Renzo thought, watching Nägeli rest the papers on one knee. Deciding perhaps that he'd tried Renzo's patience long enough, the treasurer said, "I'm sorry I haven't been able to help you much so far. But I may have a piece of useful information after all. Hannes had a private account at the Burghers' Bank that he diverted a small part of his surgeon's income to. It won't have been turned over to the police, because officially it belongs to the *Tuchleute*. He'd had the account for years, since before his first marriage, even though the rest of his banking was done through UBS. He was quite open about it—told me he'd kept the account at the Burghers' Bank to hide it from his wives and used it to pay out a certain sum every month. He asked me if I could help him to make it even more private. I saw no harm in it, so I incorporated his account under the *Tuchleute* umbrella. A fine game as long as he was alive, but now, given how he died, I need to tell you about it."

At last Nägeli held his sheaf of papers out to Renzo. "Here's the data on every penny that has gone into and out of Hannes's account. It must deal with a very youthful indiscretion, since the first payments— rather small ones at that point—began over fifty years ago, when Gurtner was twenty-one."

Renzo tried not to grab the stapled list of payments out of Nägeli's hands. My God! Could he have been supporting a mistress or an illegitimate child all these years? Starting to read, Renzo saw no recipient's name, only an account number. "Who's been getting the money?" he asked the treasurer.

"I don't know—I've decided to respect Hannes's privacy, as I did when he was alive. The bank will tell you the name on my say-so, though, since it's a *Tuchleute* account. Shall I make the call?"

Does he think we're in a James Bond film, Renzo thought, but he played along, nodding gravely instead of rolling his eyes at the delay. Everyone needed a bit of excitement. The treasurer removed his mobile from his jacket pocket with what Renzo perceived as a certain slow solemnity and pressed a button. At least he had the bank on speed dial. "Yes, this is Nägeli; I'm passing you to Herr Donatelli. You have my permission to provide him with the information we discussed." Renzo took the phone; his notepad and pen were already resting on the little table at his elbow, half-covering its top of inlaid wood.

"Hello, Donatelli here," he said and confirmed that he needed the name of the person receiving Gurtner's payments. He wrote it down and then passed the phone back to Herr Nägeli, who thanked the speaker and ended the call. The smile he gave Renzo then was boyish. "I've never provided a clue in a murder case before. I hope what I've given you is helpful." Then the grin disappeared. "I may be enjoying this interview with you, but I hope you realize that I'm very sorry about Hannes. When we were teenagers we were thrown together by our families, but during the last three years I got to know him better. Perhaps we were even friends. His death is a great pity."

Renzo remembered Giuliana's interest in the inscription on the watch, from mother but not father. "You say you knew his family. Were he and his father estranged?"

Nägeli shrugged. "If they were, they kept it quiet. I don't remember any talk, and in those days Hannes wouldn't have told me himself. Too private. Besides, I was always more interested in his little sister Bri!" Nägeli gave another mischievous smile, and Renzo tried to look beyond the scarce hair, wrinkled skin, thinning lips, and faded blue eyes to imagine the youngster who'd flirted with Gurtner's sister at long-ago *Tuchleute* parties.

Time to call this new information into the office. He took leave of Nägeli, ran down the stairs and, on his way back to the station, dialed Giuliana. "I've got a name for you to start asking about." He explained about the hidden bank account and the decades of regular payments flowing out of it. "It's not a name I've run into yet during the case: Norbert Wittwer. That's who was getting secret money from Gurtner."

22
Before

" N orbert's joining you later?" the inn's hostess said to Jakob. "I'll put you at this bigger table for when he gets here. *If* he gets here," she added. "He's much worse since last time you were here, Köbi. It's not the drinking; I'm amazed at how he's cut down. But he looks . . . well, it's hard to believe he'll make it till Christmas. Even though the doctors have said he should get six more months. According to him."

Markus saw the older woman exchange a look with Jakob that said a lot about what they thought of Norbert's grasp on reality. It also suggested how well they knew each other. As she went off to get them each a pint of beer and a plate of food—Jakob had advised Markus to let her serve them whatever she thought was the evening's best, and he'd been glad to agree—the older man said, "Heidi Stettler is our younger daughter's godmother. I've known her since I was nine, and I introduced my wife to her before we got married. They've been friends ever since."

For the next couple of hours, Jakob and Markus drank and ate and talked, to each other and to the people who stopped at their table, all of whom called Jakob "Köbi." Markus lost count of the number of times he stood and shook hands with men and women over sixty, as Jakob, having greeted someone, said, "Look, I've brought one of Karli Gurtner's three sons with me—this one is Markus. He's a photographer."

The evening gave Markus an interesting perspective on his friends in Bern. The people he usually hung out with acted as if enthusiasm had been banned: what counted was cleverness and disdain. These oldsters at The Lion were different. They clasped his hand warmly and welcomed him to Heidmatt, with many of the men clapping him on the shoulder. Two separate people made a point of asking what his Aunt Bri was up to, and, after he told them about her charity work, remembered her warmheartedness from primary school. Another man reminisced about Markus's grandfather coming to his house several times when his little brother was ill, adding, "My mother always said your grandfather saved Walti's life. She made me bless old Doctor Gurtner in my bedtime prayers for about a year after that! At the time it put me right off the poor man." Markus thanked people for their comments and memories. He couldn't remember the last time he'd felt such uncomplicated pleasure among a group of strangers—or perhaps even a group of so-called friends.

Quite a few of the diners and drinkers that night sat down at Markus and Jakob's table, tried to buy them more beer, and stayed on to tell Jakob a piece of news about their families or jobs, generously including Markus in the conversation. Then, when Markus was halfway through his second and last pint, Heidi ushered a shrunken figure to their table that Markus realized must be Norbert. Maybe the man had been five foot four or five in his youth, but now he was shriveled and bent to the size of a twelve-year-old, skin taut and yellow, hands trembling, clothes drooping off his frame. He was also completely bald, and his large brown eyes gleamed with a childlike inquisitiveness that contrasted strangely with his haggard face and skeletal body. Standing up to greet him, Jakob became a giant. Gently, he took Norbert's arm and helped him into the chair next to his. Markus, who'd stood, too, watched his father's former bear take his seat tentatively, his eyes fixed on Jakob.

"I'm getting worse, Köbi," Norbert said. The waiter had already brought him a pint of something that wasn't beer.

"I'm sorry." Jakob lifted his mug to Norbert, who touched his glass first to Jakob's and then to Markus's. "*Zum Wohl*," all three said, and each took a sip of his drink, before Norbert spoke again.

"Are you sure? That you're sorry?"

Markus stared first at the little man and then at the big one. However, Jakob seemed to understand Norbert's strange question.

"We've talked about this before, Norbert, and every time I've told you the same thing. I'm not angry. Remember how I drove you to Bern, and you talked to a lawyer? I was very grateful you did that. I still am. You don't have to feel bad about the past anymore."

Norbert nodded and smiled, but Markus thought he still looked worried. "I've got a friend here who wants to meet you," Jakob told him then. "His name is Markus, and he's Karli Gurtner's son. He takes photographs for a living."

Norbert turned to Markus as if he hadn't noticed him before and stared long and hard into his face with the open curiosity of a small child. It was uncanny in an elderly adult. "Karli's son's a grown-up man?" he said. "I guess . . . How many children does he have?"

Markus couldn't get over how odd it was to hear his father referred to by this childish name. "Three, all sons. I'm the second one. I'm thirty-five. My younger brother's only eighteen."

Norbert's face was skeptical. "You don't look like Karli," he said.

Markus was used to this. "My big brother Patrick looks a lot like him, but—you're right, I don't." He paused. "Köbi said you're one of my father's oldest friends."

"Yes, I am," Norbert confirmed, with an enormous smile. "He told me if I stuck to him he'd take care of me, and he did. He's younger than me, but he's smarter. Did you know that?" Markus started to say something, but Norbert went on. "Pesche and Karli were the smart ones. They liked Heidi. You liked Heidi, too," he elbowed Jakob in the ribs, "but you were too young. And Müller liked her, but he was too old. Remember Müller, Köbi? He was a bad 'un." Norbert stopped abruptly like a rundown wind-up toy and took a sip from his mug. Markus had decided his drink was probably sweet cider.

"Müller was the schoolmaster in our class with your father, along with Heidi and quite a few people in this room," Jakob explained. "I've told you about him. Your father used to challenge his authority, which we pupils loved. It got him into trouble, though. Not much trouble—Müller was too scared of your grandparents—but . . ."

Norbert interrupted. "*You* got into trouble, Köbi. You and Pesche. Müller hated Pesche."

"Isn't Pesche the one with the puppy?" Markus asked, and Jakob started to say something. But Norbert took hold of his arm and began a rambling story about a chemotherapy treatment during his last visit to the hospital. Markus stopped listening. He wanted Norbert to say more about his father, something that would explain the anger in his old man's voice when he'd barked at Norbert that night at the gallery. If they were such good friends, why was Norbert supposed to phone Paps according to the rules of their "deal?" Did it have something to do with money? That fit what Norbert had just said about Paps taking care of him.

Markus was convinced there was a secret here, and he wanted to know it.

Just then, Norbert banged a fist on the table. "I need to see Karli!" he announced. "I want to see him before I die. I've asked him to come here, and he's said he will, but I don't believe him anymore. So, I'm going to Bern to find him."

Jakob appeared to take this pronouncement seriously. "You told me on the phone you had something to give him, Norbert, but you didn't say what." Norbert nodded his head up and down repeatedly, as if he'd forgotten he was doing it, and answered, "The watch. I want to give it back."

"What watch?" asked Markus. His father, who'd never given any of his sons a watch, had given one to Norbert?

Norbert looked surprised but answered readily enough. "Karli's father the doctor gave him a special watch when he was thirteen. Karli gave it to me and told his parents he lost it in the river. He got a bad beating with a leather belt from his father for that, believe me. I still have it, that watch. I used to wear it, but now I keep it in the back of my wardrobe."

Markus had never heard any of this, which wasn't surprising, since his father never talked about his childhood. So, his grandfather had beaten his father with a belt? Well, the apple hadn't fallen far from the tree. Still, the knowledge was like peeping through a newly built window into his father's soul and seeing the view from an unexpected angle.

"Are you giving back the watch so Paps can pass it on to one of us? Since you don't have any children of your own, I mean. That's thoughtful of you." Markus smiled at Norbert and then glanced at Jakob, expecting him to echo the praise. But Jakob's expression was far away. Meanwhile, Norbert was silently moving his lips, as if reciting a mantra. Markus looked back and forth between the two of them and knew he was missing something.

"Köbi knows why I'm giving the watch back," Norbert said at last. "Right, Köbi?"

Markus saw Jakob's expression sharpen as he seemed to return to the present. He put his arm around Norbert's shoulder and left it there. "I think I do, *Alter*. I think I do. It's a good idea. When did you come up with this plan?"

"Heidi put it into my head," Norbert admitted. "Once it was there, I couldn't get it out. I kept thinking, 'The sooner, the better,' and when you called about us getting together tonight, I decided to tell you about it."

"Well, good for you!"

"You'll have to help me, though, Köbi. I can't figure out how to do it by myself."

"Maybe *I* can help," Markus volunteered. He was coming to see that there was no point sitting in The Lion with Norbert and asking him for anecdotes about his father's schooldays or hoping he'd explain the "deal" with Paps. The little man didn't seem to think in a straight line. But if he spent more time with him, helping with this watch-returning project of his, maybe the information he sought would spill out—like the story about his father getting the belt. He imagined escorting Norbert to meet his father—now *that* would give the old bastard a surprise. Shock the hell out of him, probably, since he was clearly avoiding his dear old childhood friend. Markus liked the idea.

In fact, he'd enjoyed the whole evening. Being cheerfully accepted as his father's son by a roomful of people who knew nothing about his history and expected nothing more from him than a smile and a greeting was extraordinarily pleasant. Perhaps it was time to stop playing the black sheep—assuming everyone would let him—and just be a thirty-five-year-old photographer. Maybe he could even manage to be something as staid as Ada's boyfriend. *If* that was what she wanted. He didn't know, because he'd always been afraid of the answer. Perhaps it was time to ask. Sitting there imagining himself in a new role, he realized Jakob had said something. He smiled at his friend. "Sorry, I missed that."

"I wonder if you'd mind if we left. Norbert needs to go home, and we could drive him if we leave now."

Markus nodded. "I'm ready to go. It's been great, though. Thanks for bringing me." He paused and glanced over at Norbert, who was draining his mug. "Maybe after we drop him off, you could fill me in on what this watch business is about. There's obviously a story I'm missing."

"I'll do that," Jakob said, and Markus was surprised at the serious expression on his face as he spoke, before he added, "Come on; let's say goodbye to Heidi." He turned in his seat and closed his left hand over Norbert's right where it lay on the table. He held it firmly and squeezed it gently until he had his friend's attention. "I'm going to drive you home, old man, so stay right here while Markus and I go find Heidi. Did you hear me? Are you going to be here when I get back?"

"I'll be here." Norbert was frowning. "The pain is starting. I need my medicine." Then he smiled at Markus so sweetly that, for the first time, Markus could imagine why his father had befriended Norbert. "Köbi is lucky to have a good son like you."

Markus and Jakob exchanged a glance and a shrug; neither one reminded Norbert who Markus's father really was. Jakob let go of Norbert's hand, and, when he stood up, Markus did, too. The two men moved away from the table toward Heidi, who was sitting with a group of younger people, laughing. Touching Markus's shoulder as they approached her, Jakob said. "Norbert has a point, even if he's mixed up. I'm lucky to have gotten to know you."

Markus's throat tightened for a moment. "Me, too," he said.

23

Nordring police station,
Thursday afternoon, November 26

N orbert Wittwer? The name of the man Gurtner had been sending money to for decades meant nothing to Giuliana. That didn't last long. After her searches for a phone number and driver's license proved useless, Giuliana turned to Wittwer's post office account, where the payments had ended up. It took a bit of hoop jumping, but within fifteen minutes, Giuliana knew that Norbert was seventy-four years old and lived in Heidmatt. When she couldn't find a work history for him, she checked social services and discovered him classified as "sufficiently handicapped to be unable to pursue steady, income-generating work." He'd been getting a small pension from the government since he was seventeen.

The news hit her between the eyes. If Wittwer was disabled, there was a perfectly normal reason for Gurtner to have been sending him money. It looked as if Renzo's mysterious discovery was a dud. Still, she'd pursue it. She persuaded a secretary in the cantonal office that administered pensions like Wittwer's to dig up the old records for her. These showed him living in Heidmatt with his mother until her death sixteen years earlier, at which point he had been examined by a social worker and found capable of living on his own in the tiny cottage he'd inherited.

"Do you want me to read you the notes attached to the completed form?" asked the woman.

"Yes, please."

"Okay. The man who reviewed the case says, 'Norbert Wittwer presents several classic symptoms of fetal alcohol syndrome; I'd estimate his IQ to be in the high seventies. He is also an alcoholic and at the age of fifty-eight shows signs of liver damage. He is adamant about wanting to continue to live on his own now that his mother has died, and, when sober, appears able to take care of himself and his home well enough to live independently.'"

Fetal alcohol syndrome, Giuliana repeated to herself. She remembered feeling deeply guilty about the occasional glasses of wine she'd drunk with both pregnancies. Now she wondered how much alcohol it took to do that to your baby. She shuddered.

The social worker had had more to say; the woman on the phone read on. "'I would nevertheless recommend placing Herr Wittwer in an institution, because he is, apparently, seldom sober. However, several of his neighbors have promised to see he gets enough to eat and that he and his house are kept tidy. I've explained that they are under no legal obligation to do so, but they insist.'"

Giuliana was very glad to live in the city, but small towns had their advantages, too. Imagine a group of women—she felt sure they *were* women—volunteering to look after the old drunk next door. *Only in a village*, she thought.

The report continued. "'Should any of them be unwilling or unable to continue this assistance, Erna Iseli, age seventy-three, promises to let this department know.' That's it," said the administrator, followed by, "No, wait. There are short follow-ups every couple of years indicating that Wittwer is still coping, and then there's a doctor's report. *Ach,* what a scribble!" There was a pause. "All I can get out of this mess is that the man has liver cancer—hmm, that's sad. Let's see. The medical report is from a year and a half ago. His invalidity pension hasn't stopped, so I guess he's still alive."

"I hope so," Giuliana said. "Tell me, is he classified as a ward of the state? I mean, if the police interview him, does a guardian need to be present, or can we talk to him alone?"

This was a crucial question. If they decided to bring Norbert in for questioning, she didn't want what he said dismissed from court because he'd been denied a watchdog.

There was the rustle of paper, followed by the clicks of a keyboard until her contact said, "I can't find anything giving him protected status. Frankly, since his pension is justified by a mental disability, I think he *should* have a guardian, but it isn't in his files. Can you wait while I check with my boss?"

While she waited, Giuliana read online about fetal alcohol syndrome. The info was interesting but didn't make her feel prepared for an encounter with Norbert Wittwer, since the condition produced a whole range of different effects, and those who had it varied widely in their mental abilities and physical problems. One thing they all shared was the lack of an indentation on their upper lip—the skin there was completely smooth. She was staring at the photo of a child with this feature when the woman came back onto the phone. "He's not protected," the secretary told her. "Unfortunately."

Giuliana silently agreed that it was probably a mistake for Norbert but certainly very helpful for the police. "What's your supervisor's name?" she asked and wrote it down. "Can you ask him to send me an email confirming Wittwer's independent status? Today, please. This is urgent for us."

Giuliana set the phone down and stared at the corkboard on the wall across from her without seeing it. Had Gurtner been helping a childhood friend all these years? If so, why the secrecy? The guild treasurer said he'd wanted to hide the payments from both his wives. Some kind of bizarre modesty on his part? Or was Wittwer a blackmailer?

She wrote up what she'd learned and sent it to Erwin and Renzo. Full of misgivings but determined to follow protocol, at least for the present, she also sent the report to Toni Rossel. Perhaps the information about Wittwer would distract Toni from going after Markus Gurtner with too little evidence. But not for long—because if Norbert fit the physical type of people with fetal alcohol syndrome, he'd be too small and slight to have punched Gurtner in the eye and brained him with a rock.

She was close to finishing the report when her cell phone rang. It was the dialect expert at the University of Bern who'd been analyzing the emergency call reporting Gurtner's drowning. "Frau Professor Michel, it's good to hear from you. Any luck with the caller's speech?"

"I've got some preliminary answers," the woman said, and Giuliana noticed *her* dialect was from somewhere in the Bernese Alps. "I thought you'd want to hear them right away, even if I still have work to do on them. You asked me to tell you if the man in the recording uses a pure city-of-Bern dialect. He does not. There's some city speech present, but his dialect is predominantly Emmentaler."

Giuliana felt a quiver of excitement, before reminding herself how many tens of thousands of people lived in the Emmental. "Good to know. Can you be more specific about what part of the Emmental?"

"Yes. I'd say you can eliminate the areas around Luzern, Burgdorf, and Langenthal. More like Langnau or Bowil. Or maybe Trubsch-achen."

In a sudden burst of certainty, Giuliana said, "Our drowning victim came from Heidmatt. Could the caller have grown up around there?"

"Absolutely; Heidmatt would work just as well. Any small town ten, fifteen miles south of Langnau: Heidmatt, Eggiswil, or Röthen-bach would all fit, for example. I can't be more specific than that. When I write it up, I'll explain it in linguistic terms, so you know why I'm so sure. I assume this may have to stand up in court, right?"

"Yes, go ahead and prepare your findings as if you were going to testify—that may not happen, but we might as well be ready. Thank you very much. This is extremely helpful." Could it have been Norbert on the phone? Giuliana was thinking. With his cancer, wouldn't he be too weak to...?

"May I ask you a question?" Michel went on. "I read in the news-paper that the victim's name was Johann Gurtner. But the speaker calls him Karli. Do you think it's possible the wrong person was attacked? Sorry if I'm being nosy. It's just that I . . ."

Giuliana interrupted, unable to keep her voice from rising. "What? What are you talking about? There's no name in the call."

Professor Michel remained silent for a moment, and when she spoke a coldness had crept into her voice. "I hope we're both talking about the same recording. The one I've been working on goes as follows: 'Listen. I need you to send rescuers to Dählhölzli, near the restaurant. Now, right now. A man's drowning in the Aare. I tried to get him out, but I couldn't see anything. God, I'm sorry. I'm afraid Karli is . . . You've got to hurry.' It's perfectly clear to me—the speaker says, "I'm afraid *Karli* is,' and then he interrupts himself."

"My God," Giuliana breathed. "Frau Michel, you're terrific. You're . . . it's brilliant. All of us heard it as '*s Kerli*,' so we thought the caller was simply saying 'the guy.' But I'm sure you're right. Johann Gurtner's middle name is Karl, and all his schoolmates called him Karli, so now we know that whoever phoned the emergency number knew exactly who'd fallen into the river. This is . . . you can't imagine how useful this is to the investigation."

The professor's voice was warm again. "I'm so glad I could help. I'll need about a week for the report, though."

"Of course." Elation making her generous with the department's budget, she added, "Take what time you need" and hung up, shaking her head. My God, how had they all missed it? No, how had *she* missed it? She was the one who'd heard Gurtner's older sister call him Karl, who'd been sitting in the dining room of The Lion when Heidi Stettler had called him Karli. But when she'd listened to the emergency call, Gurtner was still "Hannes" in her mind, and "Karli" had automatically become the generic "*Kerli*." If Frau Michel hadn't asked about Gurtner's name, she'd never have noticed. This was news that had to be passed to Erwin immediately. Not only did the dialect analysis prove that the man on the riverbank was from the Emmental. He'd known Gurtner as a child, before he'd started calling himself Hannes.

Erwin wasn't answering his mobile, so she left a message about the linguist's findings, preceded by a warning not to play her words on speakerphone. Until she and Erwin had had a chance to discuss the implications, this was not to be shared with anyone. Especially not Toni. Because Markus, their main suspect, did *not* speak in a Heidmatter dialect. But Norbert Wittwer surely did.

24

G iuliana was hunched over her desk, still trying to reconcile a case against Markus with the revelations about the phone call when she realized it was time to leave for her interview with Gurtner's younger sister, Brigitte Rieder. Five minutes later and slightly breathless, she was on her way to the tiny neighborhood of posh villas across from the city's rose garden where Rieder and her husband lived.

She climbed a narrow one-way horseshoe of a street to find the house at the crest of the hill: large, white, and three-storied, with a beautifully kept lawn hidden behind a thick hedge. A red-painted front door stood at the top of a set of stairs. Giuliana climbed them and, before ringing the bell, turned to admire the city from this vantage point. She'd never been on this hill before, despite the fact that it was only a twenty-minute walk from her house. She was glad to know it existed, this precipitous little street with its elegant houses. Another of her city's secret places.

Brigitte Rieder led her into a large kitchen and seated her at a round table in front of a different view, this one toward the town of Ostermundigen and, beyond it, to the three-thousand-foot Bantiger. Not far past this small mountain was the beginning of the Emmental, where Brigitte had grown up. Chatting to Giuliana about the NGO she worked for, the older woman moved around the kitchen making coffee in a large glass pot with a funnel and a paper filter. Brigitte was as thin as her older sister Charlotte, but that appeared to be all they had in common. This woman had none of her sister's tall, intimidating elegance. Short and quick, with a cap of straight gray hair and no make-up, Brigitte didn't need Charlotte's cool distance to make her mark. Giuliana decided that the younger sister was formidable, too, but in her own way—perhaps feisty would be a better word for her. In contrast to her sister's classic suit, Brigitte wore wide-legged cargo pants and a slim tunic patterned in shades of green. Around her neck were blue-framed reading glasses on a blue cord. Even the brisk way she spoke differed from her sister's careful tones.

What struck Giuliana most, though, was how low-pitched Brigitte's voice was, almost raspy. She'd just stopped speaking. When she started again, after a slight pause, she came straight to the point. "I know you want to ask me about my brother. I've spoken to Kathrin and Nicole about you. To Markus, too. Both my sisters-in-law seem to trust you, and so does my nephew, who's also my godson. Markus doesn't do trust, Frau Linder," she added, looking up from measuring coffee to smile at Giuliana, "so consider yourself honored."

Giuliana nodded at the compliment, noting that even though Markus might very well have killed his father, she still felt pleased to have won some portion of approval from Gurtner's fragile son.

Brigitte turned her back on Giuliana to pour water through the coffee grinds. Her next words surprised Giuliana. "My husband Hene and I couldn't have children, so . . . well, I guess that's made Karl's sons particularly dear to us. We've stayed close to both of Karl's families for that reason. I never stopped seeing Kathrin after she and my brother broke up; we've been friends for over forty years. As for Nicole . . . it took me a while to forgive her for being the other woman, but I've grown fond of her, too."

Brigitte carried two red coffee mugs to the table, followed by a milk carton. No porcelain cream pitchers for her. Giuliana watched her energetic movements around the kitchen and decided to let her have her say before beginning to question her. This speech had been planned, and Giuliana was curious to see where it was going.

"What I'm saying is that over the years I've seen a lot of my brother's family. But I wasn't close to *him*. I'm shocked that he's dead, and I'm very sad for Nicole and the children. Most of all for my sister Charlotte, because our brother was always at the heart of her existence. But," the word rang out like a deep-noted bell, "I'm *not* going to pretend to be overwhelmed by grief."

This speech must have coincided with the last drop of water running through the ground coffee, because Brigitte brought the pot to the table, filled the mugs, and sat down across from Giuliana, her back to the window that looked out toward the Emmental. Her piece said, she folded her hands and waited for questions.

"Thank you for that explanation," said Giuliana, wondering why it had been necessary. Perhaps the younger sister felt guilty for not being as sad as she knew the older one must be. "Even though you and your brother weren't close, I'm still going to ask if you can think of anyone who would have had a reason to attack him."

"I have no idea. Believe me, I've thought about it a lot since Nicole called me with the news, and I can't offer you a single insight. I'm sorry." Brigitte shrugged before pushing one of the red mugs closer to Giuliana and pulling the other closer to herself.

Giuliana hadn't expected anything else—her job was rarely made so easy for her—and she went on. "The other way you can help is by describing your brother. I know he went away to school when he was thirteen and you were only eight, but I imagine you can still tell me quite a lot about what he was like—as a child and more recently, too."

The older woman added milk to her coffee and stirred it vigorously, the clink of the spoon filling the quiet kitchen. Giuliana waited. Eventually Brigitte took a sip from her mug, set it down, and spoke. Her husky voice was soft and thoughtful, and she paused often as she said, "My brother was who he was because . . . because of his

relationship with our parents. Maybe one way to put it is that he was
... the conduit for my parents' anger with each other. My mother was
more than a decade younger than my father and ... I think he married
her because he found her frivolity enchanting. She probably admired
his dedication to medicine. Then ... well, they got fed up with the very
qualities they'd originally been attracted to. Once Karl came along,
each saw the other as 'spoiling' him by trying to shape him to fit their
own ... needs."

Brigitte cocked her head, frowning slightly at Giuliana, who'd just
taken a sip of coffee. "I hope I'm making sense. I've never tried to sum
all this up."

Giuliana set her mug down. "It sounds like your mother was
trying to raise a charming aristocrat and your father wanted a future
doctor."

Brigitte laughed, not bitterly but with real amusement. "If only
they'd made it a joint enterprise, it might have worked out just like that.
Instead, they used Karl to undermine and punish each other. My father
was too harsh with Karl because he was convinced my mother let him
get away with ... well, with everything. Meanwhile, my mother treated
him more like a friend than a son. I don't think she ever disciplined him
... although, since I wasn't born until he was five, how would I know?"
Her chuckle was as deep and raspy as her speaking voice.

Nodding, Giuliana waited while Brigitte drank some coffee before
asking, "So, what did this upbringing do for your brother?"

"Nothing good. Poor Karl." Brigitte didn't speak again for a while,
and Giuliana buried her impatience in her coffee mug. For this much
insight, she had to pay with time.

"On the surface," the older woman said at last, "you could say
both parents won. Karl was very intelligent, which was something
both wanted; he became a doctor, if not a village GP; and he could
be extremely articulate and charming. Charm," she said, in what was
almost a growl, filling the word with contempt. "It's such a two-sided
gift. Karl always had a lot of charm, with all the cleverness and deceit
that implies. Plus ... what? A strong power of attraction, I guess."

Brigitte stopped again and topped up their coffee from the glass pot on the table. Giuliana added milk to her mug and said, "Everyone we've talked to about him agrees that he attracted friends and followers."

Brigitte, who'd just lifted the milk carton herself, set it down again and said, "That's it! His charm had something to do with gaining control over people. I don't think he actually enjoyed cruelty," here her voice sank almost to a whisper, "but if making someone afraid of him would bring them under his thumb, he'd use it. Fear, I mean."

Giuliana was unobtrusively taking notes. She looked up and met Brigitte's eyes. "Is that what he did with Markus?" Brigitte started and frowned, but before Giuliana could follow up, the doorbell rang. She waited for Brigitte to go the front door, but instead there was the noise overhead of a chair scraping, followed by the thump of feet on the stairs.

"Excellent!" a male voice said. "Thank you. Have a good day." Seconds later, a stocky man with gray hair like a monk's tonsure appeared in the kitchen doorway carrying a padded Amazon envelope, which he set down on the countertop. He wore wide-wale corduroy trousers and a pumpkin-colored turtleneck; in style and age, they looked like they could have been at Woodstock. "Hello," he said. "You must be the policewoman."

"Giuliana Linder," she responded and stood; he crossed the kitchen to shake her hand as her brain cast around and supplied a caption for the face: Heinz Rieder, called Hene, retired biochemistry professor.

"Enough coffee for me?" Heinz asked his wife, peering at the glass pot on the table.

"Not hot," she warned, but he poured himself a little, added a lot of milk, and stuck his cup in the microwave.

"Bri's giving you the lowdown on Karl, huh?" he said, leaning against the wall as he waited for the coffee to heat. "I'll tell you one thing about him—he hated to lose. Man, did it piss him off! A chess match, a political discussion, anything. I'm sure it made him a good surgeon—he hated to lose a patient, too. But it made him a pain in the ass as a brother-in-law. Lousy father, too, if you ask me." The microwave pinged, and Rieder grabbed his coffee, not forgetting to pick up his package on his way out. "Domenico Scarlatti's complete sacred music," he called to his wife as he left, waving the envelope and grinning.

"Have fun," she said, with an answering smile, and his feet clumped back up the stairs.

Brigitte was still smiling when she said, "Hene and Karl were civil to each other at family get-togethers, but that was the best they could manage. Both alpha dogs in their own ways." She shook her head. "He couldn't stand the way Karl spoke to . . . the boys."

You mean Markus, Giuliana thought. She was glad Brigitte had given her a way to get back to the middle son, since Rieder had interrupted her first attempt to bring him up. "So, tell me about your brother and his sons."

Brigitte's smile disappeared. She shifted in her chair and drank the last of her coffee before saying, "Three boys, three ways of coping with a father who wanted to run their lives. The oldest, Patrick, figured out a way to say, 'Yes,' to his father's demands—or at least imply it. Then he turned around and did more or less what he'd wanted to do in the first place, but without flaunting it."

Brigitte was moving things around on the kitchen table. The spoons clattered in the mugs, and the mugs clinked as they were clustered roughly together and pushed to the far side of the table. They were joined by the milk carton. This done, Brigitte focused on the scene outside the window, seeming to study the distant television tower that crowned the Bantiger. Giuliana tensed. Was she going to shut down the interview to avoid the topic of Markus?

At last the deep voice began again. "Markus wasn't like Patrick. He wouldn't accept his father's authority, and he wouldn't pretend to, either." Another pause. "When he was alone with his mother, he was as kind and obedient as the average kid. Kathrin listened to him and took his ideas seriously. But Karl never stopped insisting on obedience. There wasn't much reason behind most of his demands, once Markus was a teenager—it was simply a matter of Karl winning."

Giuliana kept her expression sympathetic, even as she wondered why Markus's mother and aunt, who clearly loved him, couldn't stop dwelling on why he'd hated his father. And, by extension, perhaps wanted him dead. She'd need to confront Brigitte about the possibility of Markus's guilt—but not yet, since it risked blowing up the interview.

"What about the youngest son, Philipp?" she asked. Saying his name reminded her that she needed to find out if his dog had turned up.

Brigitte gave one of her gravelly chuckles. "I'd say he's profited from his father being older and less energetic this time around—Karl is . . . was . . . much more lenient with Philipp. Still, since fifteen, Philipp's become rebellious. It goes with his age." She fiddled with her mug, sighing. "I imagine their recent conversations were mostly angry, which has probably made his father's death a lot harder for him to deal with."

Giuliana nodded and decided to see what a bit of silence might draw out of Brigitte. She glanced around the kitchen. Walking in, she'd had a strong sense of color, but until now she'd been concentrating too hard on the interview to register what a riot of different patterns the room contained. A wooden floor with rag rugs in primary hues, a solid turquoise countertop, green-and-blue swirls on the kitchen cabinets, and a variety of different greens, blues, and yellows in the wallpaper, the tiling, the curtains, and the cushions on the kitchen chairs: it all fought for her attention. Or should have done. Instead, Giuliana found herself liking the exuberance of it. From upstairs she could hear intertwined voices singing what she assumed was Professor Rieder's newly arrived Scarlatti—the music seemed to work its way into harmony just like the extravagant colors in the kitchen did.

Apparently comfortable with the silence, Brigitte said nothing. Giuliana moved on. "During this investigation, a man called Norbert Wittwer has come up as someone your brother knew. Do you recognize the name?"

"Norbert," Brigitte murmured to herself. Then she repeated the name, but with an emphasis on the "bear" sound in the word:

"Nor-BERt." She paused briefly before adding, "My brother was in school with a boy named Norbert, but I never knew his last name. He lived in Heidmatt and was ... small for his age. Odd, too."

"Were they friends?" Anything about Norbert at this point seemed important, so Giuliana persevered. "Did they visit each other's homes, for example? Or ...?"

Giuliana's next question dried up as Brigitte shook her head vigorously, a crooked smile on her face, and said, "Even now, it embarrasses me to remember the way we castle children were kept separate from our classmates. The only way my father could get my mother to go along with us attending the village school was by accepting *her* demand that we only associate with our classmates at the schoolhouse and nowhere else. In first and second grade, I managed to have a best friend named Beatus. He was a farmer's son." She paused, and when she continued, her face was soft with memory; Giuliana wondered what picture of her seven-year-old self she was seeing in her mind. "Beatus and I spent all our breaks together, and our whispering in class had us in constant trouble with our teacher. For a while, we planned to run away together. In any case," she went on, her voice brisk again, "I can assure you that Karli never brought school friends home and never went to their houses."

So, that was all Giuliana was going to get on Norbert Wittwer. Her next move would be to track him down in Heidmatt—assuming Renzo or Erwin hadn't already done it. That decision made, her mind went back to Markus. Meanwhile, Brigitte was again staring out the window at the TV tower. Before Giuliana could change the subject, the older woman said, "I remember one incident with Norbert that happened during break time." Her voice was far away, and she seemed to be talking as much to herself as to Giuliana. "It was in the fall, not too long before Karl and I were taken out of school for good, in the middle of the year. The youngest class, my class, was going on a bus-trip—I can't remember where—and a teenager named Heidi, whom we all knew, was coming along with us to help out."

Heidi? Giuliana remembered the hostess at The Lion. But now wasn't the time to interrupt. Brigitte was immersed in her story.

"When we came out of class, Heidi was standing on the playground, and quite a few of us ran and hugged her; we little ones loved her. Then the older pupils came out of their classrooms, and my brother walked over to Heidi. He started telling her how he'd been to the Bern-Belp airport. I remember wishing he'd go away, because *I* wanted to talk to Heidi, and I was sure she wanted him to go away, too, because she didn't look the slightest bit interested in hearing about all the landings and takeoffs he'd seen."

Brigitte turned from the window to look at Giuliana as she spoke, but her expression was still distant. "Then a boy from Karl's class came over to us, and Heidi hugged him. I knew his name was Pesche, because sometimes he helped kids from all three classes—even the oldest ones—with their homework. Heidi moved away from Karl and took Pesche's hand, and we younger kids moved closer to Heidi, too, so Karl was left standing there by himself. But not for long, because other boys came over, and he went back to talking about airplanes."

Giuliana had to ask. "Are you talking about Heidi Stettler who became innkeeper at The Lion with her husband?"

Brigitte's small reminiscent smile broadened. "Exactly. You know her! Isn't she lovely? I drop in on her at The Lion whenever I visit my sister Lotti, just to have a chat. A tiny piece of me still wants to sit on her lap whenever I see her! At the time I'm talking about, when I was eight, she must have been fourteen or fifteen—you can't imagine how pretty she was then. I realized later that Karl must've had a crush on her. He was only thirteen, but I guess his hormones were already stirring. I'm sure it drove him crazy that Heidi'd picked Pesche over him. Pesche was smaller and didn't have Karl's good looks, but even at eight, I could tell that Pesche was a young man, not a boy. He wasn't that much older than Karl, I suppose, but he was much more mature . . . probably because he was a *Verdingbueb*, orphaned and working for his keep. I remember that he had very striking brown eyes. Anyway, he and Heidi were in love; anyone could see that."

Why had Heidi Stettler claimed to know nothing about the Gurtners, Giuliana wondered. She'd not only taught and played with Bri, she'd also known Hannes—or Karl, as Giuliana was now coming to call him in her mind—well enough for him to be attracted to her. Was her refusal to talk about Johann Gurtner suspicious? Or was she, like most people, simply averse to telling the police more about any subject than was necessary? Most people, that is, except Brigitte Rieder, who seemed to be an exception to that rule.

Brigitte talked on, still relating her childhood memory. ". . . switched over to talking about boxing," she said. "Our father had insisted Karl learn to box, so he went to Langnau twice a week for classes. All the boys, even the littlest ones, got into scuffles with each other, and some trained for the local wrestling competitions, but my brother was the only one who knew how to hit people professionally. That fascinated the others, so he talked about it a lot. Bragged about it, I'd say now, but at the time I just knew it made me uncomfortable."

As if that long ago discomfort had returned, Brigitte jumped up to clear the table. She put the mugs in the sink and the milk carton back in the fridge before continuing her tale from the kitchen. Giuliana watched her from a distance as she said, "The worst part of the boxing business was that Karli would demonstrate the holds and punches he'd learned on this boy you asked about, Norbert, although he was definitely undersized for his age. He'd stand there, and Karl would pat his shoulder and say how brave he was before demonstrating a left hook, or an uppercut, or whatever the term was. Usually he just tapped Norbert on the cheek or the diaphragm, but sometimes he got carried away and hurt him."

Giuliana looked up from a note she'd made to see that Brigitte's mouth had twisted again, and she was shaking her head from her slouched stance against the kitchen counter. "This particular time he socked Norbert in the stomach so hard that the boy doubled over moaning, and Pesche yelled, 'Why don't you hit someone your own size, Karli? What a way to treat a friend!' Something like that. Karl stalked over to Pesche and said, 'Well, you're not my friend—I'll hit you. This is a jab,' he called out to the other boys and put his fists up. Before he could hit out, another boy pushed Pesche to one side and took the punch himself, on the side of his head. Karl yelled and stepped back, cradling his knuckles, and the boy came at him and hit him under the chin so hard that he flew backward into a bush. That was lucky for Karl, because part of our playground was paved—he could have landed much worse."

The picture Brigitte had painted was vivid in Giuliana's mind: the fall day, the schoolchildren in their little groups, the play fighting flaring into something serious, and Karl tumbling backward into the shrubs edging the schoolyard. The scene seemed fresh to Brigitte as well, since she added, "I can still see the way that other boy stepped toward Karl where he lay in the plants, waiting to see if he was going to get up and fight. He was filthy and bruised and barefoot, and his clothes were too small. Pretty much rags, in fact. I remember how he stood there looking down at my brother without a word, his face full of contempt. None of us moved. Afterward, I felt bad that I hadn't run over to see if Karl was all right, but at the time no one did a thing. Except Pesche—he walked over to the raggedy boy and put an arm around him. Just then, our teacher, Fräulein Kämpf, came outside and rang a handbell to tell us that break was over, and it was time for us little kids to go on our bus trip with her and Heidi and for the bigger ones to go back to their classes."

It was a revealing story. "So, Norbert was not only your brother's friend but his victim, too?" As soon as the words were out of her mouth, Giuliana was sorry for them. It was too provocative a question. Brigitte just nodded, however, her lips set in a line. She returned to the table and slipped into her chair. Once she was settled, Giuliana asked another, more important question. "The boy who took the punch meant for Pesche: do you remember his name?"

"No," she said. "I must have known it then but not anymore. Sorry. I don't think Karl had much to do with him, in any case."

Maybe not, but Giuliana wanted to remember him. She made a quick note and then turned back through the filled pages of her notebook, checking dates. "It was fall when this fight happened, you said, so let's assume it happened in October. By January, you were continuing second grade in Langnau, and your brother was at boarding school in Thun. What happened?"

Brigitte opened her eyes wide and spread her hands. "I can't tell you. I just don't know. All I can say is that toward the end of November Karl was suspended from school. My father gave him such a whipping that he couldn't sit down, I remember. I also know Father met with the school board. Soon after that, I was taken out of my class. It made me very angry, and I protested to my parents, but it was useless."

Giuliana felt Brigitte's sadness over this long-ago injustice descend on her again. She remembered Beatus, the farmer's son. Had Brigitte ever seen her childhood friend again?

"It was Advent," said the older woman, "which was usually a happy time for our family, but that year I was miserable. We all were. My mother was crying off and on, which scared me, and Father ignored me completely. He went around looking like he'd never smile again. Those weeks puzzle me, even now. Karl's suspension from the village school doesn't seem like a big enough crisis to justify my parents being so upset, not to mention me being taken out of a school where I was happy, to be driven every day to another town. I can see why they sent Karl to Thun a semester earlier than planned. But why did I have to change schools? In the middle of second grade, too?"

Giuliana nodded. "It does seem odd. Have you asked your sister about it?"

"Many times. Charlotte always starts by saying that everyone at the Heidmatt school resented Karl for excelling, and that made it a terrible place for both him and me. I think she has convinced herself with her own reasoning, but that doesn't make it true." Brigitte glanced at her watch. "My God, it's five-thirty. I didn't realize we'd been talking so long. Are we almost finished?"

"Almost. I'd like to ask you if you think your brother stayed in touch with any of his old friends from the village school. Norbert, perhaps. Or Heidi."

"Certainly not Heidi, because I see her now and then, and she would have mentioned it. In the case of other people, I doubt it. I don't think he set foot in Heidmatt after he left the school. He had to drive through the village to get to the castle, first to see our parents and then to visit Charlotte, but as far as I know he never spoke to anyone local again. He shook off that part of his life as if it had never happened."

Except for paying Norbert hundreds of thousands of francs over the years, thought Giuliana. But she kept that to herself. Thinking about how late it was getting, she decided with an inner sigh that it was time to ask Brigitte about Markus again, even if it proved counterproductive.

"One last thing, Frau Rieder. Since your brother's death, the police have talked to literally hundreds of people who knew him. The most obvious enemy he appears to have had was your nephew Markus, who has a history of violence and substance abuse. Do you—?"

"No," interrupted Brigitte. She'd leaned forward, her pleasant face transformed. "It doesn't matter what your question is—the answer is no. Markus would not kill his father. He had a bad time when he was young, but that's over with, and I won't hear a word against him. Please." Her voice was trembling now. "I've tried to help you understand my family. Please don't twist what I've said and . . . use it to hurt anyone."

Brigitte Rieder wouldn't be the first person to say too much to the cops and regret it afterward. Giuliana was sorry to see her distress, but not at all sorry for how the interview had gone. She got up from the table and quietly gathered her notepad and pen into her purse.

"Thank you, Frau Rieder, for being so honest with me," Giuliana said to the older woman. "The police will take your good opinion of Markus Gurtner into account, I promise."

Brigitte, her lips pressed into a thin line, didn't answer. She escorted Giuliana to the front hall and saw her out without a handshake. At least she didn't slam the door.

Still staring at the closed door, Bri took a moment to try and control her trembling. Suddenly the kitchen seemed far away, and she needed to sit down. Walking stiffly into the living room, she crumpled into the nearest chair, closed her eyes, and hung her head. What had she done?

How could she have been so idiotic, chattering away to a cop about Markus? Karl, now—Karl was another story. She'd seen no reason not to be honest about him. Besides, she hadn't just revealed her brother's faults—she'd talked about the unjust way he'd been treated by their parents. But why hadn't she been more careful about Markus? She should have realized he might fall under suspicion, but she just didn't think . . . besides, she'd talked to him on the phone after he'd been interviewed by this same policewoman, and he'd sounded perfectly calm about the whole thing.

She shook her head as she reminded herself that Markus's calmness might not be the best way to judge the seriousness of a situation, since he was always calm now. It was impressive the way he'd come to grips with his temper; she hadn't seen him fly into a rage in years. His episodes of violence were definitely behind him.

Even as she was reassuring herself with these thoughts, her mind betrayed her, digging up a picture less than a year old of Markus punching a man in the stomach and then knocking him down. As the incident came back to her, she put her hands over her face.

She'd invited Markus and Ada to dinner for her April birthday, and they'd accepted. During the dinner, Markus had surprised and delighted her by asking if she wanted to come with him on a photo shoot. A Swiss designer had created a new collection of women's clothes. Not exactly doublets, tabards, and tunics, but outfits that, combined with multicolored leggings, suggested medieval costumes. To further evoke the Middle Ages, the models were to be photographed in the village of Gruyères in three days.

"We have permission to use the castle," Markus told her, "with access to sections that aren't usually open to the public. Of course, you might get bored; you know how tiny and touristy the village is, and there'll be lots of hanging around while the women change clothes. But the weather should be good, and there are walking trails nearby, if you get tired of watching the shooting. Why don't you come? Hene should come, too, if he wants to. I can pick you both up; I'm renting a car for the day."

She hadn't even asked her husband to join them; she was too eager to have some time alone with her godson. The day had been perfect; she'd walked, read, poured Gruyères's famous double cream into her coffee, and basked in the early spring sunshine. She'd been touched by how much time Markus had found to spend with her, explaining the planning and lighting of fashion photographs in general and these Gruyères ones in particular.

Late in the afternoon, as she sat on a bench watching Markus photograph one of the models so that she cast an enormous shadow, two men began to harass the young woman. They whistled and catcalled before adding obscene hand gestures and pelvic thrusts. Their comments in English and German were limited but included both "fuck" and "*fick*," which shed light on what they were probably saying in their own language. At first the work crew ignored them, but then one of the two walked into a shot. Speaking English, the artistic director asked them, first politely and then harshly, to stop making a disturbance. The result was more obscenity. The tourists were so drunk that reasoning with them was useless.

A local man sitting on the bench next to Bri watched all this with growing anger. Eventually he stopped muttering to himself and burst out, "I'd call the police, but we don't have any, not till summer brings more tourists. All we get are two security guards who make rounds a couple of times a day. Now that we need them, who knows where they are? *Gopferdammi*, it makes me mad."

While her companion on the bench was speaking, Markus had set down his camera and picked up another, very small one. He walked toward the two men, filming the artistic director being treated to one last lewd gesture and loud comment. Several feet away from the men, he stopped and spoke in slow, clear English. "Gentlemen, as you can see, I'm filming you. I'm also asking you, as my colleague just did, to be quiet and stop disrupting our work. If you don't, I'm going to call the police. I'm also going to show this film I'm making to the Finnish Embassy and find out who you are. Maybe someone you know back home would like to hear how you behave when you're out of town."

Oh, so they're Finns, thought Brigitte. Markus was good at recognizing languages. She hoped the two men wouldn't . . .

One of them turned away, but the other lurched forward to grab the camera. Markus sidestepped him, transferred the camera into his left hand, and hit the Finn in the stomach with his right. When the man doubled over, Markus did something—she couldn't see what— that made him fall heavily to the ground. He lay there curled on his side, vomiting loudly. Markus paid no attention; he was already focused on the other man, who'd turned back to face him. The second man held up both hands, palms out, in a gesture that clearly meant, "Not me. I don't want a sock in the gut," and said in loud English, "He's the Finn. I'm Estonian." His nationality clarified to his satisfaction, he left the clearing with as much dignity as he could muster, staggering only a little over the cobblestones.

"Aren't you going to take your friend with you?" Markus called after him, but the Estonian ignored him. In the meantime, the Finn had stopped retching and was making other noises. Brigitte sat close enough to recognize after a moment's reflection that they were snores. The man had passed out. Markus bent over him, grabbed his waistband and the back of his collar and dragged him back until he was clear of the pool of puke. With quick movements, he pulled a handkerchief out of his pocket and wiped the man's nose and mouth clean. Dropping the square of cloth next to him, Markus turned to talk to the artistic director.

Markus's intervention had happened so fast that some of the models and make-up people never realized what had happened. He hadn't even raised his voice, Brigitte reminded herself, as she pictured that very one-sided fight. Then she remembered him shifting the camera from one hand to the other, calm as a summer's day, and viciously sinking his fist into the drunk's broad middle. Not that she hadn't approved of his quick action at the time, she had to admit it. But telling herself that Markus was no longer violent: no, she couldn't do that.

25
Before

Jakob stopped in front of a run-down cottage at the end of a road on the outskirts of the village. When he got out of the car, so did Markus. Together, they helped Norbert down the path.

"Do you want your pain medicine first?" Jakob asked, as they stood just inside the front door across from a steep staircase. The entrance was so crowded with three men in it that Markus stepped into the small parlor to the left of the stairs and turned on a lamp. The room contained the kind of old-fashioned settee, armchairs, tiny tables, and knickknacks that Markus had seen in the homes of many of the aged *Verdingkinder* he'd photographed. Here the furniture was particularly worn and shabby, but the room was very neat. In fact, it resembled a stage set, with no sign that Norbert ever used it.

Norbert led Jakob into the room to the right of the stairs, where he snapped on an overhead light. Markus followed them into what he saw was a small kitchen, with a square table and three chairs on one wall and a tiny bathroom opening off the far end. Norbert answered Jakob's question at last. "No pills yet. First, we get the watch down. I want to show it to Markus." Norbert took hold of one of the sturdy kitchen chairs and dragged it away from the table. "We'll need this to fetch the watch." He glanced up at Jakob, all six feet six of him, and giggled. "Even you'll need a chair to reach the back of my wardrobe, Köbi."

"I'll get it," said Markus, trying not to roll his eyes at the idea of these two old geezers, one of them dying, clambering up onto the furniture. He seized the chair, carried it up the alarmingly narrow and badly lit staircase and stepped into the bedroom that had to be Norbert's, since the other was clearly a woman's room. Or had been. He thought of the old man living with his mother in this tiny house, the two of them looking after each other until her death, and Norbert then keeping her room, with its droopy lace bedspread and flowery curtains, just as it had been. Perhaps there should have been something morbid about the picture, ludicrous even, but Markus could only find it sad. Unbidden, his own mother's face flashed through his mind. Why in God's name hadn't he invited her to the opening of the *Verdingkinder* exhibition, he found himself thinking? What exactly was he punishing her for?

Jakob appeared at the head of the stairway, Norbert lying across the big man's arms like a sleepy child; he was nattering away about someone named Marie. Jakob set Norbert on his feet and turned toward Markus, who stood by the wardrobe with his chair. "So, tell Markus what needs doing," Jakob said, "and then I'll get you to bed."

The little man opened the double doors of the old wooden wardrobe and, ignoring his meagre collection of shirts, trousers, underclothes, and socks, pointed to the large top shelf. "The watch is up there," he said, "in a box."

Markus positioned the chair, climbed onto it, and saw two folded wool blankets—army surplus, from their color—and a wooden dump truck painted in bright colors. Behind the truck, he could see a small chocolate box and, all the way at the back of the shelf, what looked like a walking stick. He passed the chocolate box to Norbert, who said, "That's it, that's it." Markus reached back into the wardrobe for the stick, thinking Norbert could use it for getting around. He lifted it over the blankets and stepped off the chair, still holding it horizontally across his chest. Jakob had stretched a hand out to steady him as he climbed down, and when his eyes fell on the stick he froze. His hand rose instead to his cheek, and he leaned back against the wall.

It was an expensive-looking walking stick made of dark wood, as thick as a child's wrist at one end and tapering slightly to a metal tip at the other. It had a large brass knob incised with a pattern and, below that, a kind of collar, also brass, engraved with delicate writing. Norbert looked up from the watch in the chocolate box, saw the cane—and gaped at it.

"I forgot," he whispered. "I forgot, Köbi. Don't look." Norbert himself covered his eyes with his free hand and turned as if to show Jakob how.

Markus shifted the stick to an upright position and was about to grab the knob when Jakob cried, "No. Don't touch anything. Just set it down on the floor." At this, Norbert began to sob, even as he gasped out, "I forgot it was there. I never wanted you to see it again. But I'm stupid—I'm so stupid."

Markus walked to the other side of Norbert's single bed and laid the cane on the bare floor there. What the fuck was going on? He frowned at Jakob, who said, "Sorry I yelled at you. I swear I'll tell you everything on the way home." As he spoke he led the crying Norbert to the bed, and they sat down on the edge, while Markus went to prop one shoulder against the wardrobe; he crossed his arms and watched the two old men curiously.

"How long have you had the stick?" asked Jakob. His voice was gentle, his arm around Norbert's shoulders.

Norbert swallowed a sob and stuttered, "Always; I found it after he threw it away."

"It's very important, you know—more important than the watch. I wish you'd given it to me a long time ago."

Norbert, his head hanging almost to his knees, tears still falling, mumbled. "I'm sorry. I'm so sorry. I hid it, and then I forgot."

"I'm going to take it now. Is that all right with you?"

The little man raised his head, and Markus saw his swollen face.

"Of course you should take it. I don't even want to look at it. I don't want the watch, I don't want the stick, I don't want the money. I just don't want you to hate me again, Köbi."

Markus straightened suddenly as Norbert's words replayed: "I don't want the money." What money? He thought again about whatever "deal" his father'd had with Norbert. Did this stuff—watch, stick, and money, wherever *that* was—all have to do with the deal?

Jakob reached into his pocket, pulled out a pack of tissues, and handed it to Norbert. "Clean your face now, and we'll get you ready for bed. Nothing between you and me has changed, I promise."

Fumbling with the plastic, Norbert took a couple of tissues out of the pack, blew his nose, and began to wipe his eyes. "Can I show Markus the watch before I go to bed?" he pleaded, his voice muffled.

"Do it quickly, then," Jakob said. "We want to leave soon. Tell me, is there any newspaper in the house?"

"By the woodstove in the kitchen," Norbert answered without curiosity. "Marie keeps it there for starting the fire."

Jakob went downstairs. Norbert looked up from his seat on the bed and patted the empty place at his side with one hand as he picked up the box with the other. "Come see your grandfather's watch," he said, as if offering Markus a treat.

Aha, thought Markus, *he's remembered that I'm Karli's son and not Köbi's.* He didn't particularly care about seeing an old watch, but he sat next to Norbert, who pulled the lid off the blue-and-white cardboard box and lifted out something wrapped in an old dishcloth. He handed it to Markus, as though allowing him to do the honors. Markus opened the bundle to find a large, traditional-looking man's watch with a brown leather band. Bending over it, Markus saw it was a Breguet. He turned it over and read, "Matthias Gurtner 1908."

Norbert was watching him eagerly, so Markus said, "Very handsome," adding, "It's nice of you to give it back." He smiled at the old man, who didn't smile back, only nodded and said, "I have to." Markus heard Jakob on the stairs before he saw him: he was carrying a small stack of newspaper and wearing his winter gloves. He spread sheets of paper out on the bed, picked the cane up from the floor, and wrapped it carefully in the paper, making sure the knob was well covered. Then he took off his gloves and handed them to Markus. Fishing his car key out of his pocket, he said, "Would you mind taking this down to the car and putting it in the trunk while I help Norbert? Wear my gloves, in case the paper slips off."

"No problem." Markus quickly re-swaddled the Breguet in its dishcloth and thrust it back into the box, which he handed to Norbert, stood up, took the gloves, and put them on. Norbert giggled. Markus's hands swam in Jakob's gloves: over an inch of empty leather hung off each of Markus's fingers. He wiggled them playfully at the little man, then picked up the newspaper-swathed cane and brought it down to Jakob's car. By the light in the trunk, he unwrapped it and saw that the metal collar under the decorative knob was engraved with a now-familiar name: Matthias Gurtner. Watch and stick, they were part of his father's story and, somewhere along the way, there was also money. Finally, Jakob was going to explain what the hell this was all about, and then, maybe, for the first time in his life, he was going to know something important about his father that the old man didn't know he knew.

Markus rewrapped the cane, slammed the trunk door, and took off the enormous gloves. As he headed back into Norbert's cottage, hugging himself against the cold, he felt excited. Whatever Jakob told him, it would give him the upper hand. What was he going to do with that advantage over his father?

26

t was almost six! As soon as Brigitte Rieder's door closed behind her, Giuliana dialed Ueli's cell. She didn't know what was waiting for her back at the office, but she felt sure that she was going to have to work past dinnertime. She hated when she was forced to let Ueli know so late in the day that she couldn't make it home, but he always coped. At least the last time was over a month ago, she reminded herself.

"What's up, love?" Ueli sounded cheerful. That probably wouldn't last long.

"I'm sorry to screw up your evening, but I have to work late, and I don't know when I'll make it home. Will you be okay?"

"Dinner won't be a problem," Ueli answered, "but tonight is the class meeting on bullying at seven-thirty—parents and kids. Think you can make that?"

"Shit!" She'd forgotten.

"Lukas and I will go, and you can try to get there, even if you have to come late."

"It's in his classroom, right?" She'd read the notice two evenings ago, and now she couldn't remember a thing.

"Yep. Isabelle already asked me if she could spend the evening with Quentin, and I said yes, as long as she's home by nine-forty-five. Lukas and I will grab a kebab and go on to school. If you don't make it, we'll see you at home."

"That's great, Ueli. I'm really sorry. It's . . ."

"I know. No big deal. Bye."

"Bye!" She wanted to do more than bleat about being sorry, but . . . her work took precedence over his; that was how they made their family life function. She sighed. If she could manage to get to sleep at a decent hour on Saturday night, she could get up early on Sunday, take Lukas out for breakfast, and keep him busy somewhere so that Ueli could sleep in. Isabelle would probably do the same: the two of them could snooze away in perfect silence until noon. Maybe she could make it work.

When she got back to the little case room on the homicide corridor, Erwin wasn't in. She was about to phone his mobile when she saw a message on her desk in Erwin's writing: "Philipp Gurtner," followed by a phone number. She shook her head over Erwin's carelessness, wondering how long ago the boy had called and why Erwin hadn't told him to call her mobile. Sitting down at her desk, she got out her phone and dialed.

"This is Fippu," she heard.

"Hello, this is Giuliana Linder. You called me. What's up?"

"Oh, hello. I've got two things to tell you. One is that Polo's back. Less than two hours ago he showed up at our door barking. He's not hungry, and his coat's not ratty. His leash is on, but it's clean—doesn't look like he's had to drag it around. Someone must have been looking after him. I guess when they saw one of my flyers with our address, they brought him back."

Giuliana grabbed a slip of paper from the box on her desk and made a note. "Were you home when he got there? What time was it?"

"Yeah, I was here; it was about four-thirty. I don't think whoever returned him rang the bell. I mean, I heard the barking right away, but no bell. It's great Polo's home, but I think it's weird someone dropped him off like that. I looked up and down the street right away, but I didn't see anyone. You said to tell you."

"Yes, thanks. And I agree; that *was* odd behavior. I'm glad you've got your dog back, though." She waited, but Philipp said nothing. "You said there were two things."

"Yeah, well. This . . . this isn't something I want to tell you. But . . . my mother said if I didn't, she would. God, I can't believe I said anything to her. Now you're going to . . . going to think . . . even though Markus would never . . ." Philipp stopped.

After a moment, Giuliana said, "It's clear you're upset. Why don't you tell me the facts first, and then you can explain why you didn't want me to know."

Still Philipp was silent. Then it came out. "It's about Markus. My brother. Normally we talk on the phone once a month. Maybe more often. Sometimes I call him, sometimes he calls me. Or we text. He sends me photos he's taken. So, like . . . it's perfectly normal for him to call. About three weeks ago, we were talking about . . . a lot of different stuff. He asked me how Paps was. Then he wanted to know which days Paps walked Polo. Where they went, what time. He said . . . he said he wanted to discuss something with Paps, and it would be easier to pretend to run into him while he was out with the dog than make an appointment, because, well, Paps might not show up for that. So, I told him. By now you must have figured out that Paps . . . he . . . um . . . he treated Markus like shit! Even my mother doesn't trust Märku because . . . well, years ago he did some stuff that . . . but I think he's brilliant."

The boy's voice rose on the last, emphatic word. Giuliana kept calm, despite all the bells and whistles going off in her head. The kid felt bad enough about betraying his half-brother to the police; no need to grind his nose in it. Her tone was flat as she said, "Thanks for letting us know that, Philipp. As for Polo, I think we should check for fibers in his fur and fingerprints on the collar and leash. I'm going to ask someone to drop by your house during the next hour to pick up the dog, and you can go along if you want, even though we already have your prints. It won't take more than an hour—can you do that?"

"Sure." He sounded calmer, now that no one was talking about

Markus. "I guess I should put gloves on to unbuckle the collar, huh? I'll put it and the leash someplace safe."

"Perfect. Put them in a paper bag; paper's better than plastic for preserving DNA traces, just in case there are any. And don't brush the dog—we need anything that's stuck to his fur. "

"Listen," he said, "you have to understand that Markus would never hurt our father."

"I hear you," she said, which didn't mean the same as "I believe you." When she remembered those light-blue, husky-dog eyes staring into hers, she thought Markus was capable of . . . a great deal.

"Please," the boy added, his voice sharp and shaky at once.

That was all he said, and Giuliana ignored his plea. "I'll call someone to pick you and Polo up. Thanks again. Bye."

She phoned Erwin. Before she could share Philipp's news, Erwin was bellowing in her ear. "We broke Markus Gurtner's alibi. A shop near his apartment has a CCTV camera mounted to watch the street front, and it covers three Mobility parking slots. Markus was filmed on the afternoon before his father died getting into a rental car. He lied!"

The solution to the case was starting to take shape at last. Giuliana found herself grinning as she said, "Then you'll be even happier to hear that Markus knew exactly where and when to find his father along the Aare. He phoned and asked his brother Philipp for his father's dog-walking schedule three weeks before the killing. Philipp just told me, very much against his will. His mother made him."

"*Heilandsack!*" said Erwin, and Giuliana snorted, wondering from what depths of Erwin's brain that old-fashioned exclamation had emerged. "We'll go get Markus right now," he added, "and it'll be my turn to have a go at the fucker." Now that sounded like the Erwin she knew.

"Not so fast," she said.

"What? You're not still worried about his career or something, are you?"

"Nope. I just don't want you to tackle him until I tell you about a complication. This man Norbert Wittwer from Heidmatt, the one

Gurtner was sending money to. I think maybe *he* made the phone call from the Dählhölzli payphone." She told him about Frau Professor Michel and the Emmentaler dialect. "Markus may be a murderer, but he grew up in the city, and that's how he speaks. He didn't make that call. Someone from Heidmatt was with him on the Aare, and I think it must have been this old friend—or maybe enemy—of his father's."

"Where are you?" she went on. "I think we should talk. I've sent you a report . . ." When Erwin didn't break in to assure her he'd read every word of it, she added, "Wittwer was born with fetal alcohol syndrome, has an IQ of around eighty, and on top of that is an alcoholic with liver cancer. I don't see him planning a confrontation with Gurtner, but I believe he was involved in some way."

Giuliana stood now at the case room's one window, which overlooked an apartment house for seniors across the street. It was already dark, but by the light in the building's lobby, she watched a woman in a beige winter hat and knee-length brown coat push a walker out the glass doors. She inched her way to the nearby bus stop. Giuliana swore to herself that when she turned seventy-five she'd buy herself a red winter coat. Down with brown!

"I'm finishing up a chat with the *Fahnder* working on Markus's phone records," Erwin told her. "Are you in the case room? I'll be there in about fifteen minutes."

"Wait, don't hang up. Tell them to check if Markus made calls to Heidmatt or received any. This could be something cooked up by both men," Giuliana said. She watched as, across the street, the no. 20 bus paused and started up again. When it was gone, she saw that the elderly woman hadn't made it; she was still creeping forward. Around her, the passengers disgorged by the bus spread out and hurried away in all directions, braced against the cold.

"Will do," said Erwin and was gone.

Giuliana went back to her desk. She arranged to have Philipp and his dog, together with the leash and collar, picked up for testing and then tried to settle down to report on what she'd learned from Brigitte and Philipp. But she was too restless to concentrate. It troubled her to be so ignorant about Wittwer: she wanted to know more about him and his state of health before questioning him. Maybe she could fetch him from Heidmatt. Before she picked him up, she'd try to find someone in the village who'd known Wittwer and Gurtner as children to give her more insight into why one had supported the other for almost fifty years. Was a friendship based on Norbert's unquestioning loyalty and obedience enough of a reason?

Her restlessness pushed her to the window once more, this time to study the mesmerizing blotches of light cast by the streetlamps. There were footsteps in the hall, and she turned to greet Erwin. Instead, the door was flung open, and Toni Rossel launched himself into the room. His entrance was so abrupt and his expression so triumphant, if only for the second before he noticed she was alone, that she thought of Monty Python. "Nobody expects the Spanish Inquisition," she said in English, even as she wondered why she was so foolishly making fun of him.

"What?" Toni exclaimed. "What are you talking about?" He dismissed her joke with a sweep of his hand. "Where's Erwin? I thought . . ." She knew what he'd thought: he'd expected to find them discussing something they didn't want to share with him—which, to be fair, was more or less what they'd just done on the phone.

"Erwin's on his way." She concentrated on removing any emotion from her voice. "I assume you got my report on Norbert Wittwer, the man Gurtner was paying. Since then I've learned more about the emergency call, and I've interviewed Gurtner's younger sister, who gave me some excellent background. I was about to write it up." *Please hurry, Erwin*, she thought. She wasn't sure she'd be able to control her temper with Toni after such a long day.

Toni was moving toward her and, not for the first time, she wished she were taller than five foot six. She mustn't let him back her up to the window and lean over her. "What's going on with the middle son, Markus?" he asked.

She could pretend she didn't know, which might keep him from ordering Markus brought into the station before she'd had a chance to talk to Norbert. But she didn't want to play the clueless woman, even to placate Toni.

"Markus asked his half-brother Philipp for their father's dog-walking schedule a few weeks before the attack. Plus, his claim to have been at home all afternoon was false. He was caught on CCTV getting into a Mobility car near his home. I believe there may have been contact between him and a childhood friend of Gurtner's. We're going to confirm that before we pick him up for interrogation."

"We? You mean you and Erwin have already decided. When were you planning to bring me into the picture?" Toni came a step closer, frowning.

"Toni, if you want to hear anything else from me, you need to sit down." From her place by the window, Giuliana waved toward Erwin's chair like a waiter showing a guest to his seat. To her surprise, Toni sat. She remained standing where she was, and the two of them faced each other across six feet of space. "Thank you," said Giuliana, managing a smile, and told him why she thought Markus and Norbert might be working together. "Norbert isn't officially intellectually disabled," she concluded, "but it's a close thing, according to his social worker. If we talk to him first, he'll probably give us everything we need. Then we can pick Markus up and confront him with what we know. It makes no sense to grab the man too soon and let him hire a lawyer before we have the facts. So, tomorrow we'll . . ."

"No! We need to pick Markus up *now*. Maybe this retard you've dug up was with him on the river, but it's the son who's our killer. Imagine how idiotic we'd look if we gave him time to hide with his aunt in that bloody castle, and we had to drag him out of it with TV cameras rolling. Once the press found out I lost him by not acting fast enough, the shit'd hit the fan. I'd be a joke."

Giuliana noticed the shift from "we the police" to "I, Toni Rossel." Bad press had always been Toni's nightmare. Even when she'd first known him, years before, he'd worried about the public humiliation of losing a case. He had a point about the danger of Markus disappearing before they could get at him. From what she'd seen of Gurtner's son, though, she couldn't imagine him abandoning his painstakingly salvaged life and career to go underground. It wasn't as if she and Erwin were refusing to bring him in at all. Maybe they could find a compromise.

"What about . . . ?" she began. Toni interrupted her.

"Remember what I said about you trying to block my decisions? Remember what I told you I'd do? I guess you refuse to believe me." His smile was rueful; he looked like a father just before he says, "This is going to hurt me more than it hurts you." She stared at him, feeling a roaring in her ears.

Erwin chose that moment to blunder through the half-open door. He stopped, looked at Toni and Giuliana, and closed the door behind him. Then he went over to Giuliana's desk, set down his laptop and some loose-leaf binders, and leaned back, hands on hips. Ostentatiously he let his head swivel back and forth between them, examining their faces, and said, "Well, at least you two have the sense to keep the length of the room between you, so you don't kill each other. Although I'm afraid a fight would be pretty one-sided. Did you know Giuliana is an excellent markswoman, Toni? She's won prizes for unarmed combat, too. She'd have you pinned in . . ."

Toni interrupted in a prosecutor's carrying voice. "Funny you should say that, Erwin. I was just reminding Julie here of a time *I* pinned her. That was to a sofa, and she didn't resist at all. In fact, if all the noise she made was anything to go by, she quite enjoyed herself."

Giuliana's face burned. She stood motionless by the window, glad her desk lamp was on the other side of the room, leaving her in shadow. She'd known this would happen sooner or later, and at least it was Erwin Toni had started with.

Erwin didn't even glance at her. "My God, Toni," he drawled. "Are you still trotting out that old chestnut? Anyone would think you hadn't had a fuck since—when did Giuliana do her little stint as a prosecutor? In the last millennium? Ho-hum." He faked a huge yawn. "Let's talk about the case, huh? Has Giuliana had a chance to fill you in on our plans?"

At some point during Erwin's remark, Toni's gaping mouth had snapped shut to form a thin line in his angry face. Giuliana wasn't sure she'd ever felt more grateful in her life. In a voice whose calmness amazed her, she said, "Glad you're here, Erwin. I was just catching Toni up on what we've learned about Markus Gurtner and Wittwer. I told him you and I were in favor of waiting to bring Markus in until we'd questioned Norbert. He'd like to get both men now, which I consider premature."

Erwin nodded at her. "After you told me to check for calls to and from Heidmatt, I found three: one from Markus to a Heidi Stettler, and two *for* Markus from an inn called The Lion. I think that gives us more than enough cause to pick Markus up today and have a talk with him. As for Norbert, I'd like you," he glanced at Giuliana, "to bring him in for a chat tomorrow. See if he needs a guardian to be with him when we interview him."

"He doesn't," Giuliana reminded herself to check for the email she'd requested confirming Norbert's independent status. "Are you going to talk to Markus tonight?" she asked Erwin. "I'd like to . . ."

"Absolutely not," Toni broke in. "Erwin picks Markus up and sticks him in a cell, and I interview him tomorrow morning. I don't want either of you there—I'll use Julie's boyfriend. The pretty *Tschingg.* Give me his name and number, Julie."

Giuliana opened her mouth to say . . . God, she didn't even know where to begin. Then she saw Erwin raise his eyes to the ceiling and give a tiny shrug. He was right; there was no point. She nodded at him before moving to her desk to write Renzo's number on a slip of paper. As she wrote, she was already thinking through her next steps. There was nothing she could do about Toni interviewing Markus without her or Erwin, but at least Renzo would be there. Nothing to be done, either, about Markus being picked up too soon, nor about Toni letting him sit in a cell all night before talking to him. The fool must assume a night in jail would scare Markus into a confession; she was sure it would give him time to come up with a strategy instead. For now, all she could do was focus on Norbert Wittwer.

Giuliana handed over Renzo's number, and Erwin pushed himself away from her desk and asked Toni, "You coming along to pick up Markus? Otherwise, I suggest you focus on getting search warrants. I need to move now if I want to find the guy at home." He stood by the door, which he'd opened wide, making it clear Toni was expected to leave with him. Giuliana stopped hovering by her desk, sat down, pulled her laptop toward her, and opened it. She wasn't comfortable turning her back on Toni, but Erwin was there, thank God.

"We're not done," Toni said to her as he stalked out. She ignored him, except for one hand lifted in a sketchy wave. When the sound of feet in the hall was gone, she locked herself into the case room, pushed back her laptop, crossed her arms on the desk, and rested her cheek on her forearm. She felt exhausted; her whole body ached.

How long had Erwin known some version of the story about her and Toni? She couldn't get over what he'd said. On the one hand, he'd caused Toni's dramatic insult to flop. On the other hand, he already knew the very thing Toni was threatening to reveal. So, who else knew? At that moment, she felt too tired to sort that out.

And what about Toni calling Renzo her boyfriend? No big deal in front of Erwin, but if he'd started spreading that rumor . . . ? Somehow, she'd have to deal with that. She'd be damned if she'd let him spoil her job for her, though. When all this was over, she'd sit down with her boss, Rolf, and see what he recommended she do to make sure that she never had to work with Toni again. Until then, she'd try to stay out of his way.

She couldn't keep other people out of his way, though. *Get a good lawyer, Markus—you'll need the protection.* She was almost sure Markus had killed his father, but there were years of provocation leading up to whatever had happened on the river. A skilled defense attorney like her father or brother would help Markus shape his story. His lawyer would also be quick to point out that the police had no evidence linking Markus to the riverbank or his father's body. If only he had a big bruise on his nose or cheekbone or, even better, a pull-over in the same blue as that thread caught in his father's watchband.

Well, maybe he did have something blue; the search would find it, if he hadn't thrown it away.

With that distinctive, bright blue thread in her mind, Giuliana called up a pair of gloves in a similar color. Where had she seen them? Knitted blue gloves, one overlapping the other, resting on a tall, narrow chest of drawers in . . . Markus's foyer. That's where they were. She sat up and, seizing her phone, sent Erwin a text. Maybe she was wrong, but that blue was uncommon.

Satisfied, she pulled her laptop back toward her and found the email she'd requested about Norbert's status: disabled, yes, but not a ward of the state. It had been a long time since lunch, and she was very hungry, but she'd spend another hour finding out as much as she could about Norbert and then go home, eat, and get a decent amount of sleep, so she'd be alert to talk with the old man the following day.

Tapping at her keyboard, she began by searching for the number of Heidmatt's village council president. She'd start with whoever ran the village, at least on paper, and work her way down. Sooner or later, someone would tell her more about Norbert.

27

Walking into her apartment just before eight, Giuliana stripped off her coat, which was beaded with moisture from the sleet, hung it on the hall coat rack, and opened her umbrella to dry in the bathtub. As she changed into indoor shoes, she noticed the silence. Cold, hungry, and very tired, it took her a moment to remember that Ueli and Lukas were at the meeting on bullying, and Isabelle was with Quentin. She wished she was better acquainted with her daughter's . . . was he now her boyfriend? She'd had five-minute chats with him when he came by with Isabelle and when she happened to see him in town, but that wasn't much to go on. Unfortunately, Isabelle had so far refused all requests to bring him to dinner.

It was a rare luxury to have the place to herself. She changed into jeans and a pullover, filled a plate with leftover chunks of stewed lamb from one past dinner and roasted cauliflower from another, set it in the microwave, and, while it was heating, ran a glass of tap water and sliced bread from a bakery loaf. When the food was ready, she ate it at the kitchen table, glancing over the morning's newspaper. Her meal done, she finished an article about how hard it was for refugees in Switzerland to find jobs, or even apprenticeships, and glanced at her watch.

Just past nine. Too late by Swiss custom to phone anyone but a close friend, but she still hadn't reached the head of the Heidmatt council. Fetching her phone from her purse, she filled the kettle as she dialed Stefanie Egli's number.

"Egli." The man sounded annoyed. In the background, an overexcited TV voice was narrating soccer.

"Good evening, Herr Egli. Sorry to bother you so late, but my name is Linder and I need to speak to the Frau Egli who heads the village council. Do I have the right . . . ?"

"She just got the kids to bed. Can't your business wait until tomorrow?"

"For God's sake, Fred," hissed a woman. "Just give me the phone."

There was some rustling, the TV noise faded away, and Stefanie Egli said, "I apologize for that. What can I do for you?"

Giuliana wedged the phone between ear and shoulder as she got out a peppermint tea bag and a white mug. "No problem. *I* apologize for phoning you at home so late. My name is Linder, and I'm from the cantonal police in Bern. I'd like to talk to a villager of yours tomorrow, Norbert Wittwer. I know he's very ill, so before I show up at his door to bring him to the Bern police station, I wanted to ask if you know something about his state of health. Could he travel with me in the car to Bern, do you think, or do we need an ambulance? For that matter, perhaps he can't leave his house."

"Well, he manages to leave his house almost every night to walk over to the *Beiz* and have a drink," the woman said, "so unless he just had a relapse, he ought to be able to make it to Bern in a car." Giuliana smiled at her caustic tone, which softened when she added, "Actually, we have a roster of local people who drive him to the hospital in Langnau for his treatments, and he's fine with that. So, I think all should be well."

The kettle boiled, and Giuliana poured water over the teabag and stood over the mug watching the tea steep.

Frau Egli continued. "You can't let him know you're coming tomorrow, since he doesn't have a phone. If you tell me when you'll be here, I'll call the neighbor who looks after him. She can make sure he's ready in time."

"That would be very kind of you. And it brings me to the next thing on my mind." Giuliana had considered what she should reveal about the investigation and decided that offering the woman some tidbits would encourage her cooperation. "I'm looking into the death of a man who used to live in Heidmatt, Johann Gurtner. Herr Wittwer and he were close as boys, and . . ."

"Of course," Egli said. "The council just decided to send flowers to Herr Gurtner's sister; I'll be doing that tomorrow. How old was he, do you know?"

"Seventy-two. He went to your village school until he was thirteen. Can you think of anyone who might have been there with him? I know Herr Wittwer was, but I'd be interested to talk to anyone else around that age who was in the same class." Giuliana spooned out her teabag, dropped it into the compost container on the counter, stirred the tea, and took a cautious sip, inhaling the scented steam.

"Well, that's easy," Egli said. "My uncle was in Norbert's class, along with Herr Gurtner. I've heard him tell stories about the trouble he and his friends got into as kids, and Gurtner is in some of those tales. Not that they were friends," she added, "but they were in school together for six years. Karli, they called Gurtner then. And my uncle's Arnold Arm; everyone calls him Noldi. He farms across the Emme, over toward Niederbühl."

That meant nothing to Giuliana, but her GPS could find it. She took a larger mouthful of tea, outlining the day in her head. "That's perfect, Frau Egli. Do you think if I went by to talk to him tomorrow morning at eight-thirty, it would be too early for him?"

The president of the village council laughed. "That man has been getting up before five to milk cows since he could balance his bottom on a milking stool. I'll call him right now and let him know you're coming. I'll call Norbert's neighbor, Marie Iseli, too, and tell her you're stopping by to pick the old man up tomorrow. When will that be, do you think?"

"Let's say around ten-thirty. That gives me plenty of time to talk to your uncle. I really appreciate this. Could you give me addresses and phone numbers for Herr Arm and Frau Iseli? And your cell phone number, too?"

There was a flurry of contact swapping. Plans made, Giuliana had just settled down on the living room sofa, tea mug in hand and feet on the coffee table, when she heard a key in the lock and Lukas's excited voice. It was past his bedtime and might still be a long time before he fell asleep. Sighing, she got up and went to greet him and Ueli.

Lukas had already disappeared into the bathroom, and Ueli was hanging up his wet jacket. He turned to give Giuliana a kiss and said softly, "It was all pretty hard to take. The defensiveness of some of the parents was—well, shocking. They weren't willing to admit their kids were at fault in any way, even though none of them could come up with a single thing Salomé had ever done to hurt anyone. Except for one truly nasty girl, who started to make stuff up. Salomé and her mother weren't there, thank God. This little liar—"

Ueli broke off as Lukas emerged from the bathroom. "I was just telling Mam about the girl who said Salomé tried to push her downstairs." He moved toward the kitchen as he spoke, and the other two followed and sat at the table.

"Yeah," agreed Lukas. "Sandra lied in front of everyone, and her best friends wouldn't back her up when Frau Tanner asked if it was true. Frau Tanner accused her of 'being mistaken'"—Lukas rolled his eyes—"so her parents grabbed her arm and left."

"Things improved after that." Ueli's head was in the fridge; he turned toward the counter with a quart of milk in one hand and a jar of his mother's homemade elderberry jelly in the other. Giuliana raised her eyebrows at him, questioning, and he said, "Lukas and I made a deal. He goes right to bed, but only after a cup of hot chocolate and a jelly-bread."

Sitting across from her son, Giuliana watched her husband get a mug out of the cabinet and heat milk in it. Giuliana caught Lukas's eye. "You've been making drinks and sandwiches for yourself since you were seven. What's with this sudden helplessness?"

Lukas looked smug. "My fault," Ueli said. "Part of our deal is me waiting on him."

Giuliana fetched her mint tea from the living room and came back to see Lukas biting into a thick slice of brown bread smeared with butter and jewel-bright jelly. She sat back down and asked her two men impartially, "So, what solution came of all this?"

The microwave beeped, and Ueli took out the mug as he answered. "What would you say, Lukas?" He got the chocolate powder out of the cabinet and added it to the hot milk.

Swallowing a mouthful of bread first, Lukas answered, "Tomorrow Salomé will be back in class, and we're all going to look at a film about bullying, and then the kids who've called her Salami and said other mean things are going to apologize. I don't mind doing that," he added, and Giuliana, relieved, met Ueli's eyes. He smiled and nodded at her before putting the mug and a spoon down in front of his son. Lukas began stirring his chocolate vigorously.

"Lukas and I agreed on the way home that no one expects him to become Salomé's best friend,"—this with a look at Lukas, who grimaced—"but that he should do whatever he can in a normal way to be kind to her and, at the very least, call her by her real name. Frau Tanner will also start punishing anyone she hears or sees picking on the girl. The last person to speak at the meeting was the head of school, and she told all the kids and parents that Frau Tanner had her full support and that she would back any punishment, including suspension, in response to further bullying. And so would the school board. Impressive, huh? Frau Tanner came to that meeting prepared."

"Very impressive." Giuliana looked around the warm, brightly lit kitchen with its framed prints of flowers on the walls and thought about how lucky Lukas—and by extension she and Ueli—were. Lukas enjoyed going to school every day, and he and Niko, his best friend since kindergarten, were solidly integrated into the class. Imagine if she had to send Lukas off each morning knowing she was delivering him to be picked on and ostracized. She'd be incapacitated by worry, helpless to fix the situation, and gnawed to pieces by hate for the other children and their parents. Thank God she wasn't Salomé's mother. How had the poor woman been coping?

She and Ueli sat together, watching Lukas slurp down his not-very-hot chocolate milk and chew his last bit of sticky bread. Ueli's hand lay on the table, and she covered it with her own, full of an almost guilty gratitude for her own family's security. Ueli turned to look at her, and she saw the contentment in his eyes. She smiled at him. Then she heard Toni's ugly words to Erwin in her head, and her eyes dropped to her lap. How had she allowed things to come to the point where both Renzo and Erwin knew something intimate about her that Ueli didn't? Or did the whole police corps know? Oh God.

She pulled herself together. "So, that's Vati's part of the deal done," she said to her son. He'd finished his drink and was scraping some streaks of wet cocoa powder out of his mug with his finger and sucking on it. "Now comes the instant bedtime part. Call me when you're in bed, and I'll come in to say goodnight."

"Okay," the boy said, getting up and turning away from the table. Then he turned back and, with a wry smile that he shared between his parents, picked up his cup and plate with extra care and carried them to the sink, where he rinsed them and slotted them into the dishwasher. Just as exaggeratedly, his parents broke into gentle applause, and he grinned, stuck his tongue out, and scampered off to the bathroom.

"I was proud of him at this meeting," Ueli said to her softly. "He has all the right instincts, even if he has taken part in this Salomé-bashing. I don't think he'll do it again. Not that we can expect him to be the class's white knight, but he might even do the girl a kindness. We'll see."

Giuliana stood up, went around the table, and leaned over to give Ueli a kiss on the top of his head. "Thanks for going to the meeting," she said. "I'm sorry I wasn't there."

"Don't feel bad; I know you can't help it. Hmm. Maybe I'll end up doing some kind of article about this business," he said. She watched his expression grow distant. "With disguised names and places, of course. I'll have to think about who I can sell it to."

Giuliana was reading a sleepy Lukas one single page of his current bedtime book when she heard her phone ping from the kitchen. The text turned out to be from Stefanie Egli: "My uncle is expecting you around eight-thirty, and Norbert's neighbor will have him ready at ten-thirty. Why not come by my office before you pick Norbert up, in case you have follow-up questions." Giuliana confirmed the plan. She found Ueli at his desk lost in work, so she fetched her laptop and settled back in the kitchen to review that day's reports on alibis and door-to-door inquiries—with one eye on the clock and one ear on the door. Isabelle was due back from her evening with Quentin at nine-forty-five.

At nine-fifty-two by the oven clock, she heard the door open and went to stand outside the kitchen. "Hello," she said to her daughter, who was taking off her boots. She gave her mother a quick smile and looked away again, but in that one peek, Giuliana had seen a blaze of joy on her daughter's face. Oh, God, she's really in love with him, Giuliana thought, and felt her stomach clench with worry. *Be happy for her,* she chided herself, but all she could contemplate at that moment was how painful love could be when you were sixteen.

"Good evening?" she asked.

"Yeah." Isabelle's brusque tone couldn't hide her delight.

"I'm glad," said Giuliana. A hundred questions and bits of advice filled her head, along with several dire warnings. But she bit them all back.

"Tea?" she asked.

"Thanks, Mam, but I'm going to bed." Instead of offering the usual goodnight peck on the cheek, Isabelle put both arms around her mother, hugged her tight, and strode off to her room, closing the door quietly behind her. Giuliana was staring after her, eyebrows raised, when her phone pinged again. Erwin this time. "M delivered and settled in cell, ready for T and R tomorrow. Poor R."

Poor Renzo indeed, having to deal with Toni's games the following morning during Markus's interview. Then she froze. Renzo reported to *her* on this case, and she'd forgotten to tell him about the prosecutor's decision to pull him into the interrogation. They hadn't even exchanged a text since then. She glanced at her watch: after ten. Could she risk it? Two nights in a row? Cringing at the memory of Renzo's hurry to get through the previous call, she decided to send a text: "Phone me if you can. I'll wait five minutes and then write if I don't hear from you. It's about Toni." Two minutes later, her phone rang.

"Fränzi's out with a girlfriend, so I have plenty of time to talk. Tell me about Toni. And while we're at it, how'd it go with the younger Gurtner sister?"

Giuliana could hear the warmth in Renzo's voice, and she smiled in response, even if he couldn't see it. "Toni first, before the rest of it. Did you see Erwin's report about Markus's alibi being broken and his worming Gurtner's schedule out of his half-brother?" She heard his "Uh-huh," and went on. "Markus also got some phone calls from Heidmatt, we think from Norbert Wittwer. The point is, Markus is in custody now, and Toni's planning to interrogate him tomorrow morning with *you*. I'm really sorry I didn't let you know sooner."

"It's fine. I got a call from Erwin. He told me all about it. Toni didn't get in touch or send me any prep, but I guess he figures he'll see me at the eight o'clock meeting tomorrow."

Giuliana stared at a drop of chocolate milk on the kitchen table while she thought about whether to warn Renzo that Toni might be keeping him in the dark because he was hoping to make a fool of him during the interrogation. She decided against it. There was no reason to turn Renzo more against the man than she already had at breakfast that morning. And she didn't *know* why Toni had decided to bring Renzo in. But he did need more information before he sat down across from Markus. "I'd better sum up what I found out from the dialect expert and Markus's aunt, Brigitte Rieder. You need to know more about Markus—and about Wittwer." With that, she settled back as comfortably as she could in the kitchen chair and told Renzo everything she'd learned that afternoon and about her plans to meet with Arnold Arm and to interview Norbert the next morning.

"Sounds useful," Renzo said. "I'm about to read your original report on Markus, the one you wrote right after you interviewed him at home."

"I found him pretty volatile, so be prepared. And good luck with Toni, too. Don't let him throw you off balance. He can be—manipulative."

After they disconnected, she tried not to imagine what Toni might say about her to Renzo. It doesn't matter, she kept telling herself, but it was hard not to conjure up the worst. She found herself fighting hot waves of shame, even though she knew she had done absolutely nothing to be ashamed of. What was shameful about consensual sex between two unmarried adults? It was the way Toni used the fact of their having had sex to put her down to other people. The more she thought about that, the angrier she got, until she found herself pacing back and forth in the kitchen. When this case was over, she swore to herself, she'd talk to a lawyer about the consequences of going after him. This vow made her feel better, and she put in another half hour reading reports. Then, reminding herself that she was due at Noldi Arm's farm just after eight, she turned off the laptop, blew Ueli a kiss from the living-room doorway, and went to bed.

28

Heidmatt,
Friday morning, November 27

To get to the farm, Giuliana had to drive right through Heidmatt and take a winding road into the hills. The narrow track made the curves risky. Several times a stream meandered across her path and then rushed away down a gulley. So far the rain was holding off, but the clouds that tossed and teemed in the sky were dark gray, as were the boulders on either side of her and the grim stones stacked in the fields. It was clear why the descendant of a family that had worked this steep ground in the foothills of the Alps for generations might be named "Arm," which meant poor.

She found Frau Egli's uncle hefting a chain saw into the bed of his pickup. A wool cap was pulled down over his ears, and he wore knee-high rubber boots and what looked like at least four layers of old pullovers and cardigans over his already barrel-shaped chest. He wasn't large but appeared strong. "Let's go into the barn where it's warmer," he said, once they'd shaken hands. She waited while he covered the tools and equipment in his truck with a tarp. "I'm heading up to the forest to work on my trees after we talk, but I've got plenty of time for that. The trees aren't going anywhere."

She followed him through heavy doors into his barn, where he led her between two rows of cows' red-brown rumps into a tiny office. There he offered Giuliana the desk chair and took the single wooden stool. Leaning back against one wall, he crossed his arms over his thick chest. "My niece says you're investigating Karli Gurtner's drowning and want to know more about Norbert," he began. "I was in school with both of 'em till fourteen, so tell me what you want to know and I'll try to answer."

"Thank you," Giuliana said. She sat a moment breathing in the mingled scents of cow, dung, and hay, which she'd never found unpleasant. "I talked to Gurtner's younger sister Brigitte Rieder—Bri—and she told me about Karli having quite a few friends, one of whom was Norbert. I understand that Norbert has fetal alcohol syndrome and is therefore somewhat small and odd-looking and not very bright."

Arm slapped both hands on his thighs with a loud crack and said, "I don't believe it. That you, an outsider, should finally tell me what's wrong with that poor soul. All these years I've wondered if it had a name, or if he was just a strange bird. Now it all makes sense. By the time I knew his mother, she was usually sober, but my parents and their friends would talk about how wild she'd been as a girl. Man, I'm glad you came by. Ha!"

As if in response to her master's cry, one cow gave a long moo, and Giuliana could hear her shifting restlessly. Arm, with barely a glance, called, "Settle down, Blösch. There's a good girl." Well, if you only have thirty cows, you must consider each one a friend, Giuliana supposed, grinning nonetheless at his use of the cow's name.

Arm re-clasped his arms and said, "I guess you heard about Karli's pals being the Three Bears." When she shook her head, he said, "Our classmate Pesche nicknamed them that because they were called Al*bert*, Nor*bert* and *Bern*hard. Albert hung out with Karli because it gave him a chance to be the shit that he truly was. Bernhard was Albert's cousin and a decent person; I never understood why he was in that group until I ran into him in Bern many years later and realized he was gay. I guess being one of the bears was a safe place for him to hide in plain sight while growing up. But Norbert, the third bear, loved Karli—although he was afraid of him, too. The best way I can explain it is to tell you that Norbert was like a good dog with a bad master: he fawned and hung around and begged for crumbs of affection even when Karli mistreated him. Sometimes Norbert got pats and praise and treats, and sometimes he got curses and even punches, but he had no one else."

Even after Bri's story about the boxing, hearing Arm talk so casually about Gurtner mistreating Norbert took her aback. Maybe that was the reason for the payments Gurtner had made to the man—guilt about how he'd bullied him. "Poor Norbert," she said and waited to see what else Arm would say about him.

"As a child I kept my distance from him. He was strange, and that made him frightening. Once I could see him with grown-up eyes, I knew he was a victim. But," he grimaced and shrugged, "I'm afraid it didn't make me try to become his friend. And now he's dying. Jesus, some people have god-awful lives, don't they?" Arm shook his head and then met her eyes. "So, don't make Norbert's any worse, if you can help it," he said fiercely.

Giuliana wondered at his vehemence, but all she said was, "I'll try not to." The little office was starting to feel warm, so she took off her coat, folded it, and laid it across a pile of ledgers on Arm's desk. As she did, she noticed an additional sound in the background: rain was pounding on the barn's tile roof and starting to run through the gutters and drainpipes.

"One of the things Gurtner's sister told me," she said, "was that he—'Karli'—was asked to leave school all of a sudden in the November when he was thirteen. Apparently, he never came back to your class; his parents kept him at home until it was time for him to go to *Untergymnasium* in Thun. Do you know why he was suspended?"

Arm stood up and moved his stool around in the tiny office until he could lean back more comfortably against the doorframe. Then he frowned. Giuliana listened to the fall of rain and the stirring of cows and waited. Finally, he said, "I was there when it happened—and I was there all the months and years before it happened, too. Believe me, it wasn't 'all of a sudden.' I'd say it was the result of every last soul on that damned school board finally finding the guts to do something about the chaos in our classroom: first, by chucking Karli out and, more importantly, by getting rid of our bastard of a teacher. They didn't manage *that* until the following spring, but I guess it had to wait until they could hire someone to take his place."

Giuliana grinned; finally she was going to get the background she needed on Norbert's relationship with Gurtner. She wriggled in her chair until she, too, was more comfortable. Pen and notepad at the ready, she said, "Tell me how Karli got himself thrown out of school."

Noldi Arm hated the way Karli made fun of everyone when they spoke during lessons. Herr Müller was always telling them how stupid they were, but for Noldi, taking the schoolmaster's insults and beatings was part of a normal school day. Karli was a kid like the rest of them, though. Just because his parents were a big deal and he was smart, that didn't give him the right to make them all look like idiots. And, at least in Noldi's case, feel like an idiot as well.

The only kids who raised their hands were Karli and Pesche. They always knew the answers to Müller's questions, but that wasn't why they spoke up. It wasn't to suck up to Müller, either, because they both despised him even more than the rest of the class did, if that was possible. For a long time Noldi wasn't sure *why* they bothered to call attention to themselves. He assumed Karli couldn't get into any real trouble no matter what he said or did, but Pesche was always in danger of having his hair pulled, his palms smacked, or his butt caned, even though he answered correctly. Once, Müller had banged Pesche's head against the wall. But Pesche kept speaking, and Noldi understood at last that this was his way of defying the teacher, because it drove Müller nuts that a *Verdingbueb* could be so smart. Somehow, even when he appeared to be behaving, Pesche usually managed to make Müller look like a horse's ass. Noldi loved that. The whole class loved it. But it was dangerous.

Noldi knew the answers to a lot of Müller's questions. When he'd been in the baby class with Fräulein Kämpf, he'd loved raising his hand and showing off. But after only a day or two with Müller, he'd figured out that the safest thing to do was keep quiet and make himself as close to invisible as possible. Everyone did that, except for Karli and Pesche. Actually, Köbi made himself conspicuous, too, but in other ways.

Unfortunately for all the kids who didn't want to answer in class, Müller still managed to call on them. On the day Karli got suspended from school, Thomas Zürcher was the first to be tortured. "Thomas, when was the Battle of Sempach?" Herr Müller asked. "Stand up and answer now, Zürcher. The class is waiting."

"If we're waiting for Tömu to figure out when Sempach was, we'll die of old age," Karli said. His bears—and other people, too—laughed. No matter how much everyone suffered from Karli's mockery, most were prepared to laugh at his jokes. Noldi found Karli funny, too, but he never laughed. He didn't want to give him the satisfaction.

Glancing back, he could see Tömu stand up very slowly, his face a blank. Pesche, from his desk in the front, made numbers behind his back with his fingers: one, three, eight, six. Tömu stuttered out, "Thirteen ... uh ... seventy-six."

"My God, he got the century right," said Karli from the back of the classroom. "But he needs glasses to see Pesche's fingers."

"That's enough, Karli. Sit down, Thomas. You should know the date by heart—it's thirteen eighty-six. Katharina, who was the hero of the Battle of Sempach?"

"Arnold Winkelried," Käthi whispered. No one needed help with *that* question; they all knew how the brave soldier from Unterwalden had deliberately run on as many of the enemies' pikes as possible, to clear a path through the Habsburg front lines for the Swiss.

"Correct. Now, I want someone to give me the name of an earlier Swiss battle against the Habsburgs." Both Pesche and Karli raised their hands to answer, but the teacher ignored them, his eyes moving around the room. Noldi shrank down in his seat, hoping Köbi, who shared the double desk with him, would block him from view, but it was no use. Noldi could feel Müller staring at him. "Arnold. Trying to hide behind that lump Jakob, are you?" Köbi looked at Noldi with sympathy but could only shrug—he had no clue about battles. An important one started with "M." Noldi knew that. He'd known the name the evening before, but now, with Müller and Karli waiting for him to screw up, his mind was like a radio broadcasting only static. Pesche had turned around in his seat to mouth something; Köbi was looking at Pesche, too, trying to figure it out. But they couldn't read his lips.

Müller yelled, "Arnold"—which made Noldi think of Arnold Winkelried and how he'd run on the enemy's pikes, which was exactly what he was about to do. "Stand up, you cretin," he said. "Look at me, boy, not at your classmates. We talked about this yesterday, and I gave you several pages in your history book to read as homework. Only someone as stupid as you are could forget. It's the Battle of Morgarten, thirteen fifteen in Canton Zug. You will stay after class today and write 'Morgarten' fifty times on the blackboard." Noldi sat down again, grateful not to have been caned. Of course it was Morgarten. Now he'd have to stay late, and his father would yell at him for not getting all his chores done. School was shit.

Then things started to get exciting. "My ancestors were around in the thirteen hundreds." That was Karli. Sitting there in the back row, surveying the class like a prince and saying stuff like that. As if anyone gave a fuck about his ancestors.

"That's very interesting, Karl," the teacher said. Müller's voice changed when he talked to Karli, sucking up even though everyone in the class knew they hated each other.

Pesche broke in. Noldi loved when he did this, even though it always got him into trouble. "Actually, Karli, *all* of our ancestors were around then. Don't you know what the word means?"

Köbi and Noldi grinned at each other. Round One to Pesche. But Karli rallied quickly.

"Yes, but your ancestors were sleeping in pig shit. My ancestors were warriors."

Herr Müller called "Boys!" but, as usual, those two ignored him. Pesche had turned around in his seat, facing backward to talk to Karli.

"Given my last name, I guess my ancestors were baking bread. But, in any case, they were producing food, which is probably what all of *our* ancestors were doing. I wouldn't brag too much, Karli; yours were probably licking the butts of a bunch of dukes."

Müller kept saying, "That's enough," but no one was paying attention. It was much more interesting to listen to Pesche and Karli. Karli had always been a shit to Pesche, because he was a *Verdingbueb*, but everyone knew that things had gotten much worse since Pesche'd started going around with Heidi about two months earlier. Karli's parents probably wouldn't have let him go near Heidi anyway, but that didn't matter—he was still jealous as hell. Noldi was a little bit jealous, too; he figured all the boys in the class who were old enough to like girls were, because Heidi was perfect. But they weren't hateful about it, like Karli.

"One of my ancestors fought at Sempach," Karli insisted.

"Well, maybe he did," said Pesche. "But your family is noble; that's what you're always telling us. And were the noblemen on the Swiss side? No, they were on the Habsburg side. Your ancestors were the bad guys, Karli. We were fighting you. And we won." He paused. "I like that idea—my ancestor swinging a morning star into Karli's ancestor's head and then chopping him up with a battle axe. With no bears around standing guard."

Noldi liked the idea, too. He turned around to look at how Karli was taking this blow to his dignity, if not his head. Which was why he didn't see Müller heading for Pesche in the front row. But Köbi did; Köbi always had an eye on Pesche. To distract Müller, Köbi swept all the books and notebooks, his and Noldi's, from their shared desk to the floor. That made quite a crash. But it didn't do any good. Müller ignored the noise. Grabbing Pesche by the hair, he dragged him out of his seat to the front of the classroom. "I won't have this kind of insolence," he shouted at the top of his voice, "especially from a smart-ass little *Verdingbueb* like you. You have interrupted me for the last time, you *Söiniggu.*" And he whacked the left side of Pesche's face with the cane.

Noldi sat there, scared, but Köbi was already out of his chair and running toward them. As he passed Müller's desk, Noldi saw him grab up the teacher's thick wooden pointer. Jesus, Köbi, Noldi thought, you can't hit the teacher with a big stick, although a voice inside him was saying, "Well, why not? He whacks us often enough." Still, he yelled, "No, Köbi, don't! Don't do it."

Noldi wasn't the only one yelling: most of the class was screaming at Köbi, Pesche, or Müller, while the teacher bellowed curses and shook Pesche like a dust cloth.

Then Fräulein Kämpf walked in from the next-door classroom. "Herr Müller," she said, her voice sharp and cold as an icicle. She spoke quietly, but everyone froze: Herr Müller with his cane raised to hit Pesche across the face again; Pesche with his fists clenched at his sides, his face bloody and full of defiance; and Köbi holding the pointer over his head like a club. "This noise is unbearable. And you are making most of it yourself, sir. My pupils and I cannot work if you are going to lose control of yourself in this way. Now let Pesche go back to his seat. I suggest you go home and compose yourself. I will look after your class for the rest of today."

Herr Müller, his face red and his expression furious, let go of Pesche and stood there, panting and glaring at Fräulein Kämpf. Köbi had sensibly lowered the pointer in hopes that Fräulein might not have seen it, but he remained on his guard, waiting. For a moment, it looked as if Müller might defy Fräulein, but then he walked toward the teachers' room. Everyone watched him pass through the classroom without a word, except Karli, who gave one of his mocking laughs. He just couldn't keep his mouth shut, that boy.

"The old maid's got you by the short hairs, eh, Müller?" he called out. Müller ignored him. Fräulein Kämpf didn't.

"Karl," she said, walking up to where he sat at his double desk next to Albert, "that was impertinent and vulgar. You may also leave the classroom. Right now. And you should know that a letter has been sent to your father, telling him how disruptive your behavior has been for the past several months. Today you have given us another example of the kind of insolence that we are no longer prepared to tolerate."

Everyone stared at Karli, waiting to hear what he would say to Fräulein Kämpf. Noldi didn't care if Karli was fresh to Müller, but he didn't want him insulting Fräulein. The silence grew heavier; it pressed down on them all like a thick woolen blanket, and still the small woman and the large blond boy looked at each other. Instead of his usual smiling insolence, what Noldi saw in his face was amazement. Perhaps it had never occurred to Karli that what he did at school could have the slightest influence on his life.

"My father won't believe a letter from you," he said, but he didn't sound convinced.

"The letter isn't from me; it is from the men who sit on our school board," answered Fräulein Kämpf. She was very calm. "That's enough rudeness from you, Karl. Leave the classroom now, as I told you to, and go home. You are not welcome back in school today or on Monday. If your mother wants to know why, tell her I will be glad to speak with her."

The whole class waited again to hear what Karli would answer, but he was no longer staring at Fräulein Kämpf. Eyes on the floor, he got up, made his way to the student cloakroom, put on his jacket and boots, and left the building.

Fräulein gave a great sigh before she turned to the class and smiled. Noldi felt like cheering—she'd met the enemy, won the battle, and survived: the Stauffacher of the classroom war. Hero or not, Arnold Winkelried had died fighting the Habsburgs. Werner Stauffacher had lived. "Now, children," she said, "there's another hour before you go home for Saturday lunch, and I think it's time for an art lesson. Bernhard, you draw very well, so I suggest you take over the class." Bernhard was the nicest of the bears and drew fabulous and obscene caricatures of Müller, although Noldi doubted Fräulein knew about those. "I will come in to check on you all now and then, but while you are on your own, I don't want to hear any noise. Please come to my room to get drawing paper and colored pencils, Bernhard. We will set up a still life on the desk for you pupils to copy, but if any of you prefers to draw something from your imagination, that will be fine." She looked around the room, still smiling. When she'd been their teacher, she'd been strict, but she'd never raged or insulted anyone like Müller. "Do your best," she said, "and afterward we'll hang some of your drawings on the wall."

Since it was Saturday, school was over at noon, but none of the pupils rushed home. They were too excited. The kids from the younger class, and even the big ones in the older class, wanted to hear about Karli and Herr Müller. Noldi's older brother Klaus and two of his friends ran over as soon as they saw him, and he made a dramatic tale of it. The chilly forecourt of the schoolhouse was full of children; the vapor from their chattering mouths gathered over their heads.

At last Fräulein Kämpf came outside with Herr Gerber, who taught the fourteen-to-sixteen-year-olds. "All right, children," she said. "It's time for you to go home." She locked the schoolhouse door and set off for her own little house, while Herr Gerber, who was only twenty-four, walked away toward the farm where he boarded. Noldi left his brother horsing around with his friends and headed for home, as well. He couldn't wait to tell his parents about the Battle of Karli and Pesche, followed by the Battle of Müller and Kämpf. Thinking of battles reminded him that he was supposed to be writing "Morgarten" fifty times on the blackboard, which meant that he'd won the Battle of Morgarten. He ran home laughing.

Giuliana was laughing, too. "So, you got out of your punishment!" She and the old farmer smiled at each other, as the cows munched and mooed in the background, shuffling their feet in the straw. One pissed loudly. Turning serious, Giuliana asked, "Did you see Karli again?"

"Oh yes, around the village once or twice before he went off to Thun for school in January and perhaps ten times over all the years after that, when he happened to pass through the village with his parents or sisters. But we never spoke." Noldi shifted restlessly, and Giuliana realized that her own body was stiffening. Imagine how uncomfortable the old man must be crouched on that stool. The tale of Karli's exit from the village school had been longer than she'd expected, but she'd enjoyed it. Now she needed to get them both moving. A glance out the office's small window showed her that the downpour had settled into a light drizzle. "And what about Norbert?" she asked.

"The whole village knows Norbert." Noldi got up off his low stool with a suppressed groan, stretched his back, crossed to the window, and leaned against it, his bottom resting on the sill, before saying, "He's something of a local feature. He does odd jobs for people, and quite a few of us are used to finding him dead drunk somewhere and getting him home. He hangs out at The Lion, and the graveyard isn't far from there—that's a place he tends to sleep it off if he can't make it home. It's a miracle he hasn't frozen to death; I guess that's because Heidi and Ändu, who run the inn—or used to, till their daughter and her husband took over—keep watch over him. You're going over to his place now, aren't you? Well, let me warn you: he's sometimes incoherent. As a kid he wasn't the sharpest knife in the drawer, but he could communicate clearly when he put his mind to it. But after years of eating poorly and drinking too much, plus now with all the cancer medicine he takes, he doesn't always make sense. He *can* talk sensibly, when he's sober and focused, though, so just keep trying, if you have the patience. And for God's sake don't scare the poor geezer."

Listening to Arm's advice about Norbert, Giuliana debated what to reveal to the farmer, weighing pros and cons. When he'd finished, she said, "Thanks for warning me. We'll try to keep Norbert calm and not frighten him. Now, do you mind walking back to the car with me? I need to get going, but I've got a last question." As they made their way back through the cows, Arm kept up a running chat with his girls, patting their rumps. With a tut-tut sound, he stopped to adjust the way one cow was fastened above her trough.

Giuliana spoke as he worked. "We've discovered that for at least forty-five years Karli... Herr Doktor Gurtner"—Arm looked up from where he was kneeling by the reddish-brown cow and gave a small shrug at the switch to formality—"has been sending regular payments to Norbert from a secret bank account. Can you think of a reason for that?"

Arm continued to manipulate the brace that restrained the cow, not speaking. Giuliana stared at the back of his head. Was he surprised, or had he known about the money?

"Herr Arm," she said at last.

"Oh, sorry. This adjustment is tricky," he said, grunting with effort as he got up from his knees and, still crouching a little, pushed against the cow with his shoulder to shift her sideways. "I'm surprised to hear that. I had no idea Karli was so generous, and I'd never have expected it, especially because, according to Norbert, he hasn't seen Karli for years." He left the cow, and they continued toward Giuliana's car, striding through a blend of mist and rain.

"So," Giuliana pursued, "you can't think of any reason for these transfers of cash, except charity?"

Arm was slightly ahead of her, moving to open her car door for her. "I can't imagine why Karli would send Norbert money," he said, as he tried the car door handle. He waited for her to get out her keys and push the 'unlock' button and then opened the door, all with his back toward her. She felt sure he was lying to her. But why?

"I hope I've helped," he added, as he waited for her to get into the driver's seat. "And good luck with Norbert." His smile turned to a frown. "You aren't planning on locking him up, are you? Because I don't think he could cope with jail, physically or mentally."

Giuliana prayed inwardly that nothing like that would be necessary, but in truth she had no idea what they'd do with Norbert if it turned out he'd been involved in killing his friend Karli. Settled in the car, she leaned out the driver's window, her voice infused with confidence. "We won't lock him up. We just want to question him. It's been good to talk to you, Herr Arm." She gave him her hand. "Thanks for your time." Once she'd driven out of his sight, she pulled over as best she could on the narrow road. It was nine-fifty, and she wasn't due at Norbert's until ten-thirty. In the meantime, Renzo and Toni's interview with Markus had started at nine that morning. Maybe, just maybe, Renzo had been able to pass on some information to Erwin about how it was going. She reached for her phone.

29

When Erwin's small team arrived at Markus Gurtner's apartment on Thursday night to arrest him, their quarry was not home. Erwin spent a few minutes cursing himself, his team, and Toni Rossel. Then he took the prosaic step of calling Markus and asking him where he was. He turned out to be with a woman who lived eight blocks from the police station. Erwin swallowed more curses, explained that he needed to bring Markus in, and asked him to wait there to be picked up. He and his three uniformed cops drove back across the city and, finding that Markus had not disappeared into the night, took him into custody.

Renzo knew this because Erwin had called him shortly after nine, once he'd turned Markus over to be processed and put into a cell. "Jesus, why me?" Renzo complained, when he heard that he was going to be teamed up with Toni for Markus's interview the next morning. If only it were with Erwin or Giuliana; then he'd be excited.

"Well, I wish I could tell you it's because Toni's heard a rumor that you're going to be named Swiss Cop of the Year, but I think it's because he wants to see if he can use you to get at Giuliana or just plain screw with you because he knows you two are pals. But maybe I'm wrong. He

could be hoping you'll admire his superb interrogation techniques."
Erwin blew a raspberry at the end of this statement, although honesty
apparently got the better of him, because he added, "I've never sat in on
an interrogation with him; he could be good."

"Well," said Renzo, "knowing how much he loves to hear his own
voice, I imagine I won't do more than sit there taking notes. I'm glad
to get a chance to observe him, though, because I want to make up my
mind if he's playing with a full deck."

"Hmm," Erwin murmured. "A card or two missing there, yeah,
maybe especially when it comes to his way with women. Or at least
with Giule." Erwin paused. "You know about him and her, right?"

Was Erwin talking about the infamous quickie in the prosecution
office? If he wasn't, then Renzo couldn't reveal it, but if he was, then—
what? Unsure how to answer, Renzo had only managed an "Um . . ."
before Erwin added, "Okay. I guess not. Look, you don't want to hear
this from—"

At that point, Renzo broke in. "Giuliana told me yesterday that
Toni banged her once ages ago and is now threatening to tell half the
police force if she doesn't toe the line."

"Yeah," Erwin said. "He already said something to me this afternoon, in front of her, and I could see she let it get to her. I don't understand why she gives a shit. She needs to toughen up."

Renzo didn't think that would solve the problem; Giuliana was
plenty tough already. How the hell was he going to get Toni to leave
her alone? "So, he's making good on his threat now, huh?" he asked,
surprised by how calm he sounded.

Erwin snorted. "At least she's in good company—the guy never
nailed a woman he didn't blab about, and to hear him tell it there's a
new one every five minutes. What an asshole! Haven't you ever heard
him going on about—?"

"No, thank God. I haven't. So, um . . . thanks for the warning. I'll
watch my back."

"With him, always," said Erwin. "Oh, yeah, something else. His
threat to tell every cop who knows Giule about their little party on the

sofa? Well, guess what? He already started doing that years ago, with periodic updates for newbies. She just doesn't seem to know it."

"What?" Renzo yelped. But Erwin had hung up as abruptly as he always did.

Friday morning's staff meeting lasted only fifteen minutes. Toni didn't show up, Giuliana was off talking to her Heidmatt farmer, and Hansruedi had a meeting with the woman who'd found Gurtner's watch on the path. Erwin began by announcing that Markus was in custody. Renzo summarized what he'd learned at the Cloth Handlers' Guild, which didn't seem very relevant anymore. The third *Fahnder*, Walter, who'd supervised all the investigations in Gurtner's neighborhood, confirmed that a search of Nicole's, Philipp's, and Gurtner's own clothing had revealed nothing that matched the fibers found in the watchband.

"Speaking of that," Erwin said, grinning, "Markus Gurtner's apartment is being thoroughly searched this morning, but thanks to a tip from Giuliana we've already got a pair of blue knitted gloves. The lab is doing the comparison, but I'm sure it's the same stuff."

Renzo felt a twinge of disappointment that the case was almost over, but he couldn't help being excited about confronting Markus, even if it had to be with Toni. He didn't get to be part of homicide interrogations often. He only wished Toni'd had the courtesy to explain his planned approach, so Renzo didn't blunder out of sheer ignorance. He sighed. It was looking more and more like Toni's idea of his role was keeping the second chair warm.

Just as Erwin was ready to end the morning meeting, Rolf, the homicide boss, said, "Markus Gurtner has been chatting with his lawyer since seven-forty-five this morning."

"Oh, shit," said Renzo. "That's bad news—unless it's Giuliana's brother?"

They all laughed. It had happened a few times over the years that Paolo Linder, not knowing his sister was involved in a case, had shown up to represent a client and been forced to go away again. This occasionally resulted in an interrogation taking place without the suspect bothering to get another lawyer. It made the police very happy.

"No such luck," said Rolf. "It's Jordi."

Walter groaned. Oliver Jordi was considered the best defense lawyer in Bern, now that Giuliana's father had retired and Paolo hadn't quite filled his shoes. But Renzo and Erwin eyed each other smiling, eyebrows raised. "What's funny about Jordi?" asked Walter.

It was Erwin who answered. "Much as we'd like to find out what Markus Gurtner knows about how his father died, I think Renzo and I would like it even more if Toni Rossel fell on his ass. I imagine Jordi could be a big help with that."

Walter looked shocked, but Rolf smiled faintly. "I didn't hear that," he said, and Renzo understood that he and Erwin weren't the only ones who found Toni objectionable. "Hope the interrogation goes well, Renzo," Rolf added, as he got up to go back to the homicide office. "I haven't told our favorite prosecutor about Herr Jordi's arrival. I'll give you that pleasure."

Renzo walked down the hall to the case room and called Toni from Giuliana's desk.

"I understand I'll be interrogating Markus Gurtner with you at nine," he said in his best I'm-just-a-humble-*Fahnder* voice. "I'm looking forward to that." Which was true, he thought, just not for the reasons Toni might suppose. "I called to ask if there's anything in particular I need to know beforehand or anything you'd like me to do before you arrive."

Toni was all bonhomie. "Renzo! Super that you called. No need for a special briefing; I'm sure we'll work well together. Erwin must have explained that I picked *you* especially for my partner on this." Even with no one in the room to see him, Renzo stuck his finger down his throat and mimed gagging. "If you could just make sure we've got the room I requested and someone to take notes. Have Gurtner brought in there a little before nine and let him sit. No coffee. We don't want the little shit feeling comfortable, do we?" He chuckled.

"No coffee for Oliver Jordi either?" Renzo asked, all his glee hidden behind the concerned question.

"What?" Toni's voice sharpened. "Are you telling me Jordi's there with Gurtner?"

"Yes, he's been here for about an hour. I thought you knew." Contrite voice, with hints of reproach.

"How the hell would I . . .? Right. Well, get them both settled in, but for God's sake don't say anything to either of them."

Gee, thanks for the trust, thought Renzo, and decided it was time to end the jokes. He *did* want to solve Gurtner's killing.

"Something you need to remember," said Renzo, with no humility at all. "Erwin and Giuliana will bring Norbert Wittwer in by noon. They expect to be able to get everything out of the old man"—*which is why you should have waited before tackling Markus, you pinhead,* he thought—"as long as he's not lawyered up. So, it's crucial we don't mention anything about Norbert being on his way. Otherwise—if Markus and Norbert really are accomplices—Jordi could simply walk next door into Norbert's interrogation and totally fuck it up."

Toni was quiet just long enough for Renzo to speculate that perhaps the prosecutor hadn't thought the situation through as clearly as he should have, no matter how well-known he was for getting convictions. Then he snarled, "Are you telling me how to do my job?" which was more or less what Renzo had expected him to say.

"Just making sure we're on the same page," he said, trying to speak matter-of-factly through his broad smile.

Renzo studied the two men on the other side of the metal table. Both were elegant. Oliver Jordi was in his late fifties—Renzo had looked him up online—but money, and the excellent tailoring and grooming it could buy, made him look younger. He was blessed with thick gray hair, dignified features, and a wiry physique, and he wore a beautiful suit that Renzo, feeling a pinch of envy, identified as Ermenegildo Zegna. Next to him, Markus Gurtner in his blue jeans should have looked grubby but didn't: the jeans fit perfectly, the blue-and-white running shoes were clean, and with them he wore a white crew-necked T-shirt under a blue V-necked pullover. Giuliana's report had described Markus's dangling earring, but today all he wore in his ear was a tiny blue stud. When he turned his head sideways, his long, straight hair touched his back, even in its high ponytail. He sat in as relaxed a pose as the straight metal chairs made possible, but Renzo felt him vibrating with tension. His lips smiled, but his ice-blue eyes bored into Renzo. Renzo, refusing to look away, smiled at him, a real smile. The man interested him. Not to mention that anyone who managed to overcome a period of serious addiction had his respect. But studying Markus now, he saw no reason to doubt that the photographer had deliberately met with his abusive father on the Aare, tried to discuss something important with him, lost his shit over yet one more insult, brained the old son of a bitch with a rock, and pushed him into the river. Which made him a murderer.

Toni didn't look bad when he made his entrance, Renzo had to admit it. He could see why women found him attractive. It wasn't just the blond curls and chin dimple, but the way he carried himself. To Renzo's eyes, though, he was stagey. The way he strolled into the stark white interrogation room was exaggeratedly breezy, as if the four of them were about to plan a weekend in the Alps. Clearly the presence of Jordi influenced Toni's tactics, whatever they were. So, perhaps, did Markus's appearance. Despite Giuliana's reports, maybe Toni had been expecting a down-on-his-luck ex-junkie whom he could intimidate.

Renzo stood at Toni's entrance and so did the other two; Markus was not handcuffed to the chair. "Jordi." Toni's voice was so warm it was hard to believe the two men were about to confront each other. He gave his opponent a two-handed handshake and a big smile. "It's great to be crossing swords with you again."

Oliver Jordi, more restrained, said, "Hello, Rossel. Let me introduce you to Markus Gurtner." Markus also held out his hand, and Toni shook it austerely, saying, "Thank you for making yourself available, Herr Gurtner," as if Markus hadn't been picked up and forced to spend the night in a cell. Markus's left eyebrow shot up in a perfect expression of derision, but he said nothing. Instead he sat down and folded his hands on the table, as if to say, "Let's cut the bullshit and get to the questions." The two lawyers and Renzo sat, too.

"It looks like Donatelli forgot to offer you coffee," Toni said, giving Renzo a scolding shake of the head. Aha, so he was here to be the whipping boy. Good thing Erwin had prepared him. His expression remained pleasantly neutral.

"He offered, and we turned down food and drinks, thank you," said Jordi, "so why don't we get on with it? I'd like Herr Gurtner to be out of here as soon as possible. He has already been humiliated by an unnecessarily public police pick-up that very much resembled an arrest, for which you don't begin to have enough evidence of wrongdoing, and he has also been forced to spend a night in jail, which was completely uncalled for."

Toni, still smiling, said, "I disagree. In fact . . ."

"Excuse me for interrupting, Herr *Staatsanwalt*," said Markus, "but I have a statement. Herr Jordi and I have agreed that it would be efficient if I presented it to you before we proceed." He took the neatly printed sheets of white paper that his lawyer had just drawn out of a leather folder and began to read.

"On Wednesday morning, November twenty-fifth, I stated to homicide detective Giuliana Linder that I was present in my apartment all afternoon and evening on Monday, November twenty-third, when my father drowned in the Aare. I had previously made the same statement on the telephone when asked for an alibi. In both cases, I said I didn't leave my apartment until just before seven in the evening. This statement is not true, and I apologize for obstructing the investigation with my lie, which was the result of a desire to avoid involvement with the police. The truth is that I left my apartment at around one-thirty on November twenty-third, walked to the nearest place in my neighborhood for picking up a Mobility car, and drove to Heidmatt in the Emmental. There I went straight to the home of Norbert Wittwer, a former primary-school classmate of my father's. Norbert is dying of cancer, and he wanted to return an heirloom watch in his possession that had belonged to my great-grandfather. I know Norbert, so I agreed to set up a surprise meeting of the two men along the Aare, where my father walks the family dog every Monday; my half-brother Philipp told me where to find him. Herr Wittwer not only planned to return the watch; he wanted to see my father, who was his best friend in childhood, one more time. In fact, he'd previously phoned my father himself several times to set up a meeting between them but wasn't successful."

Renzo was impressed. So far the story made sense, and it seemed to fit the evidence the police had collected—the sightings of Markus on CCTV, Markus's call to Philipp, and probably the calls from The Lion in Heidmatt to Markus's mobile, if Norbert had made them. Every word would have to be checked for discrepancies, though. Markus read the statement with utter calm, as if it were a weather bulletin. His hands did not shake, he did not look to his lawyer for support, and he glanced up from the paper periodically to meet either Toni's or Renzo's eyes. It was a skillful performance.

Markus had paused, giving Renzo and Toni a long, level stare. Looking down, he read on, as coolly as before. "I got to Herr Wittwer's just after two-thirty, which—if we'd left then—would have given us plenty of time to get back to Bern, park near the part of the Dählhölzli forest where my father walks the dog, and find a bench along the Aare where we could sit and wait for him. I was quite concerned about how far and how fast Herr Wittwer would be able to walk, so I wanted plenty of time to reach the place we'd chosen for meeting my father. I hoped to be there by four-fifteen at the latest."

"So, what time did you get there?" asked Toni. Renzo slid a glance at him and saw that he looked calm and focused. He might despise the man, but apparently he hadn't won his reputation as a good prosecutor for nothing. It looked like when he finally started doing his job, instead of jerking his colleagues around, he did know his ass from his elbow. "And where is that bench? I'd like to know the point between the Elfenau nature-reserve pond and the Dählhölzli restaurant where you waited."

"We never made it," Markus answered and then looked down at his statement and kept reading. "Norbert has many years of alcoholism behind him, but since he was diagnosed with cancer, he has greatly reduced his drinking. Still, when I got to his house, I found him extremely drunk. I thought I'd drive him to Bern anyway, but he didn't want to come. I tried to persuade him, but he kept refusing and, eventually, at about three-thirty, he passed out." Markus looked up again at Toni and Renzo and said, "I was extremely annoyed about it." Back to his text: "I waited ten minutes to see if the old man seemed in danger of vomiting, because I didn't want him to choke. Then I drove back to my place. I wasn't home until about four-thirty. I'd wasted a whole afternoon, and I have several photography jobs I'm preparing—that part of what I told Frau Linder is true—so I just went back to work at my computer, and I worked all evening and into the night. I didn't know anything had happened to my father until my father's wife Nicole called and told me he was missing, which was around eight that night, I think. Later I got the news that he'd drowned."

Markus's voice stopped, and he handed the pages he'd just read across the table to Toni. "That's all I have to say."

"I'll email a copy of the statement to you as soon as we're finished here," added Jordi.

Renzo had questions about the statement. The "surprise" meeting bothered him—why hadn't Norbert been able to set up the meeting with Gurtner himself? It was obvious Markus had planned to lie in wait for his father. But why? And how the hell had Markus gotten to know Norbert, who from what Giuliana said had the mind of a child? They were very unlikely confederates. He knew better than to start the questioning, though. Swallowing his impatience, he waited for Toni to begin.

The prosecutor squared the edges of the statement's pages and set them down at his elbow, smiling. "You're telling me you were never on the Aare that evening, with or without Norbert Wittwer, and that you had nothing to do with your father's death."

"That is correct," Markus answered.

"So, why was wool from a pair of knitted gloves belonging to you found snagged in the band of the wristwatch that was torn from your father's wrist on Monday night?" Toni's smile had turned complacent, his voice triumphant.

There was a moment of silence before Oliver Jordi said, "I know nothing about these gloves. You'll have to present us with your evidence."

There was no evidence yet; the gloves were still in the lab. But Renzo could understand why Toni wanted to confront Markus with the damning news. It had worked, too; the photographer was no longer calm. He'd caught his lower lip between his teeth and scrunched his brows together, while his eyes darted back and forth between Jordi and Toni.

"It's not possible," he said. "I wasn't there."

Toni produced a photograph. "We found these gloves in your flat. Are they yours?"

"They look like mine," Markus said. "I wasn't wearing them that Monday when I drove to Heidmatt to pick up Norbert, though."

Renzo was getting tired of sitting at the table without saying a word. By failing to brief him, Toni had also neglected to tell him when and how he was supposed to assist with the interrogation. Which meant, in theory, he was free to make his own decisions. "What interests me, Herr Gurtner," he said, "is that your statement doesn't give you an alibi. You say you left Heidmatt at around three-thirty and drove back to your apartment, where you stayed for the rest of the afternoon and evening. You could just as easily have driven straight to Dählhölzli, met your father on your own, fought with him, and killed him. You had plenty of time."

"My statement is the truth," said Markus, glaring at Renzo. "If the truth doesn't give me an alibi, there's nothing to be done about that, is there?"

Jordi put a restraining hand on Markus's arm, which Renzo hoped Markus would ignore. Even the best defense lawyers were helpless when their clients lost their tempers and forgot to keep their mouths shut.

"And then there's your mobile," Toni said smoothly. "Your phone shows no evidence of your having been in Heidmatt that day."

Renzo glanced at him, before facing Markus and Jordi again. What the hell? Erwin hadn't said anything about this. Had Toni gotten hold of some extra piece of information and then blocked it from reaching the cops? That would be just like him, the tricky little shit.

This time Markus turned to Jordi before speaking. Seeing the lawyer nod, he said, "That's because my phone was dead. I took it with me when I drove to pick up Norbert, meaning to charge it in the car, but I forgot the cable."

Renzo glanced surreptitiously at his watch; it was after ten. Good. Giuliana would pick up Norbert at ten-thirty, they'd arrive about an hour later, and by then this interrogation would be done, and he'd have had time to brief Erwin on Markus's story.

Jordi had straightened in his chair and was looking imperious, something he was very good at. "My client has offered you a reasonable statement explaining his whereabouts on Monday afternoon," he said. "You've produced no evidence of his presence on the Aare at the time of his father's death. Release him—now."

"No," said Toni, all his initial joviality gone. "When the lab finishes with the gloves, we will have clear proof that Herr Gurtner attacked his father. Until then, he waits here in custody, and I can assure you that he'll remain in custody afterward as well, under arrest."

"Nonsense," said Jordi. "Even if you can show the gloves were at the scene, which I doubt, that doesn't prove that my client was there, as you perfectly well know."

Markus no longer looked as though he was paying attention to the exchange—his eyes were distant, and he was frowning slightly, the fingers of one hand resting against his chin. "Do I understand," he asked, breaking into the lawyers' confrontation, "that my father's watch—the one he wore regularly—was found near his body, and the band has a piece of yarn caught in it that you claim comes from the same wool as my gloves?"

He didn't sound like a suspect refuting an accusation, Renzo noticed, but more like someone circling in on the solution to a puzzle.

"Exactly, Herr Gurtner," said Toni.

"I'd like to see the paperwork on the fiber comparison as soon as it's ready," Jordi said. The lawyer sounded as relaxed and confident as ever, but he and the two policemen knew that, because of the gloves, the police could keep Markus for forty-eight hours at least.

Markus's expression was hard to read, but he still looked like his mind was elsewhere. He leaned over to whisper to Jordi, who asked Toni, "Are you considering other suspects?"

"We don't need to." Renzo winced inwardly at the boastful way Toni said it, especially since he found the question intriguing. He wondered who Markus had in mind.

Markus was led away by the guard outside the door. Oliver Jordi went with them, while Renzo and Toni stood in the hall watching them go. Then Toni said, "That went well. Now I need you to . . ."

Renzo looked at him. "What you need me to do is brief Erwin and Giuliana, so that they know what to ask Wittwer. If you want me to do anything after that, take it up with one of them." He turned to walk upstairs to homicide. To his surprise, Toni didn't call after him.

30
Before

*In Jakob's car between Heidmatt and Bern,
twenty-two days before Gurtner's death*

Leaving Norbert in bed with the lights out and his threadbare curtains closed, Jakob and Markus set off for Bern. Markus waited for the explanation he'd been promised. As Jakob continued to drive in silence, Markus turned to him several times. At last he said, "Why aren't you telling me about the stick?"

Jakob gave a deep sigh. "I've been sitting here trying to begin. It's a long story that involves your father, as well as several other people, and it's going to upset you."

"So does knowing you're keeping things from me. I want to know what happened."

"From the beginning, all right?" When Markus nodded impatiently, Jakob blew out a loud breath and said, "Well, I guess you could say it begins with Lässu. Remember that puppy I told you about, the one I saw when I went to eat dinner with Pesche at the Fankhausers'? Well, I got it. It took all kinds of behind-the-scenes wheeling-and-dealing, but Pesche convinced his Master to persuade my Master that he needed a dog to help him bring in his cows. You can't imagine what it meant to me, not being alone anymore on the farm. The Haldemanns never spoke to me except to tell me what to do or chew me out for doing it wrong, so I was lonely. Lässu—that was my dog—really changed my life."

Markus didn't see what this dog had to do with the watch, the cane, and Norbert, but he couldn't resist asking, "What kind of name is Lässu?"

Jakob gave a single, quiet chuckle. "I'll tell you."

Köbi and Pesche always walked home from school together, although their ways parted after about twenty minutes. Now they were talking about the puppies. Fankhauser had decided in mid-October that they were old enough to leave their mother, and Haldemann had taken his. It was the dirty-brown one that had slept on Köbi's foot; Pesche had made sure of that. For over a week now, the pup had been in the barn with Köbi, who was telling Pesche about his attempts to teach it not to foul the straw around the cows.

"I'm warning you," Pesche said, "I don't think this is going to work. Haldemann barely feeds *you*; you think he's going to feed a dog, too? And shitting in the straw? The first time he steps in a pile of dog poop, he's going to brain that pup with a shovel. He loves hitting things, you know that. He could pound that puppy to pulp in two seconds flat."

"I'm keeping him safe from the old fucker," Köbi insisted. He didn't even want to imagine anything happening to his pet. "Listen, I've decided to call him the same name as the dog in the movies that the kids at school were talking about."

Köbi had never been to a film, but several classmates had described a movie they'd seen in Thun about a dog that rescued people.

"Lassie? Köbi, you can't call him Lassie. It's a bitch's name."

"How do you know? It's not a Swiss name, so you don't have any idea what it means. You always think you know everything, but you don't. I can call my dog Lassie if I want to." Köbi's voice rose to a yell.

Pesche shrugged and walked along. The scornful expression on his face made Köbi feel like a boneheaded baby. Sometimes he got tired of Pesche being so smart. He glowered. But then he began to worry. Pesche usually knew what he was talking about.

"Is Lassie really a dumb name for him?"

"Yes."

"Okay, then I'll call him Lässu. You know, like Chrigi is a girl's name and Chrigu, a boy's. I'll call him Lässu, so everyone will know he's a boy."

Pesche laughed and punched Köbi on the arm. "If you want to call that pup Lässu, go ahead. He'll be the only dog named Lässu in all of Switzerland. But don't get too fond of him, because I think he won't survive two weeks at Haldemann's."

It was true that Pesche was usually right about everything, but he turned out to be wrong about the puppy. He survived. Haldemann called him "Dog," much as he called Köbi, "Boy," or else threw at him one of the same obscenities he used for Köbi. But Köbi overheard Frau Haldemann calling him Lässu, too, as she gave him the chicken innards she would normally have added to the soup. Frau Haldemann didn't know that Köbi saw her feed Lässu and he didn't let on, because he knew it would make her angry. But he was glad.

Whatever chores Köbi did, he shared with Lässu. True, the puppy was constantly in his way, worrying at the shovel when Köbi was digging, annoying the cows when he was milking, trying to climb into the pigs' slop buckets. At first Köbi was terrified that Lässu, with his endless curiosity, would be eaten by one of the huge sows or kicked to death by a cow. Luckily, the pup had some sense of self-preservation. The worst danger was Haldemann, as Pesche had predicted. Köbi came home from school twice to find Lässu cowering in a corner of the barn, favoring one paw and licking his side, and he knew Haldemann must have kicked him. He burned with anger, but it was good training for Lässu. The sooner he learned to stay clear of that shithead, the better.

About five weeks after their conversation about Lässu, Karli was suspended from school. That Saturday afternoon Pesche had permission to visit Heidi at the inn, and Köbi hurried home to do chores, so they had no time to rejoice together over Karli's downfall and speculate about what would happen to Herr Müller. They agreed to meet at their place on the river at three-thirty that afternoon. They'd found a kind of natural hollow along the bank of the Emme that sheltered them from the wind and to some extent from curious eyes. They'd dragged flat rocks to the area for seats and recently tried building a fire there, only to be defeated by damp wood.

The early part of November had been very busy for both of them because of the *Metzgete,* when animals were slaughtered. But by late November, with the meat cured and the fruit and vegetables all gathered and preserved, there was little to be done apart from milking cows and caring for them and the other livestock. It was a time of comparative leisure on the Heidmatt farms, so Pesche and Köbi managed to meet at least twice a week.

By three that afternoon, Köbi had already set out for the river. Haldemann and his wife were away: he at the inn playing cards, she visiting one of her daughters. Before leaving, they'd both loaded him with chores: equipment to clean, hedges and fences to check, wood to chop, ashes to clear out of the stoves. But he wasn't worried—it would all get done eventually. As he walked toward the Emme, he felt happy. He hated Haldemann but knew he could endure life on the farm until he was old enough to leave. At eleven, he was bigger, stronger, and better at evading the farmer's blows than he'd been two years before, and he had the company of Pesche and Lässu and even, at times, the Fankhausers to cheer him up. The farm work was not as grueling for him as it had been when he'd first arrived, and some of it—like milking—he even enjoyed.

Köbi hoped he'd be able to leave the farm when he was thirteen. He'd need Pesche's help, though. Lately, Pesche had talked about becoming a teacher. Köbi wanted it to work out for Pesche's sake, but he was sure it wouldn't, because Pesche couldn't afford to stay in school past fifteen. He'd have to start earning money. And if Pesche got an apprenticeship as a carpenter or a mason somewhere in the Emmental, as most of the boys of fifteen Köbi knew about had done, he could move into an apprentices' hostel, and Köbi might be able to move in with him. He'd be too young to apprentice to anyone, but he'd find a way to earn money somehow. Perhaps someone would give him a job fixing things.

Köbi knew he'd never become a farmer. When he considered what kind of work he wanted to do for the rest of his life, the idea of repairing tools and machines always came to mind. All his life, at home with his mother and now on the farm, he'd seen how worried people got when things broke down, because replacing them was so expensive. If he could repair equipment, he'd never go hungry or be without work. Even if people couldn't pay him, at least they'd always feed him in return for his fixing their stove or hay baler or radio. He wouldn't do a crap job, either, with bits of wire and tape, the way Haldemann did. No, he'd learn to repair things properly and make them almost as good as new.

Köbi was thinking about his future as a machine-fixer, wondering what the job was called and how you could apprentice for it, as he and Lässu trotted to the riverbank to meet Pesche. Along the way, he threw sticks for Lässu to fetch. The puppy always raced after whatever Köbi threw but hadn't yet grasped the concept of bringing things back. He grabbed a stick in his teeth and dashed off, eventually stopping to chew on it. Pesche'd reminded Köbi that some dogs were bred to retrieve and some to herd, and Lässu was obviously not a retriever. Still, Köbi was convinced that all dogs could be taught to bring back sticks.

In the meantime, he had fun racing after Lässu and trying to wrestle the sticks out of his mouth. Sometimes the pup would let go suddenly, and Köbi would tumble over backward. Then he'd lie there laughing at the puppy's puzzled look. "What are you doing down there?" the pup seemed to ask, as he brought his cold, wet nose up to Köbi's, which was now equally cold and wet. "Here, let me jump all over you and lick your face—maybe that will help."

Köbi arrived muddy and breathless to his and Pesche's special place on the Emme, with Lässu panting at his heels. A figure stood on one of the rocks that the boys used for seats, but it wasn't Pesche. Köbi stopped and stared. What was Karli doing in their hollow, and where was Pesche? Could he have invited Karli to join them? Pesche'd never do that, would he? Maybe he had, though—he surprised Köbi by being nice to the weirdest people sometimes. Like telling Karli not to pick on Norbert. Why would Pesche care about *him*? Köbi himself couldn't stand Karli's most loyal bear. Köbi had to do what he was told by Haldemann because he was *verdingt* and had no other place to live, but Norbert seemed glad to obey Karli like a *Meischter*, even though Karli hit him. Köbi despised Norbert for that.

Because he wasn't sure if Karli was supposed to be there or not, Köbi crept up to the hollow as quietly as he could, Lässu locked in his arms. He didn't want his dog anywhere near Karli. In fact, Köbi felt like running off, and he didn't feel ashamed to do it. He might be big and strong for eleven, he might even have knocked Karli down in the schoolyard a couple of times, but the older boy was still a threat. Or was he here for a friendly reason?

"Why are you here?" he yelled. "Where's Pesche?" The older boy just stared at him, and he saw, with increasing fear, that Karli had a stick at his feet, the kind of metal-knobbed walking stick used by old men. This one was thick and sturdy, and the shiny knob on the top was very big. Karli had been crying, and he wasn't trying to hide it. His eyes were red and swollen, his nose was snotty, and sobs shook his body now and then, as if he had no control over them. He looked like he'd been crying for a long time. That didn't comfort Köbi at all. Karli in tears was a strange sight; Köbi desperately wanted things to return to normal.

"I don't know where he is, but when I see him, I'm going to kill him. He's the reason my father punished me. He said I was a disgrace, and . . ." Karli broke off, and his body shook with another deep sob. "I hate Pesche."

Köbi thought about saying more, but talking to Karli was Pesche's job. So Köbi didn't say a word; he simply stood his ground. As soon as he saw Pesche, even at a distance, he'd yell out a warning and they'd run off together. He couldn't leave Pesche to face Karli alone. That was the only plan he had, but he felt it was a good one.

Lässu wriggled in his arms. He tried to keep the puppy still, but

Lässu didn't want to be held. He squirmed until he managed to deliver a particularly firm kick to Köbi's chest, freeing himself and slipping to the ground. The dog scrambled up and dashed over to where Karli's stick lay on the ground. In a moment, he'd grabbed it in his mouth and begun struggling to drag it away.

"No, Lässu, no!" screamed Köbi, and he started toward his dog. Karli was faster. He lifted the puppy by both ends of the walking stick, which protruded from either side of Lässu's muzzle. The dog dangled down, clinging to the stick with his teeth, growling and wagging his tail in appreciation of this new game. With one hand holding the dog high in the air by the stick, Karli used his other hand to grab Lässu's rope collar, which he twisted very tight. In surprise, Lässu let the stick fall from his mouth. Before Köbi could reach for Lässu, Karli sprinted to the edge of the riverbank, and Köbi saw a ray of light glance off the older boy's hand: the sun reflecting off the face of his fancy watch. Then Karli swung the little dog in an arc and flung him as hard as he could into the center of the frigid, fast-flowing Emme. Within seconds, the pup was carried downstream, although Köbi thought he could still see a little head bobbing along as he was swept away.

All thoughts of Pesche flew from Köbi's mind. With a scream of fury, he lowered his head, ran at Karli, and butted him in the chest. Leaving the older boy on his back, wheezing, Köbi took off running along the Emme after his dog. There was no path, so he slipped and slid and dodged, tripping several times to fall flat, only to rise and continue his race against the river's current. In no time, his and Pesche's hollow by the river was out of sight. "Lässu," he called a few times, but then he stopped yelling and saved his breath for his desperate run.

Even before his first tumble by the riverside during his wild pursuit of Lässu, Köbi had caught a glimpse of Norbert above him on the higher section of riverbank, moving in the direction of his and Pesche's special place. Moving toward Karli. He felt a rush of hatred for Karli's bear, and then he forgot about him.

* * *

Jakob and Markus sat in the car outside Markus's building for the last ten minutes of Jakob's story. As he described running down the bank of the Emme after his dog and seeing Norbert sneak past him toward Karli, Jakob's voice caught, and he fell silent.

Markus hadn't allowed himself to think about how this story was going to end, but now he could think of nothing else. He was afraid to hear it to its conclusion. Next to him sat Köbi, hands at ten and two on the wheel, staring through the windshield without moving; the old man inhaled and exhaled deliberately. But Markus could feel his own self-possession slipping away, his breathing becoming shallow, his chest tightening. In a squeezed, breathless voice, he asked, "Did Lässu drown?"

Köbi looked straight ahead as he said, flatly, "*Lässu* was fine."

Markus dropped his face into his hands, dread churning inside him. Yet he felt a weird spike of triumph, too. It was as if the small boy who lived deep in his brain was gloating. It wasn't *Markus* who was no good—no, it was Paps. He was the one who was bad. Paps had tried to grow up to become Hannes, but it hadn't worked; Karli had stayed inside him. Karli was inside Markus, too, in his genes, in his blood. So, whose fault was it if he, Markus, was also bad?

He opened the car door and stepped out onto the sidewalk. It was windy, but not raining, and there wasn't another figure in sight. Two cars drove by, soft swishes against the damp pavement. He breathed in a great mouthful of cold air and crossed the sidewalk to perch on the low wall in front of his building. He closed his eyes, and a picture invaded his mind: a man sprawled on the ground. In the dim light of streetlamps, the man's face was black, and Markus knew the black was blood. All around the man's body stood legs in jeans and sneakers, and one pair of legs was Markus's own. He watched his own foot draw back slowly and then shoot forward and connect with the bloody man's cheekbone. He thought of Karli with his stick and then of his own blood-flecked shoe and didn't know what to do with his self-loathing and sorrow.

No, that wasn't true—he did know what to do. He needed to confront his father and tell him that Karli wasn't a secret anymore. Markus knew all about Karli now, and he wanted his father to know that he knew.

In fact, he couldn't wait to tell him.

31

Heidmatt,
Friday morning, November 27

After the heavy rain that had fallen while Giuliana was talking to Noldi Arm, the rivulets crisscrossing the track down to the village had swollen to streams. Giuliana returned to Heidmatt's center at a crawl, spraying sheets of water as she went. Her tortoise-like progress reminded her of one of the few police training courses she'd almost failed: driving. The instructor had grudgingly given her a passing mark but told her never to engage in a car chase. So far she'd never had to. What she was chasing here was the truth, and so far it was eluding her. She thought Arm had been genuinely surprised to learn about the money flowing from Gurtner to Wittwer, but she was sure he'd been lying when he said he could think of no reason for the payments. Which pointed back to blackmail. Yet it didn't sound as if Wittwer would be *able* to blackmail anyone. And if he could, what secret about Gurtner did he know? Well, hopefully Wittwer himself would answer all these questions. Perhaps he was more capable than she'd been led to expect; she should know better than to underestimate anyone.

Still, it wasn't Wittwer she was considering as she drove toward the village, but the people who had featured as Johann Gurtner's enemies in both Brigitte Rieder's and Arnold Arm's stories: the teacher Müller and the indentured farm boy Pesche. If she was looking for someone from the heart surgeon's childhood who might have wanted to kill him, either one fit the bill. She should have asked Arm how old Müller was at the time of Karli's suspension. He had to have been at least ten years older than his pupils, which would make him over eighty today—not a very realistic attacker. Still, she'd ask Stefanie Egli about him. As Karli's classmate, Pesche must now be in his early seventies, and he'd probably speak Heidmatter dialect, like the man in the emergency phone call. Where was he?

She sighed and took one hand off the wheel to rub her right eye. It was hard to make herself care about new suspects with her sights fixed on Markus and Norbert. There were other names scattered through Arm's reminiscences that she should consider, though. Finding herself at the crossroads in front of The Lion, she turned into the inn parking lot to check her notebook. Arm had mentioned Heidi Stettler, of course, and another girl, Käthi, but she couldn't picture an elderly woman committing this crime. Who else was there? She found a Thomas in her notes, but a more important character in the story was Arm's desk mate, Köbi, who'd raced to the front of the class with the pointer, ready to brain Müller. He certainly sounded bloodthirsty, although in this case heroic, too. Something about him sounded familiar as well, but Köbi was a nickname for Jakob, and so far there'd been no Jakob in this case.

It was a two-minute drive from The Lion to the administrative building where she was meeting Arm's niece, Stefanie Egli, the community president. Giuliana made her way up the stairs to Egli's office on the second floor and found her behind a computer at a large desk covered with papers and folders in neat stacks. The woman was in her mid-forties, buxom and pleasant-faced, but any resemblance to a traditional Emmentaler farm wife ended there; Egli wore a tailored jacket instead of a pinafore. Walking out from behind her desk to shake Giuliana's hand, she said, "I hope my uncle was helpful. Did he leave you with any unanswered questions?"

"Not exactly," Giuliana answered, "but I could use a favor. That is, if you have time. It would help me if you could track down two people. The first is your uncle's teacher, Herr Müller. Is he alive and, if so, where is he?"

"Oh, the infamous Müller. *Onkel* Noldi's not the only one who still talks about him. The school must keep records; I'll see what I can do. Who's the second person?"

"There was a *Verdingbueb* named Pesche in your uncle's class. Both Gurtner's sister and Herr Arm mentioned him. Can you get his full name for me and, if possible, his current address? The police could track him down, but you might be able to find everything out with one call to Heidi Stettler."

"I'll try. Anything else?"

Giuliana thought about the other names, Thomas and Köbi, and decided to let them go for now. "Nothing else, except to thank you for the support," she said and left the woman to her stacks of folders.

A few minutes later, she pulled into the driveway of a small, well-kept cottage with beautiful flowerbeds. The resident had clearly been keeping an eye out for her, because before Giuliana stopped the car, she'd stepped outside. As she came down the path from her front porch to the driveway, Giuliana got out of the car to greet her. Marie Iseli, Wittwer's guardian angel, was stout with obviously dyed blond hair and looked to be in her mid-sixties. For eight years, she'd looked after a disabled, alcoholic man she wasn't related to, assuming her mother's role as his main caretaker. Why, Giuliana didn't know, but she imagined it was quite simple: the woman was a good person. There was a lot to be said for village life, she thought, as she walked around the car to greet Frau Iseli, who'd already started talking.

"Norbert's house is only just down the road, but since you're here I'll drive with you. He's so excited about talking to you, Frau Linder. Says he has a lot to tell you. I don't know what that means. He enjoys being secretive about his business, and why shouldn't he be?"

"You don't get the impression he's worried or afraid about coming to the police station?" Giuliana asked.

The woman struggled into the passenger seat. "Not so far. Except for his trips to the hospital, the poor man barely gets out of Heidmatt, so Bern's an adventure for him."

"He does know that Johann Gurtner's dead, right?"

"It's been the talk of the village. Norbert's trips to The Lion keep him up to date."

Five houses away, at the end of the road, was another small cottage that had probably once been identical to Frau Iseli's. Now the contrast between the two buildings was striking. This one hadn't had maintenance work done on it for decades, and the front garden was nothing more than a mass of weeds. The paintwork was faded and cracked, and the tiny front porch sagged.

"It already looked like this when Norbert's mother was a girl, my mother told me," said Iseli apologetically. "My husband takes a scythe to the weeds now and then, but that's all we've ever done to keep the place up."

Stopping in front of the rundown cottage, Giuliana turned toward Iseli and said, "It's enough that you've helped him all these years. Much more than enough. No one could expect you to invest money in the cottage as well. I think you've done a terrific job."

The older woman looked pleased even as she shrugged. "Until the cancer started to wear him down, Norbert looked after himself pretty well, in spite of his drinking and all. He took care of his mother till she died, and I guess she taught him how to keep things tidy. I'm only saying that I don't deserve *too* much praise. My Mam was the one who wanted to help her friend Rösli's boy, and she kept her eye on him for ages. I only took over after Mam got dementia and had to go into a home. And now she's passed, the dear soul."

During these remarks, they'd walked up the cracked concrete path and the front steps to the door. After Iseli rang the bell, they stepped down two steps. A tiny, emaciated old man, completely bald and bereft of eyebrows, opened the door. As she'd expected from her readings on fetal alcohol syndrome, his upper lip had no indentation. His eyes were large and lively, and he looked cheerful. Standing in the doorway, he smiled at the two women.

"Are we leaving right now?" he asked Giuliana. Because of his small size, his deep voice was incongruous. "Or do you want to come in? Hello again, Marie," he added. "You've come to see me off to Bern." He chuckled.

Norbert wore a warm down jacket, red sports shoes, and what appeared to be brand-new jeans; under his jacket, he had on a red T-shirt and a blue cardigan, half-buttoned. Giuliana took one step up, so that she could hold out her hand to him. "Hello, Herr Wittwer. I'm Giuliana Linder from the police. I'm the person who's driving you to Bern. I also want to ask you some questions about your friend Karli."

He shook the hand she offered but looked troubled. "Would it be okay for you to call me Norbert? I don't like being Herr Wittwer."

"I'll be glad to call you Norbert," she said quickly. "I'm ready to leave right away, if you are. It should take us about forty-five minutes to drive to Bern."

Norbert came down the steps and seemed to notice the car in his driveway for the first time. "Aren't we going in a police car?" he asked her, his whole face sagging with disappointment. Giuliana was astonished at how easy it was to read his emotions. In that sense, and in the direct way he talked to her, he was like a child. But don't treat him like a child, she reminded herself. She was going to have to feel her way.

"I'm not the kind of policewoman who wears a uniform," Giuliana said, "and I don't drive an orange-and-white car with special lights and a siren. But maybe I can arrange for you to be driven back from Bern in a real police car. I can't promise anything, though."

"Okay," said Norbert. "Can I sit in the front?"

"Please do," she said. "Go ahead and get in. I just want to thank Frau Iseli, and I'll be right along." Nodding, Norbert walked to the car and got into the passenger seat, as Giuliana said goodbye to Norbert's neighbor, who handed her a small, sealed envelope, saying, "These are the pills he should take with lunch; don't let him forget."

Five minutes later, they crossed the covered bridge out of Heidmatt and were on their way back to Bern through the Emmental. Giuliana told Norbert about the room they'd be meeting in and explained that Erwin would join them for their discussion. "He doesn't wear a uniform, either," she warned Norbert. "But he used to. So did I."

"Too old for the fun stuff now, are you?" said Norbert, which was, Giuliana reflected, the first adult-sounding remark he'd made.

"Well, I don't miss herding football hooligans and running after bad guys," she answered, "but I'll bet Erwin does." She smiled. "He has medals for doing brave things when he was a young cop, like jumping into the Aare in the middle of winter to rescue a drowning woman. Not that *he's* ever told me about his medals, but other people have."

They were silent for a while, and then Norbert said, "I'm not brave. I never was."

"That's not what I heard," Giuliana said, taking her eyes off the road long enough to smile at the old man beside her—a smile he didn't see because he was staring out the window. "I heard from Johann's"— she corrected herself—"from Karli's little sister Bri that Karli used to demonstrate how to box using you as his opponent and sometimes landed real punches. And you stood there and took it, even when he knocked you over."

"That wasn't brave," Norbert said, his voice full of scorn; "that was stupid."

Giuliana cursed herself for not thinking to turn on a recording device before they began the ride. Without it, anything relevant to the murder case that might come up in the car wouldn't be available later. They were driving on a country road, not a highway, so she pulled onto the shoulder and got out her phone. She explained to Norbert about recording their conversation, and he agreed, so she placed the mobile between them, set it to record, and had him repeat his consent. He insisted she play it back and laughed aloud, saying that he'd never heard his own voice like that before.

Back on the road at last, she asked, "Why did you just tell me that you thought it was stupid of you to let Karli punch you when you were kids?"

"Well, don't you think it's pretty dumb to let yourself get hit for no reason?"

"I guess so. But I thought you were doing it because Karli was your friend and he wanted you to."

"That *is* why I did it, but that doesn't make it smart."

"Okay," Giuliana conceded, "but I think it's still brave. Do you think Gurtner was brave? Karli, I mean."

"I thought so when we were in school together. I thought he was brave and smart and my best friend. But since I got sick and stopped drinking so much, I've been remembering when I was a kid, and talking to folks at The Lion, especially Heidi, and now I don't know what to think."

Norbert seemed so comfortable that Giuliana decided to risk the most important question. "Karli has sent you a lot of money over the past fifty years. Why did he do that?"

"You know about that?"

Giuliana turned toward Norbert; he was open-mouthed and wide-eyed, like a small child whose uncle has just pulled a coin out of his ear. "How *can* you?" His deep voice was suddenly shrill.

In her most matter-of-fact tone, Giuliana said, "It's hard to move a lot of money around without leaving a trace. Karli got a bank to send payments from his account to yours, and the bank has to keep a record of that. When the police look into someone's death, like we're doing with Karli's, we check what the dead person has done with their money. That's how we found your name."

Norbert nodded as if he understood, but he didn't say anything. Giuliana risked repeating, "Why did he send it to you?"

"I . . . I don't want to talk about that. I know I have to, but I don't want to."

"Okay." Giuliana hoped her disappointment didn't show. "Let's wait and talk about it when we're with Erwin Sägesser. That's the brave policeman I told you about." They drove a while in silence before she asked, "Who's the bravest person *you* know?"

Norbert didn't answer, and after a silence of over a minute, she let it go and decided that unless he volunteered something, she'd stop asking him questions without Erwin. They were past Worb now and out of the Emmental, perhaps fifteen minutes from Bern.

"The bravest person I ever knew was Pesche."

Pesche was the Bernese nickname for *anyone* named Peter. Still, there'd been only one Pesche in this case so far. "Do you mean the Pesche in your class at school?"

"Yeah." Norbert was turned away, staring out the window, and his answer was almost inaudible. So much for the recording. Still, she went on.

"Bri Rieder—that's Karli's little sister—and Noldi Arm told me Karli and Pesche didn't like each other. And neither of them liked your teacher Herr Müller, did they?"

Norbert turned back from the window. His voice was still low, but now she thought her phone would catch it. "That's why Pesche was so brave. He had two bad enemies, and they were both mean to him, but he always stood up to them. He was never afraid."

"Do you remember Pesche's real name?" She was afraid he might balk at the question, but he gave her a scornful glance, which she caught out of the corner of her eye.

"Of course I do. Peter. Peter Beck."

In Arm's story, Giuliana remembered how Pesche had said to Karli, "*My ancestors were bakers.*" That would have to mean a surname like Pfister, Becker, or Beck. Well, now she had the information—she just hoped Frau Egli wouldn't spend too long searching for it.

"Do you ever see Pesche?" She turned to look at the man beside her as she asked this and found him staring at her inquisitively, as though there was something in her simple yes-or-no question that had to be deciphered. Still, he answered easily enough. "I guess I see him a couple of times a month. Sometimes I go with Heidi."

She was elated. As soon as this interview with Norbert was over, she'd find Peter Beck, who must live in Heidmatt, if Norbert saw him so often. How had they gotten this far without including him in the investigation? She should have put someone onto tracking him down as soon as Bri mentioned the way he'd stood up to Karli in the school-yard when Karli punched Norbert. Maybe the voice in the emergency call really was Pesche's.

They were less than ten minutes from the police station now, so instead of asking Norbert more questions, she turned off the recording app on her phone and began to explain what would happen when they arrived.

"Can I pee first?" was all Norbert asked when she finished.

"Of course," she said. Just then her phone rang. Renzo. Against all regulations, she lifted it to her ear and drove on, as he told her about Toni's interview with Markus.

32

G iuliana parked at the police station. It wasn't quite noon, but men and women were already strolling out of the station on their lunch breaks, and Norbert got out of the car faster than Giuliana would have thought possible. He stood in the middle of the parking lot staring at all the police in uniform moving around him. Then he walked over to one of the orange-and-white cars with "POLICE" in large letters and the Canton of Bern coat of arms on the front doors and peered inside. Giuliana hurried after him. His eyes were wide, but with excitement rather than fear. "I hope it works out for me to go home in one of these." He beamed at her.

I hope it works out for you to go home at all, Giuliana thought. Now that Renzo had revealed Markus's statement—that he'd set up a meeting with his father so Norbert could return Karli's watch—she was more than ever convinced that the two men had somehow caused Gurtner's death. No matter how carefully Markus had schooled Norbert to reproduce the story of their never arriving at the Aare, she didn't believe he could lie successfully enough to keep himself and Markus out of trouble.

Five minutes later, Giuliana was able to imagine Erwin with

the grandchildren he occasionally mentioned, thanks to his gentleness with Norbert. He guided the older man to the door of the men's toilets, took him into the cafeteria to pick out a sandwich and a drink, had a more comfortable chair brought into the interrogation room for him, and explained about the cop who'd be in the back of the room taking notes as they talked. When the three of them were finally sitting around the table ready to begin, Erwin said, "People who talk to us, Norbert, some of them need advice about what to say, so they ask for a lawyer. We can get you a lawyer, too, if you want one. Would you like us to do that?"

"I wish someone was here to advise me, but not someone I've never seen before."

"It's a lawyer's job to help you, even if you don't know him. Or her." Erwin turned to Giuliana and waggled his eyebrows at her to be sure she noticed his use of both pronouns. "Shall we ask one to join us while we talk?" Erwin asked Norbert again. "We might have to wait a while for the lawyer to get here, but that's all right. We don't mind."

Norbert shook his head. "No, I want to talk now. I already told Frau . . ." he looked at Giuliana, embarrassed that he'd forgotten her name.

"That's okay, Norbert," she told him. "Would you like to call us Giuliana and Erwin, since we're calling you Norbert?" When he nodded, she said, "Okay. So, you already told me . . .?"

"I told you I'd talk about everything I didn't want to say in the car, so I will."

Erwin nodded enthusiastically. "That's great."

Norbert's anxious gaze switched to Giuliana, who smiled at him and said, "Yes, we're both eager to hear what you have to say." Norbert nodded at Giuliana and took a big bite of his sandwich. As soon as he'd swallowed his mouthful, Erwin said, "You know that Herr Doktor Gurtner, the man you call Karli, drowned in the Aare five days ago, on Monday evening."

"I know. I found out Tuesday night at The Lion. I was upset. He was my friend; that was one reason. But it also meant I couldn't give him back his watch. I'd been planning that for a long time, and then he died before I could do it. And . . . and before I could talk to him about it."

Here was the heirloom watch, cropping up already in Norbert's tale.

"When did he give you the watch?" Giuliana asked.

"When we were kids. It was important, and he told his father he'd lost it." Norbert's eyes moved back and forth between Giuliana and Erwin, his expression wary.

Erwin picked up the thread. "First, Karli gave you his watch, and soon after that he started to give you money, didn't he?" Norbert nodded. Erwin said for the transcriber, "Herr Wittwer just nodded," and went on, "Did you ask him for money?"

"No," said Norbert, his voice steady. "I was really surprised the first time I got an envelope from him. It was after he'd gone away to Thun for school. A five-franc note was inside. No letter—that made me sad. But my mother was happy about the money. And, after that, he always sent some. First cash and later money that went straight into a bank account at the post office. He told me to open that account, just so he could put money into it."

Was Norbert telling the truth? It certainly sounded that way. But an important piece of the story was missing.

"Why did Karli give you the watch?" she asked. Norbert's cautious eyes were suddenly fearful. His mouth opened and closed several times, and his hands flew to his face.

"I don't want to tell you," he wailed. "I don't want you to know what I did. You'll hate me, like Köbi used to, and maybe you'll put me in jail." His hands were snaking uselessly around his face and body, and he twisted in his seat, agitation filling his entire being. Then he gave a great sob and put his forehead down on the table.

Giuliana registered the name of Noldi Arm's desk mate, Köbi. So, Köbi'd hated Norbert once, and now he didn't. What had changed? She looked at Erwin, and he pointed at himself, a question in his eyes; she nodded. He got up, went around the table to crouch beside

Norbert and put an arm around his shaking shoulders. "Listen to me. No matter what you did when you were a boy, no one can put you in jail for it now. It's *verjährt*. That means so many years have passed since it happened that you can't be punished anymore. So, it's okay to tell us about it."

"We promise not to hate you," Giuliana added, hoping she was telling the truth.

Norbert raised his head, plucked a tissue from the box on the table, wiped his eyes, and took a deep breath. Then he picked up his paper cup and drank some Coke before saying, "I knew I'd have to tell you; I knew it all along. But I'm afraid to. Because I told a bad lie."

As Erwin moved back to his side of the table, Giuliana nodded and said, "Why don't you start at the beginning, Norbert. Tell us what happened before you got the watch."

Norbert sat up straight and folded his hands on the table. His voice when he began to speak had a singsong quality, as if he were reciting, but after a few sentences, he sounded normal again. His eyes were distant, however, as though the events he was considering were drawing him into the past. This, Giuliana anticipated, would be the truth.

"Karli told everyone that Pesche fell off the footbridge railings into the Emme, and that he and I got wet when we waded in to save him. But what really happened is that Karli waited for Pesche on the river with a big, fat stick. He walked there from the castle, even though it was a long way, and I was watching for him, like I did most of the time, and I followed him. Then I hid. Köbi got to the place first"—Köbi comes up again and again, Giuliana noted; he's right in the middle of this—"but Karli made him run away. Then Pesche came, and Karli screamed at him and hit him with the stick, and he fell down. That's when Karli dragged him into the Emme. That's how Karli got wet."

Norbert was agitated again. The hands he'd clasped on the table when he started to speak were everywhere—one rubbing his nose while the other pounded on his thigh; one scratching his head while the other hugged his stomach. But he kept talking. "You remember in the car when you said I was brave to let Karli box me?" he asked Giuliana. "I'm not. I'm a coward. If I was brave, I'd have done something to help Pesche. Pesche was Karli's enemy, not mine. He never did anything mean to me. Or to anybody. But I was scared."

"It's okay to be scared, Norbert," Erwin said. "Every man is afraid of someone bigger and stronger who has a weapon. That's not cowardly; that's common sense. If you'd come out of your hiding place, Karli might have hit *you* with the stick, too."

"He almost did," Norbert said. "Because when I saw him pulling Pesche into the river, I ran out of my hiding place on the bank and yelled, 'What are you doing?' Karli dropped Pesche then and ran at me, and I . . . I screamed."

"That was smart, screaming for help," Erwin said. He leaned toward Norbert, both forearms on the table. Giuliana was distracted by Norbert's talk of Köbi. She remembered Arm's description of the classroom fight. It was Köbi who'd grabbed the pointer to defend Pesche against the teacher. Did that mean he was the ragged boy in Brigitte's story, too—the one who'd taken a punch for Pesche?

"Maybe screaming *was* smart," Norbert told Erwin, "because Karli stopped running toward me and asked me to come and help him put Pesche in the Emme. I said no; it was just an excuse for him to get close and hit me."

"Good thinking," said Erwin. Norbert smiled, although his hands were kneading one another ceaselessly.

"So, he went back to what he was doing, pulling and pushing Pesche till he . . . floated away. Karli came at me again, and I yelled, 'No stick.' He stood there a while, and then he threw it somewhere along the river—but not into the water. He was too busy climbing up the bank to see where it fell, but I saw. After that, I got ready to run as fast as I could, but when he got to the top of the bank, he sat down on the grass and cried. He cried on and on. I sat there, too, not next to him but nearby. I didn't know what to do."

Norbert stopped talking. His mouth went slack, and his eyes lost focus.

"What happened when Karli stopped crying?" Giuliana prompted.

Norbert seemed to come only halfway back from whatever scenes he was replaying in his head. His hands were still, his eyes strange. "Karli told me he'd say Pesche was walking on the bridge railings—the way some boys did, because of a dare—and fell in, and that he and I tried to get him out. I had to tell the lie, too. No, I had to agree with *his* lie. I've never been good at lying and he knew that, so he didn't want me to talk, just agree. I said no, because I knew we'd get in trouble, but he said he'd hurt me if I didn't do it, and he'd give me his special watch if I did."

Norbert looked back and forth between the two detectives, and Giuliana noticed again how childishly expressive his face was: she could see sadness in every feature. "It was always like that with him. I never knew if we were friends because I was afraid of him or because he was good to me, since he went back and forth all the time between mean and nice."

"So you took the watch," Erwin said, as if this were the most reasonable decision in the world. Under the circumstances, Giuliana thought, it had been.

Norbert nodded. "First, I had to go into the river and get wet like he was, even though it was very cold. Then he gave me his watch." Norbert stared down at the table and spoke without looking at either cop. "He told me never to wear it, but after he left for Thun, I wore it to school once, and all the kids knew it was Karli's. So, they knew I'd had something to do with what happened to Pesche. After that, they all hated me. Especially Köbi."

Giuliana noted Köbi's name again, but something else was bothering her. "Why didn't you ask Pesche to tell them what really happened?"

Norbert looked at her with his mouth open. She went on. "The Pesche who got hit and pushed into the Emme is Pesche Beck from your class, right? You told me on our drive here that you see him a couple of times a month. So I thought he kept living in Heidmatt after he recovered."

Erwin was staring at her, too, and in that moment of suspended conversation, she replayed Norbert's words, "Karli told everyone Pesche fell off the bridge railings," and matched them with a memory of Charlotte Gurtner saying, "A village boy fell off a bridge." So, Giuliana knew what Norbert would say before he opened his mouth and explained, "I can't ask Pesche anything because he drowned when Karli hit him and lugged him into the river. He's buried in the Heidmatt graveyard. I used to be afraid to go there, but since I got so sick and started talking to Heidi about those days, I visit his grave often. Heidi mostly goes by herself to see him, but sometimes we go together. I tell Pesche I'm sorry. Sometimes I tell him other stuff. Like I said, he was always nice to me."

The three of them sat for a moment in silence, but Giuliana's mind was anything but quiet. Her eyes wandered around the off-white walls of the small, windowless room without noticing anything, as she considered Karli Gurtner killing Pesche Beck and what that might mean for the boy named Köbi who'd rushed to Pesche's aid at least twice that she knew about. Did Köbi still live in Heidmatt, too? It was time to find out.

The silence was broken when Norbert blew out his breath with obvious relief. "Are we finished now?"

"I'm afraid not," Erwin said. "We need to go back to what happened on Monday afternoon. Because someone hit Karli on the head and made sure he ended up in the Aare, just the way Pesche ended up in the Emme after Karli hit *him* on the head. And we think you know who it was."

"I wasn't there," whispered Norbert. "I meant to come to Bern, I really did, not to hurt Karli, just to give him back the watch and tell him that killing Pesche was bad and I wish I hadn't lied for him. I've been planning what to say for weeks. But when the day came, I got so scared that I bought a pint of schnapps and drank the whole thing. When Markus came to get me, I was too drunk to go. I went to sleep. No, that's a lie—I passed out. Markus tried to make me come with him, but finally he took the watch and left. I guess he went without me."

Giuliana sat up straighter, her mind on alert. Norbert had just confirmed without any prompting Markus's story about his drinking and passing out. But what was this about Markus taking the watch and going to meet his father on his own? Had Markus mentioned that? Not according to Renzo. "Does Markus know his father killed Pesche when they were boys?" Giuliana asked.

Norbert looked up at the ceiling. "I think so," he said at last.

Before she could follow up, Erwin broke in. "So, Markus went to meet Karli alone and did to him what Karli'd done to Pesche." He spoke conversationally, as if Markus's behavior made perfect sense.

Norbert half-pushed himself up from his chair, shaking his head madly, his eyes wild. "Of course not," he said, his voice shrill. "You forgot that Karli was Markus's father. *Nobody* would kill his own father." Norbert dropped back into his seat and leaned forward, glowering at Erwin, as if he wasn't sure he could be trusted anymore.

Erwin and Giuliana intercepted each other's glances. Erwin's was grim. "How silly of me," he said, "to think a son could kill his father. Or a father his son." His gravelly voice was infinitely bleak, and she was sure that he, too, was thinking about a case the department had handled just three weeks before, of a quiet insurance broker who'd used his semi-automatic army rifle to wipe out his wife, two sons, and baby daughter before slitting his throat with his bayonet. "Why don't you talk to Norbert for a while, Giule?" Erwin added. "I think I need a break." He gave a huge sigh and slouched back in his chair as she sat forward. "Shall I get you some coffee, Norbert?"

"Can I have one of those apple juice boxes with the straw stuck on?" Norbert asked. Erwin nodded, took a coffee order from the transcriber in the back of the room, and left. Norbert took up his paper cup and used it to try and catch a fly that kept landing on the table. Giuliana stood up, stretched, and thought about Markus meeting his father on the riverbank alone and confronting his lifelong tormentor with having killed a schoolmate and gotten away with it. Damn it to hell! She couldn't believe Toni was going to be proved right after all. Still, much as she wanted to deprive him of a victory, she could see how easily a fight between father and son could have sprung up and how quickly it would have turned deadly.

But what about the emergency call, the one referring to the dead man as Karli? Markus hadn't made that call. It was beginning to look as if Norbert hadn't either. So who . . .?

Erwin came back looking slightly less gray and handed their colleague his coffee and Norbert his juice. Norbert immediately plunged the straw into the little opening on the top of the box, and apple juice sprayed out onto the table. The older man gave Giuliana a wide-eyed look, clearly afraid of a reprimand from the "mother" in the room, but it was Erwin who pulled a wad of paper napkins out of his pocket and wiped up the spilled liquid.

Once Norbert had had a few contented sucks on the straw and things had settled down, Giuliana took charge of the interview; a nod from Erwin had given her his blessing. "I'm going to run through things one more time with you, Norbert. Okay?"

The little man nodded. His childlike qualities made it easy to forget that he was a man over seventy with lethal cancer, but, looking at his drawn face, Giuliana knew he was wearing out. She remembered Arm warning her that Norbert could stop making sense when he got tired. She mustn't let that happen.

Deliberately slowly and softly, Giuliana began to talk. "I know you and Markus had a plan to meet Karli while he was walking his dog." Norbert nodded. "Did Heidi know about it?" Norbert nodded again. "Did anyone else know about it?" Norbert shrugged this time and Giuliana saw his forehead wrinkle, so she gentled her voice still more as she said, "You were surprised I didn't know about Pesche being dead, weren't you? There's a lot about your life that I don't know. Like, I don't know if Köbi is your friend."

"He is," said Norbert, and the frown wrinkles disappeared. "He used to hate me, but not anymore. He even visits me at home sometimes."

"Köbi was around just before Pesche was killed. You said Karli chased him away. Noldi Arm told me about Köbi defending Pesche from Herr Müller. I think Bri, Karli's sister, saw Köbi knock Karli down, too, one time when Karli was about to punch Pesche. So, Köbi liked Pesche a lot, didn't he?" After what seemed a long time, Norbert nodded. He'd stopped looking at Giuliana and was staring at the tabletop, his hands hanging at his sides.

"Was Köbi supposed to be there when you gave the watch back to Karli? Were you and Markus supposed to meet Köbi on the Aare, too, before Karli came along?"

Norbert, still staring at the tabletop, shook his head like a pendulum for a long time, before announcing in a loud voice, "I'm hungry."

33

A young guard was instructed to take Norbert to the toilet, make sure he took his lunch pills, and then get him whatever he wanted to eat from the cafeteria. In the meantime, Giuliana and Erwin ran across the street to the bakery café for a quick meal of coffee and pie: plum for Giuliana, redcurrant for Erwin.

"So, who is Köbi?" Erwin asked. "And why in God's name is it so hard to get answers out of a tiny, shriveled old geezer with cancer and several screws loose?"

He looked tired, Giuliana thought, which reminded her that he was over sixty. Still, he interrogated suspects all the time without being flattened. Talking to Norbert was wearing them both down—the process didn't fit any of their usual patterns.

She swallowed a bite of dark purple plum embedded in cinnamon-and-almond-flavored custard. "I know," she said. "If he was a scumbag and said he was hungry just when we were at a key point in the questioning, we'd say tough luck. But how can you say that to Norbert? It's like telling a little boy he can't go pee."

"The way my prostate's been acting up, nobody better tell me I can't go pee either," Erwin commented through a large mouthful of pie. "Now, give me a five-sentence introduction to this guy Köbi, and we'll get back to work."

"He's cropped up in two interviews as one of Gurtner's classmates, always defending Pesche. The Heidmatt farmer I interviewed this morning, Arnold Arm—he talked about Köbi by name, and I think the boy Brigitte Rieder told me about must have been Köbi. He knocked Karli to the ground and stood over him like an avenging angel."

"An avenging angel, huh? Sounds promising." Erwin's coffee cup clattered into its saucer as he reached for the buzzing mobile in his shirt pocket. He listened for a minute and then said to the caller, "Shit! That really eats into our time window. Keep going. And text me the firm's name, will you?"

Giuliana, who'd been savoring her last bite of crust, looked at him inquiringly, and he said, "Renzo's working on Markus Gurtner's phone calls. That bastard Toni got hold of the data I'd requested from Swisscom and delayed it getting to us. Anyway, Markus's phone was off that afternoon until about four-thirty, when he made a call lasting twelve minutes that came through a tower in Bethlehem. Which doesn't leave him a hell of a lot of time to get to the Aare and do in his old man. But if he still had the rental car . . . hmm, Renzo needs to find out when he returned it." He sent a quick text.

"So, you're saying the first thing Markus did when he got home from Heidmatt was plug in his phone and call someone. That sounds relevant," Giuliana said.

"It could be, except it was an electrician. Renzo says Markus has phoned this firm off and on throughout the past year, and they've phoned back. Nothing strange about a photographer dealing with electricians. Still, it's a lot of contact." He swallowed the last of his coffee, frowning in thought. "I'd figure the electrician for a boyfriend, but you didn't get a gay vibe. Renzo didn't either. Could Markus have an electrician *girlfriend*?" So much for Erwin's gender sensitivity: he sounded incredulous. "Or is he phoning his coke dealer? He was a cokehead for a long time: maybe he still is."

They paid the waitress and started back to the station, Giuliana casting around in her mind for the name of the woman who'd modeled for the Venus photo, the woman who'd been with Markus when he'd met his father at the Bellevue bar. Ada. She was called Ada. She was gorgeous—but that was no reason she couldn't also be an electrician. "What's the electrical firm's name?" she asked, and Erwin checked his phone.

"Company's called Jakob Amsler AG, so I suppose the . . ." He stopped and looked at her, even though they were in the middle of the yellow crosswalk. "Jakob. Köbi."

Giuliana grabbed his arm and steered him to the sidewalk, before the cars waiting for them to cross started honking. "It could be a coincidence," she said, "but . . . Come on, I bet Norbert can tell us." She headed for the station door.

The man taking notes was back in his seat in the interrogation room, and so was Norbert, concentrating on a Magnum ice-cream bar. "Just like you said," the young guard at the door whispered, "he's sort of a kid, so I gave him a lot of napkins for the ice cream. He seems not to have made a mess so far. Hope it's okay."

"No problem," said Giuliana, smiling up at the lanky cop, who waited until she and Erwin were in their seats and then closed the door. Norbert gave them a suspicious look over his ice-cream-on-a-stick, licked all around it to catch any drips, and announced, "I'm not going to say anything bad about Köbi, and you shouldn't either." Despite his defiant words, he looked scared.

"Don't worry," said Giuliana. "We don't want you to say anything bad about him. We just want to check that his last name is Amsler."

Norbert thought so long about this question that his ice cream started dripping onto the table. Finally, apparently deciding that nothing about the answer could harm his friend, he said, "Yes. Jakob Amsler. His wife's name is Renata Lanz, and she's a teacher. Köbi used to be an . . . engineer,"—Norbert pronounced the word carefully—"but since he retired, he's gone back to fixing things. He fixed a broken fan for me during the summer."

Giuliana thought about Bri's filthy boy in rags and asked, "Was he a *Verdingbueb* like Pesche? Is that why they were friends?"

Norbert was now scrubbing chocolate off the table with a paper napkin in one hand, pausing for small nibbles of the ice cream bar in his other hand until it was almost gone. He looked up, confused.

"They were both *Verdingkinder*—Heidi, too," he said and took a huge mouthful of ice cream. "Köbi was Pesche's little brother," he added after swallowing. Then, slowly, he ate the last bite on the stick.

Giuliana drew in a breath, and out of the corner of her eye, she saw Erwin widen his eyes and shake his head just once, as if to say, "No, I can't believe it either." All the talk about Pesche over the past few days, and no one had mentioned a brother.

Norbert, now sucking on the bare stick, giggled and added, "Younger brother, not little brother. I don't think Köbi was ever little, because he's huge. Not just compared to me. He's bigger than everyone in Heidmatt." His eyes gleamed as he said this and his shoulders squared. "A giant, that's what he is."

Giuliana had a vision of the photograph she'd told Markus Gurtner was one of her favorites in the *Verdingkinder* exhibition: a very large and strong-looking old man with a stern mouth standing at a window, backlit by a stormy sky. Could that be Köbi? Heidi had mentioned she had a friend whose photo was in the show: Giuliana remembered that now. Pesche, Heidi, and Köbi, all *Verdingkinder*, and Markus producing portraits for the September exhibition. And by November, his father was dead. Was that a coincidence?

"Norbert," said Giuliana, and waited until the small man was looking directly at her. His hands now played nervously with the ice cream stick. "I know you don't want to get any of your friends in trouble, but you have to trust us to do our job right. You don't think Erwin and I are bad people, do you?" Norbert shook his head slowly but didn't look convinced. "We need to know if you and Markus were going to meet Köbi at the Aare, before you returned the watch. We're going to ask Markus the same question," she added, "and you know he'll tell us the truth." *At least he will this time,* she thought. *I'll make damn sure he does.*

Norbert was getting worried again. "That's good," he said softly. "Talk to Markus. Talk to Köbi. They'll explain everything." He sat back in his chair, as though he'd finished.

"But we need to hear the truth from you," Erwin said. "The man who's writing everything down needs to hear it. So, I'm going to ask you one question, and you can give me the correct answer, yes or no. Just yes or no."

"Yes or no," repeated Norbert, frowning. "Okay."

"The plan," Erwin continued, "was for three men to meet Johann Gurtner—that's Karli—on Monday, November twenty-third, in the late afternoon: you, Markus, and Köbi, whose real name is Jakob Amsler. Yes or no?"

"Yes," Norbert answered quickly. "The answer is yes."

Giuliana and Erwin exchanged a long look. It was time to find Jakob Amsler. But Markus came first, Giuliana thought. Whatever the plan had been, he'd been in on it.

"Thank you, Norbert," said Erwin. "You've helped us a lot. Now we'd like you to wait a minute in here while Giuliana and I have a chat outside in the hall."

"Okay." The little man was frowning again, but this now seemed to be because he was having trouble breaking the ice-cream stick into smaller and smaller bits. He didn't even raise his head as the two stood up and stepped out into the hall. "You're the one who should talk to Markus," Erwin said; "you've spoken to him before. See what you can get out of him. Meanwhile, I'll have someone take Norbert home, and we'll pick up Jakob Amsler."

"Sounds good," said Giuliana. "I just hope . . ."

She stopped. Toni was coming down the corridor toward them. "You've got the retard in there, haven't you?" he called to them, gesturing at the room where Norbert was waiting. "What's he told you? Fill me in. I want to ask some follow-up questions."

"Oh, fuck!" breathed Erwin. "You go find Markus. I'll deal with Toni. Just go!"

She went.

Markus was in a cell at the *Amtshaus*, the regional courthouse and justice center. It was across the Aare from the police station, and the quickest way to get there was on foot. Giuliana arrived breathless and went through the metal detector. At the bank of elevators in the lobby, she phoned a woman prosecutor she knew and organized a room where she could talk to Markus undisturbed. It was irregular to bypass Toni, but not unheard of; she didn't think it would raise any red flags.

Everything went faster than she'd dared hope, but still half an hour went by before she walked into an interrogation room to find Markus sitting at yet another small table in yet another metal chair, both bolted to the floor. Markus, handcuffed to the chair, threw her a look that was immensely weary, but not, she decided, hostile. She had the guard remove his cuffs and then held out her hand. "Giuliana Linder again, Herr Gurtner."

He stood up slowly, one eye on the guard, and shook hands. "I remember your name, Frau Linder, along with our previous conversation. What can I do for you?" He raised one eyebrow as he said this, and she grinned in appreciation of his mock courtesy. After she'd dismissed the guard, Giuliana sat down across from him; he sat as well, absently rubbing first one wrist and then the other.

God only knew when Toni might come barging in, so she got right to the point. "I've just come from talking to Norbert Wittwer and—"

Markus broke in, his voice strained. "Is he all right? You didn't—"

Now it was her turn to interrupt. "He's fine. At least he was half an hour ago, when I left him finishing some ice cream." *I hope Toni isn't yelling at him*, she thought. Surely Erwin wouldn't let him. "Herr Wittwer confirmed your story about the surprise rendezvous that you and he were planning with your father. He told us about the watch he wanted to return and the reason your father gave it to him. Do you know that reason?"

Markus squeezed his eyes shut for a moment before answering. "I know when he was thirteen my father killed Pesche Beck, and my grandfather, who was the village doctor, covered it up, helped by the lie my father told. Norbert confirmed the lie in return for the watch. So, yes, I've heard the whole story. I learned it a few weeks ago."

"Did you hear it from Jakob Amsler?" Giuliana asked.

When Markus said nothing, Giuliana continued. "You and Norbert weren't the only people ambushing"—his gaze on her sharpened at this word, but she went on—"your father along the Aare. A third man was supposed to have been there: Jakob Amsler, a former *Verdingbueb* who was in the same school class as your father and Norbert, along with Peter Beck and Heidi Stettler. You never mentioned Jakob Amsler in your statement to the prosecutor, and Norbert kept trying to avoid mentioning him as well. For some reason, both of you are very loyal to Herr Amsler. But the time has come to . . ."

"I know," said Markus. The barely tamed creature she'd visited in his apartment on Wednesday morning, who'd held himself like a taut wire and could scarcely contain his rage, seemed to have gone to ground. This Markus put his elbows on the table, slumped forward, and laid his forehead into his raised palms. He breathed in and out so steadily that for a moment she thought he'd gone to sleep. When he looked up at her, his pale blue eyes were no longer wrathful but deeply sad. They were puzzled, too, she decided. Almost like Norbert's. Here was another man-child trying to cope with a betrayal he didn't understand. But was the betrayer Karli again—or Köbi?

"My gloves," he said. "Did the wool match what you found in the watchband?"

"I don't know. No time to check. I've been with Norbert for hours."

Markus shook his head, eyes closed again, before saying, "I'm sure it will match. Jakob's wife Renata had wool left over from a scarf she knitted him, so she made me those gloves. But the yarn that got caught in the watchband wasn't from my gloves; it was from Jakob's scarf. It must be. I wasn't on the river that afternoon."

Giuliana sat absorbing this news. A case of one conspirator trying to shift all the blame onto the other? First, she'd have to find out if the scarf even existed. In the meantime, she stored the information away and went on with her questions. "You called Jakob when you got back from Heidmatt at four-thirty to tell him about the fiasco with Norbert, and he said he was going to meet your father alone." Giuliana said this matter-of-factly, so sure was she of its accuracy, but Markus shook his head.

"No." His tone was emphatic. "That's one of the things I don't understand. Jakob was upset that his plan had fallen through, but I was furious. Partly because I'd driven to Heidmatt and back for nothing when I had work deadlines. But mainly," he paused and hung his head before meeting her eyes, "mainly because I was so eager to confront my father. I wanted to stand there with Köbi, the brother of my father's victim, and Norbert, the man he'd scared into helping him get away with murder, and throw Pesche's death into his face. Ever since I knew we'd be meeting him, I've been . . . playing the scene over in my mind. And then Norbert got drunk and ruined everything."

Giuliana summed it up. "You couldn't bear that it wasn't going to happen."

Markus nodded. "I didn't say that to Jakob, but he knew. There will be another time, he promised. He *promised* me. Then he went and killed my father, and now there is no other time. Why did he do that? Why did he go without me?"

Silently Giuliana went over what she knew about the plan. Jakob's plan: Markus had just said it. There was still so much she didn't understand. Why had Jakob sent Markus to pick up Norbert? Why hadn't he gone himself, when he had a car and Markus had to rent one. "Do you think Amsler was setting you up to take the blame for the death?" she asked.

Markus didn't look shocked, but his expression grew grimmer. "I don't know. I just don't know. The gloves and scarf. Maybe. But Renata would never . . . Jakob and I met because of the *Verdingkinder* photos, and after that he called me to suggest a drink. Was he already . . .?" Markus frowned. "I don't know if he wanted to frame me for a killing he was planning or get me to do his killing for him. Or . . ." His voice trailed off, and he stared over Giuliana's shoulder, frowning in thought.

She was thinking hard herself. Despite all Markus had told her, she still didn't know what had happened on the riverbank. They needed Jakob Amsler. Still sitting with Markus, she phoned Erwin. Before she could open her mouth, Erwin was spluttering into her ear. "Amsler's missing, for fuck's sake. Can you believe it? We're at his apartment, searching the whole building in case he's hiding here. His wife's frantic—no one's seen or heard from him for over twenty-four hours. Told his wife after lunch yesterday he was going for a walk and that was it. She thinks he may have gone to Heidmatt, maybe to his brother's grave, maybe to one of the farms he worked on as a kid. She's already called people she knows in the village, and they're looking for him. We've got Swisscom trying to locate him by his phone, but . . ."

Erwin paused for breath, and Giuliana said, "I'm with Markus. He's confirmed that the plan was for all three men to be on the Aare. Has one of our people checked the crime site?"

"Yep, she just reported in. He's not there."

Unless he'd gone to Dählhölzli earlier to reflect on the murder and had thrown himself into the Aare. She knew Erwin had thought of that, too. They'd have to check the weir for his body.

"Let me finish up here," she said. "Then you can tell me what you need me to do. Oh! Markus says Amsler has a blue scarf knitted from the same wool as his gloves. Ask the wife. And see if you can find it."

Erwin grunted and was gone.

"You're searching for Jakob?" Markus asked.

Giuliana, who'd stood up to pace during her call, looked down at the man in the chair. "Missing since yesterday afternoon, according to his wife."

"God." Markus pressed a hand to his mouth before lowering it to the table in a fist. "I'm very afraid he's killed himself. He . . . well, he's not as strong as he looks."

"His wife has friends checking his old haunts in Heidmatt. Do *you* have any ideas?"

Markus rubbed his eyes with his fingertips before saying, "What about the place he lived with his mother and Pesche before he was *verdingt*? Have they tried the Altenberg?"

"Tell me where," Giuliana said.

A police car brought Giuliana to the neighborhood on the Aare where Jakob had spent his early childhood; she asked the driver to stop about a block from the old house with the attic apartment Jakob had described to Markus. She hadn't taken time to go back to the station to get her pistol, and, now, as she jogged past a brightly painted daycare center and crossed the street, she prayed she wasn't going to need it. Jakob's childhood home looked like a small farmhouse accidentally set down in the city—its upper story was half-timbered, dark beams against thick white walls, and the vast roof, with its overlapping reddish tiles, hung over small windows. The place was set on a steep incline; an alley to one side sloped upward past a half-hidden back garden with a wall around it. She walked up the alley. Was she arresting a killer or saving a man's life? Or both? In any case, she didn't think yelling out Jakob's name was a good plan if he was suicidal.

Scarcely visible from the street, the walled space—it was more yard than garden—lay between the half-timbered building and a neighboring house at the end of the alley. The gate that opened from the alleyway into the yard was unlocked, so Giuliana stepped into the shadowy space. Laundry hung on two lines stretched across it, and the pair of jeans she touched was damp. Eight mossy stairs descended from the yard to a thick wooden door that opened into the lowest story of the house; it had a modern lock set in above the old-fashioned latch. She crept down the stairs and lifted the latch as quietly as she could. The heavy door swung open with only a slight creak, and she snuck inside. She heard a washer and drier running in the small room to her right; to her left a steep staircase led to the floor above.

Many Swiss houses had a downstairs laundry room shared by the residents, but this was no efficient modern basement. It was the vast cellar of a very old building, with three-foot-thick walls and a flagstone floor. The only natural light came through glass panels in the door leading out to the garden. Moving away from the door meant walking into darkness, but if Jakob was hiding, she didn't want to alert him by using her phone's flashlight, nor by calling out. As she inched down the corridor, the smell of laundry detergent that she'd noticed upon entering the basement faded, replaced by a reek of damp stone, old earth, and apples. She reminded herself that she was in the middle of Bern, with Altenbergstrasse above her, golden in the late afternoon light, and people living all around her. But in this dark, timeless place, that was hard to remember. All she had to do, she knew, was find a light switch on the wall; there were overhead bulbs along the corridor—she'd seen them from the garden doorway. But she was still reluctant to call attention to herself. On either side of her at intervals she made out closed doors that she supposed led to storage rooms; she lifted each latch stealthily, but they were all locked.

At last she reached the outer wall of the building, where there was only a door on her left, lower and narrower than the others. It had no latch or modern lock—just a keyhole, with a massive key sticking out of it. She tugged a little on the key, the door swung outward, and she stepped into a dark room, stumbling a little as she felt the floor under her feet change from flagstones to earth. Reaching toward the wall, her fingers found rough stone and, as she felt its dampness, she heard something. She held her breath and concentrated on the darkness, willing her eyes to adjust. There it was again: a small, steady sound. Rhythmic. Someone in the room was breathing.

"Köbi," she said softly. The word sprang from her mouth, not at all what she'd have imagined she'd say to the lost Jakob Amsler. There was no answer. "Köbi," she repeated, only a little louder, "are you there?"

She fumbled her phone out of the back pocket of her trousers, but before she could press the flashlight icon, she heard the whisper, "No light. No light." As soft as the voice was, she could hear fear in it, so she answered, "Fine—no light," just as softly. It came to her as she said it that to the man in the far corner of the room, who'd been sitting in total darkness, she was a clearly visible silhouette against the open door. That's how he'd seen her get out her phone. So, she moved as quickly as she could into the black space, her back pressed against the wall until she, too, was huddled in a corner.

"In the dark," the man said, in a slightly louder voice, "I can't see the walls. The dark is bad, but seeing walls around me is . . . worse."

Giuliana wanted to get the man out of this cellar, onto the street, and into the waiting police car. But she wanted him calm when she did it. Although he was speaking softly, he didn't sound calm at all.

"This isn't a good place for you to hide if you have claustrophobia," she said to him, still keeping her voice low. "Let's go back to the street."

Köbi gave a snort. "I'm not hiding. I came here to decide if . . . if I could survive prison. But"—she heard the ghost of a giggle, too high-pitched to be reassuring—"it isn't going well. About an hour ago, I chose the Aare instead. I just haven't made it there yet. I have all the rocks I need in my pockets, but . . . I keep on thinking about things. Also, I fall asleep every few minutes. God, I'm tired." His voice cracked on the last sentence, and she heard what might have been a sob.

The river was right outside; the street ran parallel to it. Suppose she got Köbi out of the cellar and he broke away, ran across the street, vaulted the waist-high wall along the sidewalk, and leaped into the Aare? There was a fifteen-foot drop to the water. At least. Was she strong enough to go in after him—and brave enough?

"As a kid I spent a lot of time in this room," the man continued. "It wasn't so bad then, because Mam put us in here together. She'd give us cold boiled potatoes, a couple of apples, a bottle of water, a lit candle, a dirty old blanket, and a piss pot. Me and Pesche and Anna. Once Fredi came along, he'd be in here, too. He used to climb the walls: I think today he'd get a label—ADHD or something. When I was eight, Mam decided I was old enough to look after everyone upstairs in the apartment, and it was over. Pesche was in Heidmatt by then, and Edi'd been born."

Giuliana's eyes were used to the dark now. She saw a dim figure sitting on something—maybe a sack—at the other end of the wall. She tried to imagine tiny children being locked in this room. Their mother must have been out of her mind. "Why did she do it?"

"To keep us safe while she was out drinking and meeting men," the soft voice continued. He sounded calmer now, as though recounting the memories, awful as they were, had soothed him. "Mostly she'd be back after a few hours, but other times we were in here for—well, I had no idea then, but now I imagine it could have been thirty-six hours or more. Maybe she'd pass out and sleep it off, or go home with a guy and stay with him for a while. Or just forget we were in here. I don't know. We used to be terrified that something would happen to her, and we'd be locked in forever."

Giuliana started to suggest again that they leave, but before she could speak, he added, "Getting punished was different. *Then* she locked me in the wardrobe upstairs—alone. I think that's where the claustrophobia comes from. But I can't practice for prison *that* way. I'm too big to fit in a wardrobe." This time his chopped-off laugh was more normal.

Suddenly, Giuliana had had enough of standing underground in the dark listening to this old man talk about his childhood. She had a crime to solve. Plus, any minute the driver of the police car was going to come looking for her. "I need to turn on the lights now, Herr Amsler," she said, "and you need to get ready to come outside. Did you know that Markus Gurtner is in jail because of you? That your wife has half of Heidmatt searching for you? *And* we had to bring Norbert into Bern for an interrogation. All because you haven't told us what happened at the Aare on Monday night. It's time for you to pull yourself together and come with me to the police station."

She'd spoken her piece with the lights still out, but now her hand had found a wall switch in the corridor, and she flipped on the lights, closing her eyes as she did so, so she wouldn't be blinded. Köbi cried out, but by the time she'd opened her eyes he was getting up from his perch on a burlap sack full of something bumpy—apples, from their smell—and stumbling across the room toward her. She backed out into the corridor, watching him, but he didn't reach for a weapon. Still, she wasn't going to turn her back on him. Instead, she let him lurch out of the tiny room first and followed him down the dim corridor. He was even larger than she'd imagined. He had to bend his head to protect it from the ceiling all the way down the hall and through the door to the garden.

Only when Köbi was outside could he straighten up, and then, as she'd expected, she recognized him from Markus's photograph: a craggy-faced man with a shock of straight white hair, dark-blue eyes, and enormous hands. He was unkempt now, and the sky behind him was blue instead of stormy, but it was the same face. Except with a split lip just starting to heal and bruises around the mouth. Of course— Karli had punched him.

"*Guete Tag*, Herr Amsler," she said, as they stood side by side next to flapping sheets in the darkening courtyard. "I'm Giuliana Linder. Markus suggested I look for you here. He's very worried."

"And angry, too, I bet," the giant said. "I've been a hopeless fuck-up."

Giuliana got out her phone and dialed the driver of the police car, who'd been waiting for almost half an hour. "Raju, I'm in the garden of an old house up an alley across the street from the daycare center. We'll be walking toward you."

She heard the car door slam. "Right. I'm on my way."

Before opening the gate to the alley, she looked sternly at Köbi. "However much you've messed up, now is not the time to talk about it. I'm taking you to the police station, we're going to let you clean yourself up, and then you can tell us everything. Every single detail. Right now, though, before we leave this place, you only need to answer one question. Are you planning to break away from my colleague and me to jump into the Aare? I'd rather not have to put leg restraints on you. And I *really* don't want to have to jump in after you."

Köbi actually laughed. "No," he said. "I won't go into the Aare now. At least not until I've told you the whole story. You deserve that—and so does Markus." Walking through the gate into the alley, he stood on the cobblestones and began taking rocks out of his jacket and trouser pockets.

34

Renzo sat, as he had that morning, in an interrogation room. This one had a one-way mirror. From behind it, Erwin was observing Jakob Amsler's interview. Renzo was overwhelmed by the detective's generosity. No matter how gruffly Erwin insisted that he'd had enough of small white rooms and uncomfortable metal chairs after his hours with Norbert, Renzo knew that Erwin's decision to give up the place at the table next to Giuliana was pure kindness.

Things would be different if Toni were around. But Toni was in court, representing the canton in a case of extortion where the accused was a high-level bureaucrat. Like every prosecutor, he balanced the demands of twenty or thirty cases at a time, large and small. Murder took priority, but Toni couldn't just slip out of court during a trial where he was the chief prosecutor. Of course, the police *normally* did their best to schedule something like this interrogation when the relevant prosecutor could be present. Since Erwin didn't consider anything about Toni to be relevant, Jakob Amsler's interrogation was now. Renzo smiled as he thought about how pissed off Toni would be when he found out.

Everything Renzo had heard about the towering old man who'd

just sat down across from him was secondhand, based on listening to Giuliana and reading reports. At the moment, Giuliana was explaining Amsler's rights to him in her usual professional way and telling him about the transcription that would be made of their talk, but he knew from her manner that she was sympathetic toward him. Why, for God's sake? Okay, the old guy'd had a rough childhood, but so what? He'd let Markus and Norbert, two people who cared about him, get into major trouble, and he'd never come forward to tell the truth. Not to mention that he'd killed Johann Gurtner; he'd already confessed to that. Maybe revenge *was* a dish best served cold. But after sixty years? Bizarre. Renzo was glad he was around to keep Giuliana from being too soft on the man.

She began the interrogation by announcing everyone's names, adding, "Before I ask Herr Amsler about the death of Johann Karl Gurtner, I'd like him to clarify the relationship between himself and Peter Beck. Could you do that for us, please?"

Jakob, sitting quietly, his hands clasped on the table, nodded. "Pesche—Peter Beck—was my half-brother, and because he was illegitimate, he had our mother's last name. About a year after he was born, she married my father and had me and my sister Anna. My father walked out on us all when Pesche was six, I was four, and Anna was almost three. Until that point, I think I had a normal childhood, although I don't remember it. After my father left, our lives fell apart."

"You and Pesche were close?" Giuliana asked. Renzo thought she sounded more like the counsel for the defense than an interrogating police officer, but he didn't interrupt.

"Yes," the old man agreed. "Even with different fathers, Pesche and I were raised as brothers and stayed very close until his death. All my good childhood memories involve Pesche. We didn't just have fun together—we also did everything we could to help and protect each other. When he was sent away from us to work on the Fankhauser farm in Heidmatt, I was devastated. A year later, when I was nine and he was eleven, I got placed in the same village. I couldn't have been happier. Until I realized I had a bad master, that is."

Renzo might not be able to imagine living with an alcoholic mother, nor being sent away at nine to be a slave on a farm, but this closeness between the brothers was easy. His own older brother had been his god when they were growing up, and they were still devoted to each other. Renzo felt a tiny thread of sympathy for Jakob Amsler trying to weave itself around his heart and resolutely ignored it.

"Thank you for explaining," said Giuliana. She paused to drink from a large glass of water, one of three on the table. "Now we're going to talk about Monday, November twenty-third. We know something about your brother Pesche's drowning in the Emme almost sixty years ago and about Johann Gurtner's involvement in his death. We'll want to ask you about that event soon, but right now I'd like to focus on the death of Herr Doktor Gurtner. We know that a confrontation with Gurtner on the Aare path was planned for Monday afternoon. You, Norbert Wittwer, and Gurtner's son Markus were meant to be there. Markus called you at four-thirty to say that Norbert wasn't going to make it. Tell us what happened then."

35
Before

Dählhölzli, November 23,
the day of Gurtner's death

Köbi left the construction site where he was doing a few days of specialized electrical work and got to the zoo parking lot before four. He didn't get out of the van right away. It made him angry with himself, feeling so nervous about this meeting. He should be excited, he reflected, not scared—after all, he'd been waiting for this moment for almost sixty years. As a boy in Heidmatt, he didn't think he'd ever been afraid of anything, except once when his Mistress had shut him in a tiny closet in the attic. But in those days, he'd had nothing to lose.

They'd agreed to meet at four-fifteen, so about five minutes after four, he left the van and walked down the path to a bench Karli would pass with the dog. Norbert and Markus weren't there yet, but he wasn't surprised. According to Philipp, Markus's half-brother, Karli didn't usually pass here until after four-thirty, probably closer to five. There was time. He'd downloaded an article to read while he waited, something about improving efficiency in photovoltaic cells, but he didn't even get out his phone, just stared through the trees and bushes growing on the bank at the river flowing past him under a threatening sky.

More minutes passed without his friends showing up, and Köbi knew something had gone wrong. What could have happened? Why hadn't Markus phoned? At four-thirty, his mobile rang. One sentence from Markus was enough to explain the disaster. He cursed himself for not anticipating it. He should have talked Norbert into spending last night with him and Renata, even if that would have meant missing work today. Jesus, how could he have been so stupid? He of all people knew how quickly boozers could relapse under stress.

"I'm home now," Markus told him, "but I can still get there, if you want to carry on. I've been thinking about this for weeks; you know I have. I even brought the watch with me. Tell me what you want to do."

At that moment, Köbi didn't know *what* he wanted to do or even how he felt. Was he relieved or disappointed? All he knew was that keeping Karli hanging around with small talk while Markus rushed to his side would be ridiculous, and he didn't want the meeting with Pesche's killer reduced to a joke. "There'll be another time," he told Markus. They spoke another couple of minutes and then hung up. Suddenly, Köbi was exhausted. He tightened his blue scarf around his neck, dug his hands deeper into his pockets, slouched on the bench, leaned his head back and closed his eyes. *Just a moment's rest,* he told himself, *and I'll go.*

He woke with a jolt. His watch told him he'd slept less than ten minutes, but the Aare path was darker. He glanced quickly in both directions and then stared toward Elfenau, where Karli would come from. Nothing, thank God. Köbi stood up, which hurt, so he stretched. He'd started down the path toward his car when he glanced back once more, and there he was. Johann Karl Gurtner. Köbi recognized him from far away, even though he didn't look like the elegant patrician Köbi'd seen by chance the previous February, coming out of the symphony with his wife on his arm. That Karli Gurtner had stood tall in a camelhair overcoat, head bare to display his neatly parted white hair, face full of amusement at something his young wife had just said. This Karli was dressed, as Köbi was, in jeans and a dark parka with a knitted scarf and cap. His hands were in his pockets, his shoulders hunched against the wind.

Köbi knew he should go back to his car. Walk away now, he told himself. Do it. But he didn't. He sat down on the bench, even though the wind was colder than it had been, and the sky looked like it was about to drop yet another bout of freezing rain on Bern. Köbi watched Karli walk toward him. The loop of a leash was around his wrist, and he hurried his little dachshund along, only now and then allowing it to lift its leg or snuffle at the roots of the shrubs along the edge of the path. As Karli passed Köbi's bench, Köbi saw his face was drawn. There were pouches under his eyes and deep wrinkles around his mouth, and, despite the burgundy scarf Karli wore, Köbi caught a glimpse of jowls. Karli looked old.

Köbi stared at the back withdrawing down the path. What should he do? He could slink off, and Karli would never know he'd been here. Or he could confront the man who'd beaten and drowned his brother. This Karli, old and chilled, didn't make Köbi want to shake him until his brains turned to scrambled eggs. *This* man looked like he might even regret having killed the person Köbi had loved best.

For decades, the very thought of Johann Gurtner had been poison in Köbi's blood. Forgiving him would be like lancing a boil so the pus could drain out. Köbi knew that he didn't need to talk to Karli to forgive him; he simply had to do it. Let Karli walk away with his little dog and give up any dream of challenging him.

His eyes bored into the man's back. He couldn't do it.

Köbi stood up and followed Karli at a brisk pace. Man and dog were close to the river now, the dachshund sniffing at the bushes along the bank again. Köbi drew up alongside his quarry. "Herr Doktor Gurtner," he said, nodding. A flick of irritation crossed Karli's face at what he probably assumed was an encounter with a former patient. Then he offered a practiced smile. "Good evening," he said.

Köbi drew in a deep breath. "Hello, Karli. We've both been living in Bern for a long time. I've seen you before, but this time I've made up my mind to speak to you."

"Who are you?" The tone was detached, but Köbi thought it carried a note of fear.

"I'm Jakob Amsler, but you know me as Köbi. Pesche Beck's brother."

Karli's body tensed and his dog whined. Then he recovered, held out his hand, and said, "My God. Köbi. You always were big for your age, but I never would have recognized you." Köbi shook the proffered hand and didn't feel disgust, which was a good start. "What did you . . .?" Karli asked and stopped before going on. "How has your life turned out?"

Köbi wasn't interested in talking about his profession or his family with this man, but it seemed rude not to answer. "I became an electrical engineer and ended up spending most of my working life at Swisscom. Now I'm retired. I have a wife, two married daughters, and a four-year-old grandson. As for you, I know what you've done with your life. I'm friends with one of your sons, Markus. An impressive young man."

Karli's eyes had grown wide as soon as Köbi mentioned Markus, and he frowned, shaking his head. "You and Markus? That's . . ." He paused. "I'm surprised. What . . .?" Now he came to a full stop, and Köbi thought he was trying to find the right way to ask what in God's name they found to talk about. It provoked Köbi that Karli could have a son like Markus and not be proud of him, especially of the way he'd turned his life around.

"You don't like Markus very much, do you?" Köbi said mildly. "But I do. I like him a lot. We have a beer together now and then. I think he's an outstanding photographer, too."

"I . . . I see," said Karli, who obviously didn't. He was starting to turn away.

Köbi knew what he was about to say was not a milestone on the path to forgiveness. In fact, it was downright malicious, but he couldn't help himself.

"Markus knows that I grew up in Heidmatt, and he's fascinated by our childhoods. I've told him stories about those days, and we've started going to The Lion together. I've introduced him to several people from our school class. Including your friend Norbert. Norbert's very grateful to you for the money you've sent him over the years—that was exceptionally generous of you." Listening to these last six words as they left his mouth, Köbi could hear their edge. What was he trying to do, make peace or incite violence? At that moment, he really didn't care.

The long-haired dachshund was exploring Köbi's shoes now, and Köbi bent and held his hand out to the dog before stroking him gently.

Karli tightened his grip on the leash and said, "Well, Köbi, glad to have seen you; I'll head back home now. They're predicting rain again and ..."

"Before you go," said Köbi, "you should know that Norbert told me what happened that day on the Emme. He saw you beat Pesche with the brass-topped cane, and he watched you drag him into the Emme. You told me you were going to kill Pesche, and you did. Right after you threw my dog into the river. I've never doubted it, and Norbert confirmed it. I also know about the watch you gave him as a bribe so he'd back up your Pesche-falling-off-the-bridge story. Not to mention the money you've paid him all these years for his silence."

Köbi stopped speaking. He was aware of darkness and cold rising around them and the loud rush of the river a few feet away. *This is the moment*, Köbi thought. *Now that he knows I know, what will he do? What will he say?* Köbi's breath caught in his chest.

"Are you ... threatening me?" asked Karli.

It was a legitimate question, and Köbi didn't know the answer. He'd never decided what he wanted to do with the deposition he'd talked Norbert into making once his cancer was diagnosed. Nor with the stick, which he hoped had Pesche's DNA on it, as well as Karli's fingerprints. He'd thought that confronting Karli with Norbert and Markus and their rejection of him because of his crime would satisfy his need for retribution. Now that the other two men weren't here, he didn't know what he wanted. But he knew that what had passed between them so far wasn't enough.

"Am I threatening you?" he echoed. "Well, I haven't made any threats so far. I guess I was curious to see what you'd say when you found out I knew the truth and could prove it. No one in the village ever believed your lie anyway. Not even your own father. He knew you were a murderer, and he covered up the truth to protect you."

That elicited a short, bitter laugh. "No, no. My father did that for his own sake. He despised me from that day on." Karli's voice drifted far away, and he glanced off across the Aare. "I don't think he spoke a warm word to me again for the rest of his life." His reverie lasted a few more seconds, and then his eyes snapped back to meet Köbi's. "Do you want money?" he asked.

"Money? You think I would take money as compensation for my brother's death? From you? His killer?" Köbi found himself roaring the last words, and Karli moved back, almost stepping on the dog, which was cowering and growling behind his feet.

"What do you want from me, then?" Karli asked. His voice was growing angry, too, and he dropped the dog's leash.

"I want to hear what you have to say about murdering my brother. Are you sorry?"

"Sorry?" Karli sounded more surprised than angry. "Of course I'm sorry. I've never forgiven myself. How could I do something so reckless and out of control? I thought then, if only Pesche were gone, my life would be the way I wanted it to be. That I'd be able to have Heidi and get the class behind me again. Instead, I lost my friends and my home and became a demon in my father's eyes. It was the worst thing I've ever done in my life."

By the time he'd finished speaking, Karli had raised his voice and moved closer to Köbi, but Köbi didn't notice. He was replaying Karli's statement in his head. All the right words were there: sorry, forgive, demon, the worst thing. But not one of them had anything to do with Pesche dying in pain and terror and never having the chance to grow up and become the teacher he'd dreamed of being. Nor with Köbi and his loss of a beloved brother. Every word Karli had spoken had only to do with Johann Karl Gurtner and how the death had hurt *him*.

With one swift movement, Köbi reached down, grabbed the little dachshund, walked two steps to the edge of the paved path with its steep drop to the Aare and hurled the dog into the middle of the river. He turned toward Karli, who looked first shocked and then defiant.

"Think you can scare me by killing my dog?" the older man said. "Think again."

Köbi stared out for a moment at the frothing water, trying to come to grips with what he'd just done to the dachshund. It was time to stop, to walk away. But something was compelling him to act. He stepped back toward Karli, and his speed must have scared the doctor, because he put up his hands, as if to shield himself, and his watchband caught in the wool of Köbi's scarf. Köbi's hand grabbed Karli's wrist; with his other hand, he peeled off the watch, tugging it loose from the scarf. He meant to fling it into the Aare, too, but Karli hit his arm as he threw, so the watch sailed away in another direction. It was too dark to see where it landed, and the rush of wind and roar of water drowned the sound of its fall.

Karli bellowed and punched Köbi in the mouth with his right fist, then danced away at the pain in his hand.

Köbi's lip was bleeding now, but he grinned. "I see. You don't care about your dog, but you do care about your fancy watch. Why doesn't that surprise me?"

"I'm calling the police," Karli screamed, reaching into his pocket for his phone. Köbi wrested it out of his hand, and it followed the dog into the river. By now, Köbi was laughing. "What about your wedding ring? What about your wallet? Into the Aare with them."

Karli tried to hit him in the face again, but this time Köbi was ready for him and punched him in the eye. It wasn't a hard punch, just a reminder that Köbi was still perfectly capable of defending himself, just as he had all those years ago. Then, before things could escalate, he caught both of Karli's wrists and gripped them in one of his giant hands. He was so much the larger and stronger of the two men that it was effortless. Yet Köbi realized that his passionate desire to make Karli pay for his viciousness—or force him to show some remorse, at the very least—was ebbing away. Had he really expected to find a guilty conscience buried inside the man? At his core, Karli had barely changed during sixty years. He regretted the murder he'd committed as a child only for his own sake; he'd probably never given his victim another thought. This whole confrontation had no point; it had never had a point. What had Köbi been thinking? How could he have been so naïve? And cruel? The poor dog...

As all this was going through his mind, Köbi kept Karli's wrists firmly in his grip. He noticed the doctor was making a lot of noise, cursing and threatening. Since his hands were out of commission, he was kicking Köbi in the shins and trying to knee him in the crotch.

"Oh, shut up—and stop kicking me, or I'll throw your boots in the river, too." As a precaution, Köbi stepped further away from the other man, his left hand still squeezing Karli's wrists together, his right gripping Karli's left shoulder to keep him at a distance. "What are you babbling about?"

Karli was throwing his body around to free himself, but he found the breath to say, "The second I get home, I'm going to call the police. I'll wreck your life for this, I'll ..."

Köbi laughed again. The harsh sound must have startled the other man, because he fell still. "My God, you *are* full of yourself," Köbi told him. "What the hell are you talking about? You're going to wreck *my* life? The one who needs to worry about getting his life wrecked is you, you *Gigu*. Oh, that's right. I forgot to mention that Norbert has had your stick all these years, and he gave it to me. The murder weapon. Think of all the DNA and fingerprints it has on it. And you're worrying about your watch and phone. Ah, Karli, you're a piece of work. You'll go to your grave an egocentric monster. A monster who saves lives, I know that, but a monster just the same. There's nothing to be done about you, not a thing. Except to ignore you—like your father did."

With each word, Köbi registered the truth of what he was saying—there *was* nothing to be done about someone as deeply selfish as Karli. But still tears came into his eyes. So many years of dreaming and planning and scheming and now here he was, holding Karli away from his body the way a parent restrains a toddler having a tantrum.

He stood in such an awkward position that his back ached, and now it was starting to pour. What a joke! They were making complete fools of themselves, two old men scuffling like boys and calling each other names in the rain.

It was finished. Köbi'd had his moment, petty as it had turned out to be, and now it was time to go home. He let go of Karli's wrists and stepped away, his back to the river, so that the two men faced each other, four or five feet apart. Köbi thought of the dachshund and turned his head to look along the path, hoping to see the little dog trotting toward them, as he'd seen his beloved Lässu coming back so many years before on the bank of the Emme, miraculously still alive.

He caught movement out of the corner of his eye. By the time he'd whipped around, there was scarcely time to register that Karli was bearing down on him, arms outstretched, palms forward, intent on shoving him into the Aare. Köbi pivoted, but the turn brought him off balance. The pushing hands missed him, but Karli's shoulder didn't.

A second earlier, all he'd wanted to do was walk away from Karli. Now he wished he'd knocked him unconscious. But it was too late. He was in mid-air, falling onto the very edge of the bank, which was rocky. The only weapons he had to use against the man who'd just tried to drown him were his legs. In the split-second of his fall, Köbi kicked out as hard as he could at the man still bearing down on him with a face twisted in rage.

One flailing leg caught Karli mid-shin, and he tripped spectacularly, flying up into the air and over the bank where the path dropped away. The water level was high because of the rain, and many of the large stones that edged the Aare were totally submerged. Karli curled his head down and twisted his body as he fell, trying to keep himself away from the middle of the dark river where the current was fastest. In doing so, he aimed himself headfirst toward the hidden rocks. Köbi tried to yell a warning, but the fall had knocked the breath out of him. He lay paralyzed.

He heard the splash as Karli went in, but it took him several minutes to get up. The pain in his diaphragm was intense, and his lungs struggled for air. As soon as he could move, he clambered down the bank until he was over his knees in searingly cold water, calling Karli's name. He balanced precariously on invisible underwater rocks, all the time fearing to lose his footing in the current. He took off his gloves and felt around in the water with his hands, but his fingers found no sign of the man. A hint of light reached him from a distant lamp somewhere, but there was nothing to see—Karli was either completely underwater or he'd been swept downstream. He was gone.

Köbi climbed back up the bank and started running toward the restaurant. He ached all over. His back was bruised from his fall and his legs from Karli's kicks. His shoes, socks, and trouser legs were drenched, and the wind numbed his feet and legs. At least he could put his dry gloves back onto his freezing hands. As he jogged along, he passed one of the long rescue poles that were set out on brackets along the river. Instinctively, he put both gloved hands on the heavy pole and hoisted it up from its supports, thrusting its semi-circular hook out into the river and passing it back and forth through the torrent. Strong as he was, he felt the current try to drag the pole out of his hands and carry it downstream like a bit of debris. It was hopeless, he knew; he couldn't see a thing. Karli could be anywhere. He dropped the pole onto the bank and stumbled back to the path.

Phone, he thought, as he ran toward the restaurant. He couldn't find it in his jacket pockets. Then, like an apparition, he saw a pay phone mounted on a side wall of the building. He called 117, told the emergency service woman about Karli, and then bent to put his hands on his thighs, still catching his breath. How long would he have to wait for the police? They'd bring lights. He'd show them where Karli had gone into the water and . . .

At last he was able to stand up straight, and he moved out of the wind, teeth chattering. He should tell people in the restaurant that a man was in the river. They'd come out and help him search—although what could they do without light? As Köbi moved toward the door of the building, he tasted blood and put his hand to his face. His lip was bleeding from Karli's blow. He'd go into the bathroom and clean himself up before the police came. Then he remembered the dog. It felt like an age since he'd hurled the dachshund into the river, but it had been less than ten minutes. While he was waiting for the police, he'd walk downstream to see if he could find the dog. There were street-lights in that direction, between the zoo and the weir at Schwellen-mätteli. Oh, God, the weir. No dog and surely no man could survive going over the weir in this torrent of icy water, could they?

He moved along the riverside path, peering down the embank-ment and into the river. His search didn't show him the form of man or dog. He walked on, past the footbridge and away from the zoo, reaching a stretch that was better lit. He examined every dark shape he could see at the edge of the water. Behind him, he heard a siren. He needed to go back and tell the police where to look, in case Karli was caught underwater right where he'd gone in. Instead, he kept searching for the dachshund. Then, about a thousand feet from the footbridge, he saw a small mound on the steep bank, close to the water's edge, and stumbled down to it. The dog! He squatted and put his hand on its side, which rose and fell faintly. Köbi took it into his arms, and it whined feebly.

He cradled the dog and thought about the police searching for a drowned man. He'd have to explain why he'd stopped Karli on the path and how their talk had become a scuffle and how that scuffle had led to his death. An encounter he'd spent more than half a century yearning for would, in the telling of it, become a farce, the senile fool-ishness of two old men. He couldn't bear it. Freezing in his wet shoes and clothes, bleeding, bruised, and exhausted, all he wanted was to go home. The only person who could understand was Renata.

Holding the dog in his arms, he walked to his parked van. The area around the zoo was lit up by police searchlights. Up and down both sides of the river, cops in uniform and other people, too, were searching with powerful handheld lamps. No one noticed him. From the back of the van, he took the drop cloths he kept for messy electrical jobs and wrapped them around the dachshund, putting him on the front pas-senger seat. He started the car and turned on the heat, setting the vents to blow onto the little dog. He couldn't drive yet—his hands were stiff, his feet so cold he couldn't feel the pedals. As hot air slowly filled the van with warmth, Köbi sat with his head resting on his arms, which were crossed over the steering wheel.

He recalled the terrible look on Karli's face as he'd rushed toward Köbi with his arms outstretched to push him into the river. And this was what he'd wanted—to challenge Pesche's killer. Now he was a killer, too. Once again, just like when he'd run after Lässu instead of staying to help his brother, his thoughtless actions had caused a tragedy. Thank God Markus and Norbert hadn't been there to see it. Markus! He felt a jolt of adrenaline that left him weak. Jesus Christ. He'd killed Markus's father. The horror of what he'd done to Karli's wife and sons rose up to choke him, and a jagged sob tore free of his throat. Tears filled his eyes, and, bent over the steering wheel as he was, he saw them fall. Beside him, the dog whined, and he reached out, laid a hand on its head, and let himself cry. Then he straightened up and drove home.

36

The white interrogation room with its soundproofed walls was uncannily silent. Renzo could hear all three of them breathing, Jakob Amsler the loudest. The old man held himself upright in his chair, his eyes on Giuliana, his lips pressed in a line. Renzo felt that it was taking all of Amsler's will not to let his head sag to his chest.

He thought about the tale he'd heard. If it was true, then the cause of Gurtner's death was a miscalculation: Amsler's failure to understand how far a vain man might go to protect his reputation. The story made sense of the watch found along the path, the rescue pole lying on the bank, and the disappearance of the dog. It resolved the emergency phone call in Heidmatter dialect that used the name Karli; Gurtner's bruises from being hit, tripped, and restrained; and the head wound made by a rock. Remembering something else that needed explaining, he said, "Tell us what happened to the dachshund."

Amsler nodded. "I took him to the vet to make sure he was all right, kept him a couple of days to ... well, pep him up, and then drove him yesterday to Elfenau and let him out a block from Gurtner's house. He took off in the direction of home. Did he get back all right?"

"He did," Renzo answered, thinking: So that fits, too. In his notebook he wrote, "Amsler's van, dog hair." Lots of police work would be needed to prove Amsler's story, but the details would probably hold. What no one would find evidence of—because no one could—was his claim that Gurtner had tried to push him into the water, which made the death that followed self-defense. The charge against Amsler would be manslaughter, in any case; the trial would revolve around the extent of premeditation, degrees of brutality, failure to come forward, and much more. It would be messy.

Giuliana broke her long silence. "This crime occurred on Monday, and it is Friday evening. According to you, the death of Herr Gurtner was a combination of self-defense and accident. So why didn't you call the police Monday evening or, at the latest, Tuesday morning? Why did you let us conduct an unnecessary investigation, particularly when it involved making trouble for Norbert Wittwer and Markus Gurtner? Did you want them to suffer, too?"

Now Amsler, who'd sat tall through most of the interview, sagged in his chair and clasped his hands under his chin, fingers laced. He closed his eyes, and when he opened them, he mumbled, almost inaudibly, "I was afraid." Then he repeated his words, much louder: "I was afraid." He looked at both of them, one after the other, and said, a third time, in a normal voice, "I was afraid of . . . so many things. I was afraid of Markus finding out that *I* was the person who'd destroyed his chance to work things out with his father. I couldn't bear to tell Norbert, because he'd convinced himself that handing that watch back to Karli would give him some kind of . . . absolution before he died."

He stopped and rubbed his face, and when he spoke again it was hard to hear him. "I thought about having to face Karli's wife and children in court—his youngest boy isn't even twenty, you know. And of what my daughters would think of me." He shuddered and sank down farther in his chair. "Plus there was . . . prison. I was afraid of being locked in a small, dark space and not being able to get out, maybe for years."

"Your wife knew everything, didn't she?" Renzo asked. His voice was rough, as he fought to keep his heart from softening. Maybe he *didn't* want this old man to go to prison.

"Yes, and she was almost out of her mind with worry. And so angry with me for not going to the police. She finally gave me an ultimatum: either I had to tell you by today, or she'd call you and turn me in. I left home yesterday afternoon. At that point I . . . didn't plan to go home again."

"I think there's more, Herr Amsler," Giuliana said. Her soft voice sounded grim. "More that drove you into that cellar room with your pockets full of rocks." Renzo didn't turn to stare at her, but he wanted to. What did she mean? What else did she want from the man?

Amsler nodded once. He sat up straight again, but it was a long time before he spoke. Finally, he said, "As boys in Heidmatt, Pesche and I defended each other. We were a team. Then I deserted him: I ran after Lässu instead of helping him deal with Karli. I've always blamed myself for . . . what happened afterward."

Renzo thought Amsler had the look of someone stripped of all defenses: the expression in his eyes was as bleak as old bone, and he rubbed his hands back and forth before managing to still them. A few shuddering breaths later, he went on. "After Pesche was killed and I realized Karli would get away with everything, I thought I couldn't . . . go on. And then my whole life changed. The problem was that it got better. Much better. The Fankhausers—the family Pesche'd lived with—they got me away from the farmer who beat me. I stayed with them for five years, until I was sixteen, and they helped me apprentice myself to an electrician. So all I did was profit from Pesche's death— and I never stopped thinking about suicide. The only way I could live with myself in those days was to believe I would avenge him. Somehow, I'd get Karli. I never doubted it."

Renzo had read about survivor guilt before, but he'd never heard anyone talk about it. Jakob Amsler had obviously thought about it a lot.

"I finished my apprenticeship," the old man was saying. "I got a good job, and after a while my company sent me to engineering school. I married Renata, and we started a family. Killing Karli *or* myself came to seem like abandoning Renata and my two girls. But, still, I kept track of where Karli worked, where he lived, what he looked like, who his children were. I knew, someday, I'd find a way to come up against him."

Renzo could imagine how a plan of violent revenge that seemed so right at the age of twelve or twenty would slide into the stuff of fantasy as the boy became first a man in love and then a husband and father with responsibilities, surrounded by people who'd be devastated to lose him. But it would be harder to get rid of the guilt of having survived. He didn't know for sure that the old man was telling the truth, but he couldn't help identifying with his darkness. What would he do if someone killed his brother or one of his sisters and got away with it? He couldn't imagine and was glad he didn't have to, but he knew it would fill his brain with shadows. This man had carried his for over half a century.

Köbi kept talking. "Then, Monday night, it finally happened. I confronted Karli. And it was . . . pathetic. No heroics, no flaming sword, no feeling of justice being done. Just two old men yelling and swearing, punching and kicking. Until he tried to push me into the Aare, and then came my great act of revenge—I stuck out my leg and tripped him. How brave was that? An act of retribution that I've dreamt of since I was eleven years old, and it was more or less an accidental kick in the shins. While I was lying on the ground! And once again, instead of standing my ground like a man, I went dashing off after a little dog."

Jakob started to cry, and Giuliana pushed the box of tissues on the table closer to him. He wiped his eyes, blew his nose, and took deep breaths to steady himself. "I think that's all there is to say. I can't think of any more. Maybe I'm leaving something out, but right now I don't know what it could be. I'm just—done!" The old man covered his face with his hands. "What a mess!" he murmured through his fingers. "God, what a pathetic mess!"

Renzo found himself wanting to offer Jakob comfort. When he looked at Giuliana's face, he could see she did, too. "The worst is over,

Herr Amsler," she said gently. "You're here now, and the story is told. You'll have to repeat what you've told us many times—that's how it works around here—but I know you have the patience for that. Our job will be to hunt for evidence that backs up your claims, and, if you've told us the truth, we'll find it. If you've lied, we'll find the evidence to prove that, too. You'd have made our search a lot easier if you'd come to us sooner, but I promise you we'll do our best."

"Thank you," the old man said, his voice hoarse. He drank from the large glass of mineral water on the table beside him and began to look less desperate. Suddenly he blurted, "The stick! How could I forget it?" He set the glass down and leaned forward, his eyes moving from Giuliana to Renzo and back. "Norbert found the stick Karli used to hit Pesche the same day Karli hurled it away; he hid it and forgot about it. A month ago, he gave it to me. Now it's at my place, wrapped in newspaper. When I got hold of it, I planned to use it to prove what Karli had done and bring him down. Now he's dead, and Markus and the rest of his family will be the ones to suffer. I'm not sure that's what I want."

Renzo put out a hand and touched the old man's where it lay on the table, just for a second. "It's not your problem anymore," he told Amsler. "This is a police investigation, and that stick is part of the evidence, so you don't have to make a decision about what happens to it. From now on, nobody expects anything from you but the truth."

Amsler had been nodding as Renzo spoke. "That won't be a problem," he said.

37

J ust before midnight on the Friday of Jakob Amsler's arrest, it began
to snow, and it didn't stop until twenty-six hours later. On Sunday
morning, Bern glowed white in the winter sun. Ueli and Lukas hauled
two battered Davos sleds out of the basement, took the funicular
railway to the top of the city's one small mountain, and returned after dark, cold, wet, and very happy. Isabelle and her best friend Luna
joined a massive teenage snowball fight on a meadow near the Aare—
boys against girls, with lots of shrieking and rolling on top of each other in the snow. Quentin was there, and Isabelle came home glowing.

For Giuliana, the snow was simply an impediment. She got up on
Sunday after six hours of sleep and went back to the station. Monday
followed Sunday, another long, long day. Jakob Amsler and his wife
Renata Lanz were interviewed again and again, as different aspects
of their stories were checked and rechecked. So were Markus and
Norbert, along with Heidi Stettler. All of them were represented by
counsel from Oliver Jordi's office.

Erwin ran the case. Hidden behind his usual gruffness was a
grudging respect for Jakob—Giuliana could sense it. It was hard for
all of them not to admire the huge, white-haired man, as he sat there

patiently answering their questions hour after hour. The despair with which he'd told much of his story the first time was gone; all he seemed to feel now was relief. Action in the matter of Johann Karl Gurtner had been taken. Not the sort of deeply satisfying action he'd dreamed of since childhood, but action nonetheless. Now he seemed to accept that it was time to let justice take its course. It wasn't that he appeared indifferent to the legal consequences of what he'd done. But he was no longer in turmoil. Even his fear of prison seemed to have abated.

On Tuesday morning, the first of December, Bern was still a gleaming world of white, where bare branches glistened silver, and evergreens were iced like petit fours. Every roof and railing was trimmed with snow; and there were still untrodden patches of ground that shone like clean linen. In the midst of this glory, Giuliana soldiered on, barely taking time to lift her face to the sun. She checked statements and reports, new and old; made phone calls and searched for information online; took notes on what research and interviews still needed to be done; and gave out assignments. The hard work of preparing for a trial had begun, and it would take months, particularly as it would be interrupted every time she or Erwin was assigned a new homicide. From experience she knew that there would be exciting moments, when things suddenly came together as one of the team fit a piece of evidence into place that confirmed Köbi's version of the crime or definitively eliminated someone else as a suspect. But a lot of the work would inevitably be routine.

Since Erwin was the detective in charge of the case, he was the person providing the district attorney's office with the latest evidence—the confirmations of Jakob's story or lack of them—and listening to the prosecutors' suggestions of what points to pursue next. The relationship between police and prosecution was always delicate, but Giuliana generally enjoyed working with the different lawyers to prepare cases for trial. Both parties learned and profited; after all, they had the same goal, which was to make sure criminals were put away for the safety of the public. But Toni Rossel and Erwin Sägesser were definitely not benefitting from each other's expertise. By Tuesday Giuliana had already lost count of the number of times they'd clashed. The team had gotten used to Erwin's bellowing and Toni's hissing. It was often hard to tell who'd won.

Based on everything she'd learned so far, Giuliana was sure that Markus, Norbert, and Jakob hadn't known what they wanted out of the confrontation with Gurtner and hadn't allowed themselves to think about what might happen if it escalated. Markus and Jakob had certainly been eager for some kind of fight, and Norbert had at least understood that what they were doing could turn ugly, which was probably what had driven him to get so drunk beforehand. But none of this was a conspiracy to commit murder. Except in Toni's mind.

Erwin showed up at her desk that Tuesday morning at ten-thirty. Normally, he'd begin roaring whatever was on his mind from the door, but now he stood a moment in silence before saying, "Come have coffee with me."

"Sure," she said, wondering at this abrupt summons, particularly when they'd reviewed yesterday's progress and today's plans at the morning meeting only two hours before. Erwin was silent as they took the lift to the basement, stood in line, filled their cups, and found a table. When they sat down, he looked quickly around them, apparently double-checking that no one could overhear him. Finally, he leaned forward and said, "Last week, before everything went crazy, Renzo told me something. That Toni's been threatening you, saying he'll tell everyone about you and him all those years ago. Like . . . like he spilled it to me last Thursday afternoon."

Aha. Now she knew why he was acting odd. "I've been meaning to thank you for the way you reacted then, Erwin. Telling him you already knew everything. I don't know if that was true or not, but it was a perfect way to . . . well, it was like defusing a bomb. I thought you were great."

Erwin flapped his hand in front of his face like he was waving away a fly. "Forget about it. The point is I need to tell you something. I wasn't just pretending to know that story. What I want to say is that

his threat to tell every cop he knows about that ancient business, well
. . . it hasn't been a threat for years."

"What do you mean?" Giuliana whispered, but, even as she asked,
she already knew the answer.

"I hate to say this, but I doubt there's a cop in the shop who hasn't
heard about you and him on that damned sofa." Erwin grimaced and
added, "Believe me, that's just *one* of the . . . um . . . encounters he's
gone on about. If half the shit he brags about is true, it's a miracle his
dick hasn't worn down to a stub. Lots of the guys probably don't even
believe him. But what I'm trying to tell you is that you don't have to
worry about his threat. Just tell him to fuck off and drop dead."

Giuliana, elbows on the table, sank her face into her hands briefly
before raising her head to nod at Erwin. "Thanks for telling me. It's . . .
it's a relief." She knew she didn't look relieved, so she tried to smile into
his worried face. Heart-to-hearts like this were truly not his thing, and
it was noble of him to have sat her down and told her the truth. "I'm
fine, really. You did the right thing."

"Good, good. Um . . . okay then. I'm going back to work. Are you
. . .?"

"No, you go ahead without me. I'll just sit here for another
minute." She really did smile to see the speed with which he left the
cafeteria. Her eyes moved casually around the room, where perhaps
twenty people, mostly men, sat drinking coffee. How many of them
knew? How long had they known? What did they think of her? She
felt a moment of profound embarrassment, and then, just like that, it
was gone. Because the truth was that it didn't matter. For years, the
policemen she'd worked with had been sexist, unconsciously or deliberately. They'd made bad decisions sometimes. They'd often annoyed
the hell out of her. There were a few she couldn't stand. But in general,
they'd been good colleagues. If they'd heard the worst Toni had to say
about her and still made her feel at home among them, then she really
did have nothing to worry about.

So—time to get back to work. She brought her coffee cup to the
tray station and headed back upstairs. But instead of running up the

way she usually did, she dawdled, thinking about Renzo. Maybe Toni's and her past was irrelevant now, but what would happen if Toni spread the rumor that she and Renzo were having an affair? The answer she came up with, standing in the middle of the last flight of stairs was—nothing would happen. Because surely that gossip was water under the bridge by now, too. Their regular workouts and breakfast meetings and their open friendship—actually, if she was honest with herself, their obvious attraction to each other—coupled with Renzo's looks and their age difference must have generated floods of talk over the past year or two, long before Toni started making threats. She just hadn't heard any of it. Nor, as far as she could tell, been affected by it. If nothing had come of it by now, then surely it was time to put Toni and his poisonous tongue out of her mind.

Late in the afternoon, she needed to listen to a poor recording of a long phone call, so she left the detectives' shared office and moved to an empty meeting room along the corridor. An hour later, Toni found her there. He took the seat right next to hers at the long table, the smell of his cologne hanging heavily around him. She turned off the recording device and lowered her earphones. "Hello, Toni," she said. "What's up?"

The smile he gave her was smug. "Oh, I just stopped in for a little chat about the Gurtner case. I can't wait for the trial. I'll probably never get another chance to try a man for conspiring to kill his father."

"Well, the sooner you leave me alone so I can get back to work, the sooner you'll have the evidence for your conspiracy. Or not, as the case may be."

Toni narrowed his eyes, and his smile disappeared. "What does that mean?"

Giuliana shrugged. "Just what it sounds like and exactly what you already know. It's early days, and we have lots of timelines to create and people to talk to. If there's evidence that anyone planned to kill Gurtner, instead of just confront him, we'll find it. But I'm not sure the evidence exists. Erwin's already made that clear to you. So have I."

"Yes, you have. And I've made it clear to you that I won't put up with sabotage. There are consequences . . ."

He trailed off as Giuliana removed her phone from her purse, put it on the table in front of her, and set it to record. "Antoine Rossel, would you like to repeat the threat you just made to me?"

"What are you . . .?" Toni spluttered. "I never said . . ." He closed his mouth and narrowed his eyes as he glowered at her, before pushing his chair back with force and standing up. There was a crash as the chair tipped over onto the floor, followed by a bang as he walked out of the room and slammed the door behind him.

She felt shaky but elated. Thanks to Erwin's revelations, she was no longer afraid of his consequences, and if she started recording every time he came near her, he might stay away. As for his Markus-based conspiracy theory, sooner or later, when the time came to go to court, he'd have to accept that the prosecution had a weak case and back down. Until then, she'd cope.

At six, she dived into a new set of files, even as she reminded herself to leave early. She had to be home by seven to make dinner; it was her turn. Forty-five minutes later, she surfaced, looked at the time, and catapulted out of her desk chair. Seven was impossible now. At twelve minutes after seven, she flung open her front door, dashed into the kitchen without taking off her coat or shoes and opened the fridge. Her eyes ran over the shelves, and she relaxed. Chicken breasts and—she checked the freezing compartment—a bag of green beans. There was always rice in the pantry. She could have the meal ready in less than half an hour. As she transferred the packet of chicken to the kitchen counter, she called out, "Hi, kiddos. Dinner will be . . ."

Ueli walked up behind her and grabbed her around the waist, kissing the back of her neck as she straightened. "Whoa," he said. "The kids and I took a vote after I got your text from the bus, and we've decided it's pizza night. I reserved a table at Luce. So, do whatever you need to do to be ready, because we're walking out of here in five minutes. Kids," he called over his shoulder, "five-minute warning."

Giuliana turned, put her arms around her husband, and pressed her body into his. With her face buried in his chest, she felt his beard warm against her cold ear. She held onto him, overcome by a rush of gratitude and affection.

"Hey, you okay?" he asked. "Case getting to you? I know you can't talk at dinner, but I've got time later. Nothing too urgent to get done tonight, so you can tell me all about it."

She gave him one last tight squeeze and then, before she let him go, kissed him lightly on the lips. "Yeah. I could use a talk when we're alone."

It wasn't until they were together in bed with the door closed and only their bedside lamps burning that she sat up against her pillows and told him about having sex with Toni Rossel over twenty years before and what the consequences had been. While she spoke, she was careful not to touch her husband; she couldn't risk his shaking her hand off or drawing away from her; it would hurt too much. She ended by describing how she'd recorded Toni that afternoon. After a pause in which Ueli said nothing, she added, "I'm sorry I've never told you. I should have talked to you about it right after it happened, but it'd meant nothing to me, and I didn't want to risk our relationship. It means less than nothing now, but since Toni has talked about it at work, sooner or later some version of his story might find its way to you. So you had to hear it from me." She tried to meet his eyes as she finished, but he wouldn't let her.

It took an age for Ueli to look at her, and when he did his eyes were narrow and his lips tight. "What I hate about this," he said at last, "is that you two meet often, and every time you do, he can remember fucking you. You've finally told me the truth, and now I'm giving it right back to you."

Giuliana pressed her hands over her mouth and chin so hard that her lips hurt. She'd feared this could be bad, and now it was. Until this minute, part of her had held onto a belief that Ueli wouldn't feel betrayed and hurt and angry—all the normal reactions of a person whose partner had slept with someone else—because he was different. But no one was *that* different.

She'd caused him this grief, and she wasn't going to look away.

So she held his eyes and willed him to see in them that she loved him. At last Ueli put out his arms and drew her to him, until they were sitting against the headboard with their legs tangled and her cheek pressed into the hollow of his shoulder. In a much softer voice, he said, "It makes me feel sick to my stomach. But I can imagine how it must make *you* feel—especially knowing he has told this stuff to men you work with. I don't know if I can help you with this, though. I'm sure I could dig up lots of dirt on Toni. But if *I* wrote the story and there was a scandal, it would be bound to backfire on you. And meanwhile you'd still have to do your job with this bastard putting you under pressure. What a shambles!"

"I know," mumbled Giuliana against his chest.

They slid down until their heads were side to side on one pillow. Giuliana kissed Ueli very softly and drew back to look into his eyes.

"Recording him—that was a good idea," he said. "Tomorrow we'll see if there are other strategies we can come up with."

"Tomorrow," she agreed and kissed him again. This time he kissed her back.

38

" Fränzi's uncle did a great job. He went to a lot of trouble with his costume, so he really looked the part." All through his morning workout, Renzo had been looking forward to telling Giuliana about Angelo and Antonietta's visit from Saint Nicholas the evening before. Now he held out his phone to show her a photo of Angelo offering a piece of *panettone* to a man in a long red robe and a white wig-and-beard set.

He was surprised that Giuliana didn't seem impatient to leave the café, despite having finished breakfast. She took the phone and expanded Angelo's beaming face with her thumb and forefinger, smiling down at him. "The first time we had a friend of Ueli's play *Samichlous* for Isabelle, she never said a word. Just stared at him and sucked her thumb. The poor man. The jollier he tried to be, the bigger her eyes got. The next year, when she was four, it went better. Antonietta's four now, isn't she? How did she do?"

"They both seemed to be having fun. Angelo even sang!" He'd been proud of his son, who'd sung a traditional *Samichlous* song in Swiss-German, as he'd been coached to do by Fränzi, and then surprised his family with a Christmas carol in Italian that his grandmother had taught him.

Renzo was in the middle of doing house-to-house questioning about a burglary that had taken place during the night between Saturday and Sunday and was linked to a series of similar thefts in another part of Bern. He should get going, but there was something else he needed to talk to Giuliana about. He'd put it off long enough.

He waited while she finished admiring the rest of his photos from the evening before, took a deep breath, and said, "There's a project I've been working on: collecting the names of six women Toni Rossel has slept with during the past ten years or so. Actually, I've got more names, but these six are the ones I'm sure about. In two cases the women themselves told me."

All traces of good humor disappeared from Giuliana's face. "Renzo! What are you up to?"

"I'm going to pay that bastard back in his own coin. If he threatens you or even harasses you again, I'll..."

"No, you won't." Giuliana had leaned so far forward over their little table that he felt her breath on his face. He bent toward her, bringing their faces even closer, and glowered back, adding. "I won't do anything unless he does. But I'm not letting him hurt you again."

"Jesus, don't be such a..." She stopped.

"Such a what?" His anger flashed out so fast, it startled him, and he threw himself back in his chair, leaning away from Giuliana while he got a grip on his temper. Giuliana pulled away, too. They glared at each other across the distance. Then his glance flicked down to the bits of flaky pastry decorating the tip of her right breast, where she'd rested it in the little pile of croissant crumbs on her saucer as she'd leaned over the table.

He met her eyes again in a fraction of a second, but she'd caught the direction of his glance. She looked down, shook her head, and started wiping at the front of her shirt with the palm of her hand. They both tried to maintain their scowls, but it was hopeless. Shaking her head, Giuliana gave a giggle. Renzo reached out and, suppressing a grin, stacked Giuliana's empty cup and saucer on her plate, added her cutlery and deftly moved it all to an empty next-door table. Then he wiped her half of the table down with his paper napkin, sending all remaining crumbs to the floor. "There," he told her, "now you have room to get mad at me without . . . um . . . decorating your front."

"Thank you," she said and gave him such an affectionate smile that his heart turned over. But still he persisted.

"Don't be such a what?" he asked, his voice calm this time.

"Don't be so romantic!" she said, and he didn't know whether to smile or feel offended. "So . . . chivalrous. Old-fashioned. Overprotective. For God's sake, don't be such a man!"

It was funny, he knew it was—but it hurt. This was exactly why he hadn't told her about his data-collection project at the start. He'd had a feeling she wouldn't like it. And yet it seemed so fitting. A . . . a . . . what did they call it in Westerns? A Mexican standoff. Toni stood to lose a lot. His wife came from money, and, according to rumor, she had no clue how often he cheated on her. "I'm protecting myself, too, you know," he said. "Suppose he sent an anonymous letter to Fränzi about us. Or called her."

Giuliana shook her head. "Even if Toni went to Fränzi, which I don't believe he would, could you honestly blab to his wife about all his affairs? He has two young sons, you know. I think the older one is fourteen." She must have seen something in his eyes, because she said, "You see, you'd never do such a revolting thing. Never."

Ah, she was probably right. "But . . ." he began, not sure what he was going to say.

"The main point is, my dear, that it's none of your business. It's up to me to deal with Toni and, if I need help, to talk to Rolf, which I've already done, and to a lawyer, which I'm doing later this week. It is not your job to protect me. It's not even Ueli's job."

Renzo wondered what Ueli knew about the whole business, but he would never ask, and he knew she'd never tell him. He opened his mouth, closed it, looked at his watch, and stood up quickly, already putting on his sheepskin jacket. In a moment, Giuliana was ready to go, too. As they walked out of the café, she gave him another smile and, just for a moment, squeezed his hand before they both headed toward the crosswalk.

Emboldened, Renzo pointed up the street at a random building with a shop on the ground floor and apartments above it and said, "If a man ran out of there with an axe over his head and came at you, I'd try to protect you. And there'd be nothing you could do about it."

"You have my permission to protect me from an axe murderer," she agreed gravely, "assuming we don't have our guns. Otherwise, I'll protect you—since I'm the better shot."

It was true. Renzo raised both hands in surrender, and they crossed the street side by side.

39
Later

Early March was always a huge disappointment; Giuliana fell for the same trick every year. She'd feel a brush of warm sun on her cheek, see a crocus or two blooming in someone's garden, and begin to expect spring. And then there'd be another blizzard. She stood at the window staring out at the huge, wet flakes whose fall was lit by the streetlight beyond the living-room window. The wind was blowing the snow sideways. Ueli had just been out to shovel the building's front steps, yet again, and he was perched on the radiator, warming his hands along with his bottom.

He'd been quiet since he came in. Now he asked, "Has Toni Rossel bothered you lately?"

The question startled her. She'd seen a lawyer who'd been honest with her about the possible consequences of everything from a restraining order to a lawsuit, and in the end, she'd decided to wait and see. It set a bad precedent, her taking no action against him, but she hoped it wouldn't put other women at risk—she seemed to be the only woman Toni persecuted so consistently. At least Erwin, Renzo, and Rolf all knew about her clashes with Toni during the Gurtner case, and she'd recorded sworn testimony about his behavior in a deposition, in case of future need. In the meantime, she was pursuing her plan to record everything he said to her, right in front of him.

She left the window and settled into one corner of the sofa next to the radiator that Ueli had appropriated. "After those run-ins we had just before Christmas, I haven't seen him, except from a distance, and he hasn't approached me. Last week we talked about the trial on the phone, and he was civil. I'm not planning to relax my guard, but—who knows?—maybe he's not out to get me anymore."

Abandoning the radiator, Ueli plopped onto the other end of the sofa, where the pile of newspapers he'd been reading sat on the floor. Turning sideways and leaning back against the armrest, he stretched out his legs and slid his feet under her thighs. Even through his thick wool socks, she could feel how cold his toes were.

"I'm glad he's behaving," Ueli said and picked up a section of newspaper.

"Want me to rub your feet?" she asked.

"Na. This is perfect," he said, grinning at her and wriggling his toes against her skin. "You can be my hot-water bottle."

"Gladly," she told him, smiling back. She picked up her novel and went on reading about Commissario Guido Brunetti, a fictional police detective in Venice. Did his wife Paola, daughter of a count, ever warm her cold feet on him? She probably did.

40
Later

Holligen,
early Tuesday evening, March 16

Oliver Jordi, the defense lawyer, had forbidden Markus and Jakob to meet; since December they'd only seen each other in Jordi's office with counsel present. Markus had been grateful for this excuse not to have a beer with his friend. His feelings about Jakob were mixed, but the predominant one was still anger. Not that he'd had time to think about their relationship anyway. His second London show would open in three weeks, and he was bombarded with tasks from his gallerist, even as he tried to keep his freelance work humming along in the background for his regular clients. And all the while he was still threatened with a charge of conspiracy to murder his father. He knew he should be grateful to Jakob, who—after his initial failure to go to the police—continued to insist that he alone had been on the Aare that night and he alone was responsible for Johann Gurtner's death. Markus found it hard, though, to feel gratitude to Jakob for simply telling the truth, especially when he'd unleashed the whole disaster in the first place.

Still, part of Markus believed he owed Jakob something, because here he was in the restaurant near Loryplatz where they'd first met for a beer almost a year and a half before, waiting for the old man to show up. Jakob had sent him a letter, since Oliver had also forbidden them to communicate by phone. Thinking of this ridiculous embargo, Markus rolled his eyes. After all, if he and Jakob were coconspirators, wouldn't they be using untraceable mobiles? Sitting at a back table, he was already beginning to regret agreeing to this drink. Yet when he saw Jakob come through the door, he found himself on his feet, waving to get his attention. Jakob smiled at him, but after they'd shaken hands and sat down, Markus's regret returned. They ordered their beers, toasted each other, drank, and made polite inquiries about Renata and Ada. After that, an uncomfortable silence fell.

You called this meeting, damn it, thought Markus; *now tell me what you want.* But he couldn't wait for Jakob—he had to ask the question he'd been tossing around for months. Leaning forward, he looked the older man in the eye. "Why did you get me involved in this, Jakob? I've tried to tell myself it was a coincidental series of events, from you calling me after I took your picture to us deciding to meet my father on the river with Norbert. But I don't think it was. I think you set it all up. I think you set *me* up. Is that true?"

Jakob gave a twisted smile. "I've come to tell you about that very thing, and you already know it. Nobody's ever going to call you stupid, Markus."

"Well, not since you killed my father," he said and then raised his hand to his mouth. "Oh God, Köbi. I'm sorry. I never meant to . . ."

"Don't you dare apologize to me. I'm the one who's sorry. There's nothing you can say to me that I don't deserve—nothing!"

They were quiet again, but it was a friendlier silence now, and it wasn't long before Jakob, staring into his beer glass, said, "The truth is, even with what you've just said, it's clear you don't know all of it, and that's why I wanted to meet you." He paused and, with what seemed like an effort, raised his head and looked at Markus. "You see, I did everything I could to get you that photography job. You know I was one of the ex-*Verdingkinder* on the project committee with the academics and politicians, but you don't know how much I influenced them. Of course I couldn't force the decision, but I gave a presentation about you, and nobody had another photographer in mind at that point. They were grateful I'd done the work of finding someone and glad to agree with my recommendation."

Markus thought he'd been puzzled by Jakob's motives before, but now all he could do was shake his head. "But . . . why? Why get me such a good job when you hated my father?"

Jakob looked grim. "I didn't want to help you. I wanted to hurt you. Or hurt your father through you. I don't think I really knew myself, at that point."

Markus was taken aback at first, but then the funny side of Jakob's machinations struck him, and he chuckled. "Jesus, Köbi, you didn't do your research very well, did you? Thinking my father would be devastated if something bad happened to me. Didn't you know anything about the disaster I'd made of my life?"

Jakob's face started to relax. "Of course I knew what a waste of space you were supposed to be. The trouble you'd gotten into with drugs, your violent personality, they convinced me you'd be . . ." Jakob trailed off, but Markus went on for him. "You thought a thug like that would be Karli's favorite, a chip off the old block. You must have been very curious about me."

"I didn't know you, remember, so I couldn't help but think . . ." Jakob smiled, too, very faintly; the tension he'd carried into the bar with him was dissipating. "What made me wonder if I was on the right track were your photographs. To make the committee pick you, I had to learn a lot about your work, so I checked out quite a few portraits you'd done, and they threw me off. I couldn't understand how you could be an arrogant prick like Karli and still capture people's . . . people's souls."

Markus thought how much easier it was for both of them to talk about his father when they called him Karli. For Jakob, he became the bully that had killed Pesche. For Markus, he ceased to be the man he'd wanted desperately to please and was transformed into a boy he'd never known. "So, when I came to take your picture for the show, you were already planning to . . . to use me against Karli in some way," he said. "What did you have in mind?"

Jakob was trying to twirl his beermat like a top, but it kept falling over. When he glanced up at Markus, he was shamefaced again. "I . . . wasn't sure. I've always been like that—I get a lot of ideas, and I pursue some of them, but I don't always think them through. Not a good trait for an engineer. In other words, I didn't have a plan. I figured I'd meet you and see . . . what happened."

Markus waited, but Jakob didn't say anything else, so he asked another question. "So, what did you think of Karli's 'thug'?" Although he'd wanted to keep his voice light, he cringed at its bitterness, so he was surprised when Jakob smiled. "That was the problem," he said. "Even at my house that first time, you seemed like someone . . . I could respect. I was expecting charm—your father could always be charming when he wanted—but you weren't charming. You were intense. But real. And certainly not full of yourself. Apart from when you were telling me what to do to make the photo come out well, you spent the entire time listening to me talk about my childhood."

Markus gave a little bow over the table. "Thanks for the testimonial." He hoped his mockery hid what a warm feeling Köbi's words gave him.

Jakob didn't pause in his story, except to nod in acknowledgement of Markus's bow. "I decided I couldn't really form an opinion about you on the day of the photograph, so I set up our drink. Here," he swung an arm around, "in this restaurant. I thought you'd be snooty about it, but the first thing you said when I walked in was what a great place it was. That evening I talked about Pesche. Normally, he comes up only in conversations with Renata and some of the people in Heidmatt who knew him. Otherwise, I never reminisce like that. Even with my girls, I . . ."

Köbi's voice trailed away, and he drank more beer. Markus tried to catch his eye, but he looked everywhere but across the table. Deciding to order some snacks, Markus began to glance around himself, searching for their waiter. With Markus distracted, Köbi began again.

"After that first drink, I told myself I'd talked to you about the dinner with Pesche at the Fankhausers as part of my master plan for using you against Karli. The truth was that I'd enjoyed telling you about my brother and been touched by your interest in Heidmatt, even though I knew it was because you wanted to learn about your father, not me."

Markus felt the walls he'd been building against Köbi during the past three months starting to crack, and for some reason that made him angry again. "I don't understand why you told me that whole story about eating dinner at the Fankhausers and visiting the puppies without mentioning that Pesche was your brother," said Markus. It was one of the things that really hurt him. "All that time we were friends, or at least I thought we were, and you didn't tell me the truth about Pesche. Not until the night you told me that . . . Karli killed him. Was that . . . was that on purpose? Were you trying to make sure I'd become so enraged that I'd kill my father?" Markus's voice, already soft as he leaned across the table, dropped almost to a whisper as he said the last few words.

While Markus was speaking, Jakob had his palms pressed to his cheeks, back rounded and shoulders hunched. It made him look like an enormous white-crested vulture, but Markus felt no inclination to laugh. It took time for Jakob to respond, and then what he said wasn't an answer to the question. "The longer we knew each other, the more my ideas changed. I saw that you and Karli weren't a . . . a normal father and son. You were rivals. Nothing is more humiliating than having a shameful truth about yourself revealed to your enemy—it's much worse than a friend learning it. So, I started to think about us confronting Karli together, two friends against a shared enemy. That wasn't so much about using you as about gaining your support. At least, that was what I told myself."

A group of teenagers two tables away were howling with laughter, and a row of men at the small bar who were watching football on TV gave a roar. Jakob stopped talking until things quieted down. Markus opened his mouth to say something—he wasn't sure what—but Jakob went on. "I didn't think I was using you. But it's clear to me now that as long as I was planning to confront Karli without telling you about it, it was a way of setting you up. Of using you to make your father feel worse than I alone could make him feel." Jakob wasn't looking at him anymore by the time he finished his confession—he'd been focused on breaking his beermat into halves and quarters and was now working on eighths. But he raised his head and met Markus's eyes when he added, "I see that now, and I'm sorry."

The waiter appeared at last. Both asked for more beer, and Markus ordered a board of cheese and dried beef with a basket of bread. A man sitting next to them asked for the hot sauce, which was on their table, and they exchanged a few words. More time passed. Markus couldn't calm down. Köbi had offered his explanation and apology, but Markus couldn't accept them. The anger that had roiled around in his gut for months was shoving itself upward, and he couldn't control it. He saw his fists clench on the tabletop and couldn't loosen them.

When his words finally came, he managed to keep his voice from filling the room—that was the best he could do. "Then Norbert told you he wanted to return the watch. That really fell into your lap, didn't it? How could I notice I was being set up when *I* was the one who insisted you tell me what my father had done? I invited you into the apartment that night so you could finish the story—I had to persuade you to do it—and then you comforted me because I couldn't handle my father being a murderer. When I *demanded* to come with you and Norbert to return the watch, you tried to talk me out of it. That was truly clever. Yes, you played me from start to finish, and I never saw it. All through the interview with that asshole prosecutor, I kept your name out of the story. I was so worried for you. Until I heard about the blue wool in my father's watchband. Then I started to think, and after they stuck me back in the cell, I had time to think some more. The blue wool—that was the last straw."

Jakob let Markus's tirade wash over him. When it was finished, he took hold of the younger man's wrists and looked into his eyes. "No, you mustn't think the blue gloves were part of my game. God, anything but that. Renata knitted those gloves for you. They were her gift."

"Yes, but once you knew I had them you . . ."

"No, Markus, you're wrong. Even if you hate me now, you know I'm not a fool. How could I be sure you'd have those gloves on when we met Karli? How could I have predicted I'd lose a bit of my scarf so conveniently? No, give me credit: I may have set you up, but I never framed you."

Markus said nothing, but he knew Jakob was telling the truth. The business of the blue wool had made him feel paranoid, but it was a coincidence, he could see that now. He took a gulp of his second beer. Jakob clearly had more to say, but he didn't want to hear it. Nor to speak anymore himself. It was too much.

They drank in silence until the food came, and then they ate their meat and cheese and bread. It was good. He said so, and Jakob agreed, with a small smile. Markus smiled back and couldn't help imagining how much they must look like the conspirators Rossel so desperately wanted them to be.

Then something struck him as funny. Bad, he admitted to himself, but still funny, and he had to tell Köbi. "That prosecutor's twisting every word we've said and calling black white, just to prove that you and I concocted a plot to murder Paps, and we think he's crazy. But there's one way that he's right."

"What are you on about?" Jakob asked, his mouth full of bread.

"I think if the three of us had met Paps by the river as we planned, and he'd started in being haughty and insulting, trashing me and my life, patronizing Norbert, and putting you down, I *would* have killed him. At the very least I probably would have hit him or shaken him or . . . who knows what could have happened? Thanks to Norbert getting drunk and you telling me not to come to the Aare once I got home from Heidmatt, none of that happened. Which probably saved me from a return to prison. Have you thought of that?"

Jakob shrugged. "Yeah, I have. Before that Monday night, I imagined all the ways that meeting with your father could play itself out. *Since* that Monday night, I've considered all the ways it could have been different. Nothing about that scene was as I'd thought it would be, with or without you, with or without Norbert. Life just knocks us around sometimes."

There was another silence between them, and Markus decided it was time to tell Jakob something he'd known for almost two months.

"Speaking of life knocking you around," he said, and Jakob looked at him sharply. "Oliver Jordi has his people interviewing half of Heidmatt to find out more about you, Norbert, and my father, past and present. I've seen a couple of the transcripts. One was from Verena Fankhauser, a daughter of the farming family your brother lived with. I think she was sixteen or seventeen when Pesche died."

"Don't forget I lived with them, too, after that . . . so I know Verena," Jakob said, watching him warily. "She got married and moved out while I was still at the farm, but I remember her. I've lost touch with her, though. What did she say?"

Instead of answering, Markus said, "In the fifties and sixties, parents often had to pay craftsmen and even firms to take their kids as apprentices."

Jakob's face registered first surprise, then irritation. "Really? I don't remember the Fankhausers talking about that when I got apprenticed. Did they have to pay a lot to place me at Hasler?"

"They *would* have had to pay a lot, but they didn't have the money. All your expenses were paid by my grandfather, the *old* Doktor Gurtner."

"No!" Jakob said, and then he went mute. Markus drank his beer and gave him time. He wondered if Jordi would be upset that he'd revealed this secret to Köbi. As far as Markus was concerned, Jordi should have passed the information on as soon as it surfaced. For that matter, it was wrong of the Fankhausers to have kept it from Köbi all these years.

Markus had seen the transcript of the interview with Verena. "My father didn't want to take the doctor's blood money," she'd said. "We knew he was offering it to make up for his son having killed Pesche, and Papi didn't want the doctor thinking we forgave him for letting Karli get away with murder. But Mam said all that counted was Köbi having a better life, and if this money could give him that, it didn't matter if it came from the devil himself. So, Papi took it, but he swore us to secrecy. He said Köbi wouldn't go to Hasler if he knew who was paying for it. And I think he was right about that. But

Mam was right, too, because look how well things turned out for Köbi."

Jakob ate a piece of the dried beef, which Markus took as a sign he was all right. He touched the old man's hand apologetically. "No one told you about the money because they thought you'd be upset. I thought so, too, but I knew how much I'd hate it if people kept something secret from me that was about *my* life. So—now you know."

Jakob didn't speak until he'd swallowed the meat and downed the last swallows of his beer. Then he said, "You're right—I'm glad you let me know. But it makes my hate harder to hang on to. Not for Karli, I mean, but for the doctor. I was there when he let the boys tell their lie about Pesche falling off the bridge, and I heard him explaining to everyone in the room that the wound on Pesche's head had been caused by rocks. I still remember the look he gave me when I said I'd seen Karli carrying a stick with a great brass knob that I knew he'd used to smash my brother in the head with."

"You didn't tell me this before," Markus said, leaning close to Jakob.

"Didn't I? Well, maybe I thought you'd heard enough for one evening. But I can still see the way your grandfather's eyes bored into me when I described the stick. He turned his head and gave Karli and Norbert a long look. Then he asked me, 'Did you see this boy?' And I had to say no, that I'd seen the stick in Karli's hands and heard his threats, but I hadn't seen him hit Pesche with it. So, the doctor made my accusation vanish—it just disappeared. Within twenty-four hours, the official story was that Pesche had fallen off the bridge, and that was that."

"Except that Karli was sent away from home," Markus added. "My grandfather may have saved his son from punishment, but it's clear he believed you. After all, you described a cane he owned, and he must have gone home to find it missing. He wasn't willing to let his thirteen-year-old son be accused of murder and he couldn't do anything for Pesche, but he could at least help you. So he did."

Both of them had finished their beers, but Markus didn't want to leave. He felt very tired, but it was a good kind of tired, the kind you feel after a day of skiing and a good dinner. He glanced around the café and then back to Jakob, whose face was still clouded.

"Don't let it take away your feelings of success, Köbi," he said. "Maybe the old man gave you a good start, but you did the rest. He didn't make Renata fall in love with you and stay with you all these years, did he? That wasn't anyone's charity. You won her all by yourself."

Jakob smiled then—any mention of Renata made him smile—and Markus thought things would be all right. He didn't want to upset his friend yet again, but something else was puzzling him.

"I understand what my grandfather did for you," he said, "but I still don't get why my father helped support Norbert. The watch—it was obviously a bribe; even Norbert knew that. But the money? Paps . . . Karli didn't know Norbert had the stick, although if he went back to look for it and couldn't find it, he may have had his suspicions. But nothing will convince me that Norbert sent him a threatening note or made a sinister phone call. Let's face it: Norbert wouldn't understand how to blackmail someone successfully. So, why did Paps send him money?"

Jakob stared out the window of the restaurant into the back garden, where a few hearty souls—smokers, mostly—were sitting at outdoor tables under the cloudy sky. Around the courtyard, the grass was full of snowdrops. "The reasons probably weren't clear to Karli himself. He must have figured that the more comfortable Norbert was financially, the less likely he'd be to say awkward things. But I think there was affection there, too, or at least . . . *noblesse oblige*. Guilt, too, perhaps, for the way he'd treated a boy who'd repaid him with unconditional loyalty."

Markus shook his head; he couldn't see it. "Money or not, Norbert was always a threat to him. I wonder why he didn't just kill him." Seeing Jakob's eyes widen in surprise, Markus shrugged. Didn't Jakob know by now that he had no illusions about his father?

"It would have been so easy for him," Markus pointed out, "once Norbert started to drink. Midwinter, a snowstorm predicted, Paps parks at the castle and slips a flask of schnapps into his coat pocket. He meets Norbert on the edge of town, some place with no one around, and gives him the flask. Norbert drinks and falls asleep in the snow. Paps walks away, the snowfall hides his footsteps. In a day or two, someone finds Norbert frozen to death. Nothing suspicious about that. Everyone is just waiting for it to happen anyway. End of threat."

Brows drawn, Jakob shook his head. "I thought you knew Karli better than that. He wasn't a calculating killer determined to eliminate risks. He just saw red when people didn't give him his due or made him feel foolish or took important things away from him. Pesche did all of that to him, and so did you, when you grew up rebelling against his control. But Norbert? It wouldn't have occurred to him to kill someone he could manipulate so easily."

Markus could only shrug. "Maybe you're right. I've never understood my father." He never would, either. Now that the old man was dead, perhaps it was time to stop trying.

The two of them got up at last, and Markus went to find the toilets while Jakob paid. *My turn to pay next,* Markus thought to himself, and knew he wanted that turn to be soon. Thank God things between him and Jakob felt back to normal. Except that nothing could be normal while Jakob was on bail waiting for his trial and while this conspiracy charge was hanging over them both. At least Norbert was free of it all. Now that he was bedridden and not always conscious, even Rossel wasn't going to try to pin anything on him. He'd be dead before the trial occurred. Oliver Jordi had let Markus visit him the week before, and that was probably the last time they'd speak. Norbert had gone back to thinking he was Köbi's son.

He found Jakob waiting for him on the sidewalk outside the café, hands in the pockets of his jacket, wool cap on his head. They set off together toward the tram stop, two blocks away, where Jakob would ride one direction and Markus the other. They walked along in comfortable silence until Jakob said, "Renata's flying to London for your opening. That okay with you?"

Stopping, Markus turned to Jakob. "Okay with me? It's great. I just wish . . ."

"I know," said Jakob, "but the police won't let me leave the country." He paused a moment before adding, "Ada's promised to help Renata find the perfect outfit to wear that evening. Can you imagine what the two of them will come up with?"

"No." Markus shook his head, grinning. "I honestly can't. But I'm sure they'll both look spectacular. Ada didn't tell me about it, though, so I think it's supposed to be a surprise." As they continued walking, he added, "This time I've invited my mother as well as my aunt, and they're both coming. I think Renata will like them." He was going to introduce Ada to his mother, too. Jesus, was he getting serious? It wasn't coming from Ada. Maybe he was just . . . ready for it. He hoped she was, too.

They were almost at their stops when Markus paused again and faced Jakob. "I won't let you get sentenced to jail time, Köbi. I want you to know that."

It was a ridiculous thing for him to say. True, he had family money he could draw on for a long time to pay for Jordi and the rest of the defense team, but what could he, personally, do to keep Jakob out of jail? He felt himself flushing, but he met the other man's eyes anyway.

Jakob wasn't laughing, although he had a smile on his face. But it was—Markus couldn't help but notice—a proud smile, not a mocking one. A fatherly smile.

"Well, I won't let you get convicted of conspiracy, either. So there. We've got each other's backs, boy."

They stood there grinning at each other, and then Köbi put out his hand and Markus shook it before the older man turned and walked over to his side of the street. They looked at each other, not waving but not glancing away, either, until Köbi's tram came. He got on and sat at a window on the side where Markus could see him, and he held his hand up, pressing it against the glass. Markus raised a hand, too. He didn't lower it until the last window of Köbi's tram had passed him by.

Acknowledgments

Every character in this book is made up. There is no patrician family in Bern named von Eichwil and no village in the Emmental called Heidmatt. But the practice of taking children away from their parents and putting them into orphanages or on farms is not made up. I first learned about it in detail in 2009 from a Bern exhibition. That sparked the idea for the show in *Sons and Brothers* where Markus Gurtner displays photos of the *Verdingkinder* grown old.

The 2009 exhibit about Switzerland's contract children focused on the experiences of boys and girls, many of them with living parents, who were placed in institutions or on farms with strangers from the 1920s into the 1960s. One of its goals was to give visitors a sense of how neglected these children were, when not actually abused. The most powerful part of the exhibition for me were the recordings: excerpts from interviews with adults who had been placed out as children in which they described their lives of hardship and their profound feelings of loneliness. This show about the memories of elderly *Verdingkinder* traveled all over Switzerland for nine years, until the end of 2017, and broke down a barrier of silence that had kept this terrible public policy from being reexamined. Historians estimate that during the worst years of children's forced labor (1820–1960), hundreds of thousands of children were affected. There is a great deal written in German and French about *Verdingkinder*; something in English is "Switzerland's Shame," an October 29, 2014, article by Kavita Puri on the BBC News website, https://www.bbc.com/news/magazine-29765623.

While I was doing research for this book, I read many contract children's accounts of their lives but didn't interview a *Verdingkind*. I did, however, have a long and fascinating talk with two men who went to a village elementary school in the Emmental during the time that Karli, Pesche, and Köbi would have been there, and I thought they gave me a very good idea of what they experienced as schoolchildren. Luckily, they weren't taught by anyone as out of control as my Herr Müller!

I share drafts of my books with just about anyone who's willing to take the time to read them, since readers' advice so often improves my work. In the acknowledgments section of *Pesticide*, the first book in the Polizei Bern series, I thanked over fifty people for their feedback on my manuscript, and I've decided not to repeat that list of names here, although my gratitude for their comments on *Sons and Brothers* is no less heartfelt. My sister Natasha Hays deserves special thanks for her commitment. I also asked several professional editors to read sections of *Sons and Brothers* at early stages: Angela Polidoro, Nick Russell-Pavier, Jennifer Fisher, and Teresa Barker. They all gave me thoughtful advice, as did Gail Fortune and Margaret James in other contexts.

I am once again filled with gratitude for the support of my policewoman neighbor Gabriele Berger and for the contributions of my spectacular editor Kathryn Jane Robinson Price. Dan Mayer of Seventh Street Books is the reason I am a published writer, so I can never thank him enough. Thanks, too, are due to Books Forward's Simone Jung and Ellen Whitfield and to a number of people at Start Media who have contributed to designing, producing, and promoting my books, including Jennifer Do, Marianna Vertullo, Wiley Saichek, and Ashley Calvano. April Eberhardt has also been a terrific source of advice and encouragement.

Three friends who deserve special recognition are Karen Fifer Ferry, Margaret Keppler, and Julia Reid, who meticulously read this book's page proofs and noted many necessary changes that I had missed. I am so grateful to them.

Finally, my love and thanks to my husband and son, Peter and Thomas Stucker, who support me in so many ways.